THE FOG MOUND

3

SIMON'S DREAM

Also by Susan Schade and Jon Buller

The Fog Mound #1
Travels of Thelonious

The Fog Mound #2
Faradawn

THE FOG MOUND

3

SIMON'S DREAM

SUSAN SCHADE *and* JON BULLER

Simon & Schuster Books for Young Readers
New York   London   Toronto   Sydney

SIMON & SCHUSTER BOOKS FOR YOUNG READERS
An imprint of Simon & Schuster Children's Publishing Division
1230 Avenue of the Americas, New York, New York 10020

SIMON & SCHUSTER BOOKS FOR YOUNG READERS is a trademark of Simon & Schuster, Inc.
Book design by Daniel Roode
The text for this book is set in Geometric 415.
Manufactured in the United States of America
2 4 6 8 10 9 7 5 3 1
Library of Congress Cataloging-in-Publication Data
Simon's dream / Susan Schade and Jon Buller.—1st ed.
p. cm.—(Fog Mound ; bk. 3)
Summary: Thelonious the chipmunk, his talking animal friends, and Bill,
the tiny human scientist, continue to combat those who would destroy Fog
Mound, and even the Earth itself, for personal gain, while learning more
truths about the time of the Human Occupation.
ISBN-13: 978-0-689-87688-2 (hardcover)
ISBN-10: 0-689-87688-2 (hardcover)
[1. Chipmunks—Fiction. 2. Animals—Fiction. 3. Adventure and
adventurers—Fiction. 4. Science fiction.] I. Buller, Jon, 1943– ill.
II. Title.
PZ7.S3314Sim 2008
[Fic]—dc22
2007037537

FIRST
EDITION

For Ellanora, Simone, and Aven

Visit Susan Schade and Jon Buller at their website,
www.bullerooz.com.

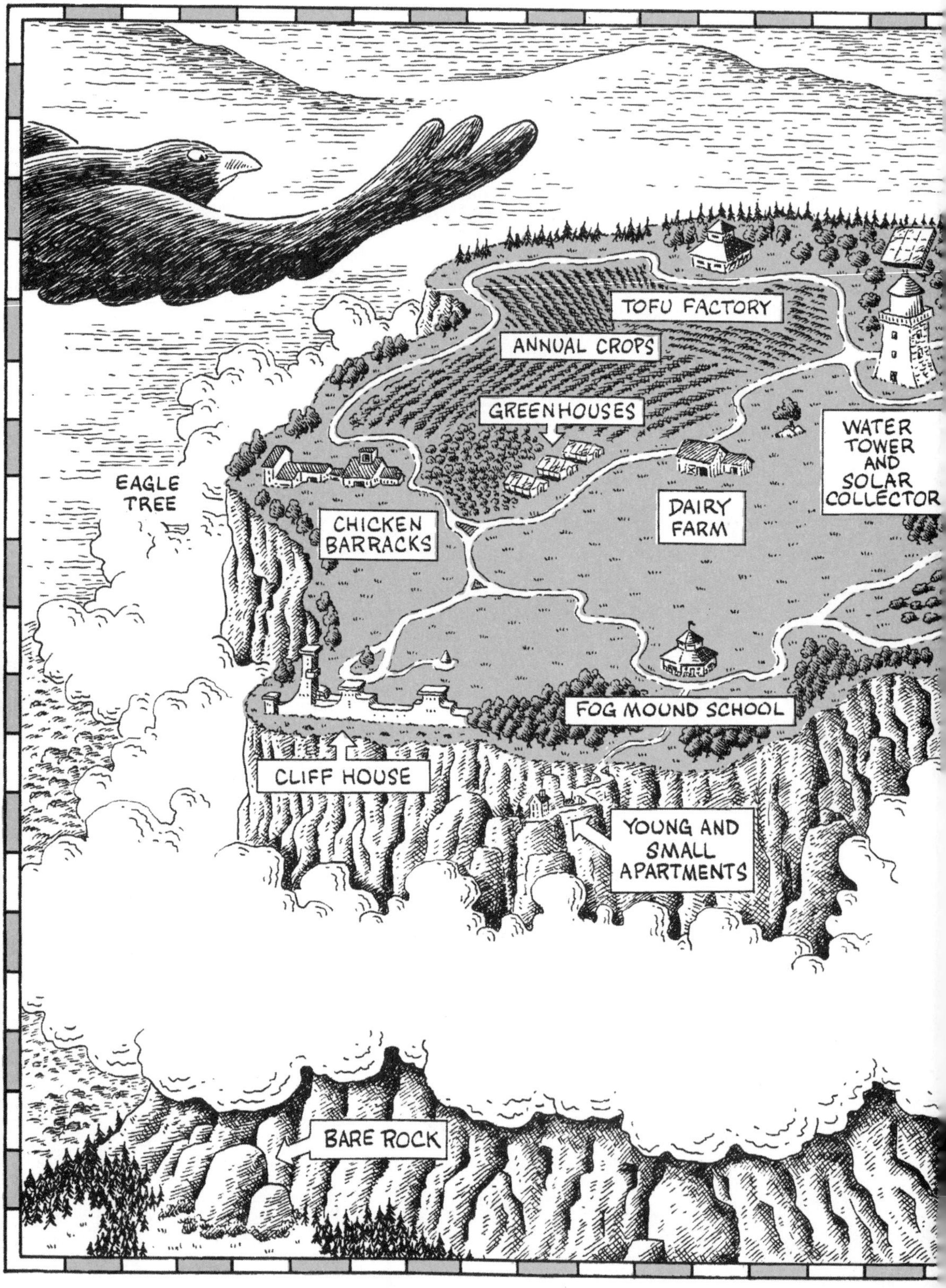
TOFU FACTORY
ANNUAL CROPS
GREENHOUSES
WATER TOWER AND SOLAR COLLECTOR
EAGLE TREE
CHICKEN BARRACKS
DAIRY FARM
FOG MOUND SCHOOL
CLIFF HOUSE
YOUNG AND SMALL APARTMENTS
BARE ROCK

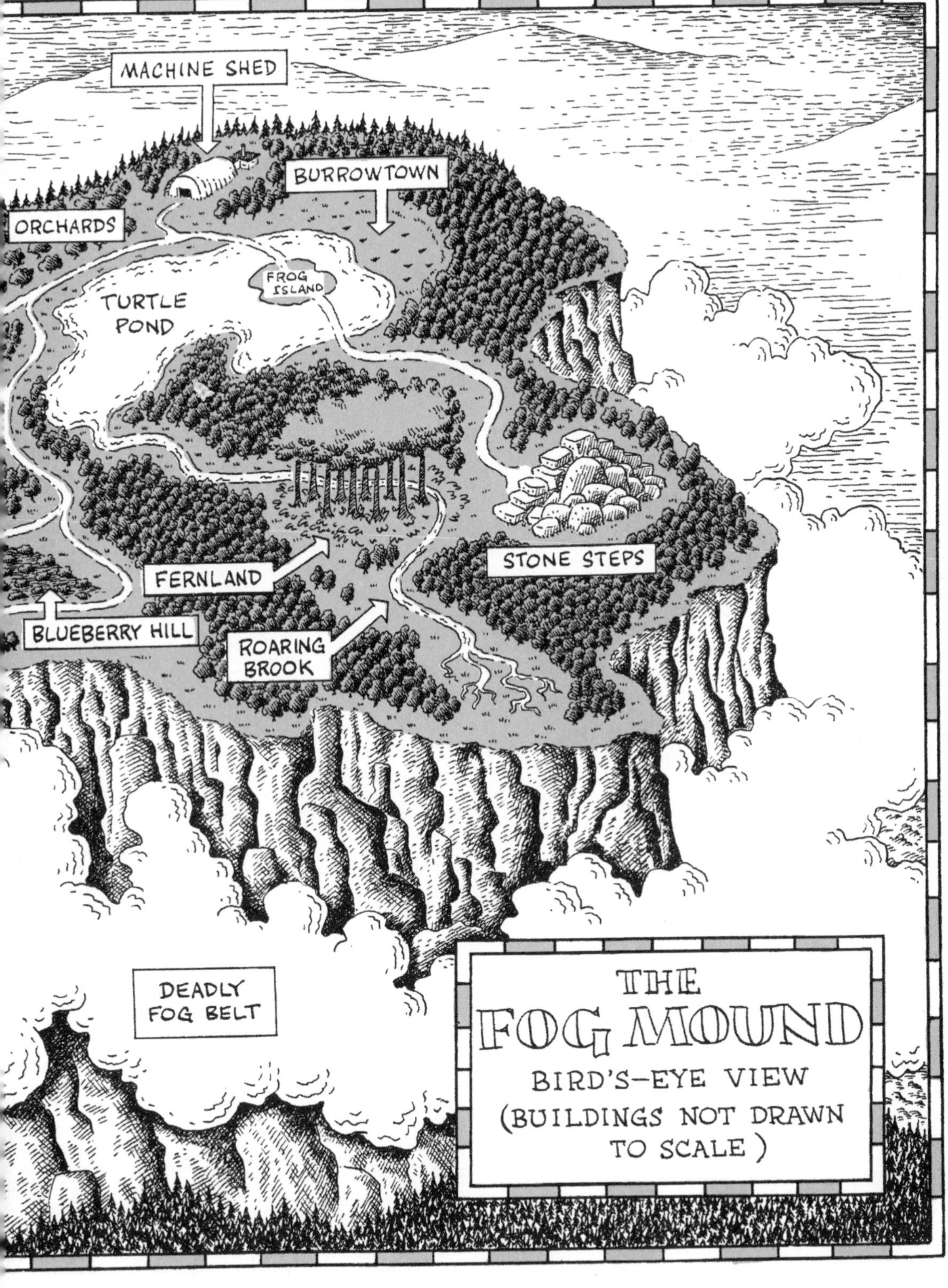
MACHINE SHED
BURROWTOWN
ORCHARDS
FROG ISLAND
TURTLE POND
STONE STEPS
FERNLAND
BLUEBERRY HILL
ROARING BROOK
DEADLY FOG BELT
THE FOG MOUND
BIRD'S-EYE VIEW
(BUILDINGS NOT DRAWN TO SCALE)

According to Chipmunk Legend, great numbers of human beings had once roamed and ruled the Earth. We call that time the "Human Occupation." After using up most of Earth's natural resources, the humans had mysteriously disappeared, leaving behind a barren, ruined planet.

There followed a period of great hardship for the few surviving animals.

But after a while seeds began sending green shoots up out of the bare dirt. Vines spread over piles of rubble. Trees reached for the sun. And once again food was plentiful.

By the time of my travels, life on Earth was prospering and varied . . .

❖   In the **Untamed Forest**, a small number of talking animals (like myself) lived under tall trees, collecting nuts, avoiding wild predators, and telling tales of days gone by.

❖   Even in the **City of Ruins**, where trees would still not grow, animals lived in the crumbling remains of human buildings, eating the delicious foods that the humans had preserved and left behind.

❖   On the **Fog Mound**, an isolated community of educated

animals grew and preserved their *own* food. And there we had found,

and thawed out, a frozen human scientist—the last human, shrunken and slightly brain-damaged, but alive!

❖   The human had led us across the sea to **Faradawn Island**, where a colony of talking birds lived on fruit and moths, while evil mutant crabs built giant robots under the water.

Was it true, as Ruby Bear feared, that some animals were beginning to make the same mistakes humans had made years ago? What were those mistakes, exactly? And would it be possible for a small band of concerned animals to put a stop to them?

As we sailed back from Faradawn Island, I wondered if we would find the answers to any of these pressing questions at our new destination: the **Mattakeunk Institute**.

1

The Time Machine

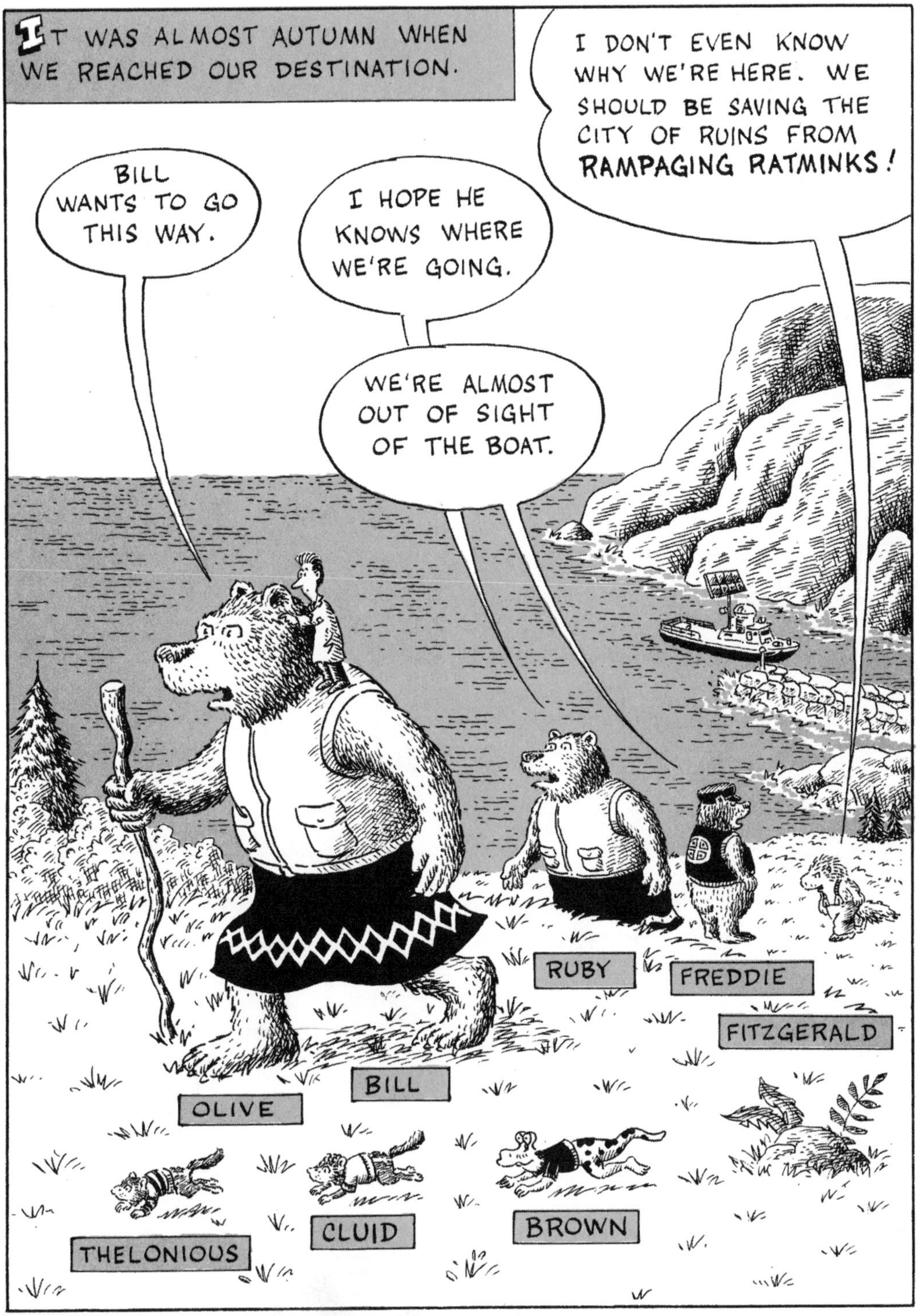
IT WAS ALMOST AUTUMN WHEN WE REACHED OUR DESTINATION.
I DON'T EVEN KNOW WHY WE'RE HERE. WE SHOULD BE SAVING THE CITY OF RUINS FROM RAMPAGING RATMINKS!
BILL WANTS TO GO THIS WAY.
I HOPE HE KNOWS WHERE WE'RE GOING.
WE'RE ALMOST OUT OF SIGHT OF THE BOAT.
RUBY
FREDDIE
FITZGERALD
BILL
OLIVE
THELONIOUS
CLUID
BROWN

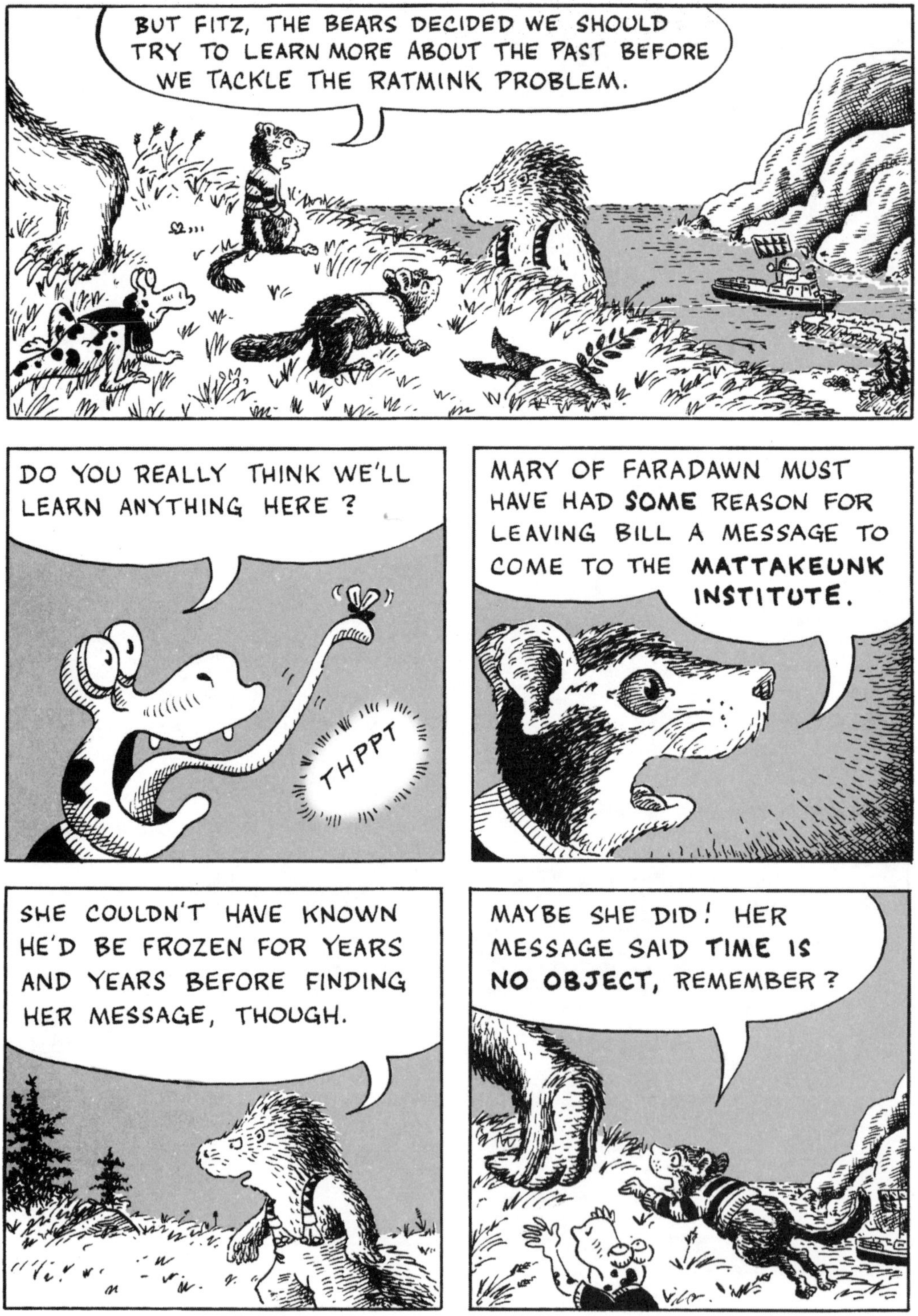
BUT FITZ, THE BEARS DECIDED WE SHOULD TRY TO LEARN MORE ABOUT THE PAST BEFORE WE TACKLE THE RATMINK PROBLEM.
DO YOU REALLY THINK WE'LL LEARN ANYTHING HERE ?
THPPT
MARY OF FARADAWN MUST HAVE HAD **SOME** REASON FOR LEAVING BILL A MESSAGE TO COME TO THE **MATTAKEUNK INSTITUTE**.
SHE COULDN'T HAVE KNOWN HE'D BE FROZEN FOR YEARS AND YEARS BEFORE FINDING HER MESSAGE, THOUGH.
MAYBE SHE DID! HER MESSAGE SAID **TIME IS NO OBJECT**, REMEMBER ?

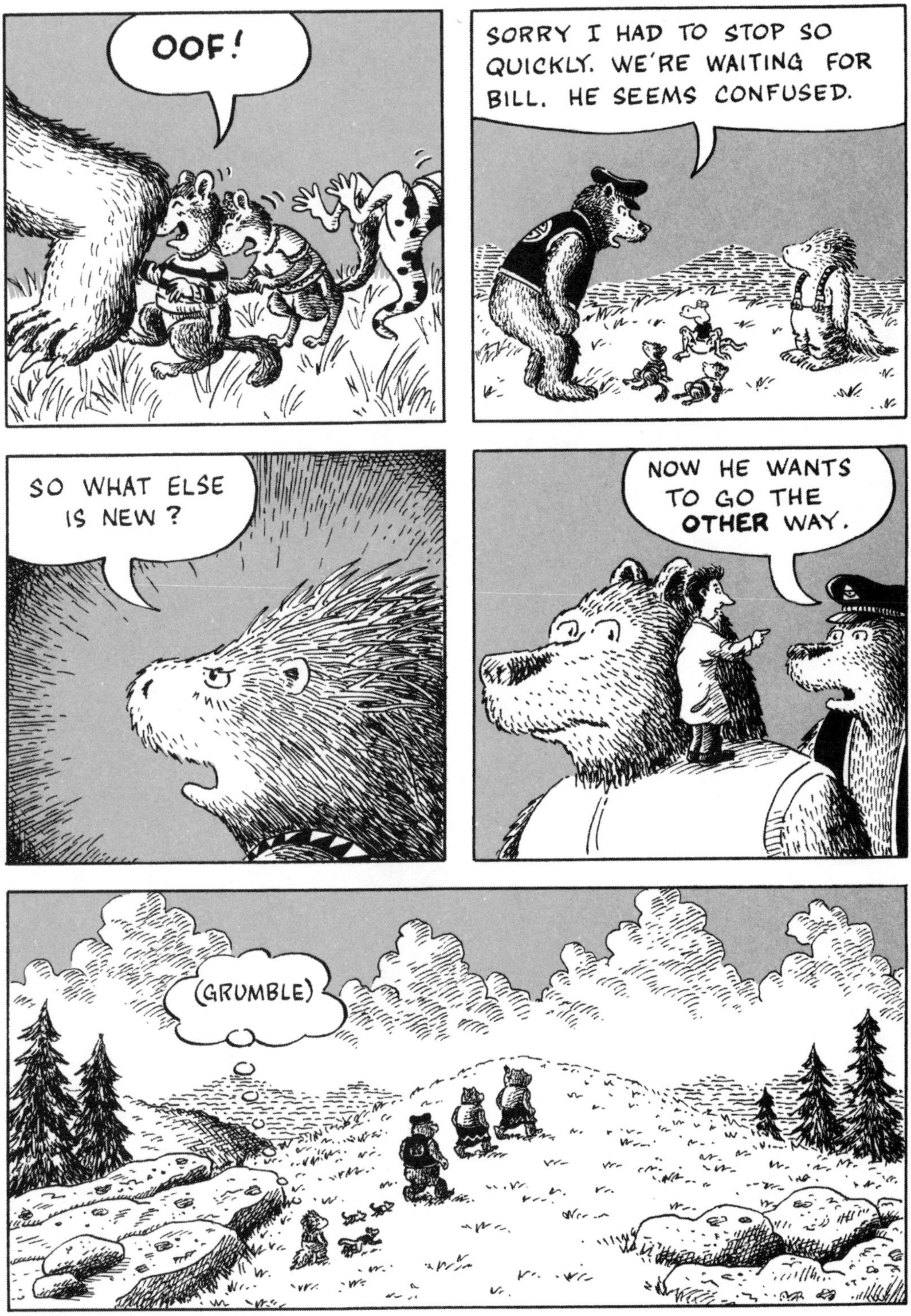
OOF!
SORRY I HAD TO STOP SO QUICKLY. WE'RE WAITING FOR BILL. HE SEEMS CONFUSED.
SO WHAT ELSE IS NEW?
NOW HE WANTS TO GO THE OTHER WAY.
(GRUMBLE)

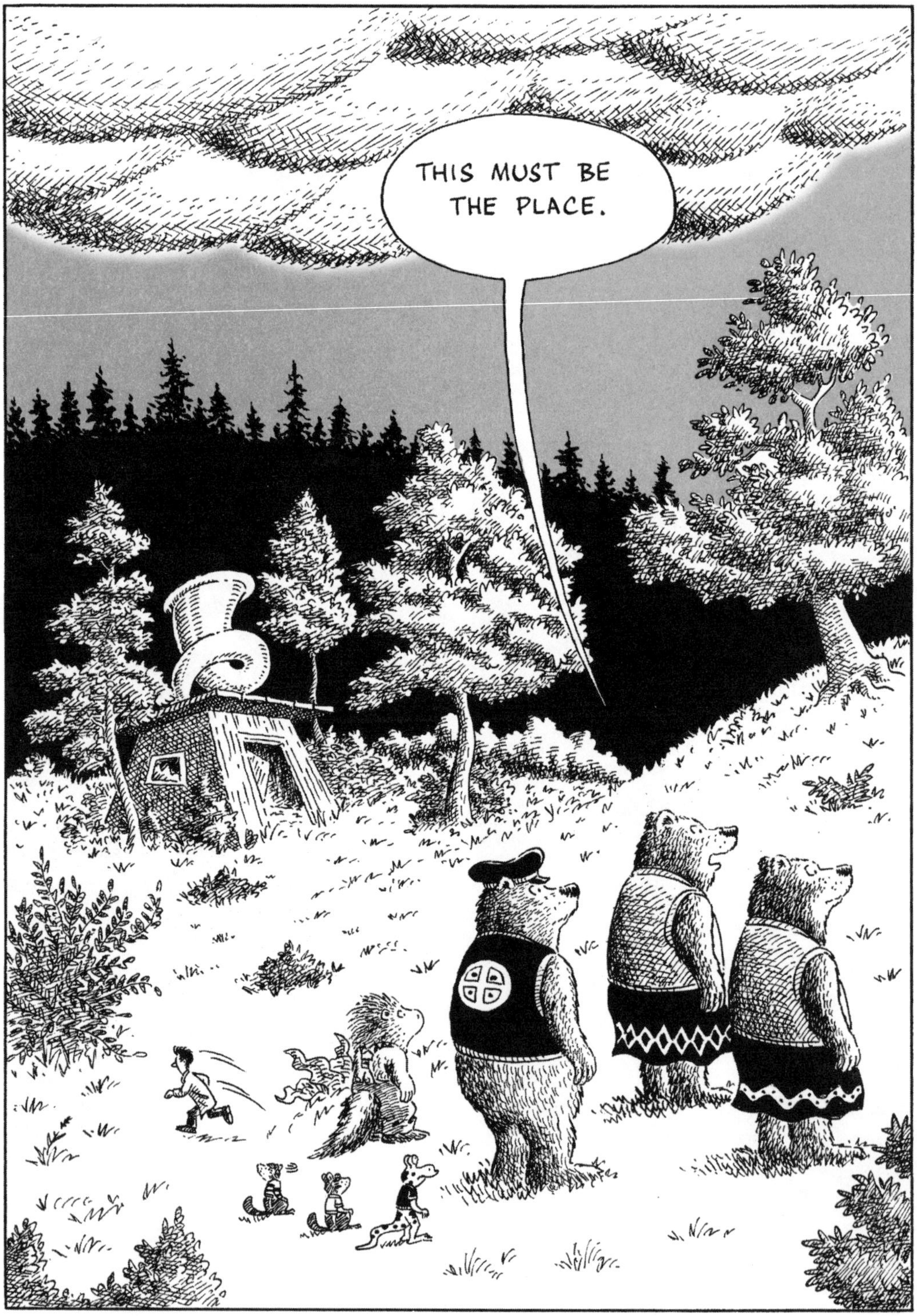
THIS MUST BE THE PLACE.

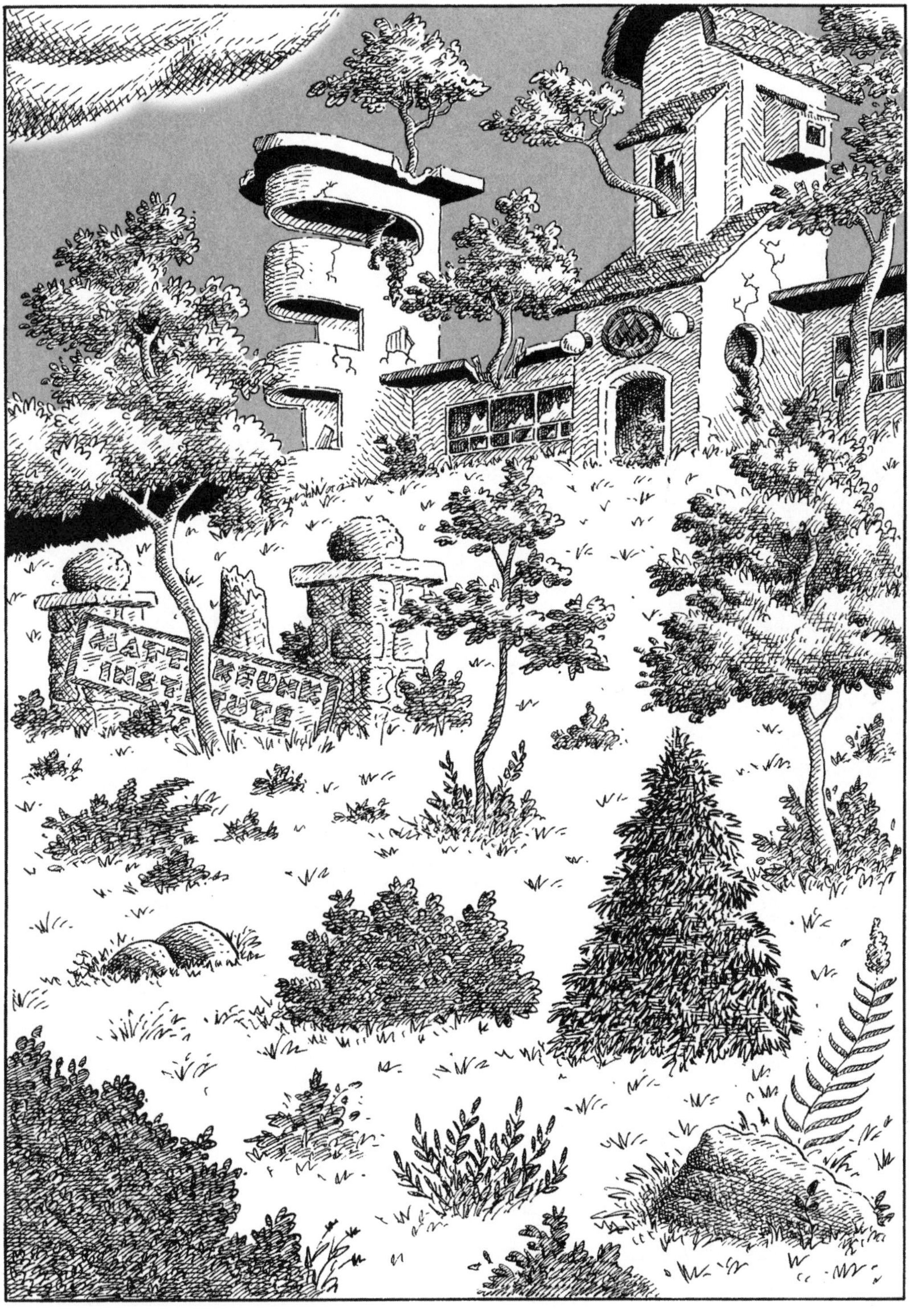
KRUNK

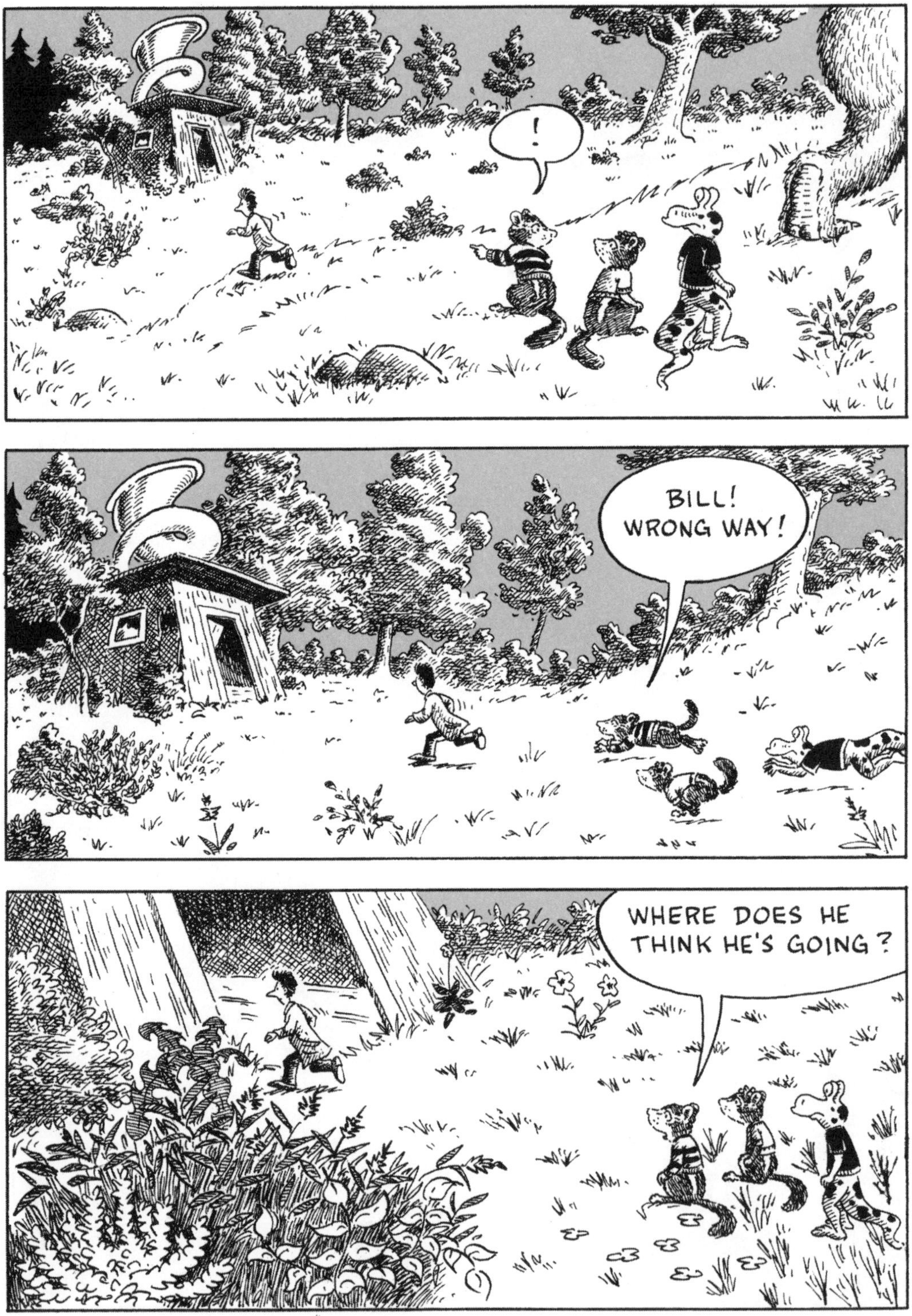
!
BILL! WRONG WAY!
WHERE DOES HE THINK HE'S GOING?

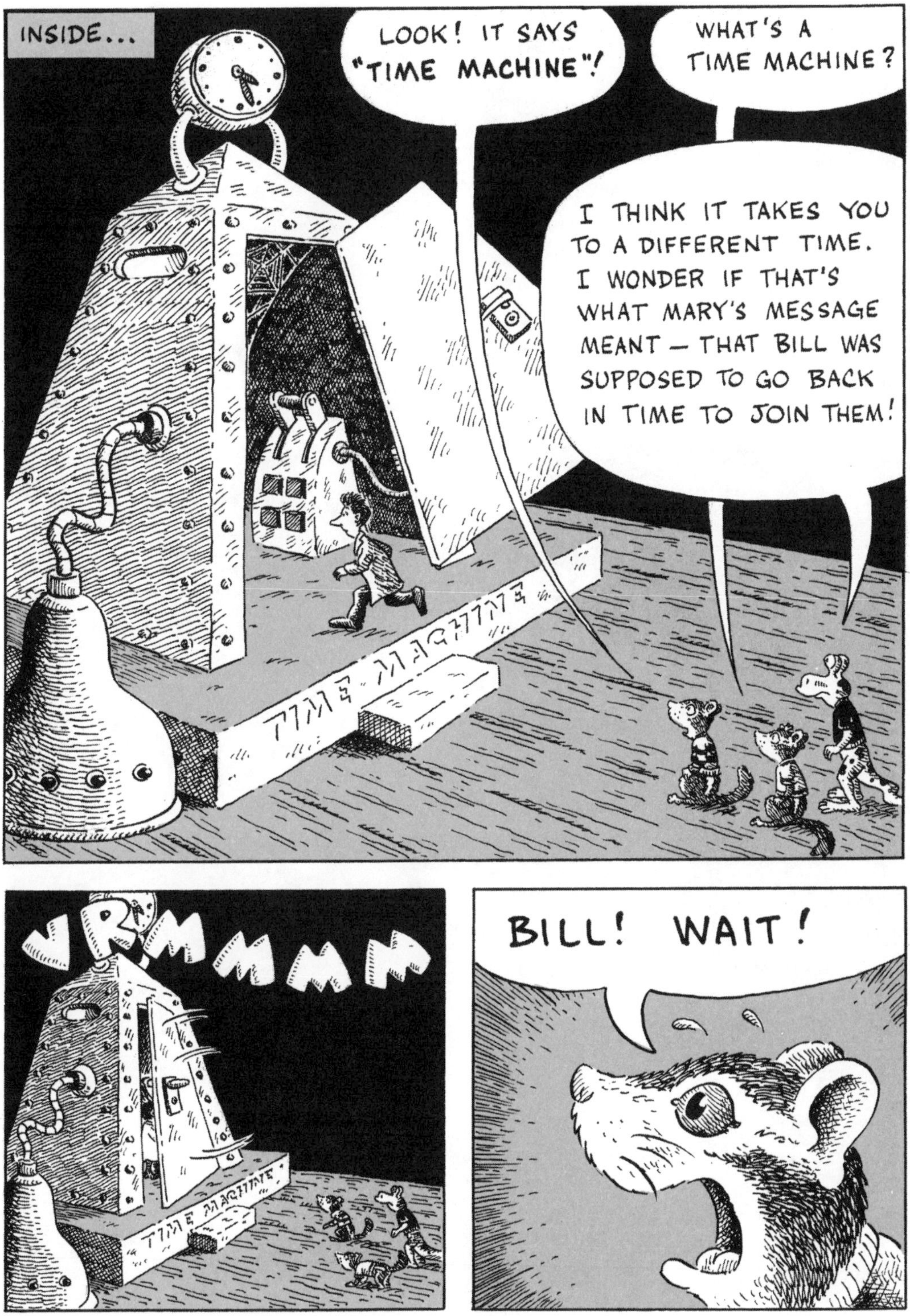
INSIDE...
LOOK! IT SAYS "TIME MACHINE"!
WHAT'S A TIME MACHINE?
I THINK IT TAKES YOU TO A DIFFERENT TIME. I WONDER IF THAT'S WHAT MARY'S MESSAGE MEANT — THAT BILL WAS SUPPOSED TO GO BACK IN TIME TO JOIN THEM!
TIME MACHINE
VRMMMP
TIME MACHINE
BILL! WAIT!

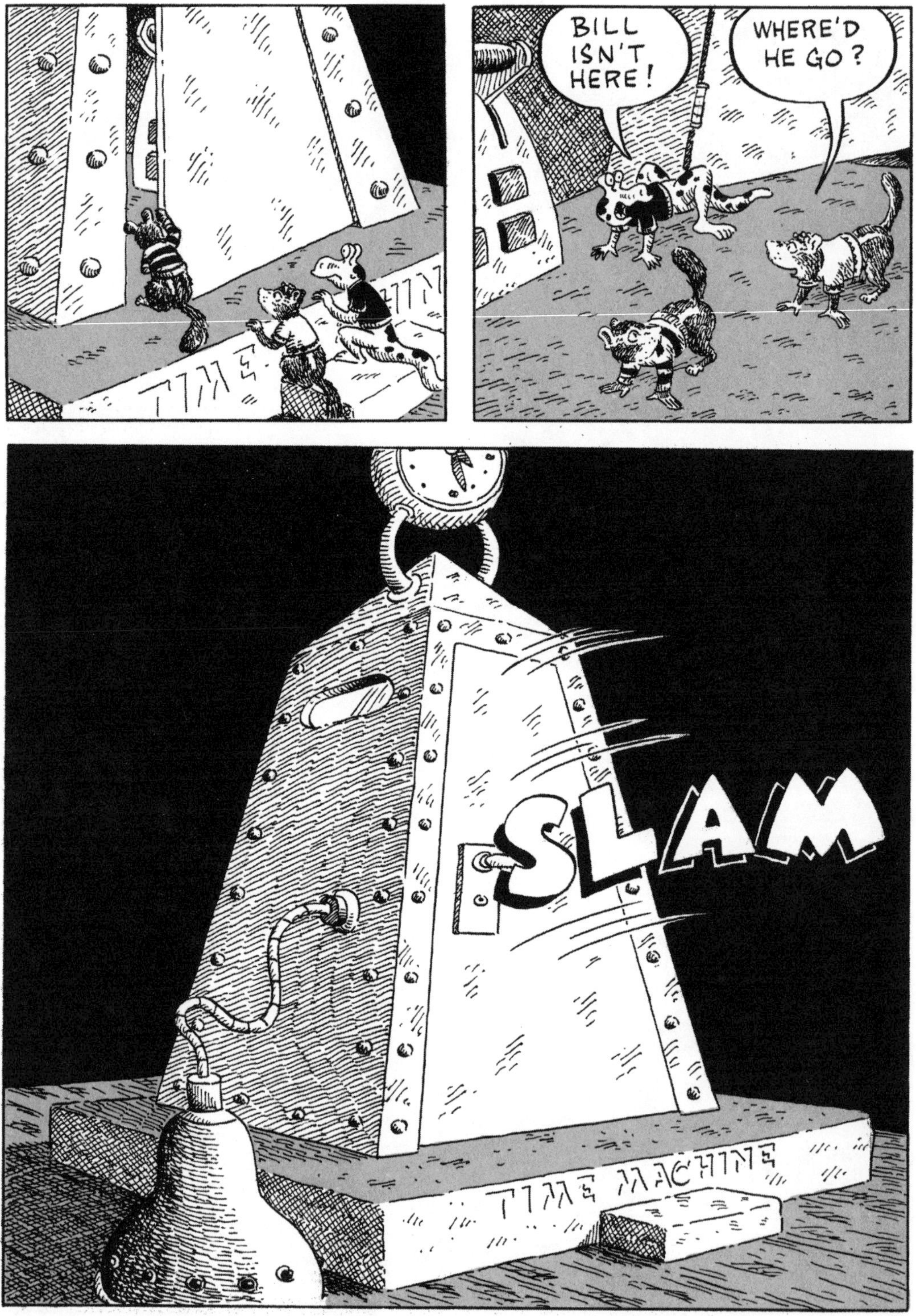
TIME
BILL ISN'T HERE!
WHERE'D HE GO?
SLAM
TIME MACHINE

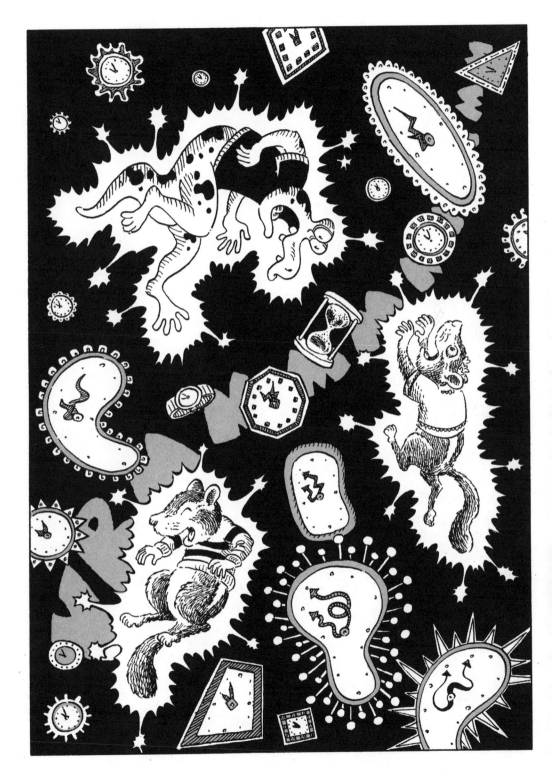

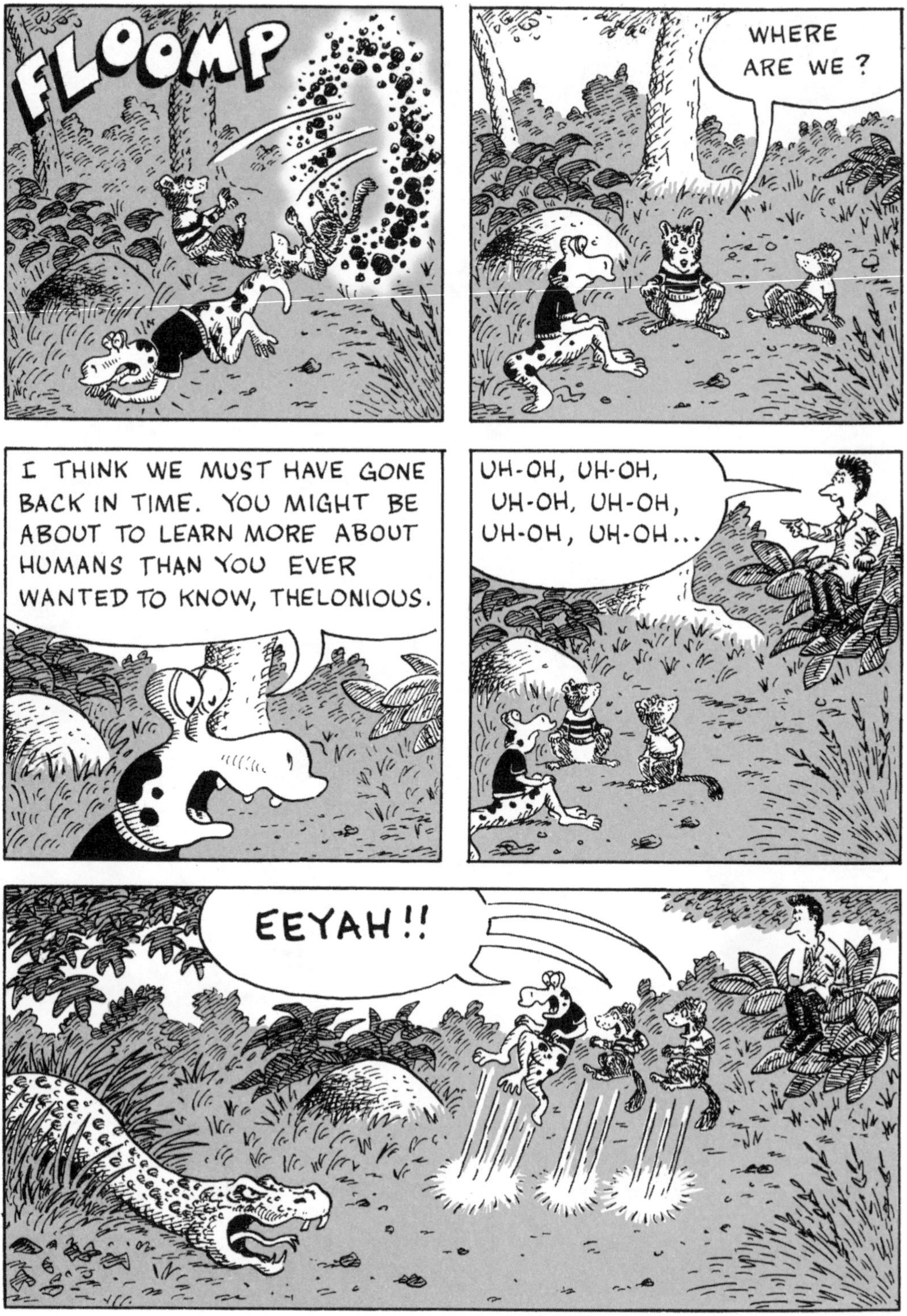
FLOOMP
WHERE ARE WE ?
I THINK WE MUST HAVE GONE BACK IN TIME. YOU MIGHT BE ABOUT TO LEARN MORE ABOUT HUMANS THAN YOU EVER WANTED TO KNOW, THELONIOUS.
UH-OH, UH-OH, UH-OH, UH-OH, UH-OH, UH-OH...
EEYAH!!

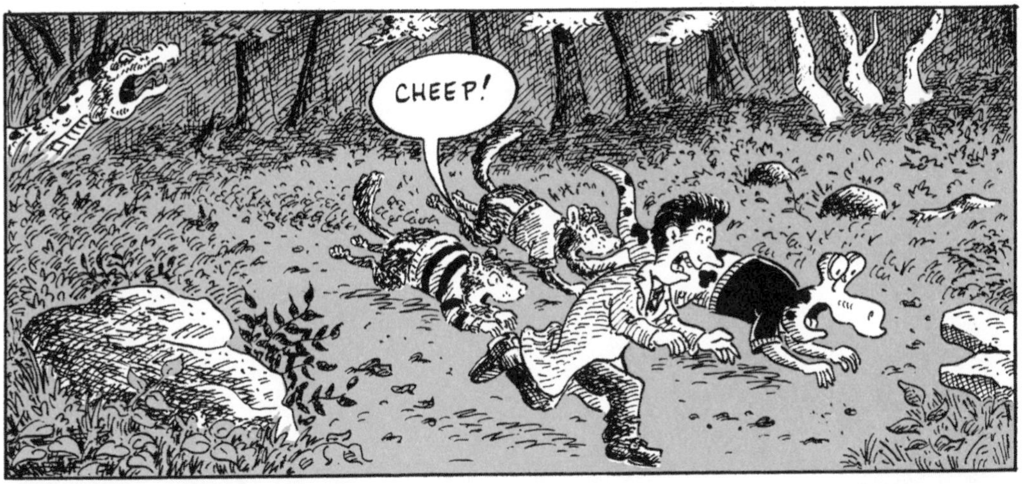
CHEEP!

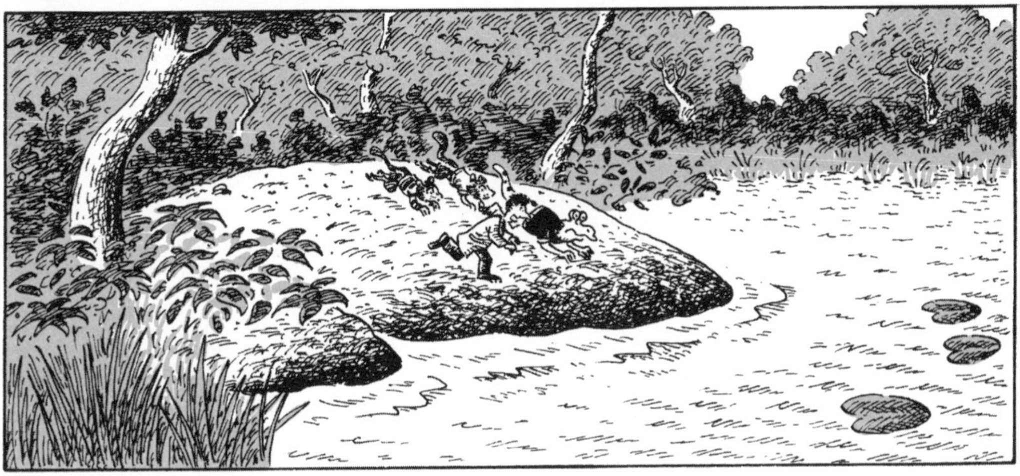

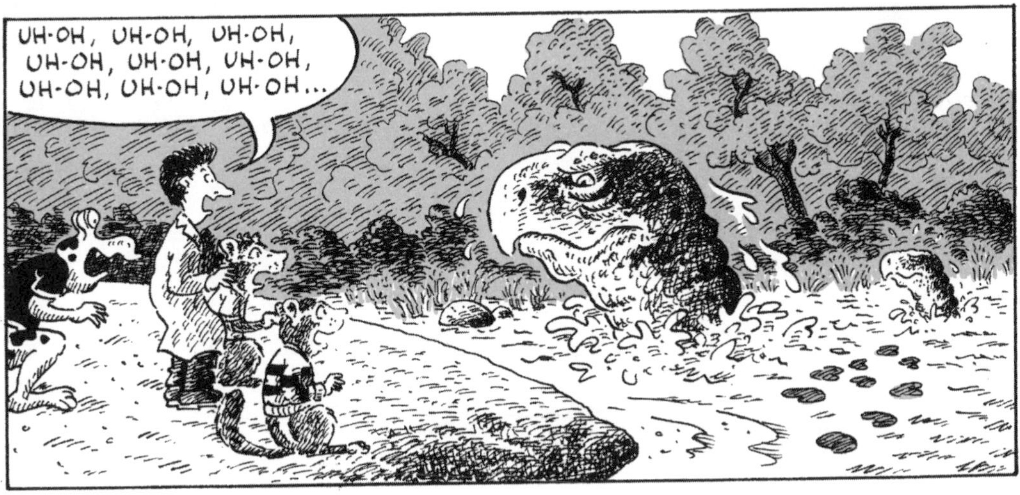
UH-OH, UH-OH, UH-OH, UH-OH, UH-OH, UH-OH, UH-OH, UH-OH, UH-OH...

2

Speaking Reptile

**"DINOSAURS!" Cluid
cried.** And we dashed behind a rock.

Dinosaurs?

I peeked out. "You mean dinosaurs
were real?"

Cluid pointed at them. "See for
yourself, Thelonious," she said.

Brown said, "If I remember my history correctly, dinosaurs were around
long before the Human Occupation. That means we've come back too far.
Way too far! We won't learn anything useful about humans here."

We all stared at the primitive animals, with their square, featureless heads
and long, leathery necks. One of them turned slowly in our direction and
opened its mouth.

"B R A A A P!"

"Yow!" I yelled. "They've seen us!"

I grabbed Cluid and Bill by their arms and backed up until we were safely hidden under some foliage. But Brown stepped forward.

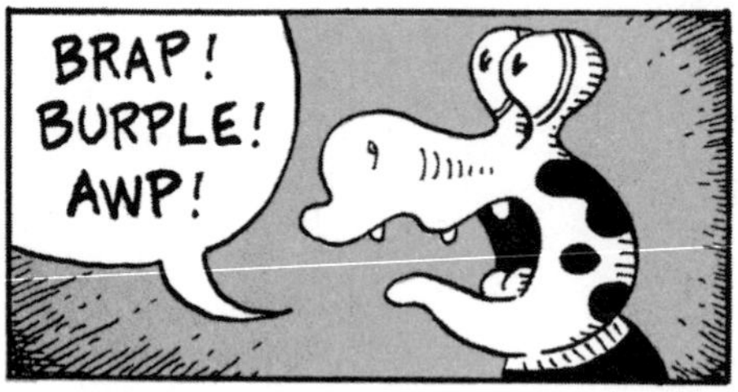
BRAP! BURPLE! AWP!

"Brown!" I hissed at him. "What are you doing?"

To my surprise, Brown made some rude noises at the dinosaurs.

The huge animals were all looking at Brown.

One of them opened its mouth. "B U R R R R P!"

"Brown!" I cried.

Brown laughed out loud. "It's all right!" he said. "They aren't dinosaurs. They're just *turtles*! They're speaking reptile!"

"I didn't know you could speak reptile," I said to him.

"Why wouldn't I?" he replied. "I'm a reptile, aren't I?"

Cluid said, "They're awfully big, Brown. Don't some turtles eat meat?"

"I'll ask them," Brown said. And he burped at them again.

One of the big creatures answered, "B L A C C H."

Brown translated. "He says they aren't meat eaters. They eat leaves and grasses and things like that."

"He didn't say all that in one *blacch*," I protested.

"Well, reptile is a pretty primitive language," Brown explained. "I was just fleshing it out for you. What he really said was more like, 'Meat, yuck.'"

Oh, well, that was good.

We came out of hiding.

Bill cleared his throat and burped, **"BLAT!"**

One of the turtles immediately rushed toward him, bellowing loudly! It came right up to the shore, with water sloshing off its huge shell and its long claws ripping into the muck.

Brown jumped between Bill and the turtle, protesting loud and fast in reptile.

The turtle grunted.

Cluid giggled. "Bill," she said, "you may have specialized in animal talk, but this time I think you said the wrong thing."

Bill cleared his throat, as if he was going to try speaking reptile again, but I clapped my paw over his mouth and pulled him back.

"Don't make the turtles mad, Bill," I pleaded. "We might be able to get some information out of them. Just don't say anything. Okay?"

Bill sighed, but he nodded and sat down.

"Ask them something," I said to Brown.

"What should I ask?" he said.

"I don't know. Ask what period of history this is."

Brown just looked at me.

"Okay, okay," I said. "Maybe that's too hard for turtles. Ask them . . . um . . . if there are any humans around."

Brown thought about it. Then he pointed at Bill and made some sounds: "URP, PSSSS?"

The turtle replied. One of the others added something, and then the turtles in the water all said, "HYONK! HYONK! HYONK!"

"What are they saying?" I asked.

Brown gave a shushing motion with his arm and listened hard until the turtles had stopped. Then he translated.

"I think they said that they used to belong to a human boy, years and years ago. They were small and the boy was big, but now they are big and this human is small. They think that's pretty funny. They said they had thought all the humans were gone until they saw Bill."

"Wow," I said, thinking fast. *They belonged to a human boy, and they thought the humans were gone!* "Do you realize what that means?" I said.

I looked from Brown to Cluid and back to Brown. *"That means they must have lived right through the end of the Human Occupation!"*

I was so excited! I had always wondered what had happened to the humans, but whenever I asked Bill, all he would say (if he said anything) was, "Unforeseen consequences." (Talking was not easy for Bill. He'd been in the freezing chamber for a long time, remember.)

I rubbed my paws together and squatted on my haunches. This was going to be good. "Ask them what happened to the big humans," I said to Brown.

"Okay."

Brown asked them.

They all spoke at once, then stopped and glared at one another.

Brown pointed to the first turtle.

It spoke.

When it stopped, Brown scratched between his eye knobs. He said, "I don't understand. But it sounds like the humans all got sick from eating green berries."

Bill stepped up and nodded, pointing at the turtle. "Correct," he said. He turned to us. "GreenBerry virus. Uh, GreenBerries not eaten, but . . . um . . . *implanted*!" He pointed at his nose and shook his head sadly.

"Implanted? Yuck!" I said. "Did *all* the humans get it?"

The second turtle started braying and bawling.

Brown listened.

"She says there was much fighting and killing among humans."

"Correct," Bill said again. "Road rage."

"I thought she meant war," Brown said.

"Road Rage War," said Bill.

"So all the humans died from green berries implanted in their noses and from road rage?" I asked.

"Quiet," said Brown.

A third turtle was speaking.

We all listened, then turned to Brown to find out what it meant.

Brown turned to Bill. "Does 'too many cleaning products' mean anything to you?"

I was more confused than ever. "Did all the people die?" I asked again.

Bill shook his head. "Many unforeseen consequences." He sighed.

"Ask the turtles," I said to Brown, "if all the humans died."

Brown opened his mouth to speak.

There was a loud splash.

All of the turtle heads disappeared at once. And Brown, Cluid, and I dashed for cover.

3

Don't Eat Us!

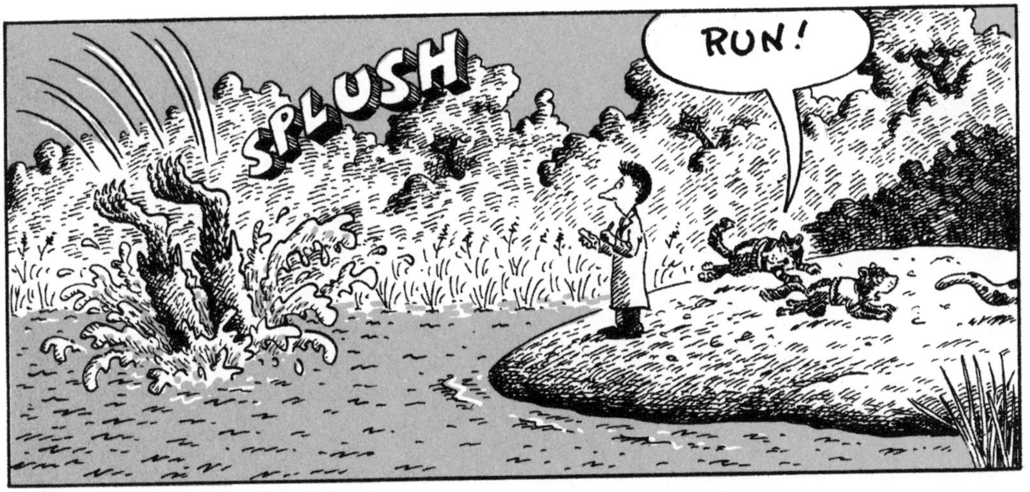
SPLUSH
RUN!

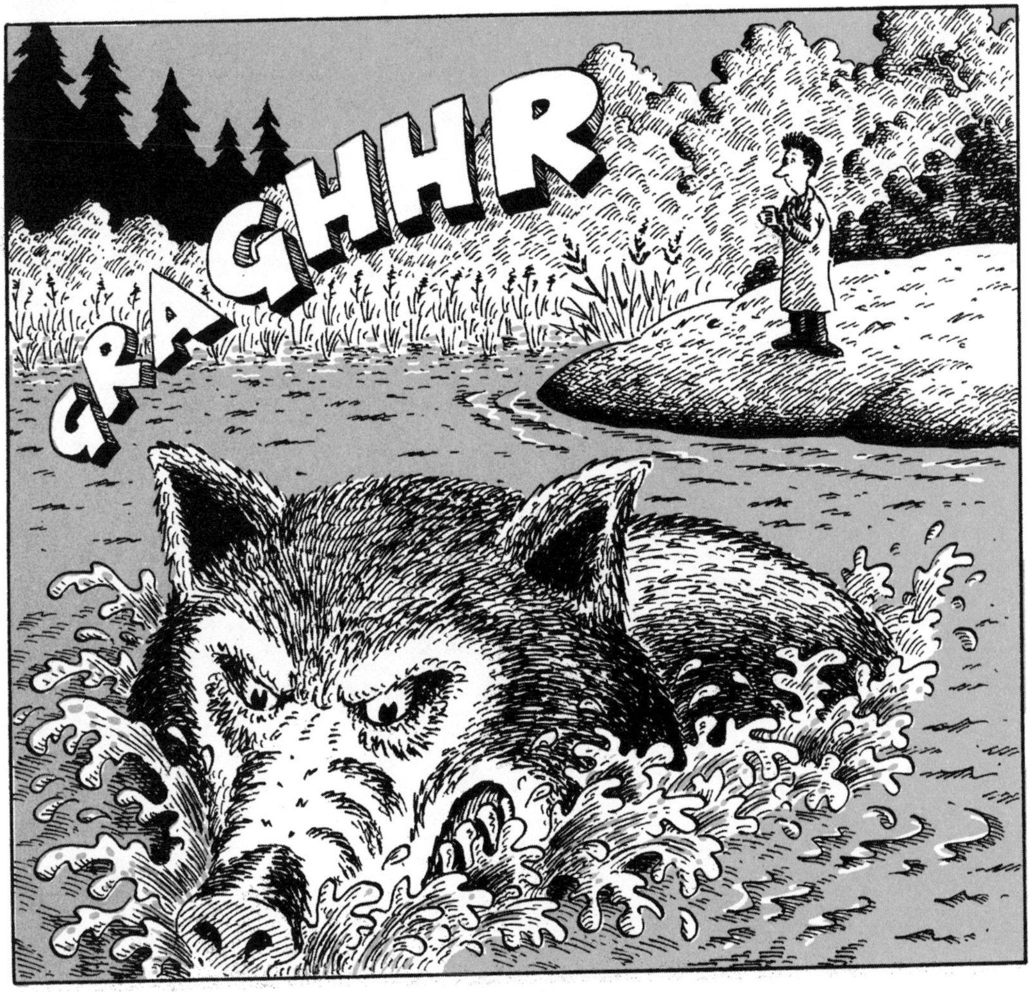
GRAGHHR

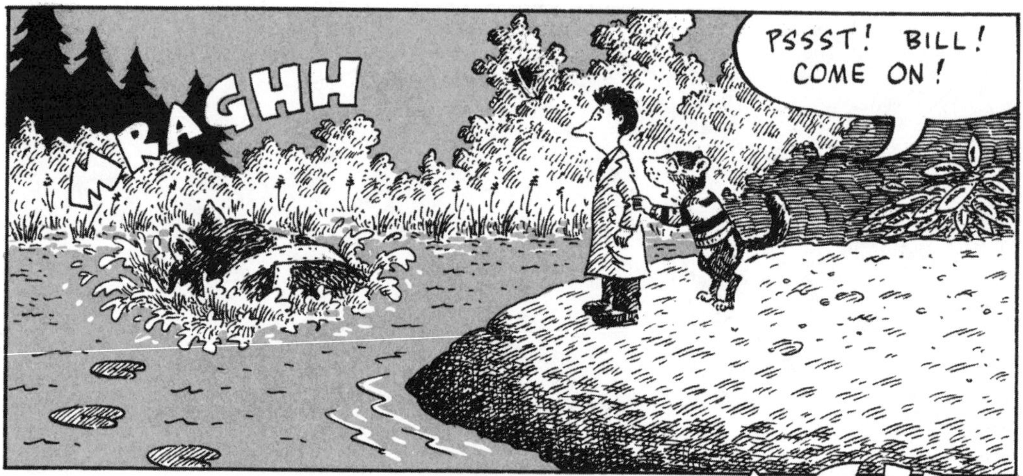
MRAGHH
PSSST! BILL! COME ON!

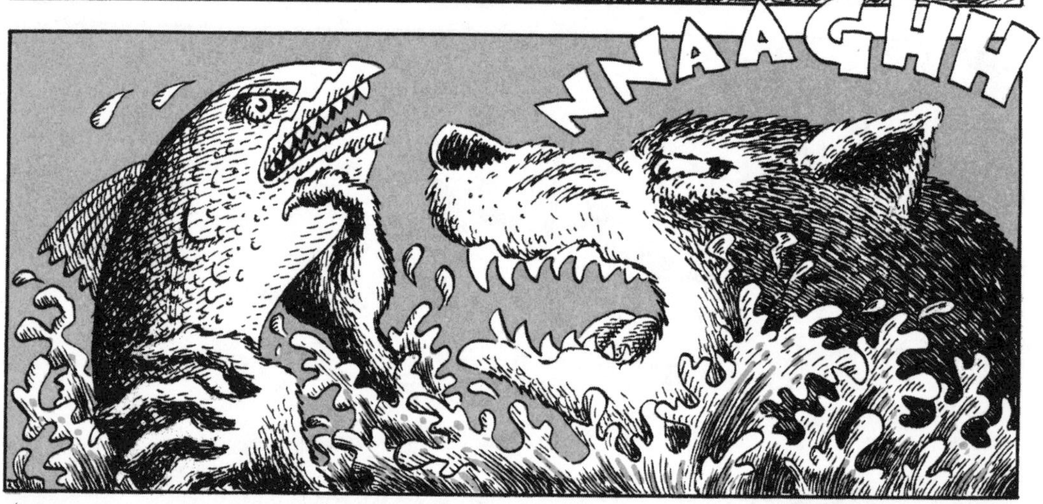
NNAAGHH

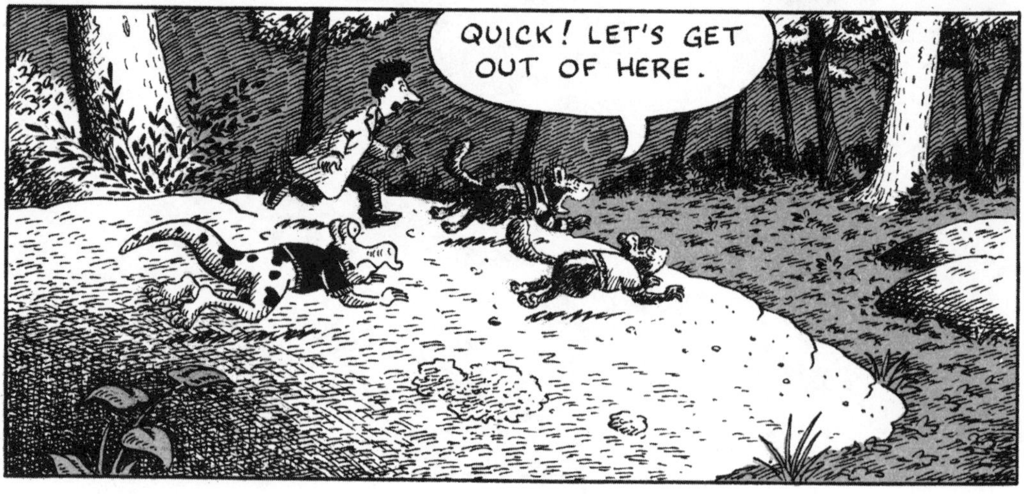
QUICK! LET'S GET OUT OF HERE.

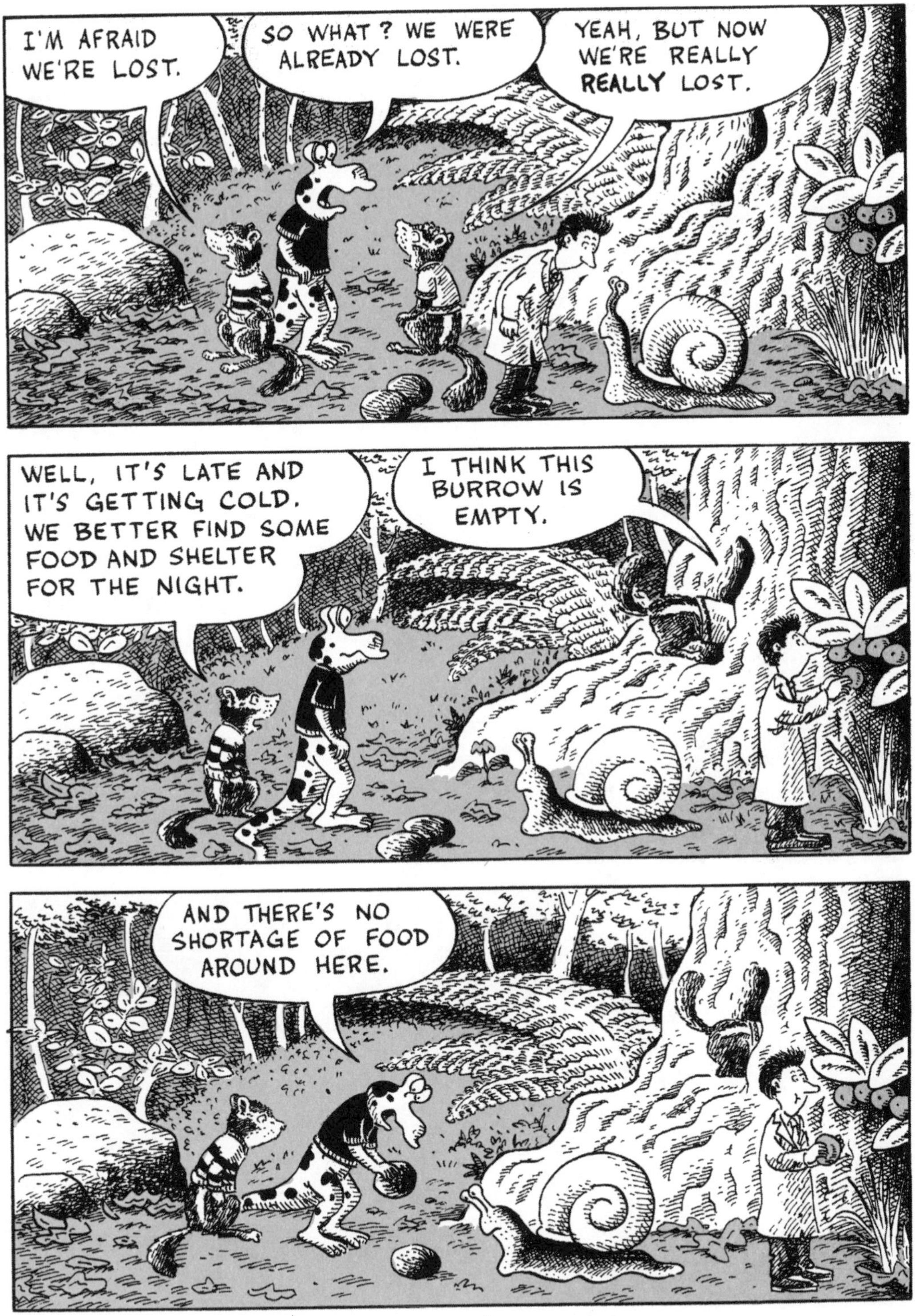
I'M AFRAID WE'RE LOST.
SO WHAT? WE WERE ALREADY LOST.
YEAH, BUT NOW WE'RE REALLY REALLY LOST.
WELL, IT'S LATE AND IT'S GETTING COLD. WE BETTER FIND SOME FOOD AND SHELTER FOR THE NIGHT.
I THINK THIS BURROW IS EMPTY.
AND THERE'S NO SHORTAGE OF FOOD AROUND HERE.

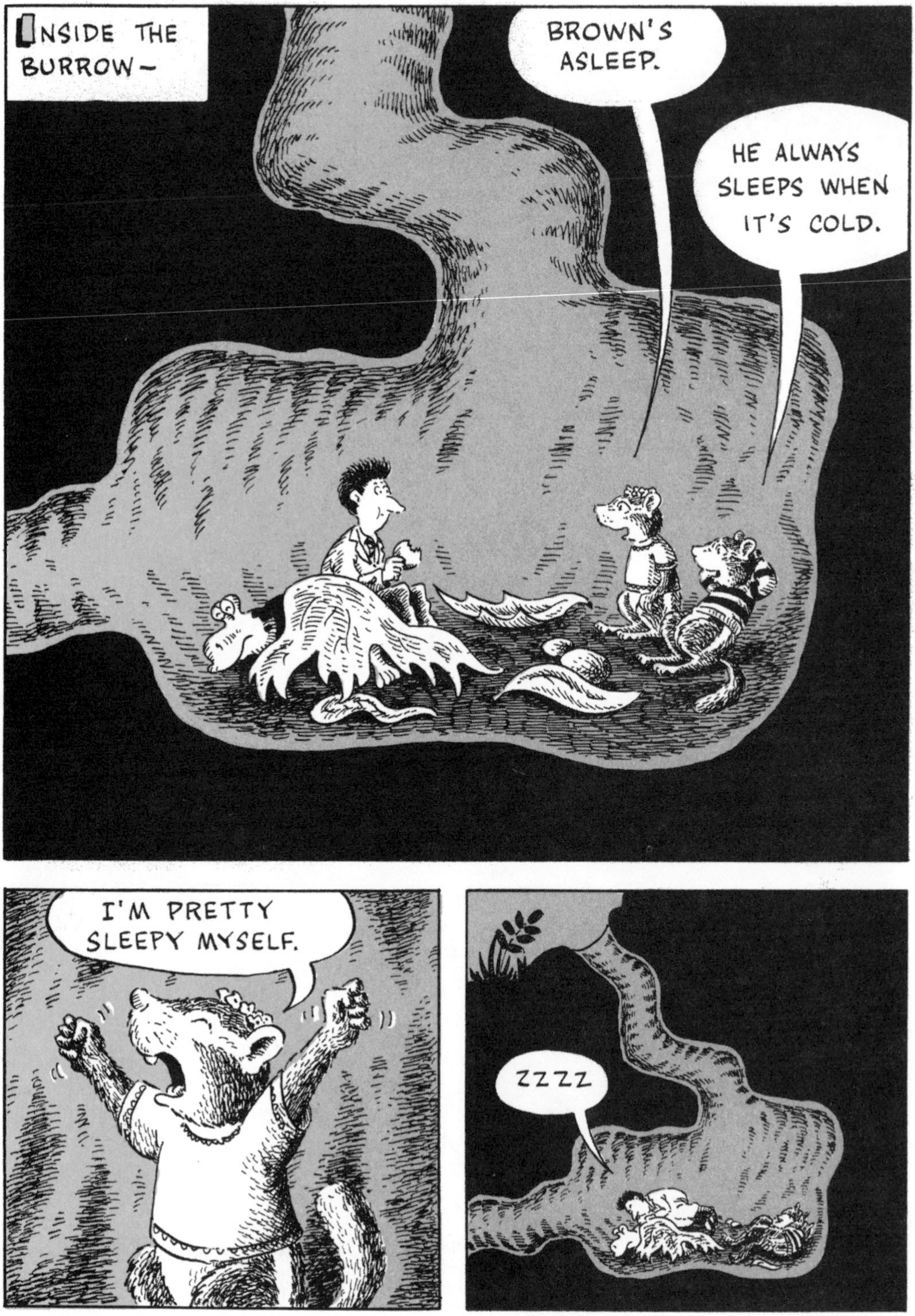
INSIDE THE BURROW—
BROWN'S ASLEEP.
HE ALWAYS SLEEPS WHEN IT'S COLD.
I'M PRETTY SLEEPY MYSELF.
ZZZZ

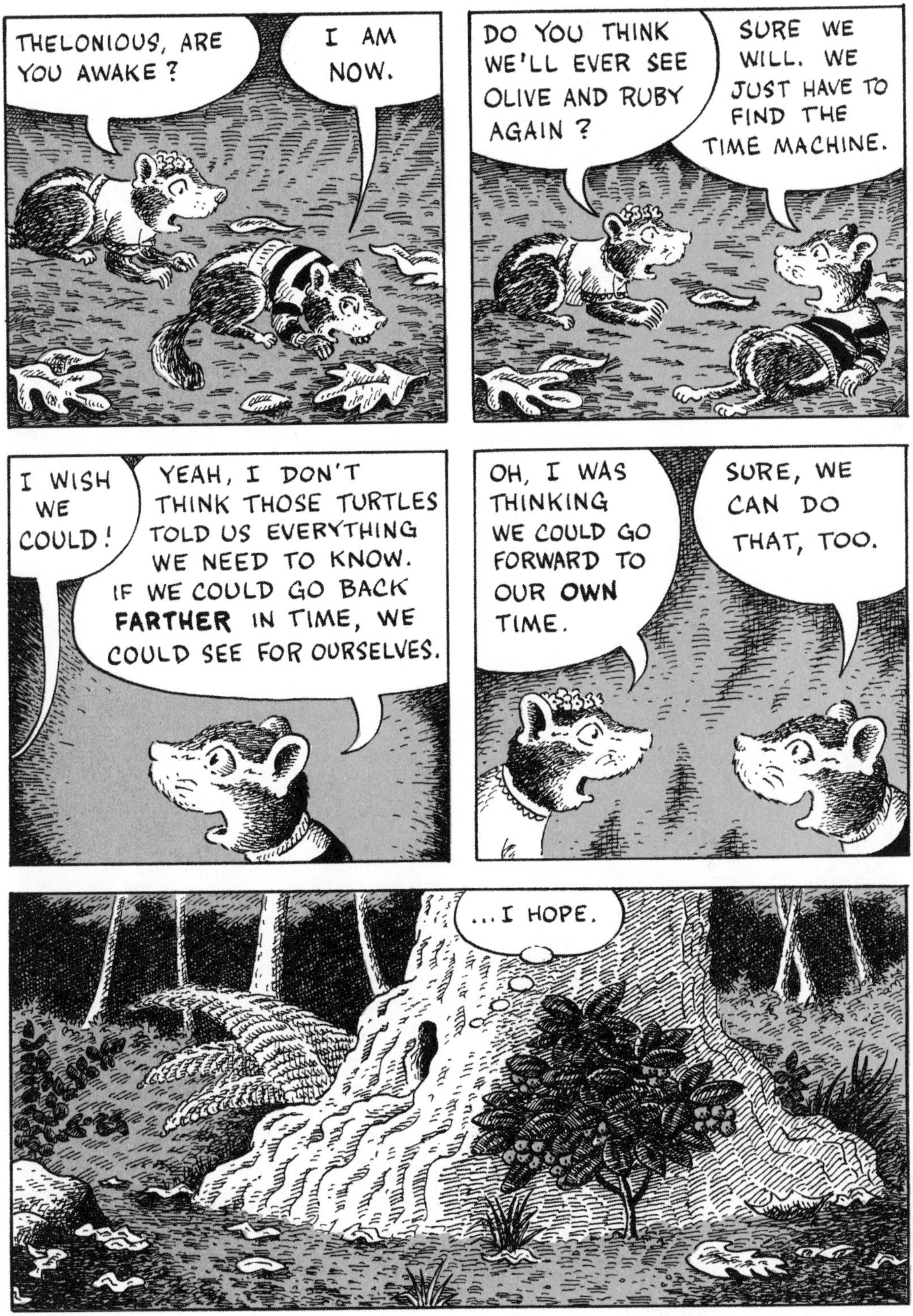
THELONIOUS, ARE YOU AWAKE?
I AM NOW.
DO YOU THINK WE'LL EVER SEE OLIVE AND RUBY AGAIN?
SURE WE WILL. WE JUST HAVE TO FIND THE TIME MACHINE.
I WISH WE COULD!
YEAH, I DON'T THINK THOSE TURTLES TOLD US EVERYTHING WE NEED TO KNOW. IF WE COULD GO BACK FARTHER IN TIME, WE COULD SEE FOR OURSELVES.
OH, I WAS THINKING WE COULD GO FORWARD TO OUR OWN TIME.
SURE, WE CAN DO THAT, TOO.
...I HOPE.

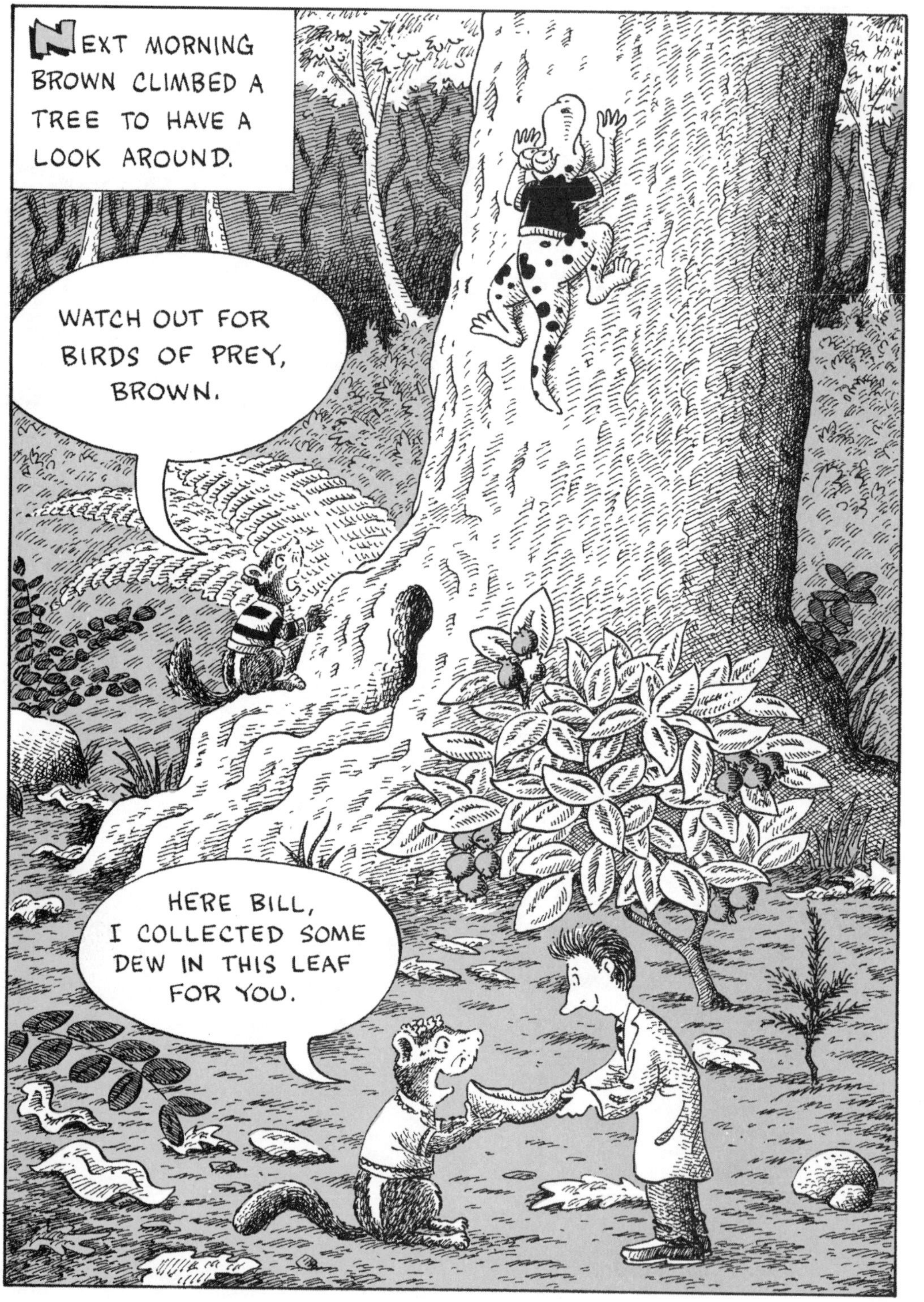
NEXT MORNING BROWN CLIMBED A TREE TO HAVE A LOOK AROUND.
WATCH OUT FOR BIRDS OF PREY, BROWN.
HERE BILL, I COLLECTED SOME DEW IN THIS LEAF FOR YOU.

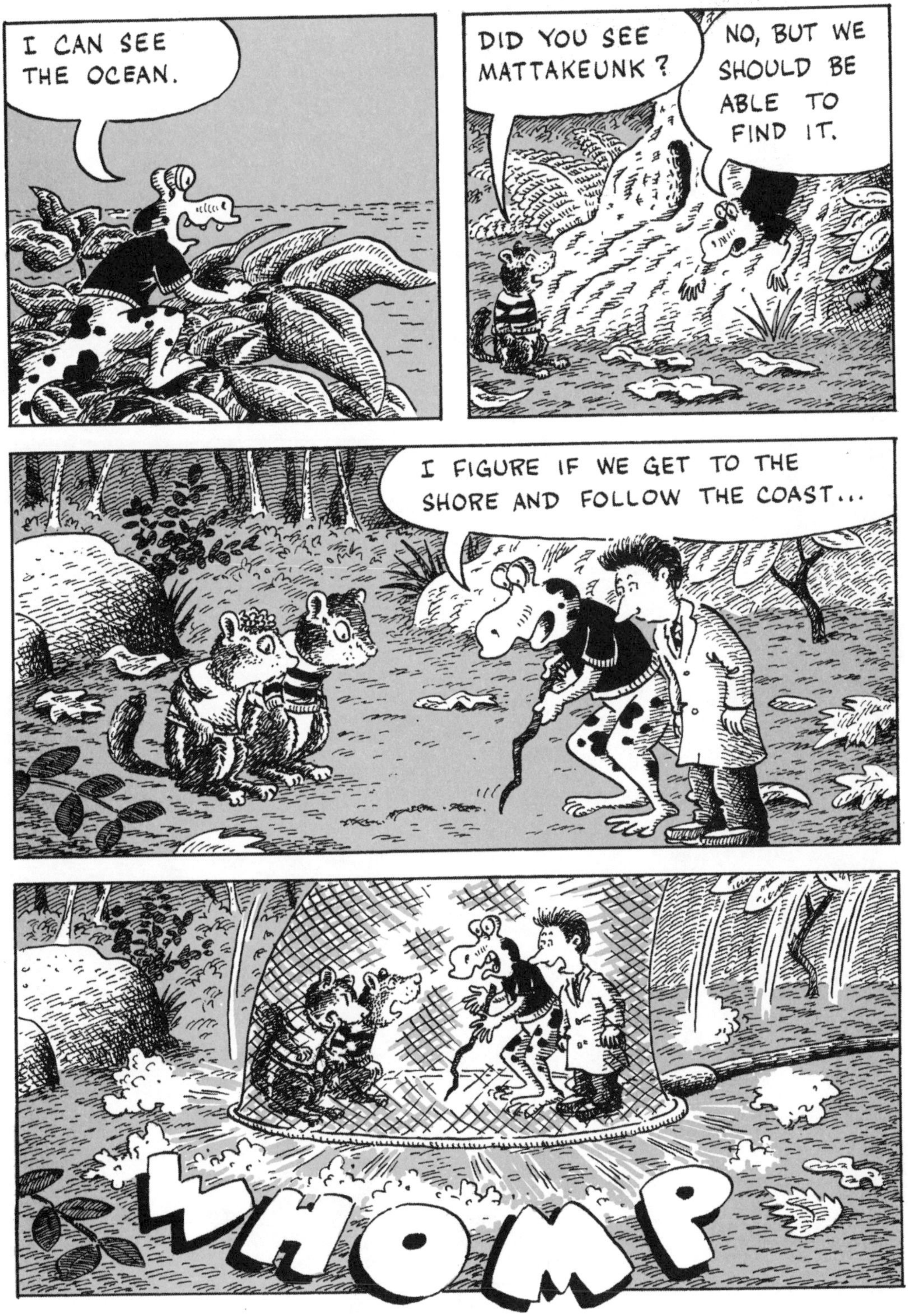
I CAN SEE THE OCEAN.
DID YOU SEE MATTAKEUNK ?
NO, BUT WE SHOULD BE ABLE TO FIND IT.
I FIGURE IF WE GET TO THE SHORE AND FOLLOW THE COAST...
WHOMP

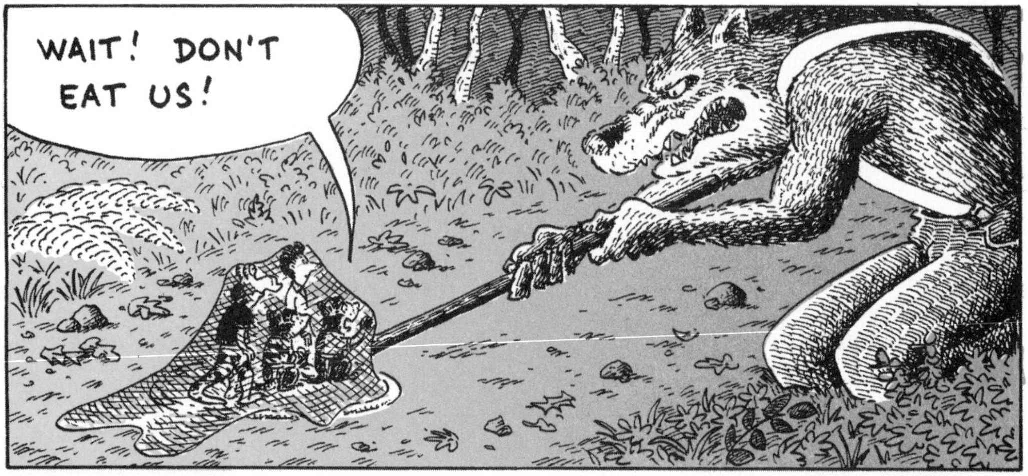
WAIT! DON'T EAT US!

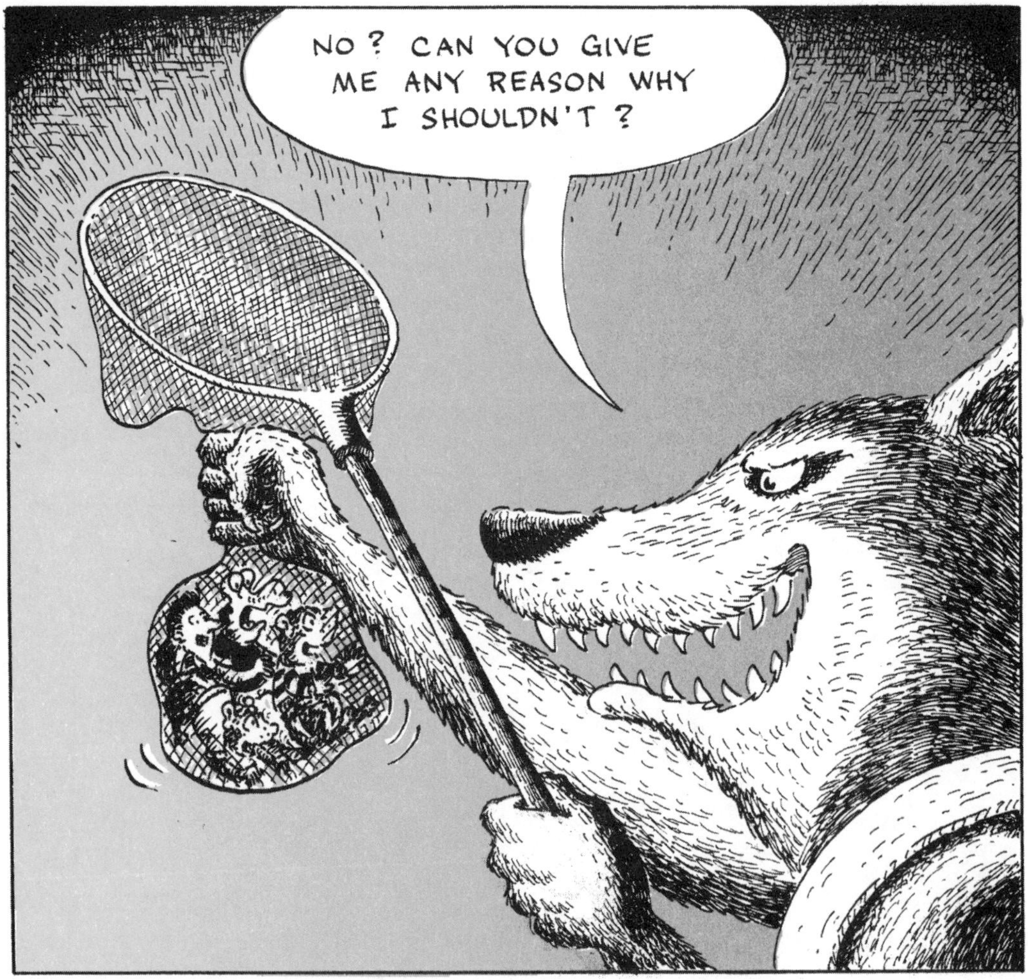
NO? CAN YOU GIVE ME ANY REASON WHY I SHOULDN'T?

4

The Wolfman

Cluid and I looked at each other. I didn't know what to say.

"He's a talker!" Cluid whispered.

I turned and said loudly, "You shouldn't eat us, because you're a talker! And *we're* talkers! It's the law of the Untamed Forest."

His lips widened into a toothy leer. "But this isn't the Untamed Forest, you know. And I follow no law but my own. The law of UPSILON THE WOLFMAN!"

He waited while I tried to think of something else to say.

"Isn't there any *other* reason why I shouldn't eat you?" he prodded.

I said, "There are *lots* of reasons!"

Brown said, "Keep him talking, Thelonious. Tell him about Bill."

I said, "This is Bill." I nodded my head in Bill's direction. "He's the last living human on Earth! You wouldn't want to eat the last living human, would you?"

The wolfman looked at Bill. Poor Bill smiled back at him.

"He's kind of small for a human, isn't he?" the wolfman said.

"He shrank in a freezing chamber," I explained.

"We're from the future. We came here in a time machine, to learn about past human mistakes so we can save the planet!"

"A time machine! HA, HA, HA, HA!"

He laughed so hard I thought he was going to fall over. His head swung back, and his large canine teeth glistened with saliva.

"HA, HA, HA, HA!"

I tried to take advantage of the moment and wriggle free.

"Not so fast, Chipmunk," he said, dumping us all quickly into a mesh cage that hung from his belt.

SNAP. The door of the cage clicked shut.

"And don't bother trying to tear your way out," he added. "This

 cage is made out of an infrangible material that I found at the Mattakeunk Institute."

I wasn't sure what "infrangible" meant, but

when I tried to bite the cage, I didn't even leave a mark.

The wolfman was watching me. He laughed. "There's a lot of cool stuff like that at the Institute, *including* a defunct old time machine. HA, HA!

That hasn't worked as long as I've been around. If it ever did! Spun you around and spit you out through an exhaust vent, didn't it?"

He gave a few more snorts of laughter. "You haven't traveled *anywhere* in time. Maybe a few miles in space, that's all."

Not traveled in time? But . . .

"Would you be good enough to tell us the way back to the Institute?" Cluid asked in a small voice.

"And give up some of the best entertainment I've had in years?" he replied. "Now why should I do that, I wonder?"

He unhooked our cage and lifted us up for a better look.

"No," he said. "I'll be having you four for lunch." He watched us closely and gave a few snickers as we gasped in fear. "As my *guests*, that is," he added, and laughed loudly.

He wound down with a few chuckles. "Forgive me. My sense of humor is a little coarse," he said. "It must be the company I keep."

He rehooked our cage onto his belt and then bounded off on all fours,

running swiftly and silently through a forest of dark evergreen trees, farther and farther from the friends who could save us.

There was nothing we could do but hold on to the soft mesh of the cage and try to keep from banging into each other.

In my mind I went over and over what he had said. *Not back in time? But what about those turtles? They said they were around during the Human Occupation. They belonged to a human boy! But they couldn't really be that old. Could they?*

The wolfman leaped over a moss-covered log, then climbed up a rocky ledge. There he stopped, looked to the sky, and howled, "AROOOOOOOOOOO!"

before continuing on his way.

I shot Cluid a worried look. I thought, *What's next? Is the wolfman really going to give us lunch? Or are we going to be lunch?*

5

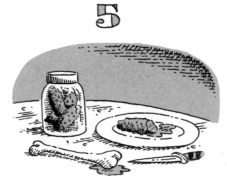

Pickles

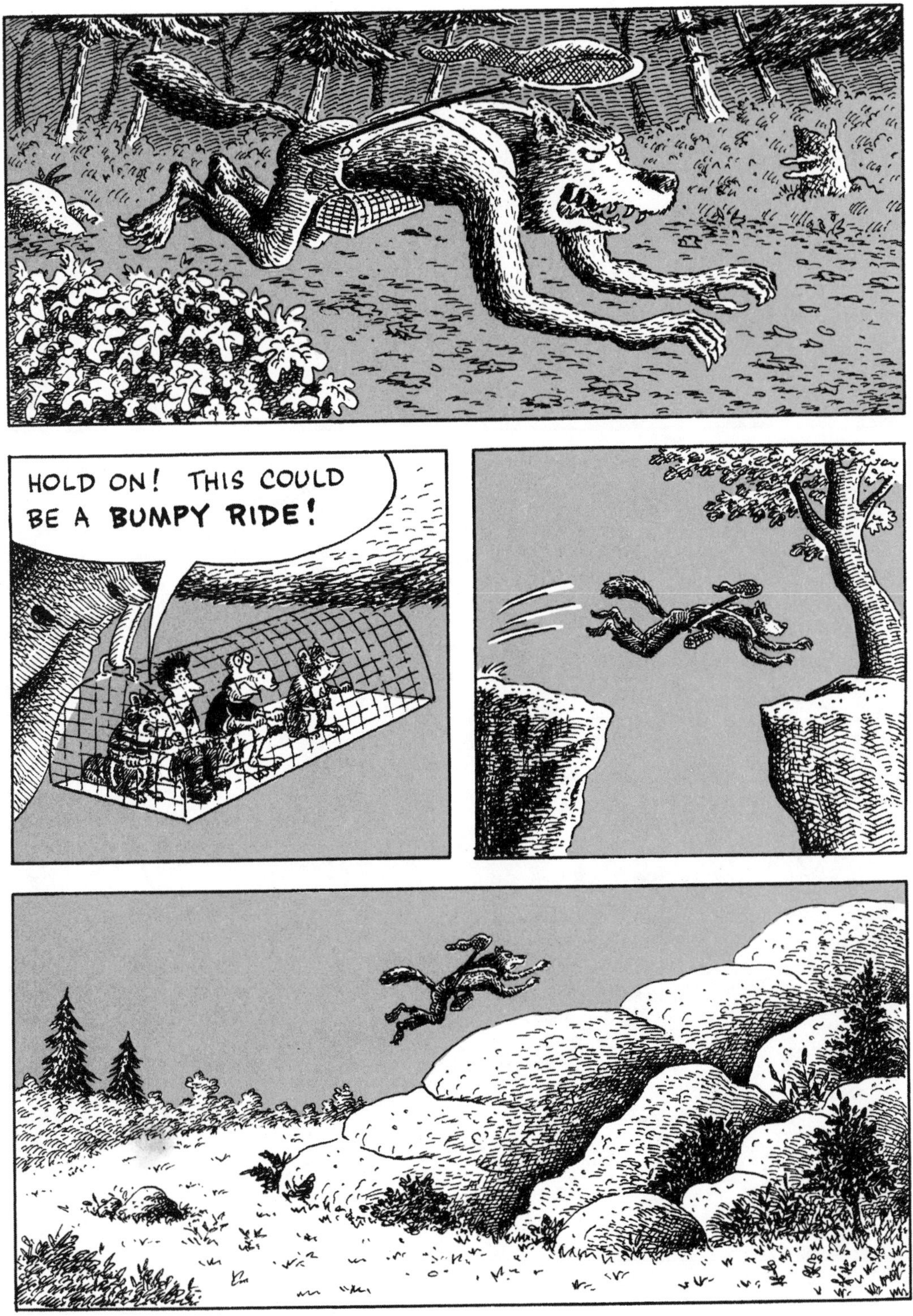
HOLD ON! THIS COULD BE A BUMPY RIDE!

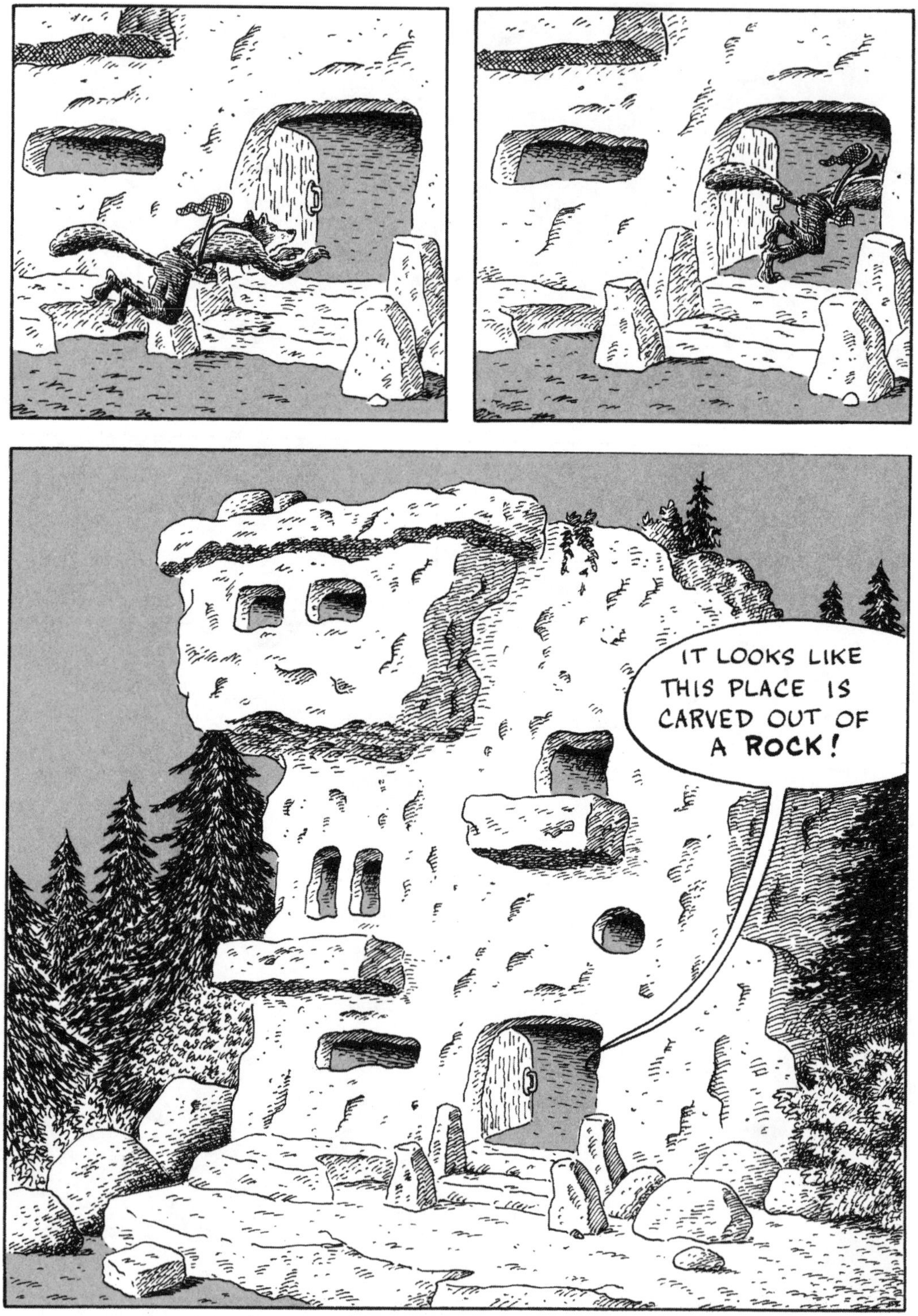
IT LOOKS LIKE THIS PLACE IS CARVED OUT OF A ROCK!

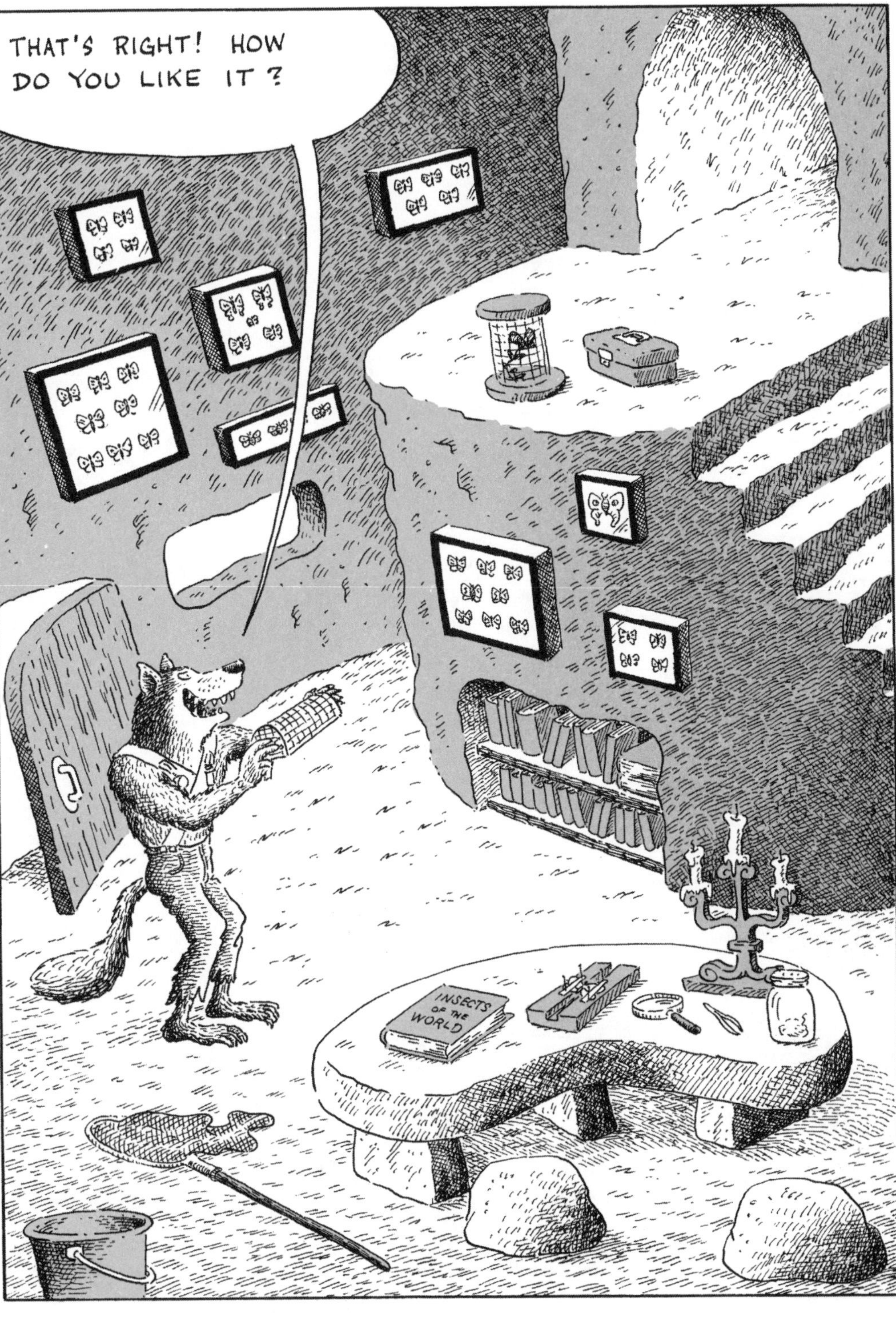
THAT'S RIGHT! HOW DO YOU LIKE IT?
INSECTS OF THE WORLD

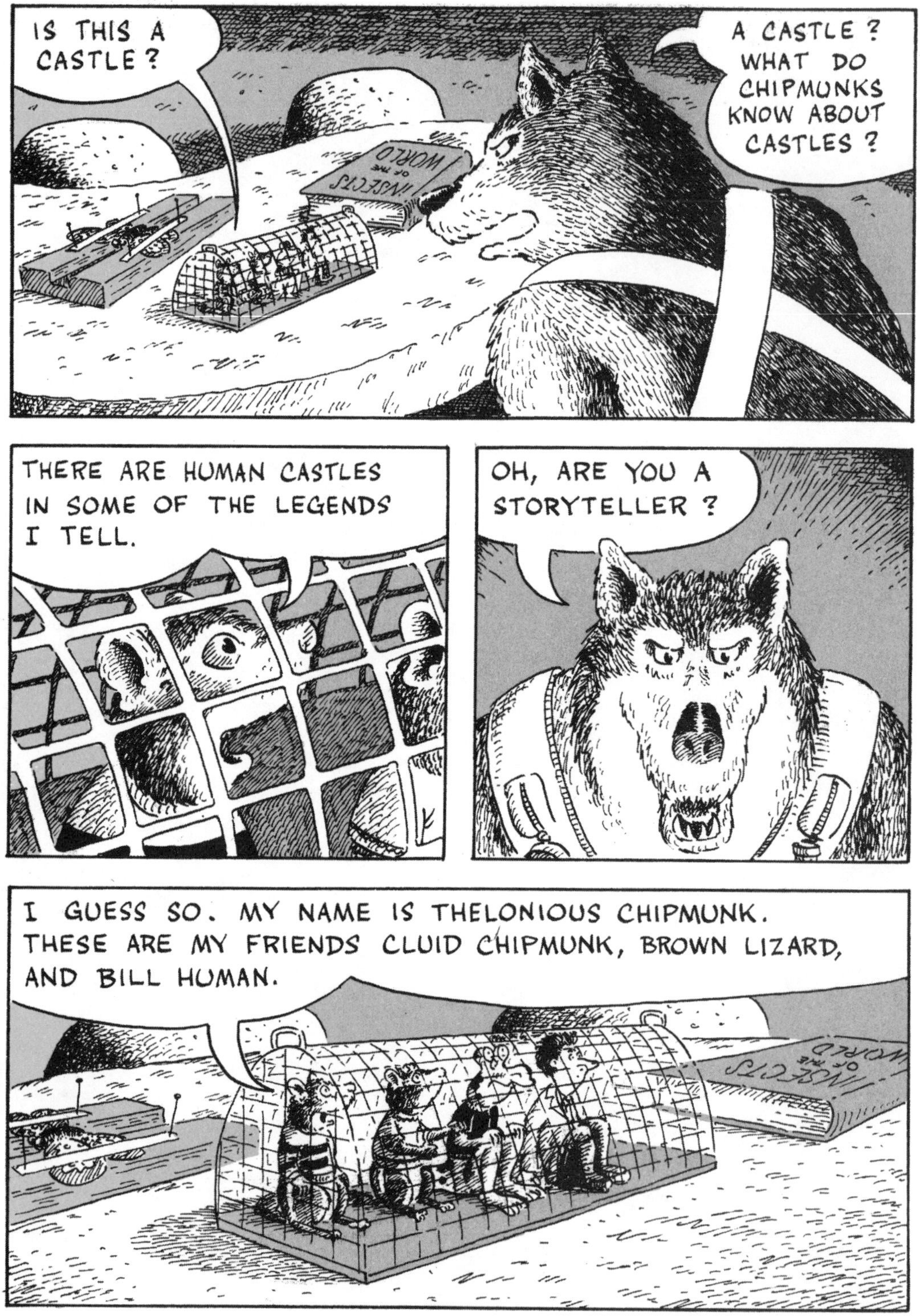
IS THIS A CASTLE ?
A CASTLE ? WHAT DO CHIPMUNKS KNOW ABOUT CASTLES ?
INSECTS OF THE WORLD
THERE ARE HUMAN CASTLES IN SOME OF THE LEGENDS I TELL.
OH, ARE YOU A STORYTELLER ?
I GUESS SO. MY NAME IS THELONIOUS CHIPMUNK. THESE ARE MY FRIENDS CLUID CHIPMUNK, BROWN LIZARD, AND BILL HUMAN.
INSECTS OF THE WORLD

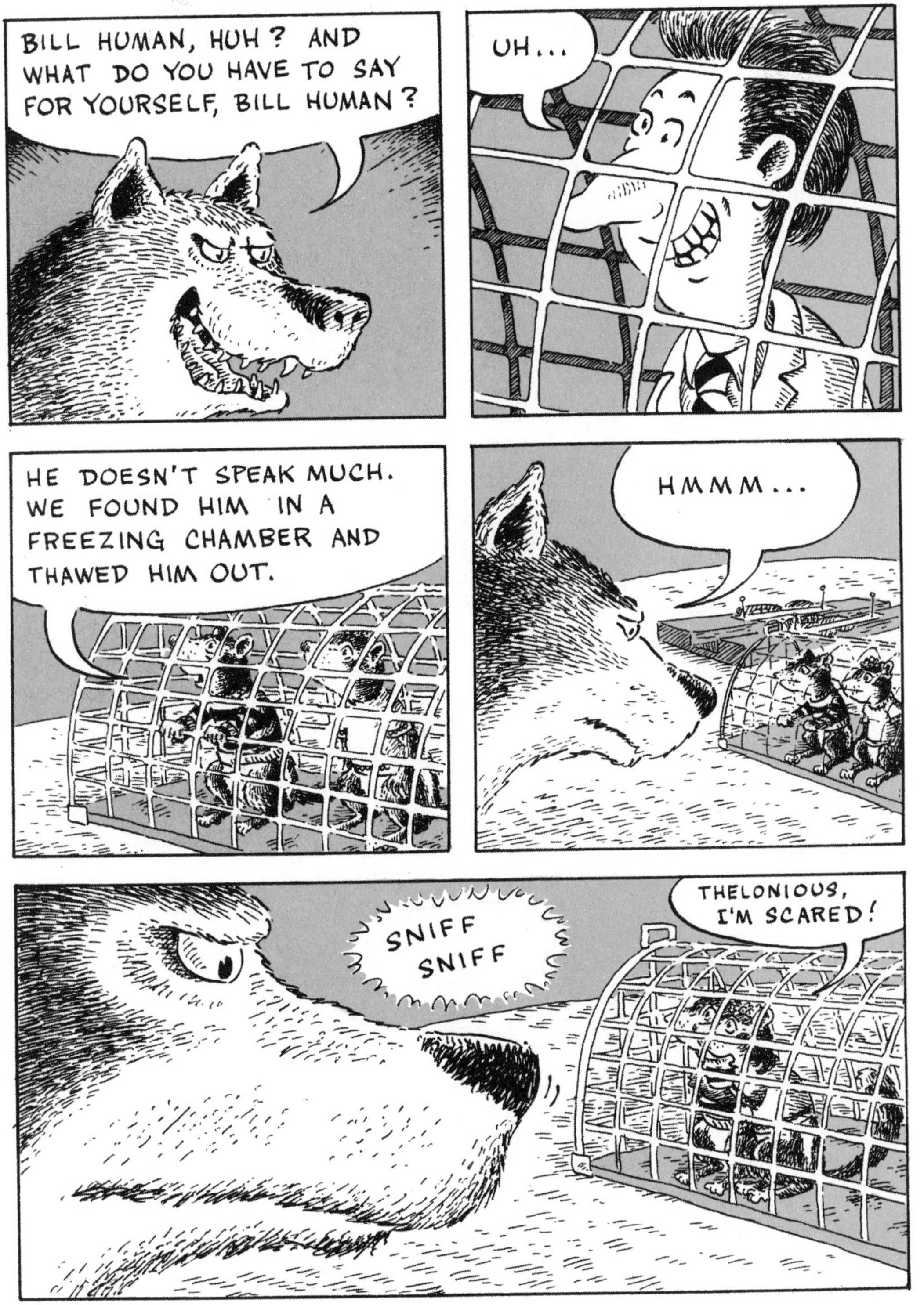
BILL HUMAN, HUH? AND WHAT DO YOU HAVE TO SAY FOR YOURSELF, BILL HUMAN?
UH...
HE DOESN'T SPEAK MUCH. WE FOUND HIM IN A FREEZING CHAMBER AND THAWED HIM OUT.
HMMM...
SNIFF SNIFF
THELONIOUS, I'M SCARED!

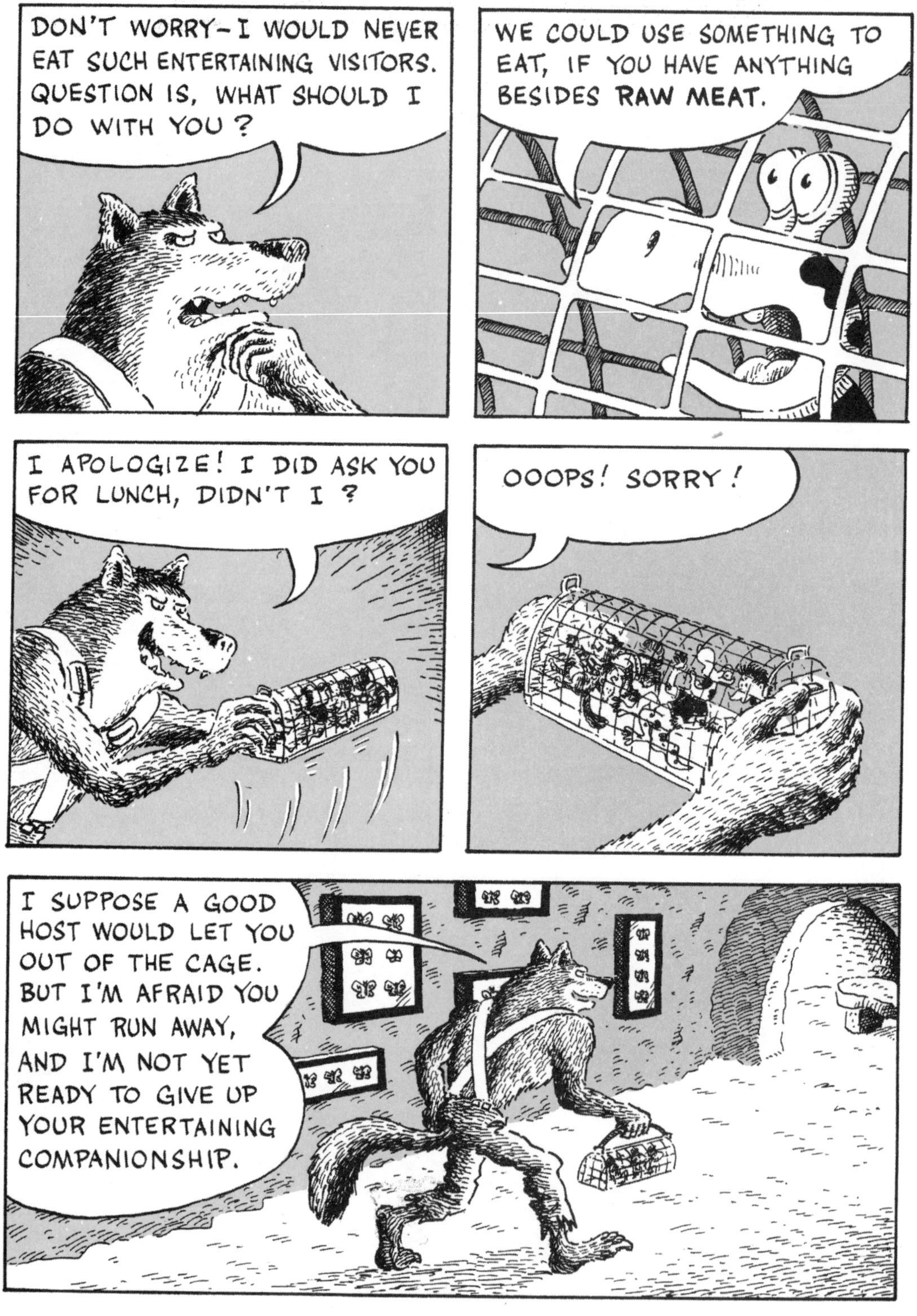
DON'T WORRY- I WOULD NEVER EAT SUCH ENTERTAINING VISITORS. QUESTION IS, WHAT SHOULD I DO WITH YOU?
WE COULD USE SOMETHING TO EAT, IF YOU HAVE ANYTHING BESIDES RAW MEAT.
I APOLOGIZE! I DID ASK YOU FOR LUNCH, DIDN'T I?
OOOPS! SORRY!
I SUPPOSE A GOOD HOST WOULD LET YOU OUT OF THE CAGE. BUT I'M AFRAID YOU MIGHT RUN AWAY, AND I'M NOT YET READY TO GIVE UP YOUR ENTERTAINING COMPANIONSHIP.

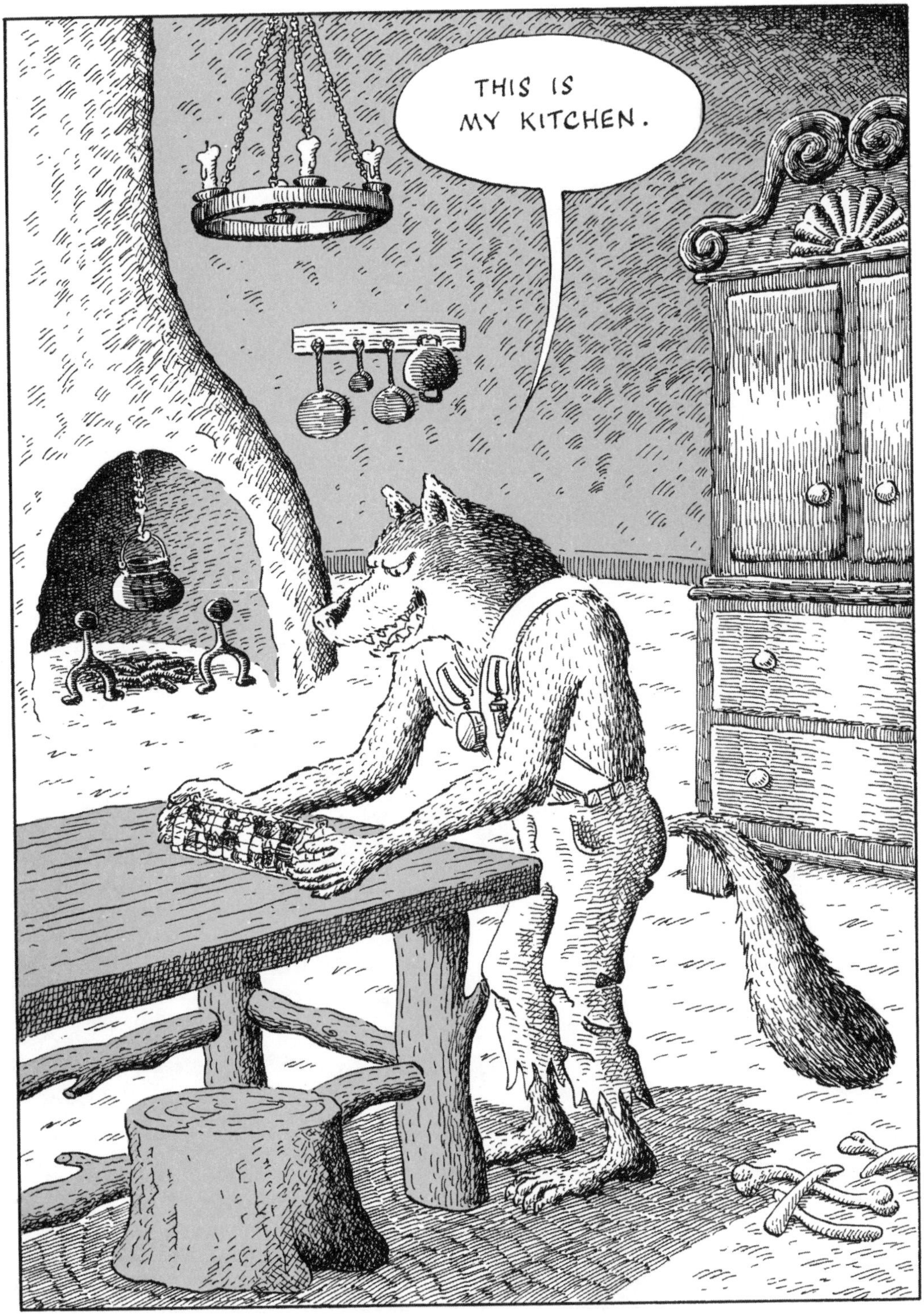
THIS IS MY KITCHEN.

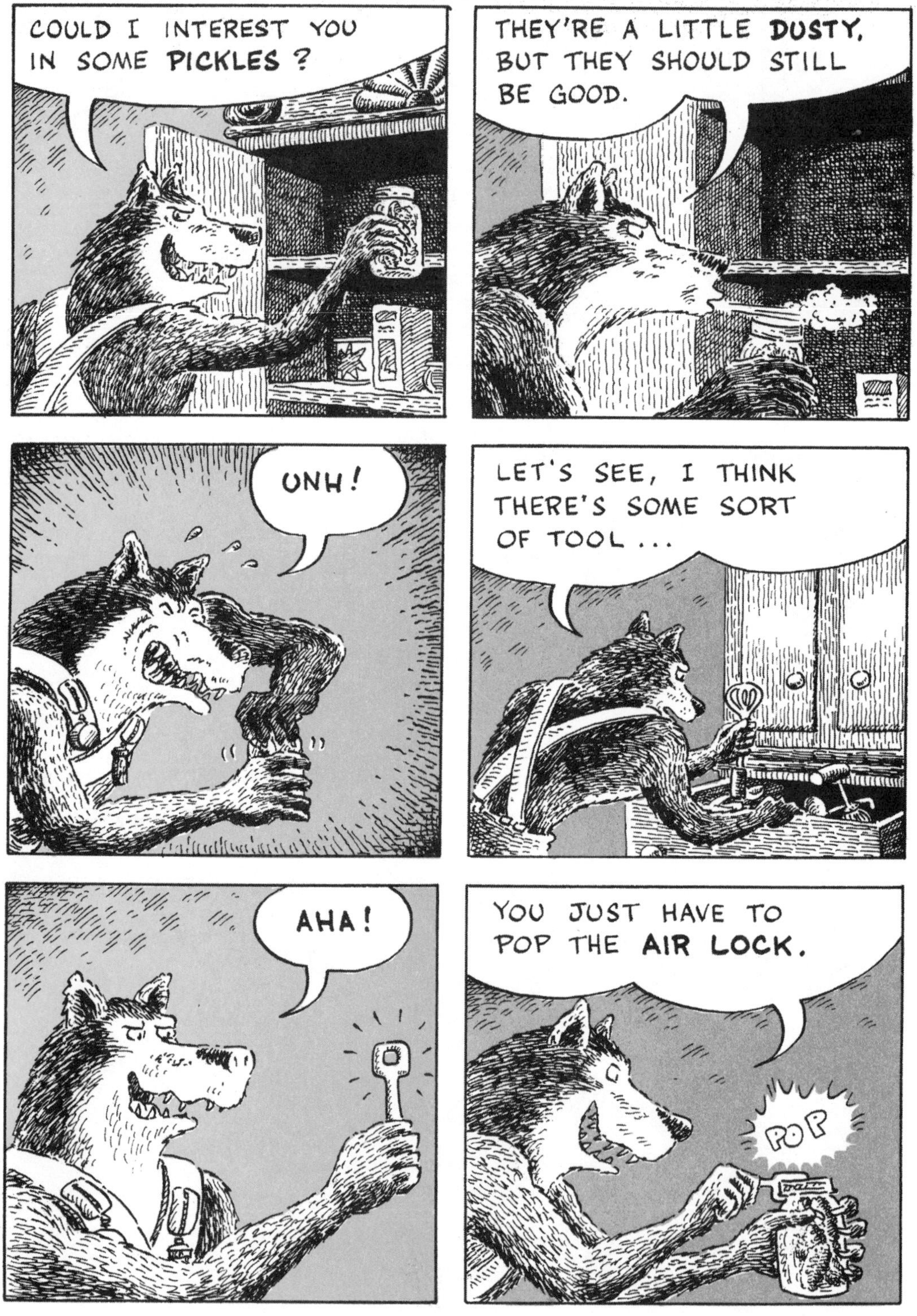
COULD I INTEREST YOU IN SOME PICKLES?
THEY'RE A LITTLE DUSTY, BUT THEY SHOULD STILL BE GOOD.
UNH!
LET'S SEE, I THINK THERE'S SOME SORT OF TOOL...
AHA!
YOU JUST HAVE TO POP THE AIR LOCK.
POP

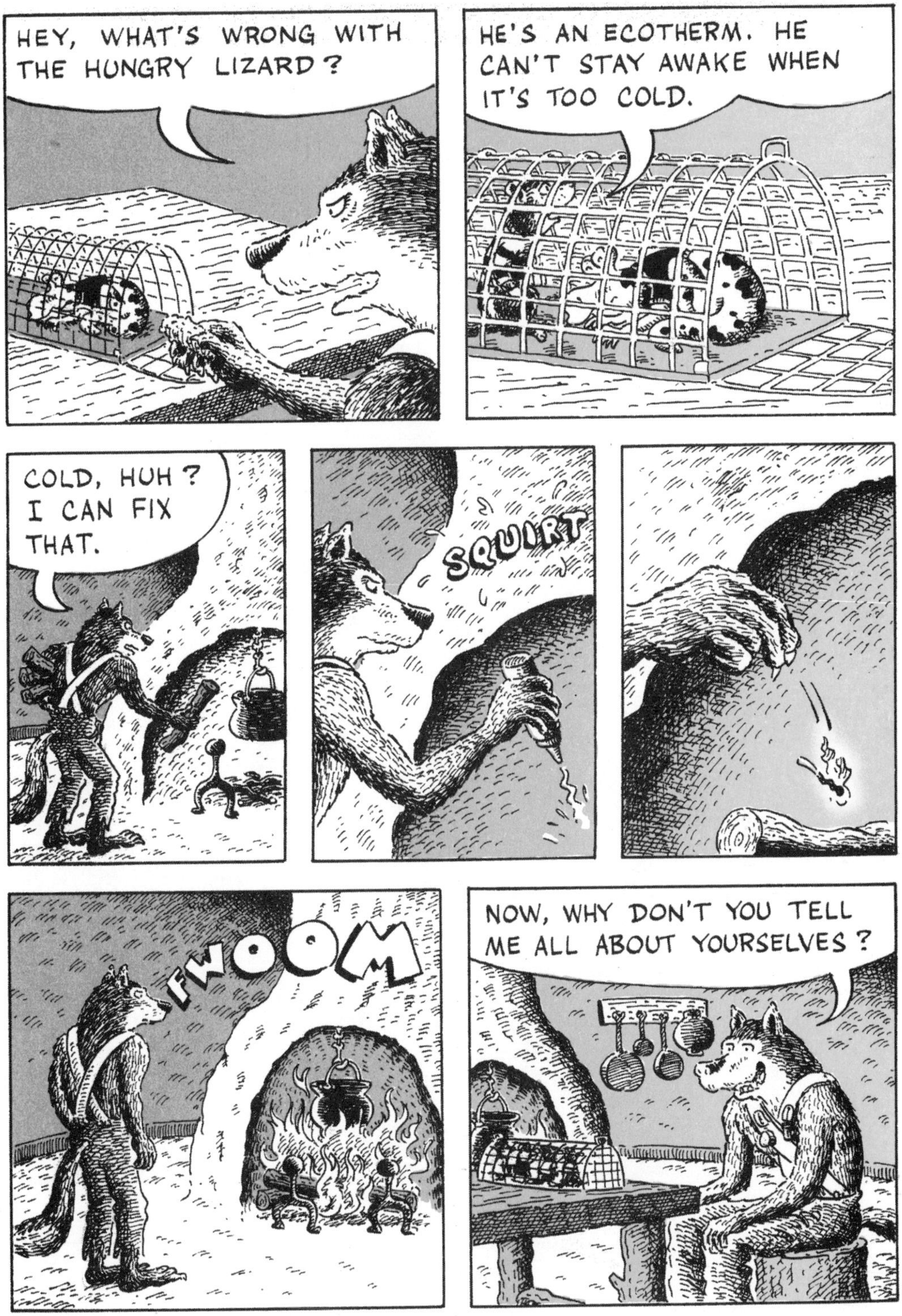
HEY, WHAT'S WRONG WITH THE HUNGRY LIZARD?
HE'S AN ECOTHERM. HE CAN'T STAY AWAKE WHEN IT'S TOO COLD.
COLD, HUH? I CAN FIX THAT.
SQUIRT
FWOOOM
NOW, WHY DON'T YOU TELL ME ALL ABOUT YOURSELVES?

6

The Crunching of
Small Bones

I didn't see that any harm would come from telling our story. In fact it seemed to me that the better he got to know us, the more Upsilon the Wolfman would warm to us. How could he not?

"Well," I began, "I grew up in the Untamed Forest . . ."

"Yes, yes, I've been there," Upsilon said. "And the others? The lizard and the shrunken human? They don't have the look of forest creatures."

"I met Brown in the City of Ruins," I continued. "He was a servant spy to the Dragon Lady."

The wolfman jumped up. *"The Dragon Lady?* Murderer of my father!" he hissed through his teeth. A low, angry rumble issued from somewhere down deep in his throat. "RRRRRRRR! I'd like to get my teeth into that monster!" He dragged his claws down a deeply scarred post and then bit into it, growling savagely and tearing out chunks of wood.

Sitting again, but on the edge of his stool this time, he glared at us. "I was so right to spare you pint-sized morsels!" He smiled and narrowed his orange eyes at the same time. "You." He pointed a claw at Brown. "Look alive! And tell me everything you know about the Dragon Lady."

Brown was awake again. He had been sleepily munching on a piece of pickle, but he swallowed so quickly he almost choked himself.

After coughing up a piece of pickle he gathered himself, looked back at the big wolfman, and said bravely, "Why should I? What will it get us?"

"You should tell me so I can wring that evil frogwoman's scraggy, jewel-encrusted neck!" Upsilon snarled.

When Brown didn't answer, Upsilon jumped up again and prowled around the room.

"How can I convince you that I won't harm you?" he asked.

"Let us out of the cage," I replied quickly.

"Oh, no." He sneered. "And have you escape? Especially now that I know you have information that I can use! I don't think so. Will you take my word that I'll let you go when you have told me all you can about the Dragon Lady?"

Brown nudged me with his elbow. I turned and we huddled. "I don't know if we can trust him," I whispered. "Your information is our only bargaining chip. What should we do?"

Bill stood up and cleared his throat loudly. (Bill spoke so seldom that his voice often needed a little loosening up.)

"Ahem." He went up to the mesh of the cage and spoke to the wolfman. "Take us to Olive," he said.

He turned to us and said, *"Then* tell."

He smiled sweetly and sat down again.

Of course! "Good idea, Bill," I said.

"Olive?" Upsilon asked.

"Olive is a bear and our good friend," I explained. "If you take us back to her and our other bear friends at the Mattakeunk Institute, we'll tell you all we know. Right, Brown?"

Brown nodded.

Upsilon narrowed his eyes and studied us. "Your *bear* friends?" he asked. "Why do I find that so hard to believe?"

"It's true!" said Cluid, holding on to the frame of the cage and sticking her snout through the mesh. "I am Cluid of the Fog Mound. We live with the Bears. They run the farm and live in Cliff House and we all work together.

Perhaps you have heard of the Fog Mound?"

He frowned. "Can't say that I have. I assumed you two chipmunks came together. This is sounding more and more strange. I'm beginning to think you're *all* storytellers!"

"Hah!" said Brown. "You haven't heard anything yet! Tell him about Faradawn, Thelonious, and the *mutant crabs.*"

The wolfman snorted.

"Shhh," I said to the others. "Don't confuse the issue."

To Upsilon I said, "If you just take us back to the Mattakeunk Institute, we will explain all."

"And that's our final offer," Brown added.

Upsilon got up and prowled around the room. After pacing for a while, with occasional glances our way, he lay down by the fire, put his head on his paws, and glared at us, without moving, through slitted eyes.

As I watched and waited, I saw him swivel one pointed ear toward the open door. Then, and only then, did I pick up the sound myself. Someone was approaching!

Upsilon rose silently, whisked up our cage, and shoved it into the cupboard.

As an afterthought he dumped the pickles beside us and pushed them up to where we could reach them.

"Don't make a sound!" he whispered urgently. "We'll talk more later!" He shut the door just as a loud voice called, "Hey, Wolfman, you old dog! How's hunting?"

The cupboard door had not latched. It let in a small sliver of light, and we could hear the whole conversation.

Upsilon said, "Blood Grey and Pinkie Fisher! Welcome. What brings you to my castle?"

"It's a castle now, is it?" someone said in a low growl.

"So I've been told," Upsilon replied.

"Dang! It's hot in here!" another animal complained in a high, whiny voice.

"What's in the sack, boys?" Upsilon asked.

"A little snack. Fancy it cooked?"

"Raw. Always raw for me," the whiny-voiced visitor said.

"You're a coarse fellow, Pinkie."

Brown jerked beside me in the dark cupboard. "Can't we get out of here?" he moaned.

"What's that?" one of the visitors asked quickly.

"Just the rats," Upsilon answered. "They won't bother us."

Rats? I turned to Cluid and saw her eyes wide with fright.

"I don't know why you don't eat those rats, Wolfman," said the one they called Pinkie.

Upsilon the Wolfman replied casually, "Oh, we get along all right. They clean up the bones for me. You want the leg, Pink?"

"Sure."

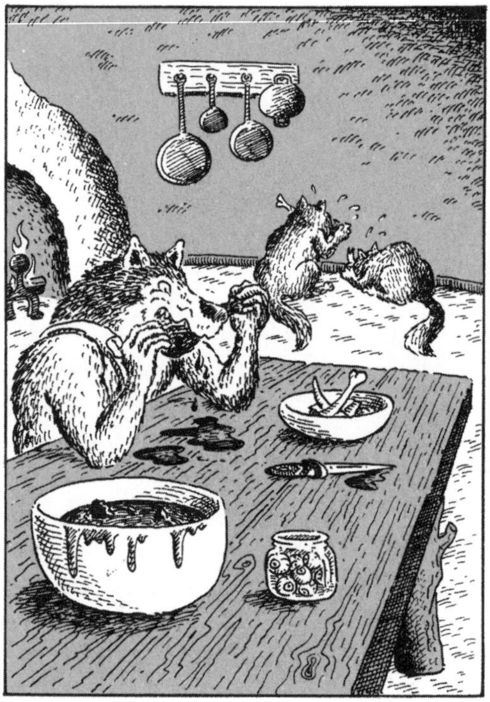

"I'll take the liver," growled his deep-voiced companion—Blood Grey.

For a while there was no more conversation. It was replaced by the gruesome crunching of small bones. *Crunch, crunch, slurp. Crunch, munch.*

"Cripes!" Brown whispered in my ear. "Do we have to listen to this?"

"Shhhh."

After a while, the growly one asked, "Catch anything good today, Upsilon?"

"So-so," Upsilon answered.

"You hunting for food or for specimens?" Blood Grey pursued.

"Whatever comes my way," said Upsilon. "Whatever comes my way." And he chuckled softly.

What little trust I had had in him melted away at that point. Of course, I hadn't been too encouraged by the slurping and crunching either.

Someone gave a loud belch. "*URP!* Not bad, huh?" It was Pinkie.

I thought nothing could be worse than listening to three large predators gorging themselves on raw meat and bones, but the silence that followed made my blood run cold! What were they doing *now*?

7

Enter the Rat

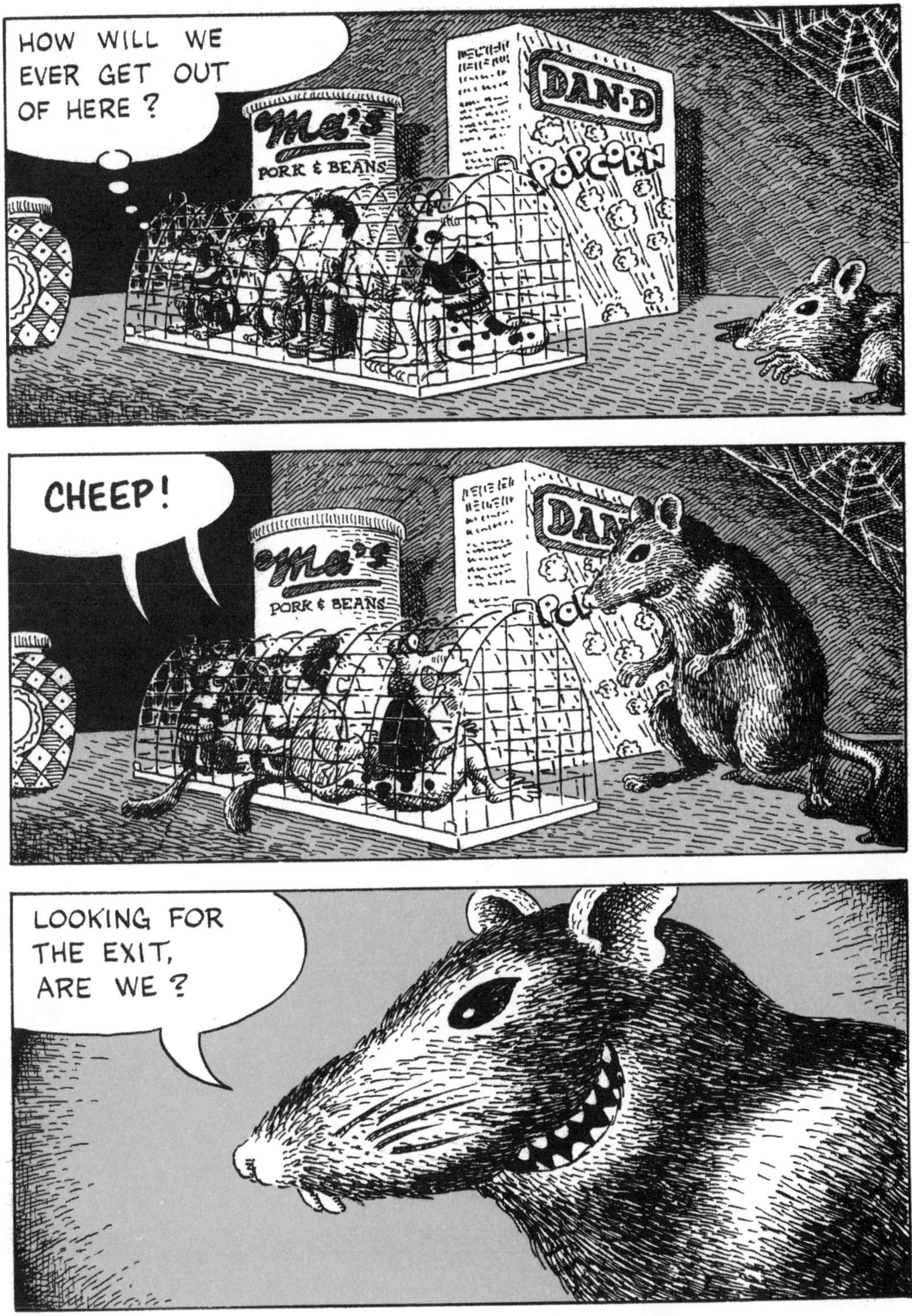
HOW WILL WE EVER GET OUT OF HERE ?
Ma's
PORK & BEANS
DAN-D
POPCORN
CHEEP!
Ma's
PORK & BEANS
LOOKING FOR THE EXIT, ARE WE ?

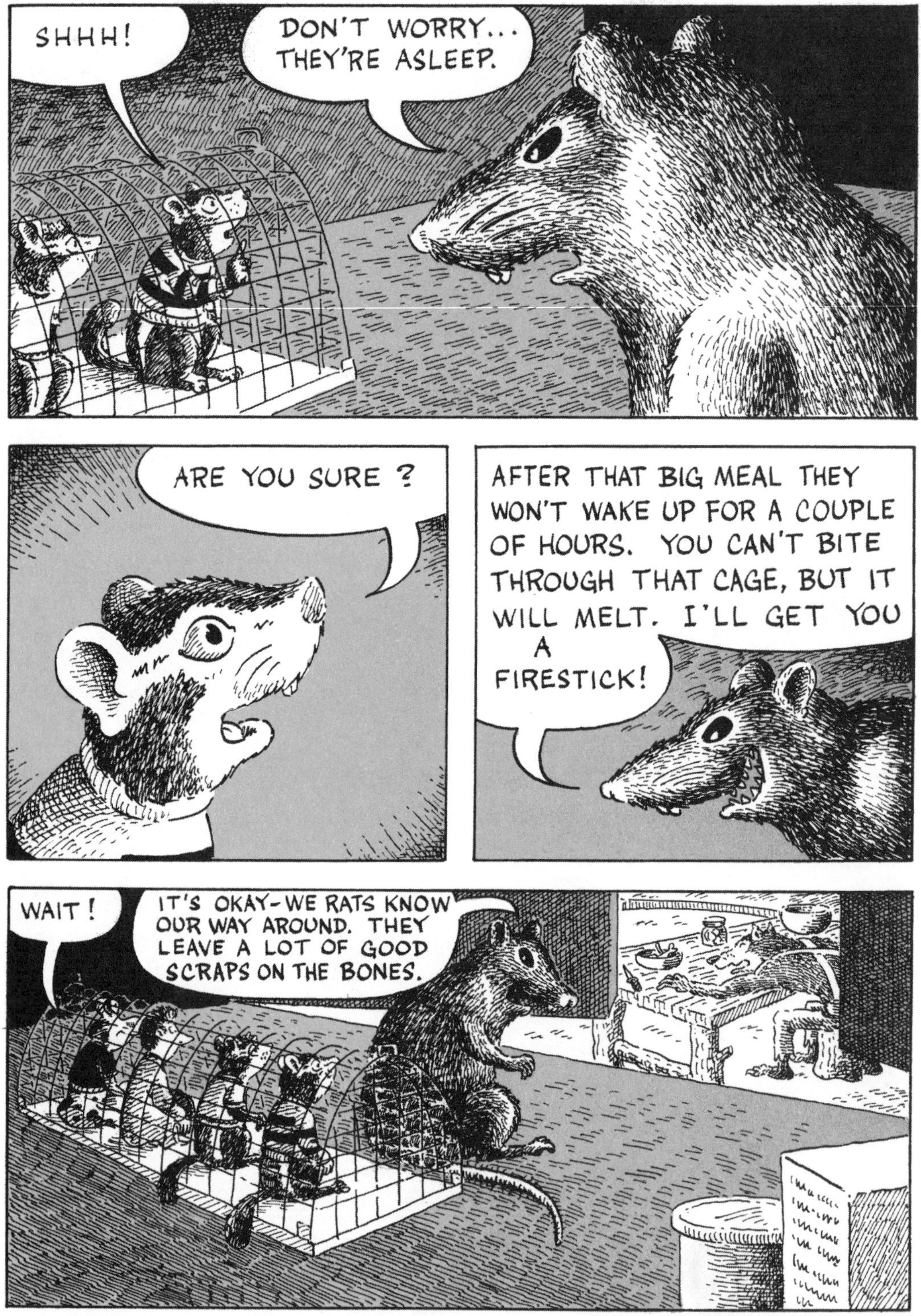
SHHH!
DON'T WORRY... THEY'RE ASLEEP.
ARE YOU SURE ?
AFTER THAT BIG MEAL THEY WON'T WAKE UP FOR A COUPLE OF HOURS. YOU CAN'T BITE THROUGH THAT CAGE, BUT IT WILL MELT. I'LL GET YOU A FIRESTICK!
WAIT!
IT'S OKAY-WE RATS KNOW OUR WAY AROUND. THEY LEAVE A LOT OF GOOD SCRAPS ON THE BONES.

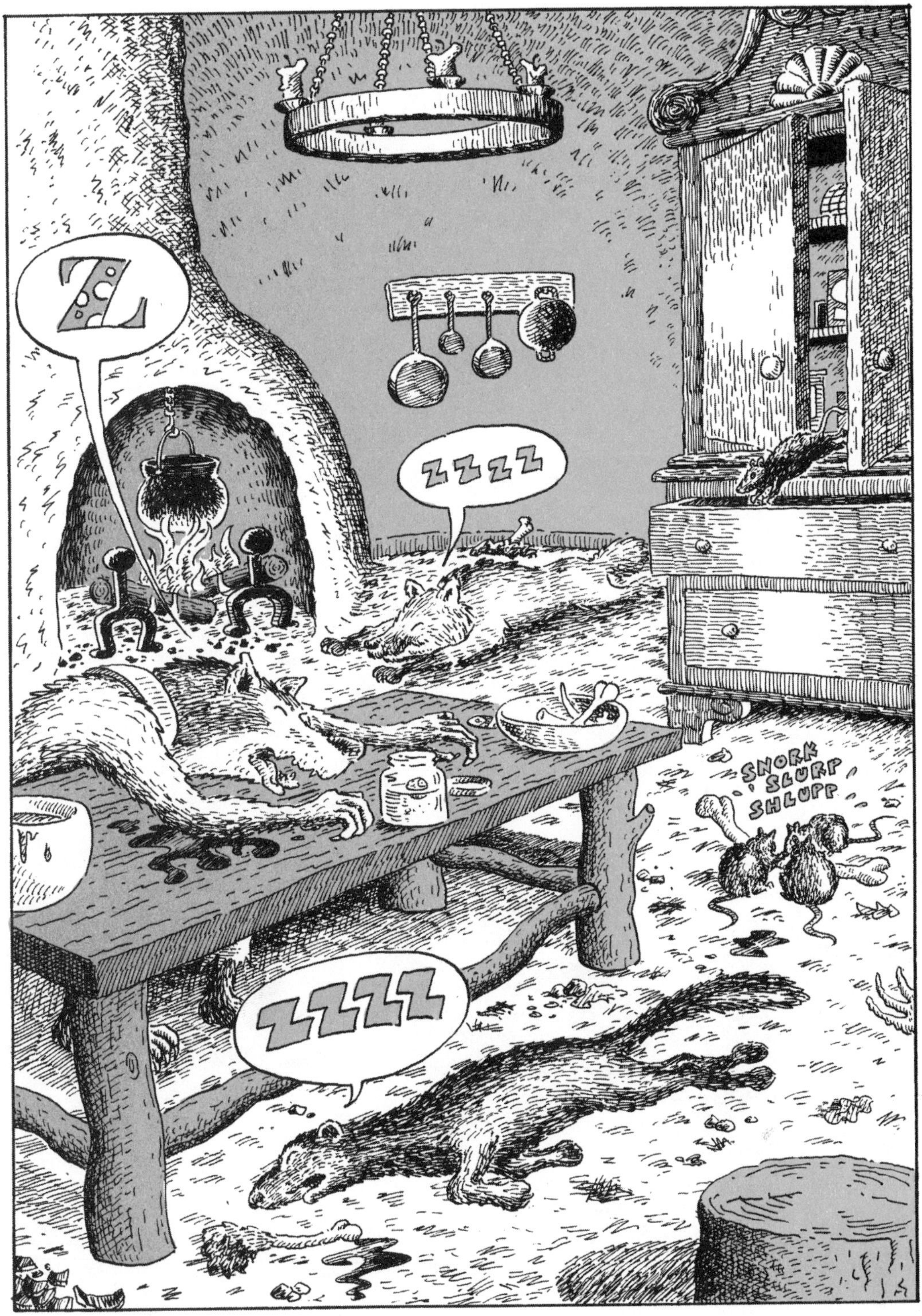
Z
ZZZZ
SNORK SLURP SHLUPP
ZZZZZ

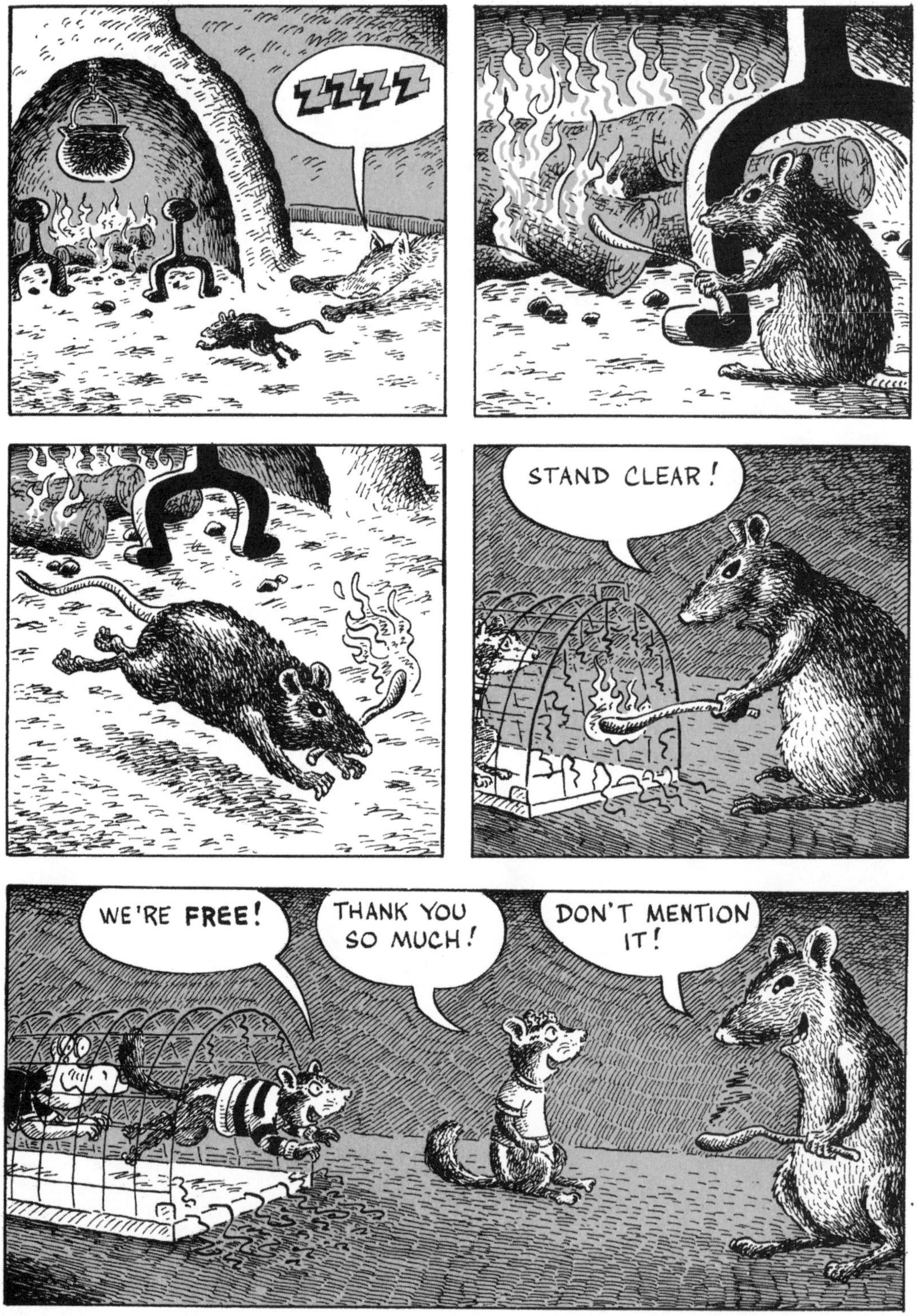
ZZZZ
STAND CLEAR!
WE'RE FREE!
THANK YOU SO MUCH!
DON'T MENTION IT!

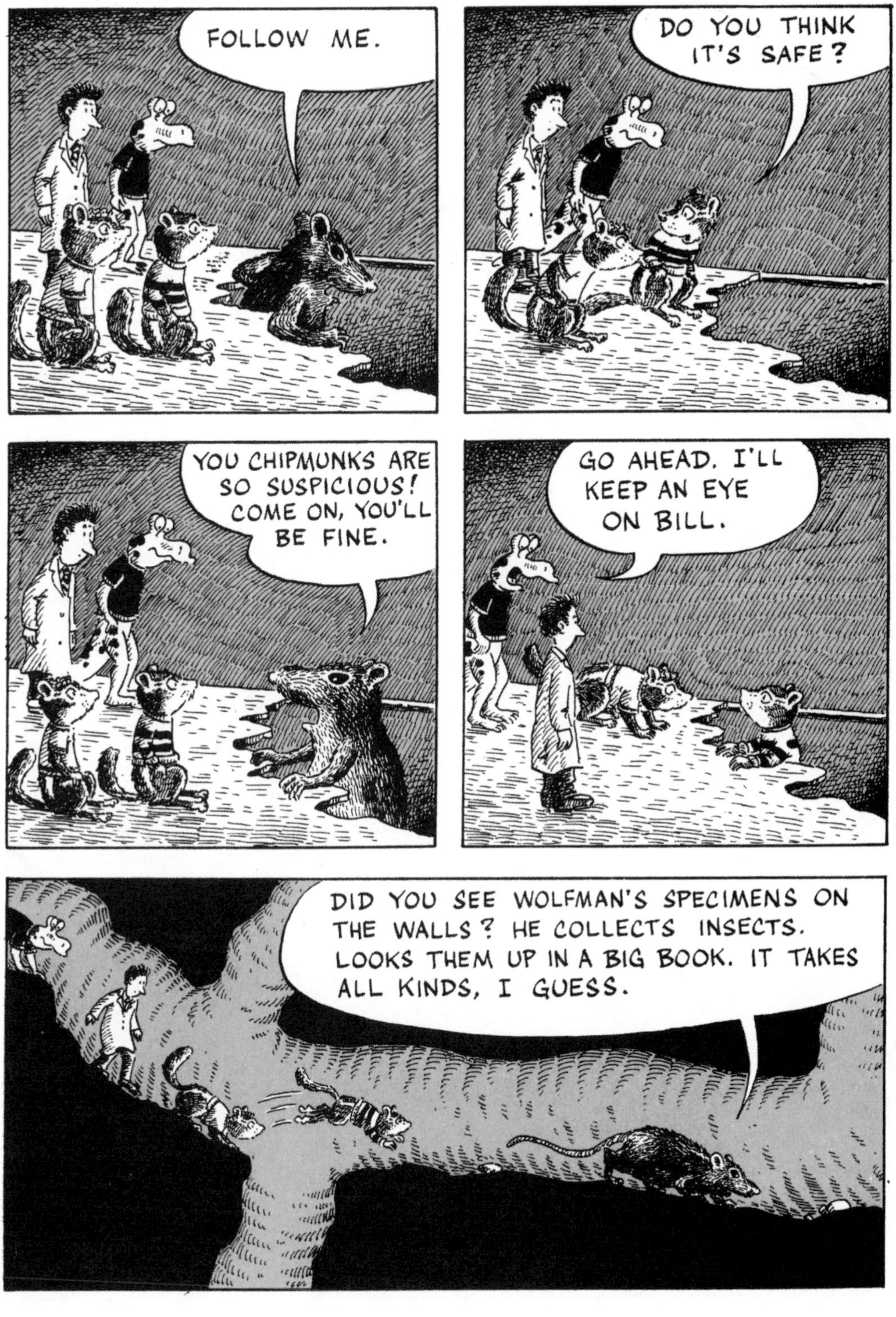
FOLLOW ME.
DO YOU THINK IT'S SAFE?
YOU CHIPMUNKS ARE SO SUSPICIOUS! COME ON, YOU'LL BE FINE.
GO AHEAD. I'LL KEEP AN EYE ON BILL.
DID YOU SEE WOLFMAN'S SPECIMENS ON THE WALLS? HE COLLECTS INSECTS. LOOKS THEM UP IN A BIG BOOK. IT TAKES ALL KINDS, I GUESS.

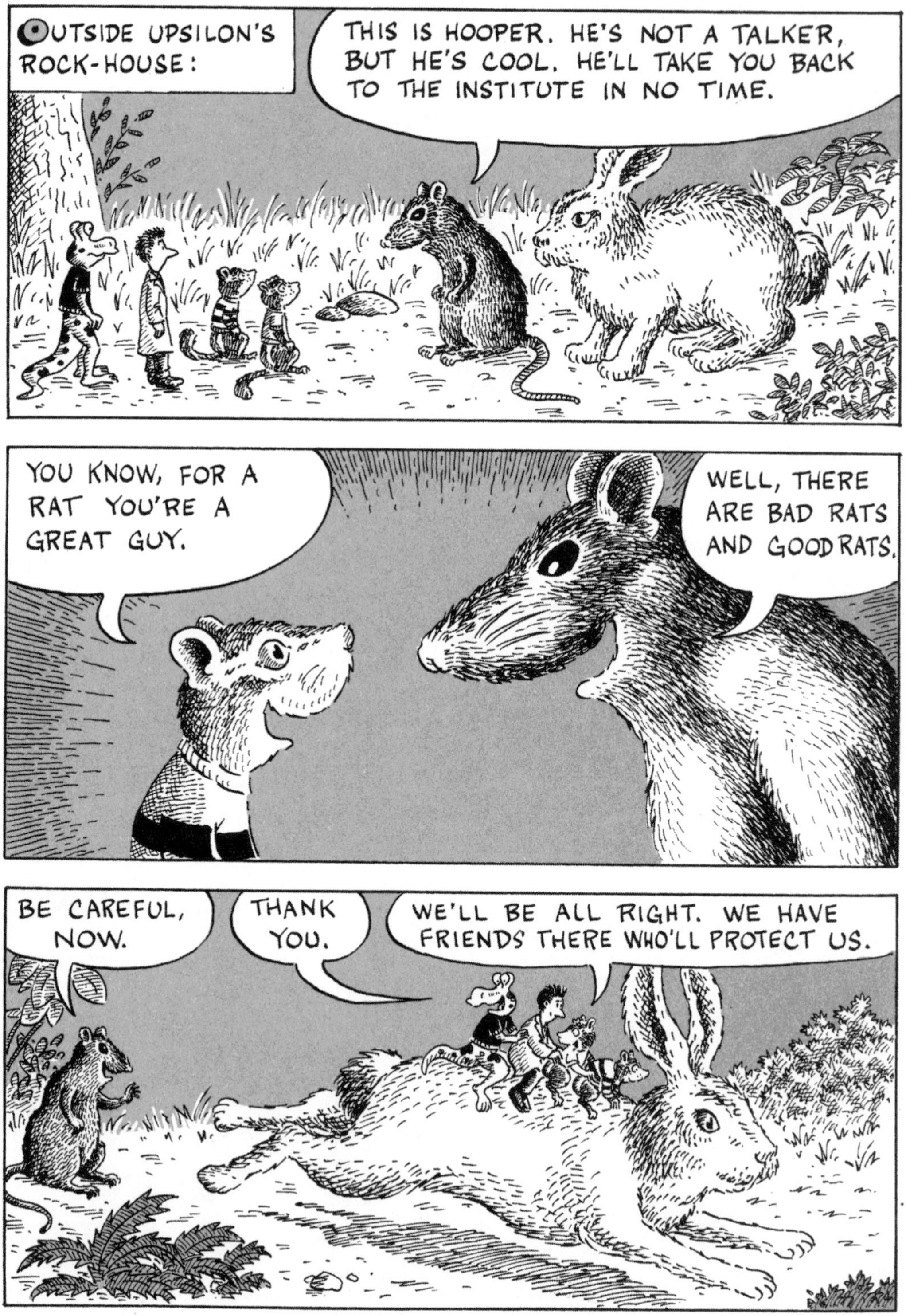
OUTSIDE UPSILON'S ROCK-HOUSE:
THIS IS HOOPER. HE'S NOT A TALKER, BUT HE'S COOL. HE'LL TAKE YOU BACK TO THE INSTITUTE IN NO TIME.
YOU KNOW, FOR A RAT YOU'RE A GREAT GUY.
WELL, THERE ARE BAD RATS AND GOOD RATS.
BE CAREFUL, NOW.
THANK YOU.
WE'LL BE ALL RIGHT. WE HAVE FRIENDS THERE WHO'LL PROTECT US.

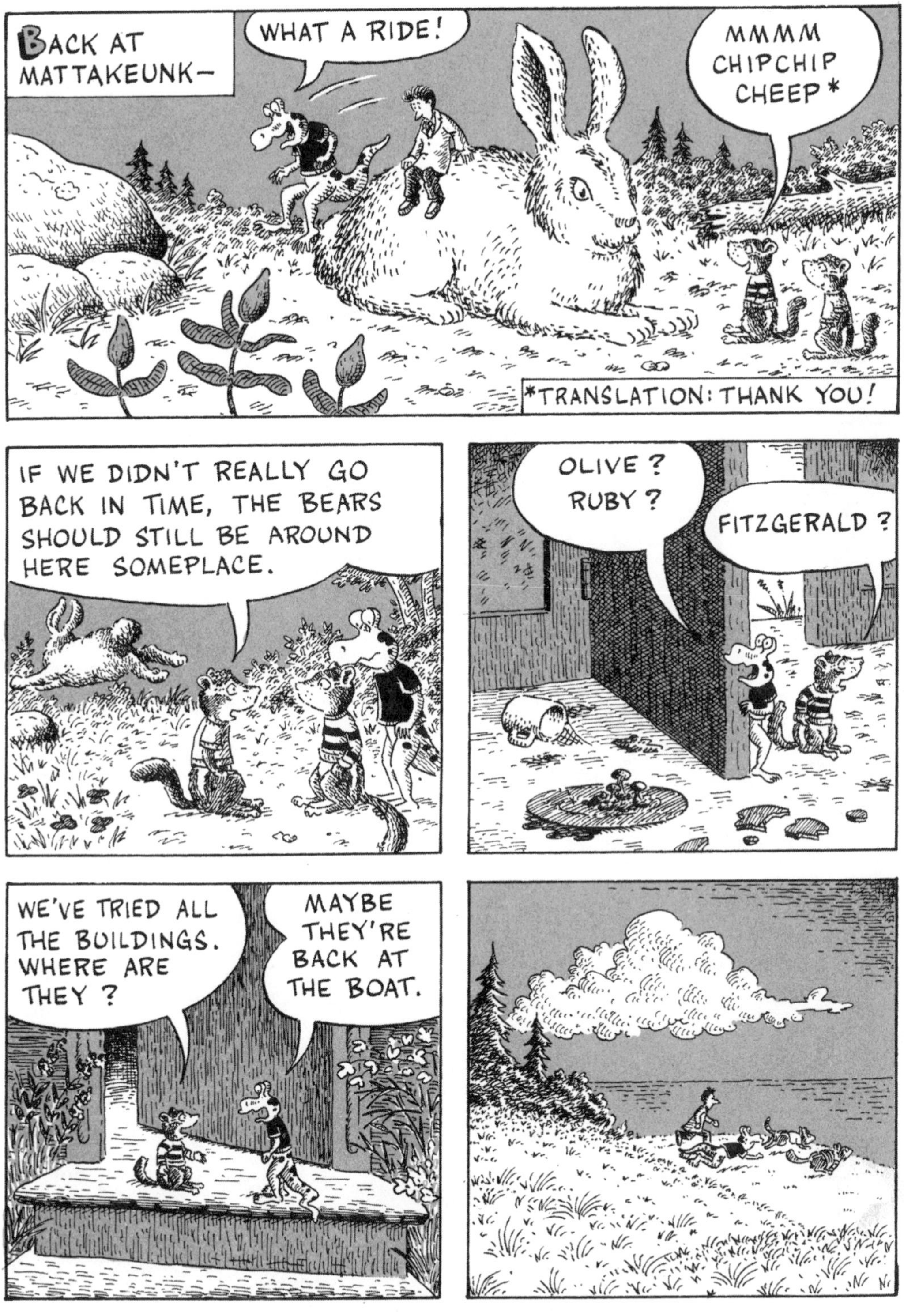
BACK AT MATTAKEUNK—
WHAT A RIDE!
MMMM CHIPCHIP CHEEP *
*TRANSLATION: THANK YOU!
IF WE DIDN'T REALLY GO BACK IN TIME, THE BEARS SHOULD STILL BE AROUND HERE SOMEPLACE.
OLIVE? RUBY?
FITZGERALD?
WE'VE TRIED ALL THE BUILDINGS. WHERE ARE THEY?
MAYBE THEY'RE BACK AT THE BOAT.

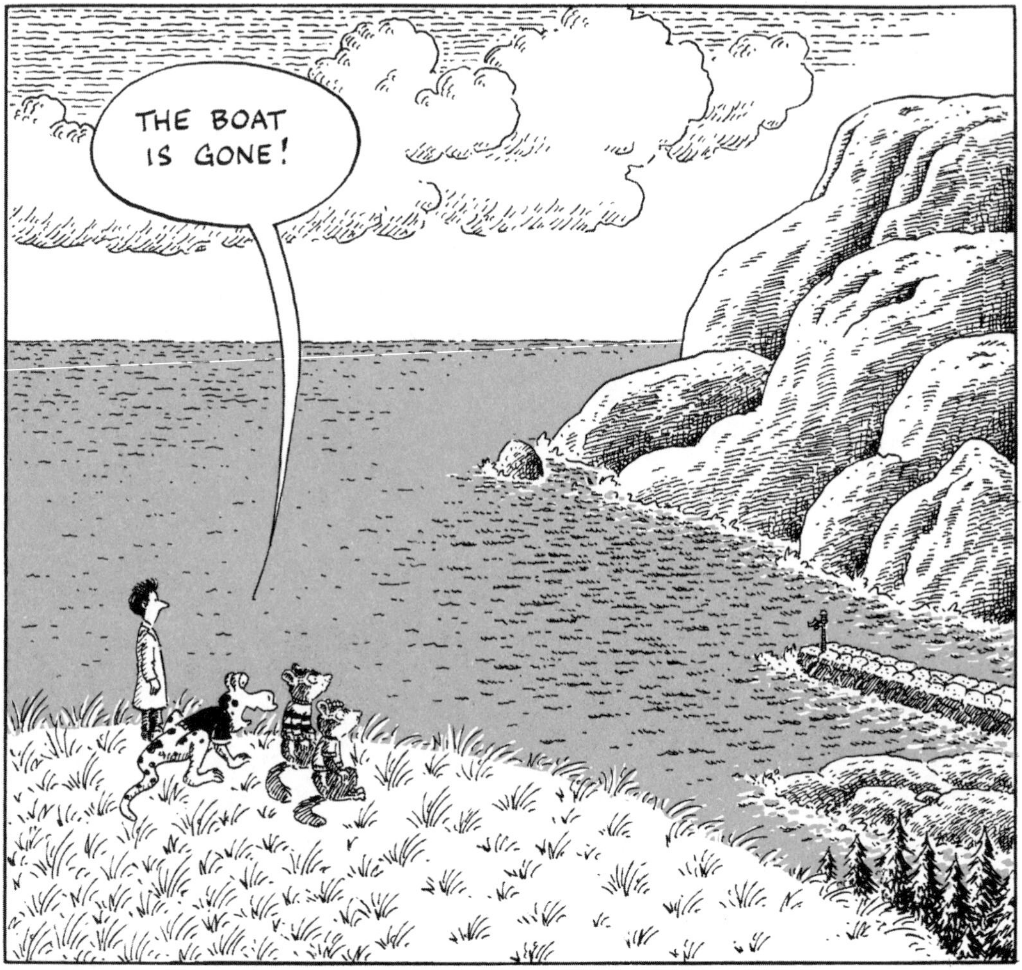
THE BOAT IS GONE!

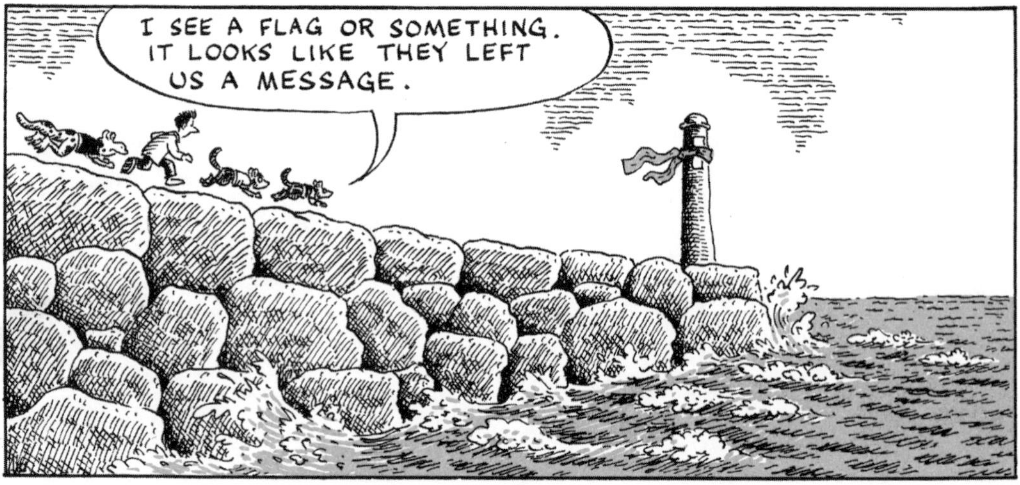
I SEE A FLAG OR SOMETHING. IT LOOKS LIKE THEY LEFT US A MESSAGE.

8

Bill Goes Off
the Deep End

I read the letter out loud:

Dear Smalls,

Where did you go? We have searched and searched. We fear the worst, but Fitzgerald is firm in his belief that Thelonious will see you through. We would not have given up searching except that we have received an urgent call for help via Mitchko Osprey.

THE MUTANT CRABS ARE ATTACKING THE CITY OF RUINS!

Bill interrupted with a loud *"HUNH! Those . . . bu . . . bu . . . bu . . . BUMBLEHEADS!"*

"There's more," I said, frowning at Bill. I continued reading:

Some of the birds and crocodiles from Faradawn followed the crabs. They will join with the beavers and porcupines to try to protect the City and all its artifacts. Wally Porcupine is asking for our help, and Fitz is anxious to rush to the aid of his friends who live there. We will return as soon as possible. WAIT FOR US. You will find plenty of canned food and everything you need in the Mess Hall.

In haste, Olive, Ruby, Freddie, and Fitzgerald

P.S. Be careful! We will return ASAP.

"What's ASAP?" I asked.

"It stands for 'as soon as possible,'" Cluid explained.

Bill was still sputtering. "Those . . . BUMBLEHEADS!" he shouted, jumping up and down on the rock. "Those . . . n . . . n—"

The next thing I knew, he was gone!

"He fell in!" yelled Brown. "Look out!"

In trying to see where Bill had gone, I slipped and almost fell in myself. Of course, I can swim. We weren't sure about Bill, though, and I didn't see his head popping up out of the water.

"I'm going in!" I said, pulling off my sweater.

"Wait!" Cluid was running back down the jetty toward the sand, pointing. "I see him! He's washing up!"

And there he was, washed ashore by the gentle waves, his lab coat white against the wet sand.

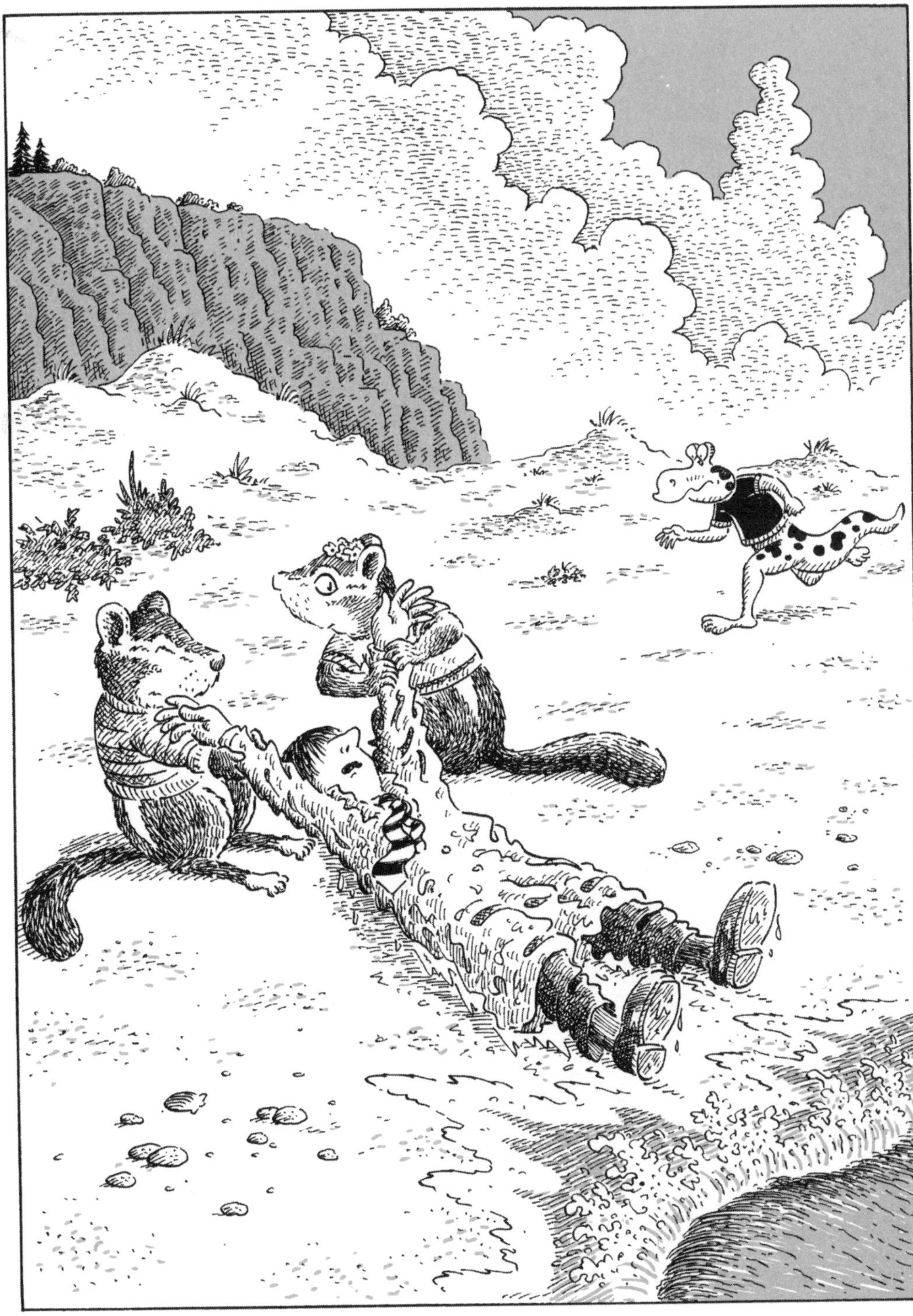

I put my sweater back on, and we ran to Bill. Cluid and I pulled his limp body onto dry ground.

"Turn him over," Brown ordered. "Squeeze the water out of him!"

I tried to follow Brown's directions, but Bill shook me off. He blew a spout of salt water into the air and said in a loud voice, "I KNEW IT!" (*Cough, cough.*) "YOU WANT TO KNOW ABOUT HUMAN MISTAKES? HERE'S ONE FOR YOU. *CARELESS EXPERIMENTATION!* I TOLD THE OTHER SCIENTISTS, 'YOU CAN'T MAKE GENETIC ALTERATIONS WITHOUT TAKING THE PROPER PRECAUTIONS!' I SAID, 'YOU AREN'T TAKING INTO ACCOUNT THE *UNFORESEEN CONSEQUENCES!*"

Bill spit out some sand and raised himself on one elbow, looking from one of us to another. "HA!" He pointed at us. "LOOK AT YOU!" he shouted.

But we were all looking at *him*! Bill was speaking like a normal animal! His dunking must have jiggled some connections in his brain.

He sat up, dripping seawater.

"Strong, healthy, responsible animals every one of you!" he continued. "Well developed! Well conditioned! Well suited to your environments!"

I straightened up and stuck out my chest.

"IT WAS NOTHING LESS THAN MALPRACTICE!" he shouted. "THE MISUSE OF SCIENTIFIC KNOWLEDGE FOR PERSONAL GAIN! Creating intelligent crabs, indeed! Those crabs have some human DNA, or I'll eat my hat! And now they're carrying on the tradition of misuse of scientific knowledge for personal gain—building gigantic robots of destruction! Didn't we have enough of that when the humans were around? And I'd like to know what commercial enterprise funded the creation of the evil ratminks! Just because you know how to do a thing doesn't mean you should do it!"

He ran his fingers through his wet hair until it was all standing on end and glared at us as if it was our fault. Then he opened his mouth as if to continue.

Cluid interrupted quickly. "But Bill, didn't *you* experiment with animals too? Didn't you make our ancestors so they could talk?"

"And have thumbs?" Brown added.

"Yes, yes, of course." Bill waved his hand impatiently in the air. "But *my* experiments were all carefully controlled. Nothing was left to chance! My animals were trained and monitored and no one . . ." He stopped. "No one . . ." He looked sideways at me and changed the subject.

"I never worked on lizards," he said, pointing at Brown.

"Chipmunks, though?" I asked.

"One of my biggest achievements," he said proudly. "The small animals were the most satisfying to me. No, no, that's not true. The bears! AHA! That was pure genius, if I do say so myself! Did you see that big bear's thumbs? Working perfectly! Why he can . . ."

Cluid smiled at me. "We must be related, Thelonious," she said quietly. "Somehow your ancestors must have left the Mound and settled in the Untamed Forest."

Bill peered at Cluid, listening. "It wasn't *my* fault they left the Mound," he said defensively. "It was my assistant! Taking it into his stupid head that the animals should be free! Letting them go—as if they weren't better off on the Mound! It's a wonder any of them survived!"

He turned to me. "I never thought I'd see so many of you living in the rest

of the world. Talking porcupines and talking beavers." He threw his head back suddenly and laughed like a madman. "HA, HA, HA!"

Just as suddenly, he stopped and frowned at Brown. "I don't know how you lizards come into it, though. Very interesting, now that I think of it. Where did you say your ancestors came from, Brown?"

"Uh, Bill?" I said, trying to get a word in.

"I never knew," Brown answered him. "But I'm not the only talking reptile. There's the Dragon Lady, for instance, and the crocodiles."

"Yes, yes. I suppose so. Hmmmm. The birds developed speech on their own, you know. No genetic intervention there. Mary was a genius with them, of course. Brilliant girl. But then, what would you expect from my daughter?"

"Bill," I repeated.

"Mary was your daughter?" Cluid said.

"Yes, of course. I taught her everything she knew. If it wasn't for that—"

"BILL!" I yelled.

"Yes, Thelonious? What is it?"

"What was your assistant's name? The one who let the animals go."

"That rascal!" Bill said. "Bob, his name was Bob. He took off with my Mary, too. He wasn't a bad boy, exactly. Just thought he knew more than I did, the young fool."

I jumped up. "I thought so!" I cried. "It's *The Story of Bob*! It's true! The lab assistant, the cages, the *mad scientist*!"

I stopped suddenly. "Um, that is . . . well . . . that's how the legend was passed down," I ended lamely.

"I wouldn't call them cages, exactly," Bill said. "Very comfortable living quarters, my animals had. They were large and clean and—"

"Bob cleaned them!" I interrupted. "That's what it says in the legend."

"Well, as a matter of fact, he did. But these stories can get distorted over time, Thelonious. You know that, don't you? You can't believe everything you hear, or read, either. I can remember . . ."

I stopped listening. Bill went on and on. In some ways I think I liked him better when he was barely speaking. But still, he had given us a lot of information. And I had a lot to think about:

Bob was a real person! And Bill was the mad scientist! My ancestors had probably come from the Fog Mound long ago, before the end of the Human Occupation. Hmmm. There's a chipmunk at the end of The Story of Bob. His name is Simon. How does it go?

In the still darkness of a moonless night, Bob the Human,

risking all, stole silently through the secret door and began unlocking the cruel cages. The first to be released was Simon, the speaking chipmunk.

"Go and be free," Bob whispered to his little friend.

"But what will happen to you, Bob?" Simon asked.

"Fear not," Bob replied. *"I too will escape—to a land where humans and nature can live in peace with each other."*

"I would choose to go there with you, Bob, if I could," said Simon.

Bob looked long and hard at the chipmunk. Then he smiled and said, *"So be it."*

Thus ends *The Story of Bob*.

Bill was still talking. ". . . used the subtraction option to remove the interference layer when I filled the memory blanks . . ."

Brown was nudging me with his scaly elbow. "Um, shouldn't we go look for the Mess Hall now?"

Brown was right. It had been a long day. I was tired and hungry. Bill was all wet. Pretty soon it would be getting dark and cold, and I didn't feel like carrying a sleepy Brown up that big hill.

"C'mon, Bill," I said, turning to trudge back up to the Institute.

". . . I didn't intend to alter the instinct pathways . . ." Bill was muttering.

"Hey, Bill!" I interrupted, suddenly realizing something. "Now you can tell us what happened to the last of the humans!"

Bill stopped mid-sentence and looked at me.

"The last of the humans? What do you think *I've* been trying to find out?

I want to know what happened to my girl Mary! I was in the freezing chamber at the time, remember?" He paused. "Of course, there were many disturbing circumstances that led me to take that step. I was pretty sure my animals would be safe on the Mound, but with the prevalence of toxiferous pestilence and the increase in the size of the encroaching zymotic cloud . . ."

"I don't know what you're talking about," I said. "I'm only a *chipmunk*, Bill."

He paused for a moment, looking at the place between my ears, then said, as if to himself, "Hmmm, I wonder if the *size* of the brain correlates with verbal capacity . . ."

I thought to myself, *Your brain isn't any bigger than mine now, or haven't you noticed?* But I didn't say it out loud.

All the way up the hill Bill kept on muttering to himself. I decided I would try questioning him again later, when he had wound down a little bit.

9

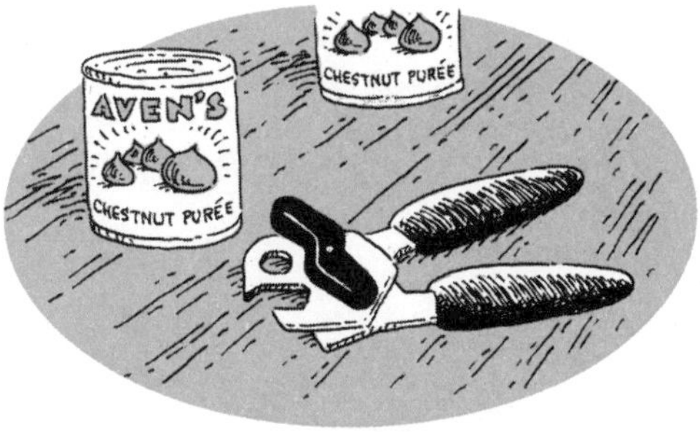
CHESTNUT PURÉE
AVEN'S
CHESTNUT PURÉE

Mess Hall

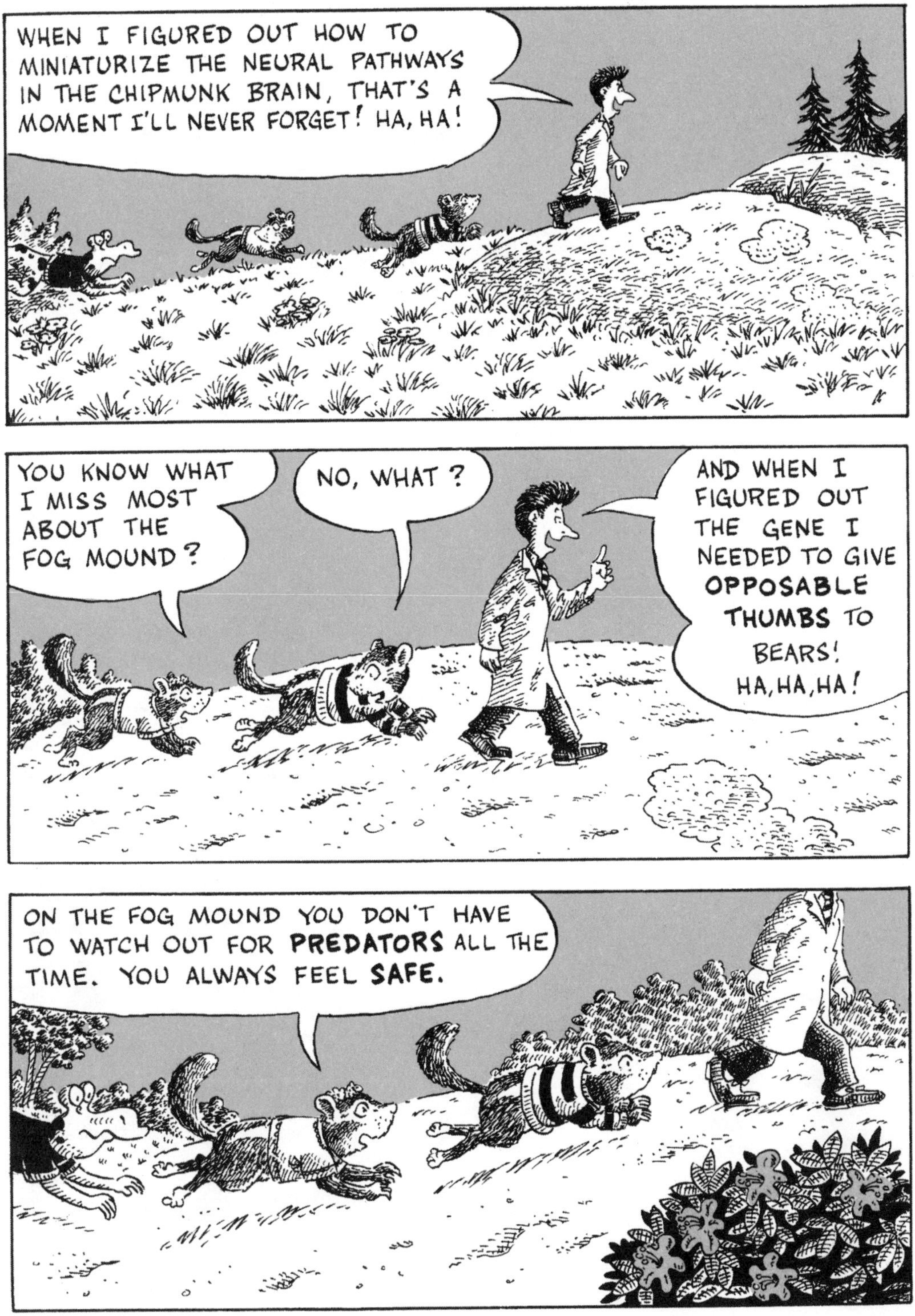
WHEN I FIGURED OUT HOW TO MINIATURIZE THE NEURAL PATHWAYS IN THE CHIPMUNK BRAIN, THAT'S A MOMENT I'LL NEVER FORGET! HA, HA!
YOU KNOW WHAT I MISS MOST ABOUT THE FOG MOUND?
NO, WHAT?
AND WHEN I FIGURED OUT THE GENE I NEEDED TO GIVE **OPPOSABLE THUMBS** TO BEARS! HA, HA, HA!
ON THE FOG MOUND YOU DON'T HAVE TO WATCH OUT FOR **PREDATORS** ALL THE TIME. YOU ALWAYS FEEL **SAFE.**

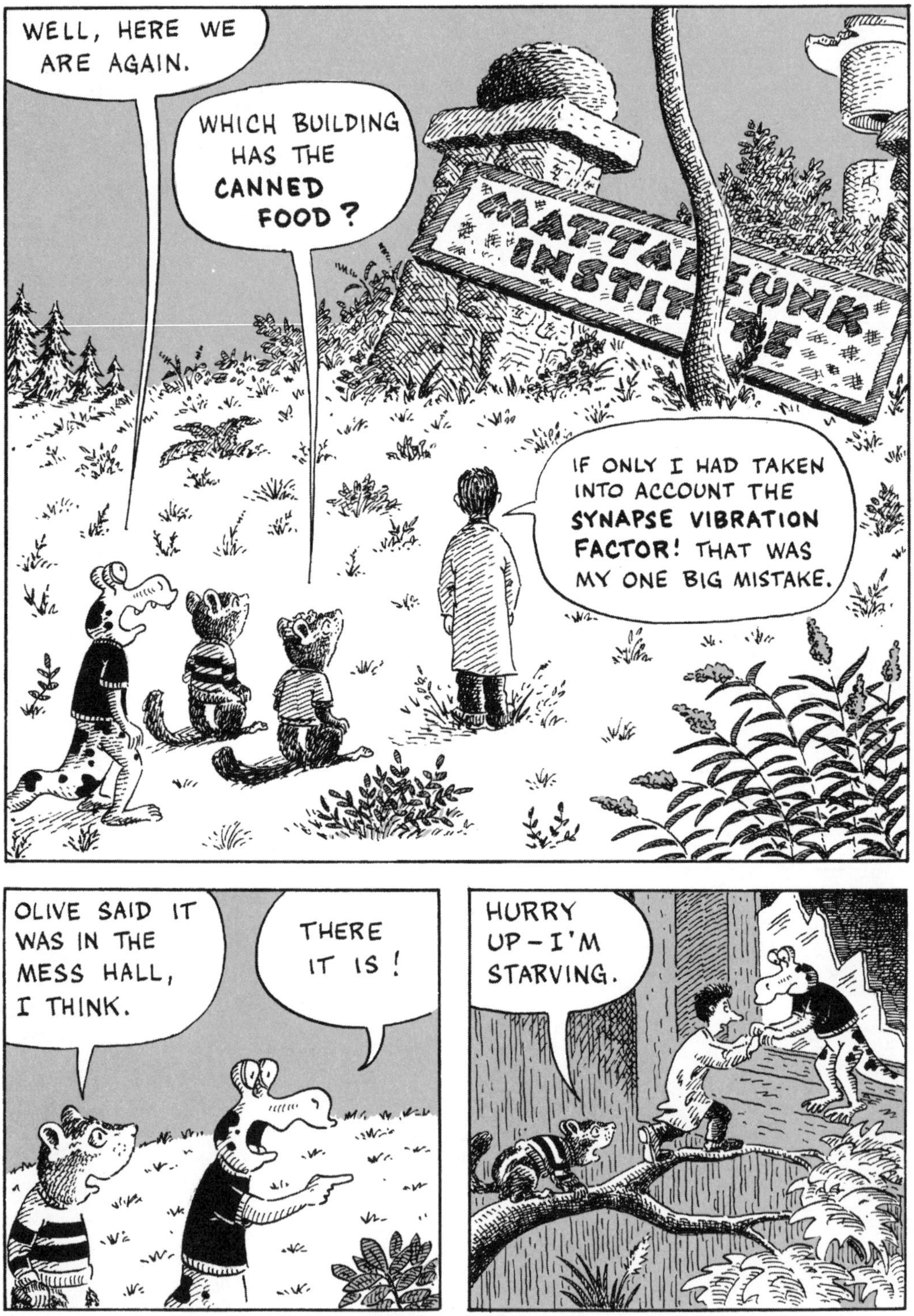
WELL, HERE WE ARE AGAIN.
WHICH BUILDING HAS THE **CANNED FOOD**?
MATTAFUNK INSTITUTE
IF ONLY I HAD TAKEN INTO ACCOUNT THE **SYNAPSE VIBRATION FACTOR**! THAT WAS MY ONE BIG MISTAKE.
OLIVE SAID IT WAS IN THE MESS HALL, I THINK.
THERE IT IS!
HURRY UP–I'M STARVING.

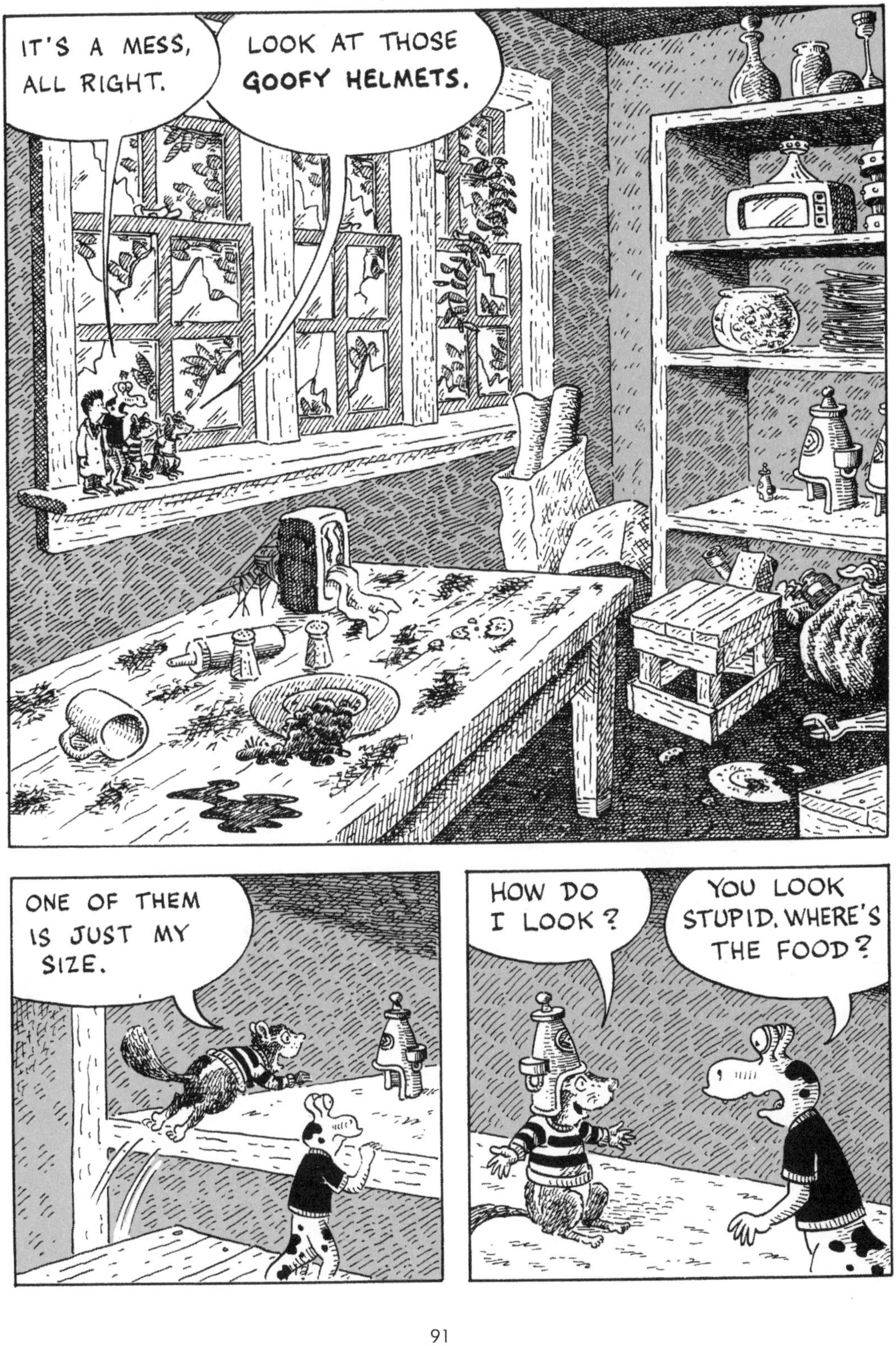
IT'S A MESS, ALL RIGHT.
LOOK AT THOSE GOOFY HELMETS.
ONE OF THEM IS JUST MY SIZE.
HOW DO I LOOK?
YOU LOOK STUPID. WHERE'S THE FOOD?

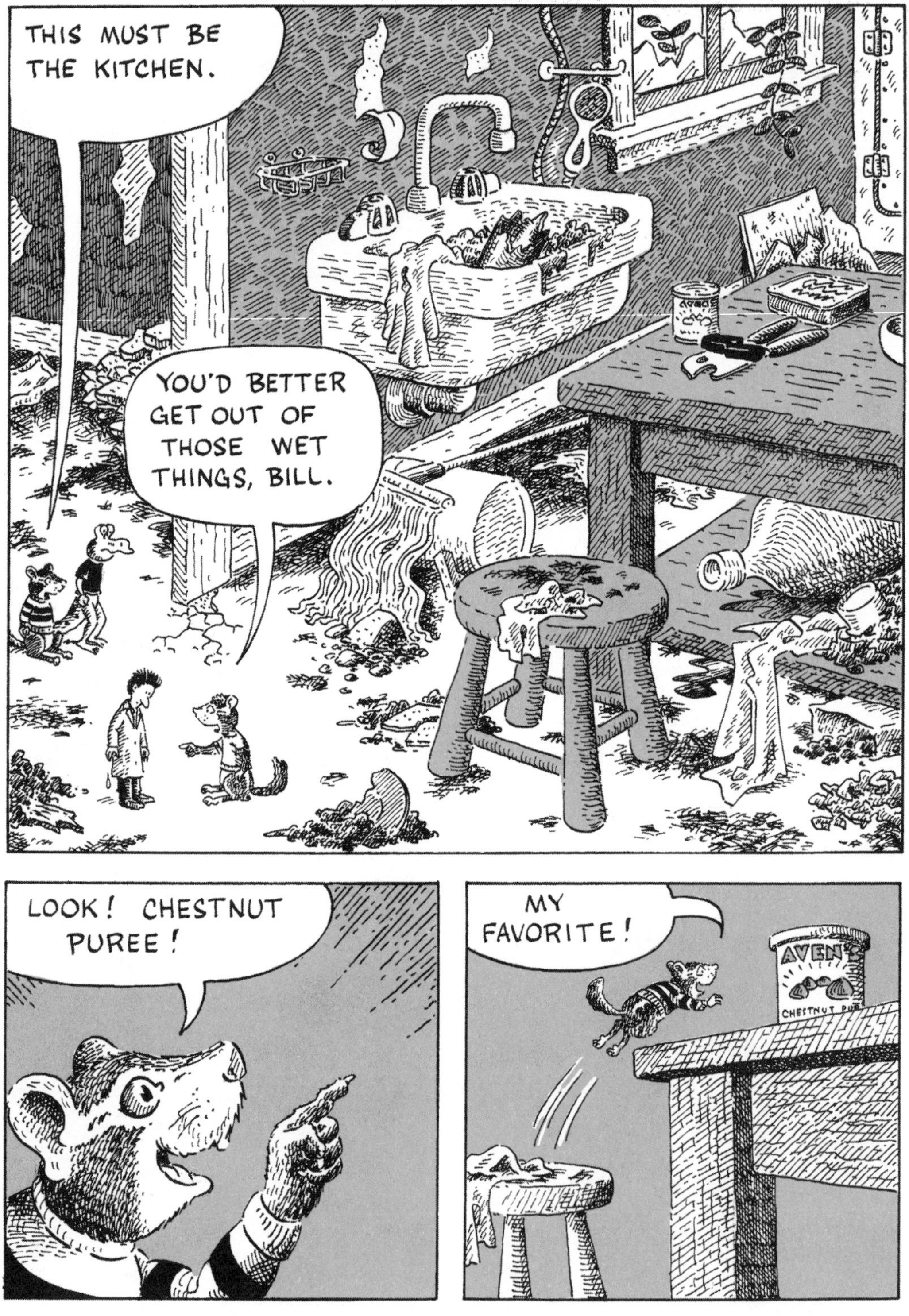
THIS MUST BE THE KITCHEN.
YOU'D BETTER GET OUT OF THOSE WET THINGS, BILL.
LOOK! CHESTNUT PUREE!
MY FAVORITE!
AVEN'S
CHESTNUT

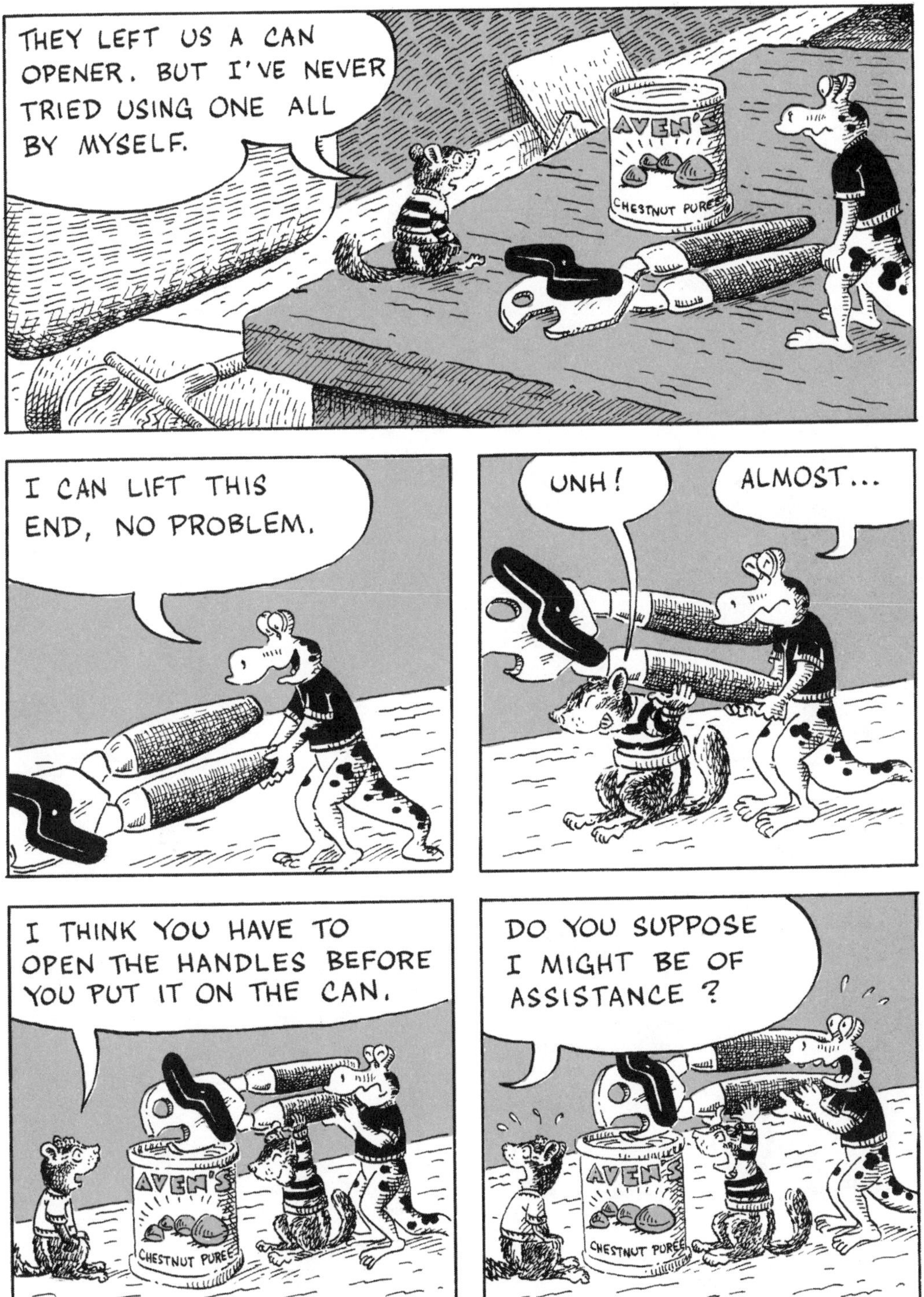
THEY LEFT US A CAN OPENER. BUT I'VE NEVER TRIED USING ONE ALL BY MYSELF.
AVEN'S
CHESTNUT PUREE
I CAN LIFT THIS END, NO PROBLEM.
UNH!
ALMOST...
I THINK YOU HAVE TO OPEN THE HANDLES BEFORE YOU PUT IT ON THE CAN.
AVEN'S
CHESTNUT PUREE
DO YOU SUPPOSE I MIGHT BE OF ASSISTANCE?
AVEN'S
CHESTNUT PUREE

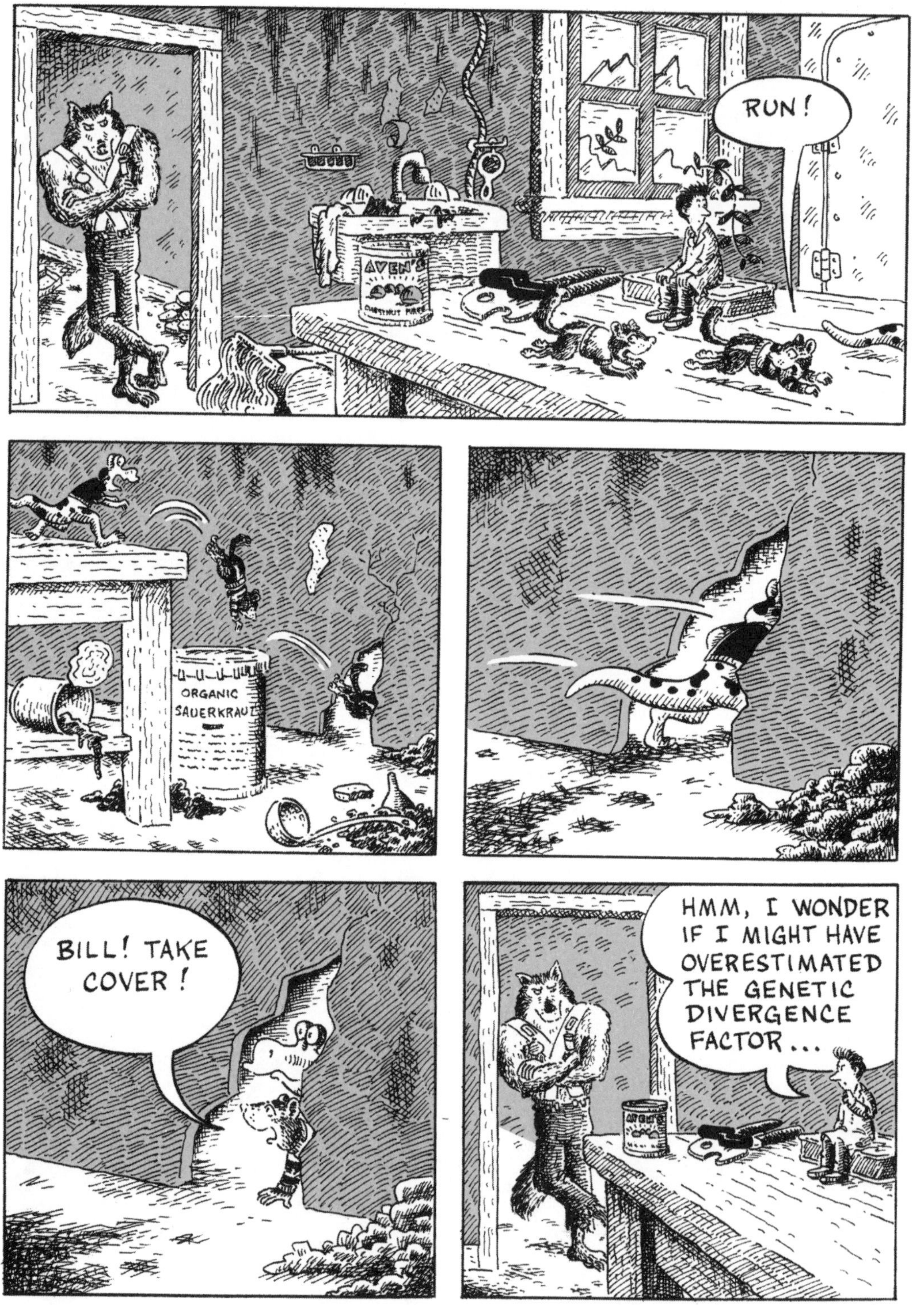
RUN!
AVEN'S
CHESTNUT PUREE
ORGANIC
SAUERKRAUT
BILL! TAKE COVER!
HMM, I WONDER IF I MIGHT HAVE OVERESTIMATED THE GENETIC DIVERGENCE FACTOR...

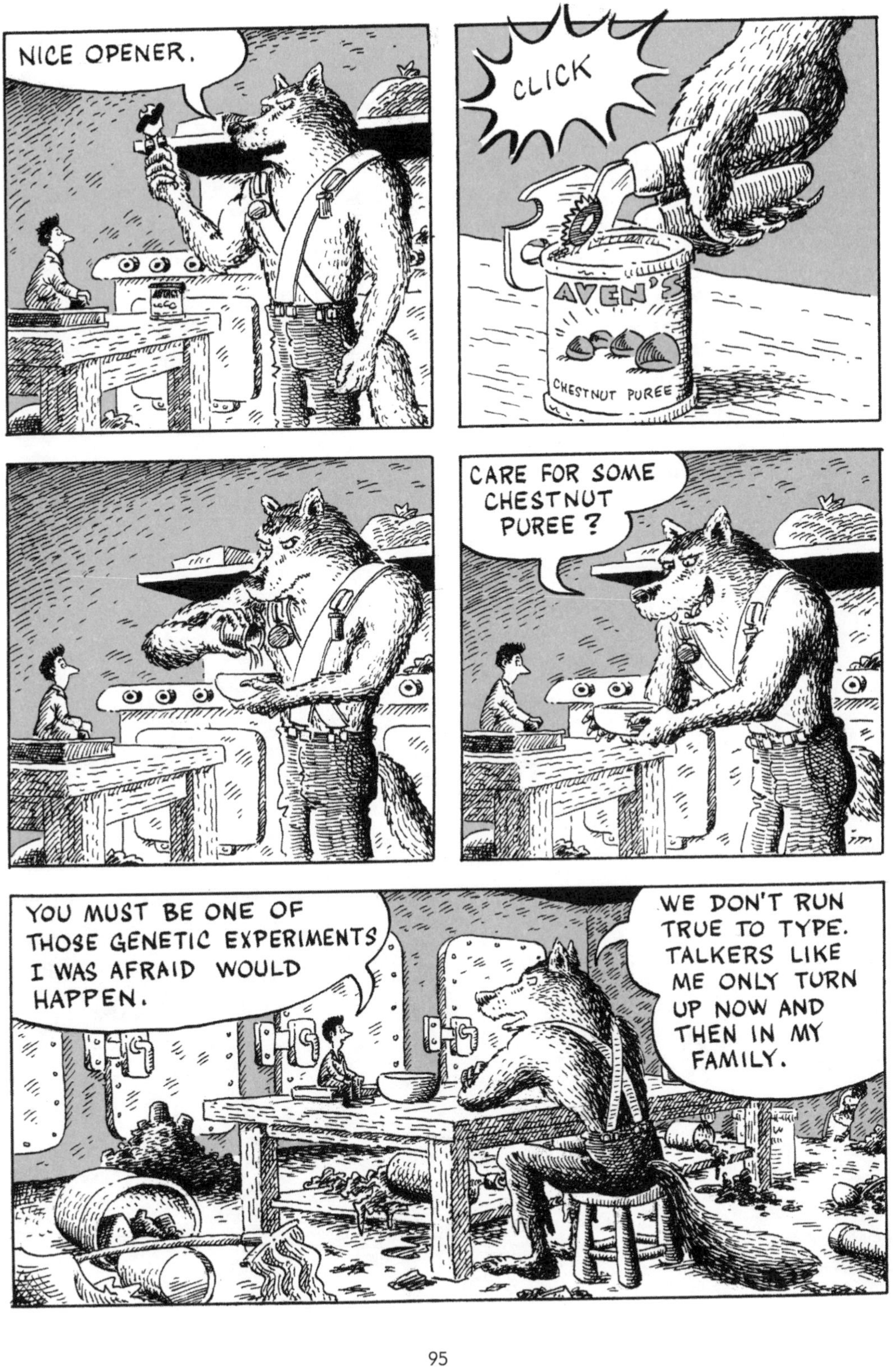
NICE OPENER.
CLICK
AVEN'S
CHESTNUT PUREE
CARE FOR SOME CHESTNUT PUREE?
YOU MUST BE ONE OF THOSE GENETIC EXPERIMENTS I WAS AFRAID WOULD HAPPEN.
WE DON'T RUN TRUE TO TYPE. TALKERS LIKE ME ONLY TURN UP NOW AND THEN IN MY FAMILY.

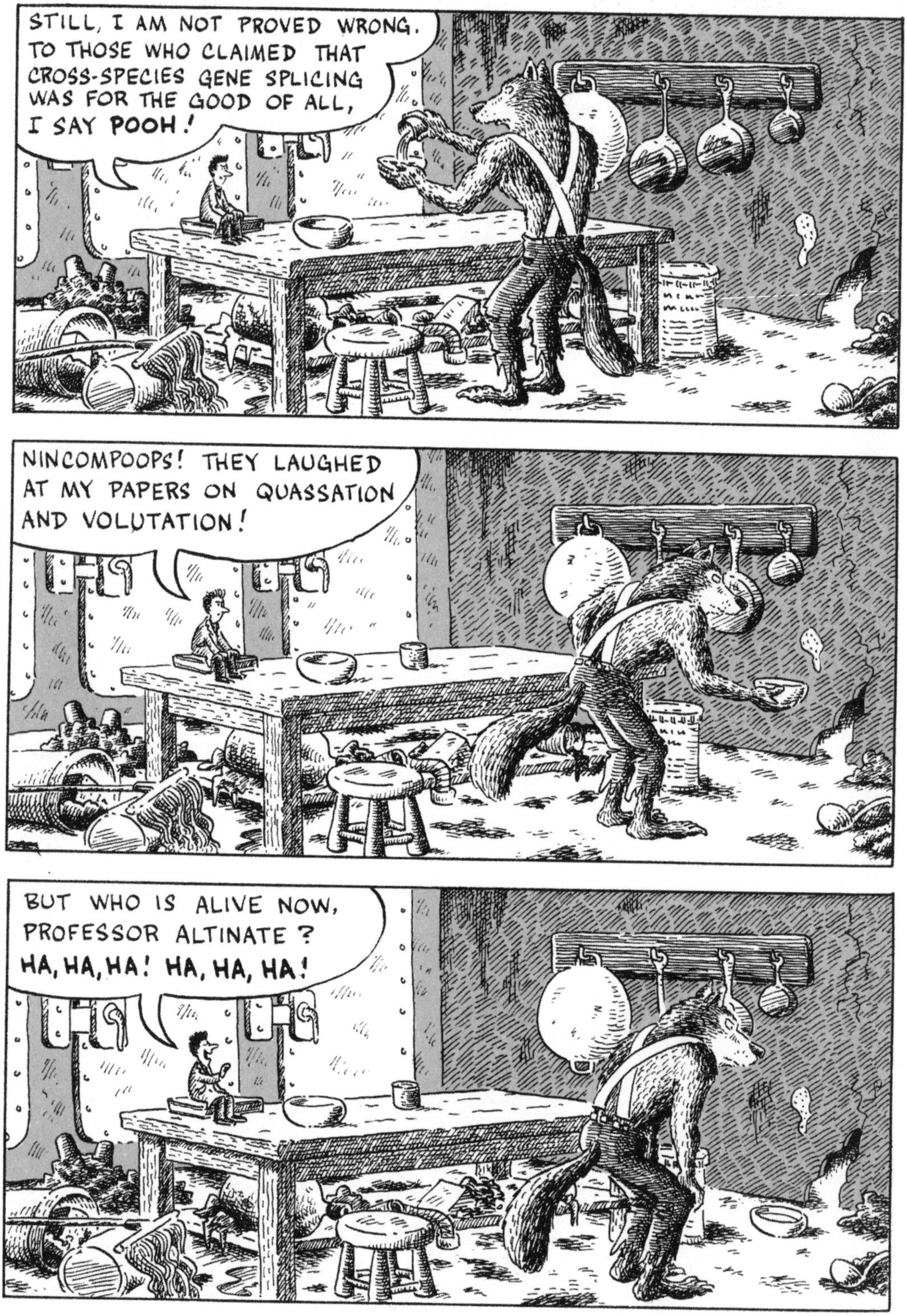
STILL, I AM NOT PROVED WRONG. TO THOSE WHO CLAIMED THAT CROSS-SPECIES GENE SPLICING WAS FOR THE GOOD OF ALL, I SAY POOH!
NINCOMPOOPS! THEY LAUGHED AT MY PAPERS ON QUASSATION AND VOLUTATION!
BUT WHO IS ALIVE NOW, PROFESSOR ALTINATE? HA, HA, HA! HA, HA, HA!

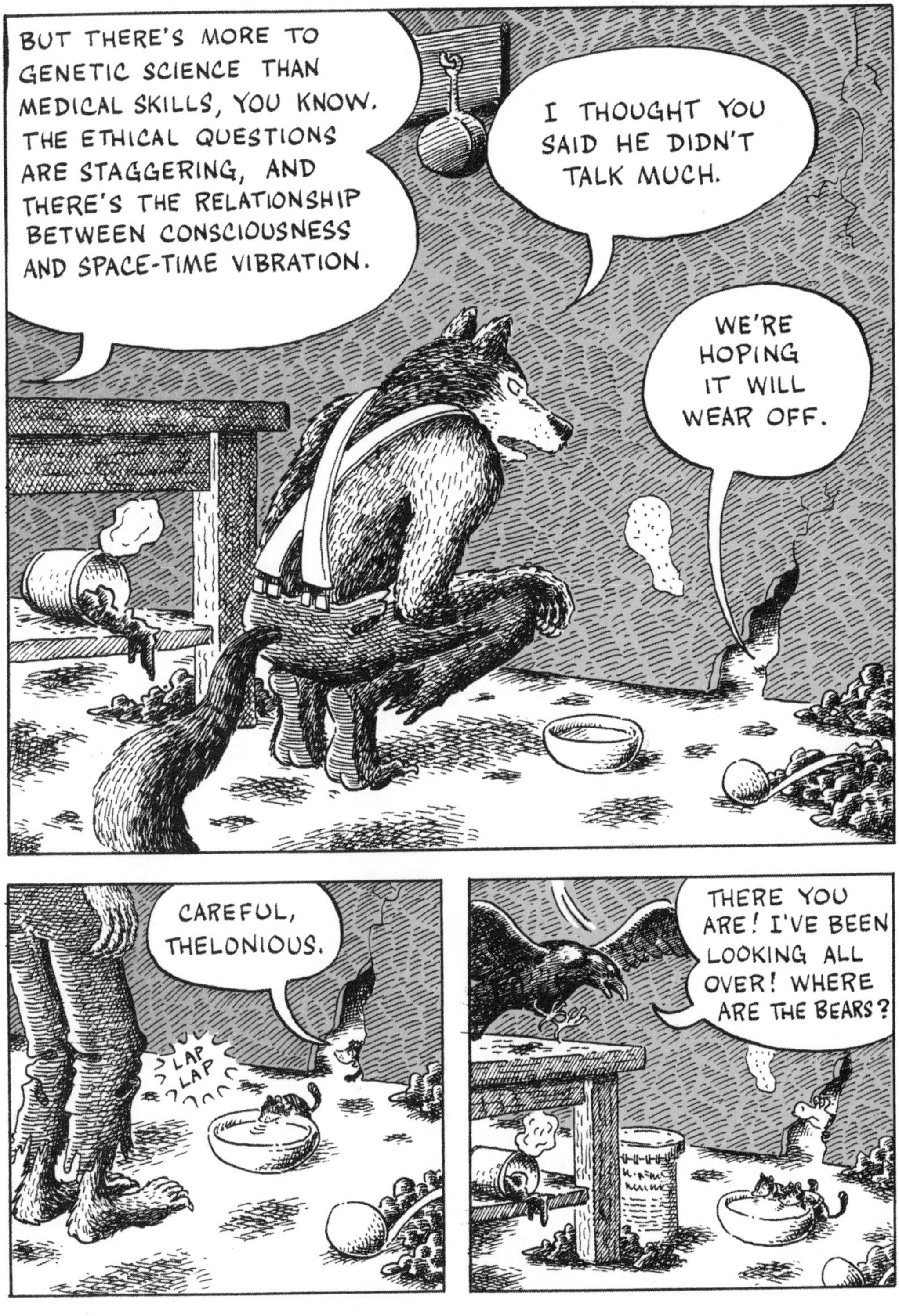
BUT THERE'S MORE TO GENETIC SCIENCE THAN MEDICAL SKILLS, YOU KNOW. THE ETHICAL QUESTIONS ARE STAGGERING, AND THERE'S THE RELATIONSHIP BETWEEN CONSCIOUSNESS AND SPACE-TIME VIBRATION.
I THOUGHT YOU SAID HE DIDN'T TALK MUCH.
WE'RE HOPING IT WILL WEAR OFF.
CAREFUL, THELONIOUS.
LAP LAP
THERE YOU ARE! I'VE BEEN LOOKING ALL OVER! WHERE ARE THE BEARS?

10

Morrie's Return

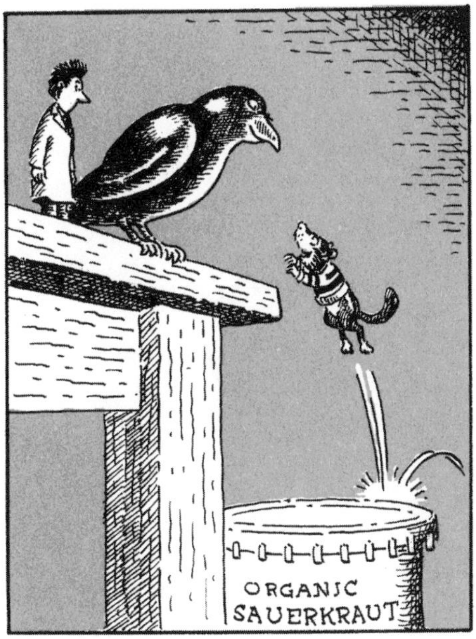
ORGANIC
SAUERKRAUT

It was Morrie Crow!

"MORRIE!" I cried, happy to see him. Morrie had traveled to Faradawn with us.

He flew in and landed beside Bill. "Hi, guys," he said. "Is this a new friend of yours?" He nodded toward Upsilon.

"Not exactly," I said.

"An interesting example of genetic manipulation; not entirely successful, but worthy of further study," said Bill.

Morrie cocked his head in surprise at Bill. I didn't blame him. The last time they had seen each other, Bill could barely speak.

"Upsilon Wolfman," Upsilon introduced himself. "Nice to meet you, Morrie. The chipmunks are still a little worried about my intentions, but I assure you, they are strictly academic."

"Meaning what, exactly?" asked Morrie.

"I just want to talk," Upsilon said. "I've learned that the lizard once worked for the Dragon Lady, and I'd like to learn more about her situation." He paused. "We have a history, the Dragon Lady and I," he added. "You

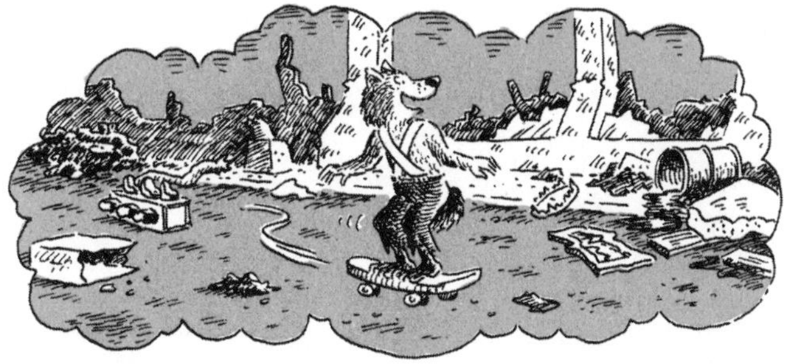

see, when I was a young wolfboy, I lived in the City of Ruins with my family. As I told Bill here, the talking gene doesn't always show up among wolfmen. Well, my father wasn't a talker, but he was a good and brave family wolf. We had the misfortune of living near the Dragon Lady's mansion. She decided she wanted our building, and knowing that my father would never show cowardice, she challenged him to a fair fight. *Fair*!" He snorted.

"Naturally, he accepted her challenge. When it looked as if he would win, the Dragon Lady called in her troop of ratminks to finish him off! If only I could get my claws into that vile, greedy, heartless, grasping, double-tongued, corrupt, egotistical, depraved, spiteful—"

Bill held up one finger. "Many characteristics of the worst of the human race," he said.

Upsilon showed his teeth.

"Of course, not *all* humans are bad," Bill added quickly.

"I'd like to rid the earth of that scheming villain!" Upsilon growled.

"You would be doing the world a great service," said Morrie. "Wait'll you hear what she's up to now!"

"What?" said Brown.

"That's what I came to tell you. You and the bears. Where are they, by the way?"

"They went to save the City of Ruins from the mutant crabs!" Cluid explained. "Mitchko the Osprey came to get them."

"Drat!" said Morrie. "I must have crossed paths with them on my way up here."

Upsilon leaned forward in his chair. "You mean these guys really do know some bears?"

"Sure," said Morrie. "Olive and Ruby and Freddie. And I hear there are more of them on the Fog Mound."

Upsilon made a whistling noise through his teeth. "Why aren't the chipmunks afraid of *them?*" he asked Morrie.

"Because they're vegetarians!" I piped up. "Unlike *you*, as we well know from being in your cupboard!"

"Vegetarian bears? I doubt it!"

"Well, you don't know everything!" I said. "They grow vegetables and fruit. And they eat milk and cheese and eggs (unfertilized, I might add). And pancakes!"

"Selective breeding, carefully managed," said Bill.

"I stand corrected." Upsilon bowed a little. "I'm sorry I missed these bears."

"Yeah, me too," said Morrie. "We need their help."

"What's going on, Morrie?" Brown asked. "Did you come from the City of Ruins? Are the mutant crabs there?"

"They were." Morrie cackled suddenly. "You should have seen it!"

11

A War of the Wicked

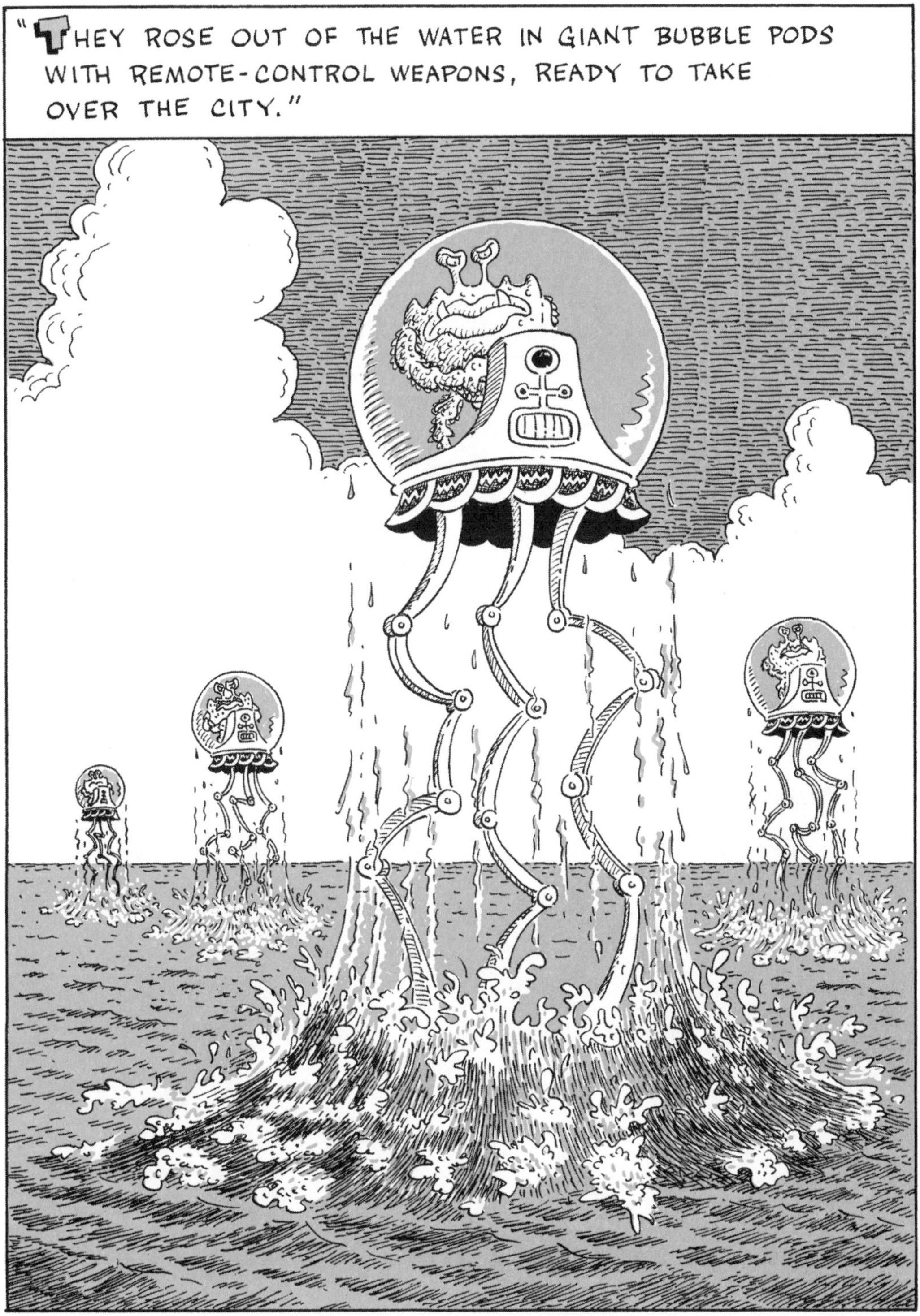
"THEY ROSE OUT OF THE WATER IN GIANT BUBBLE PODS WITH REMOTE-CONTROL WEAPONS, READY TO TAKE OVER THE CITY."

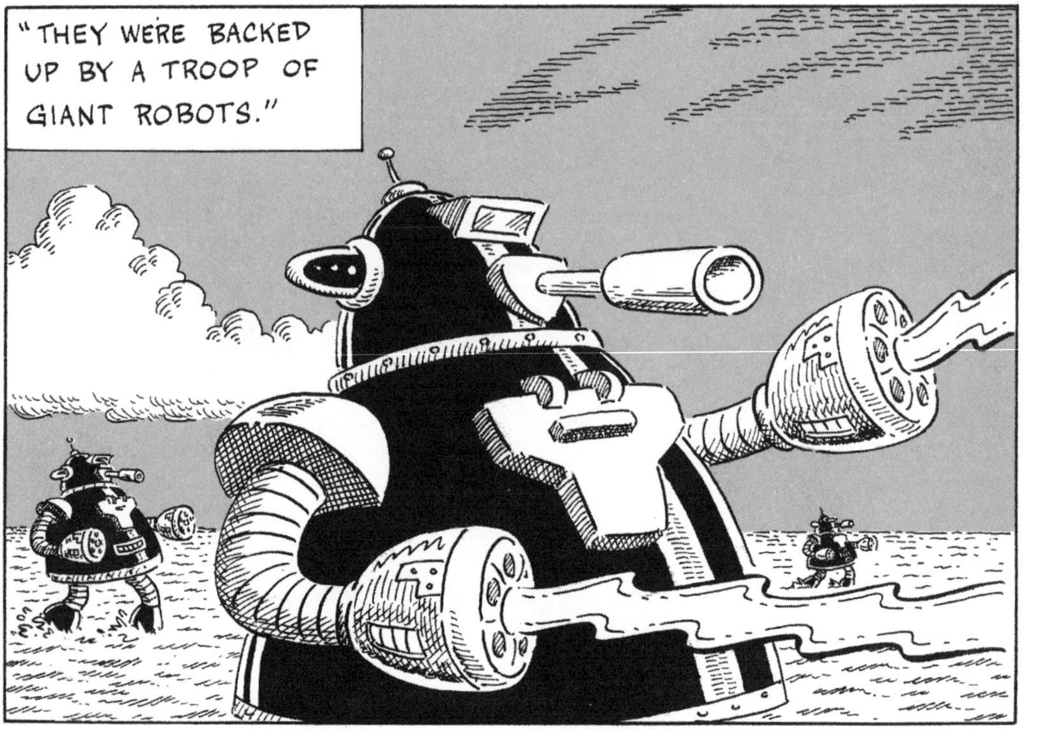
"THEY WERE BACKED UP BY A TROOP OF GIANT ROBOTS."

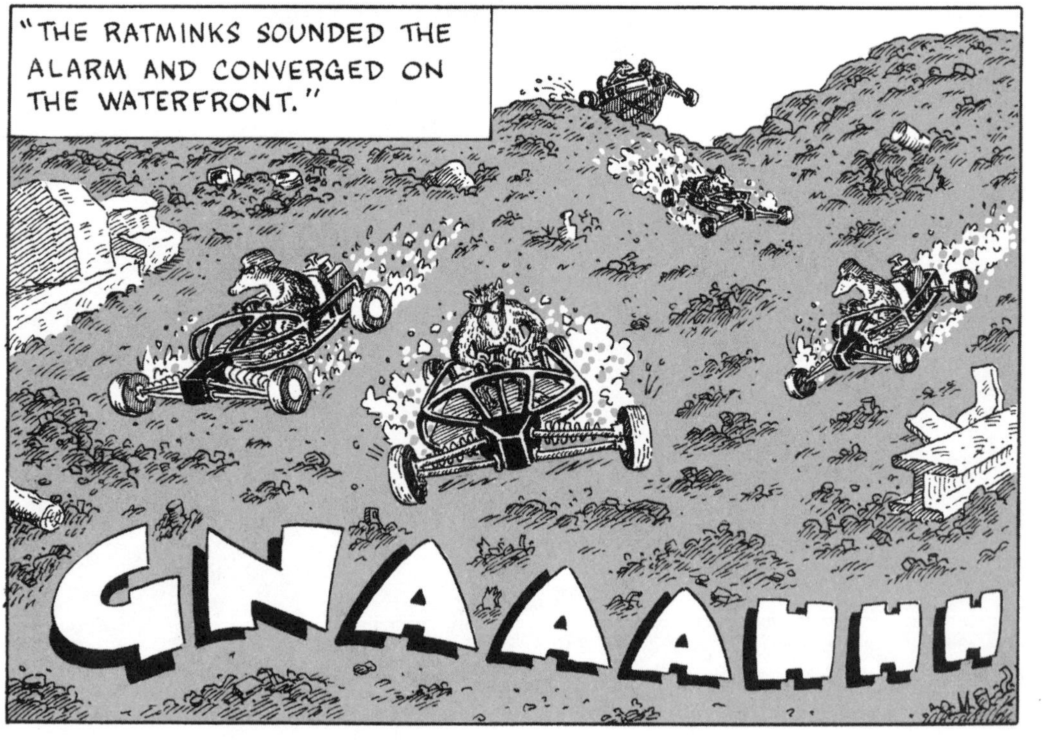
"THE RATMINKS SOUNDED THE ALARM AND CONVERGED ON THE WATERFRONT."
GNAAAHHH

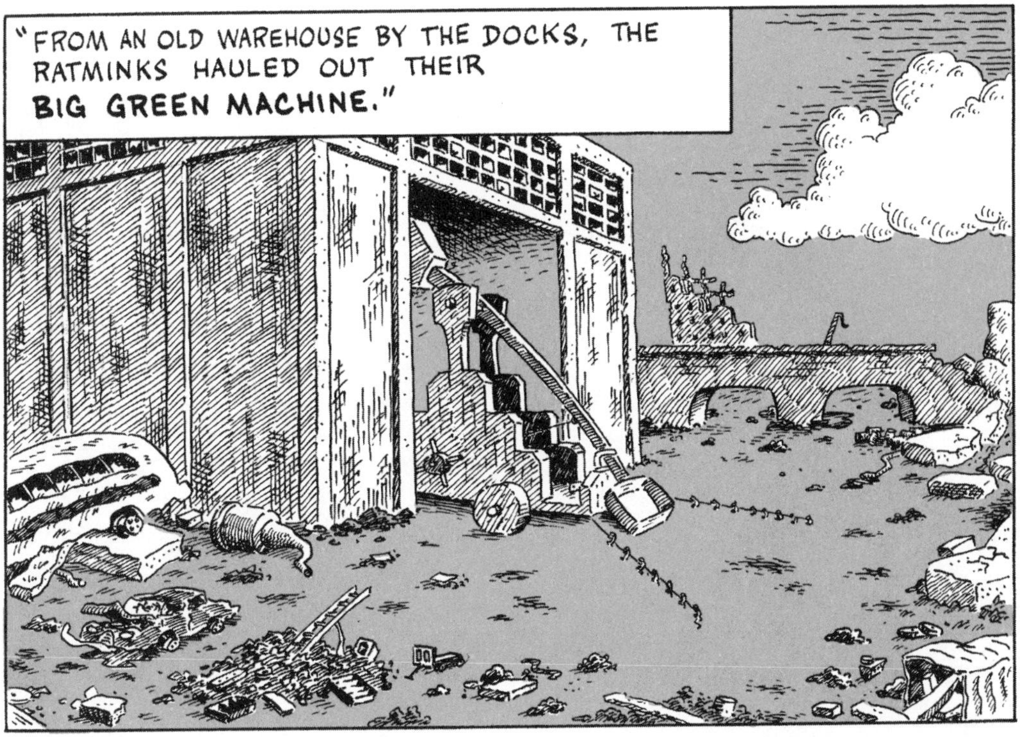
"FROM AN OLD WAREHOUSE BY THE DOCKS, THE RATMINKS HAULED OUT THEIR **BIG GREEN MACHINE.**"

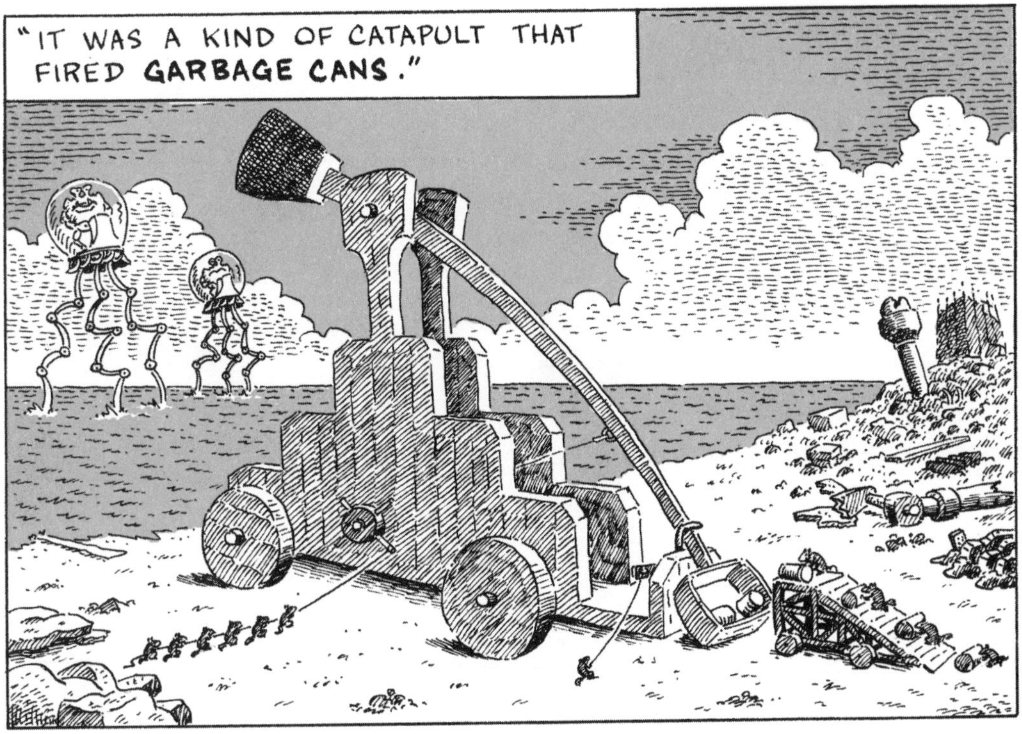
"IT WAS A KIND OF CATAPULT THAT FIRED **GARBAGE CANS**."

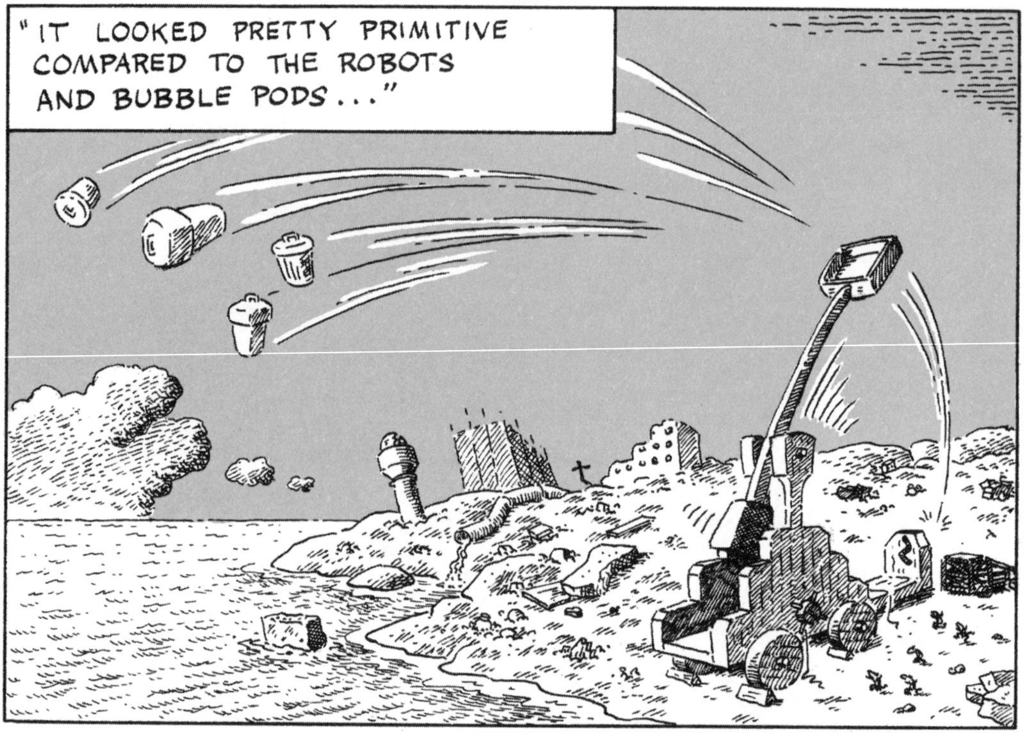
"IT LOOKED PRETTY PRIMITIVE COMPARED TO THE ROBOTS AND BUBBLE PODS..."

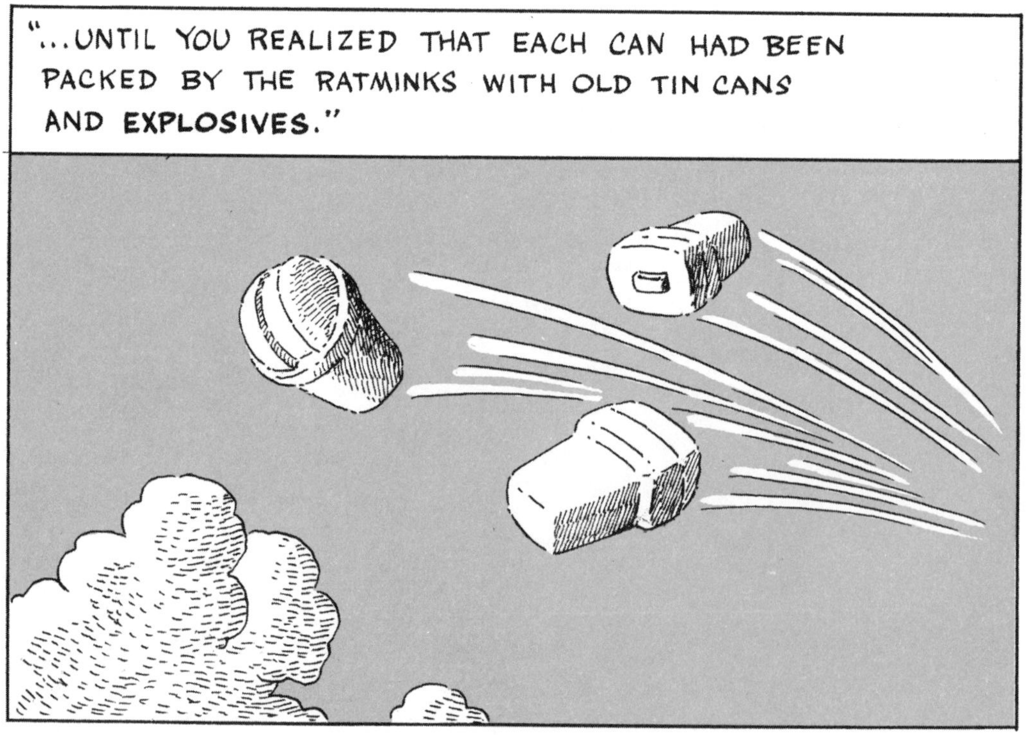
"...UNTIL YOU REALIZED THAT EACH CAN HAD BEEN PACKED BY THE RATMINKS WITH OLD TIN CANS AND **EXPLOSIVES**."

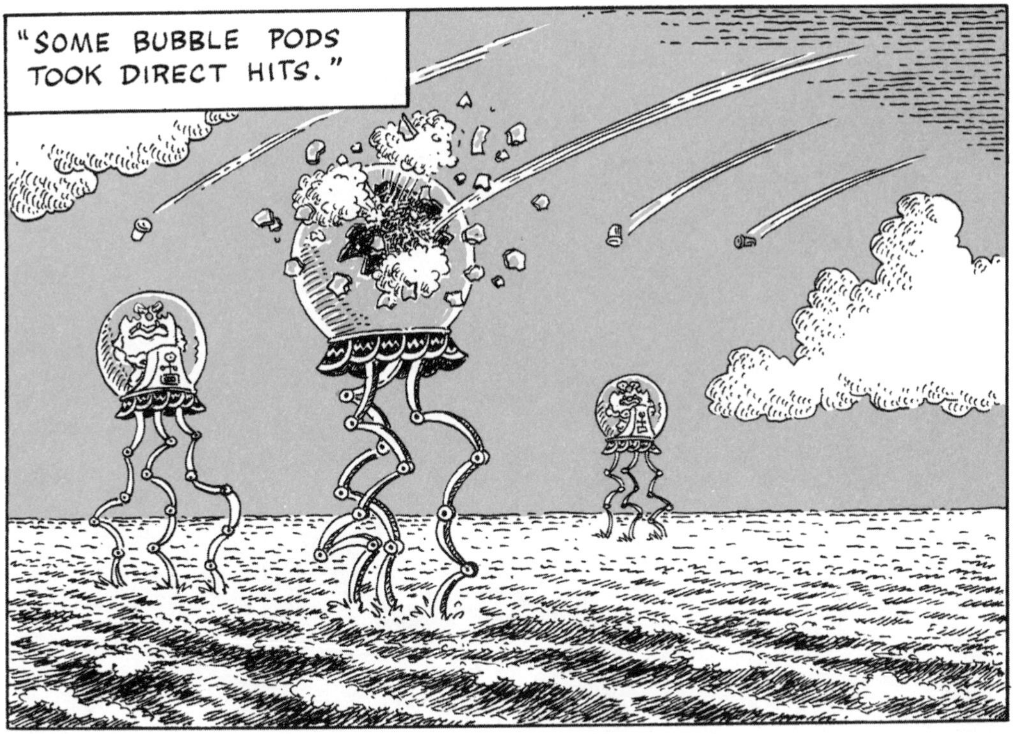
"SOME BUBBLE PODS
TOOK DIRECT HITS."

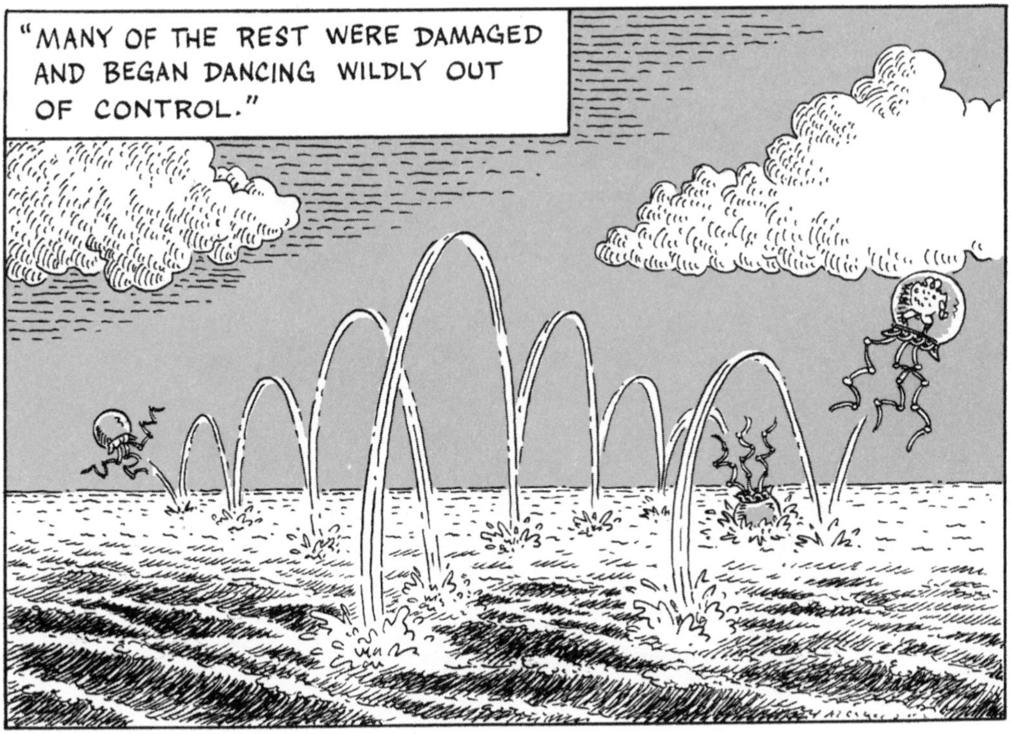
"MANY OF THE REST WERE DAMAGED
AND BEGAN DANCING WILDLY OUT
OF CONTROL."

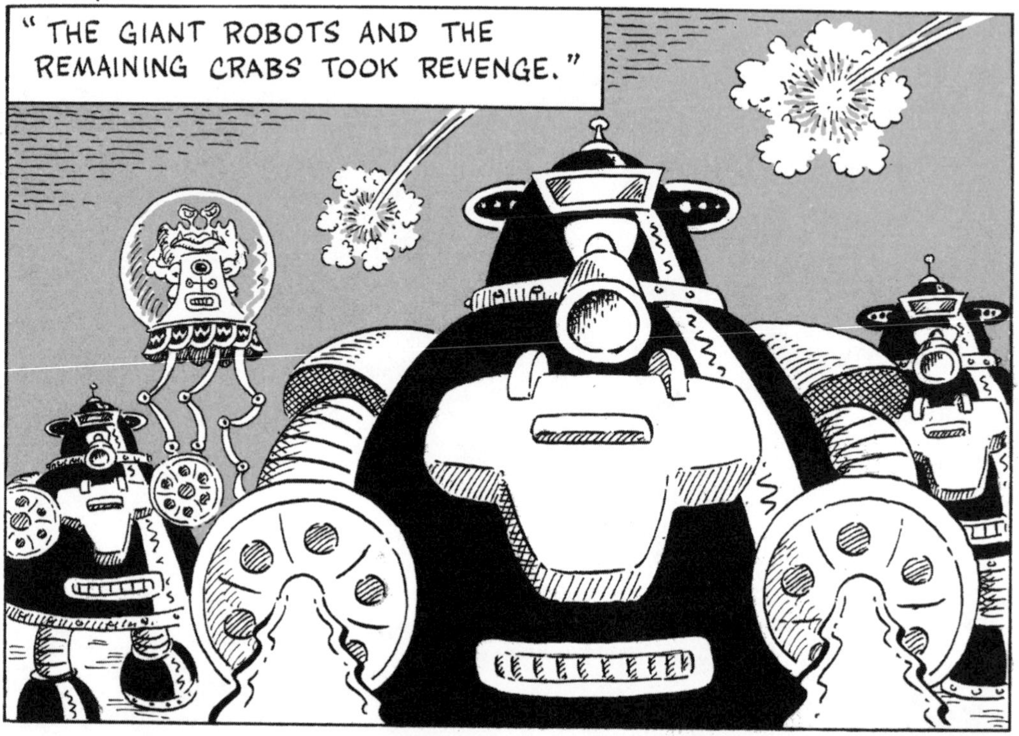
"THE GIANT ROBOTS AND THE REMAINING CRABS TOOK REVENGE."

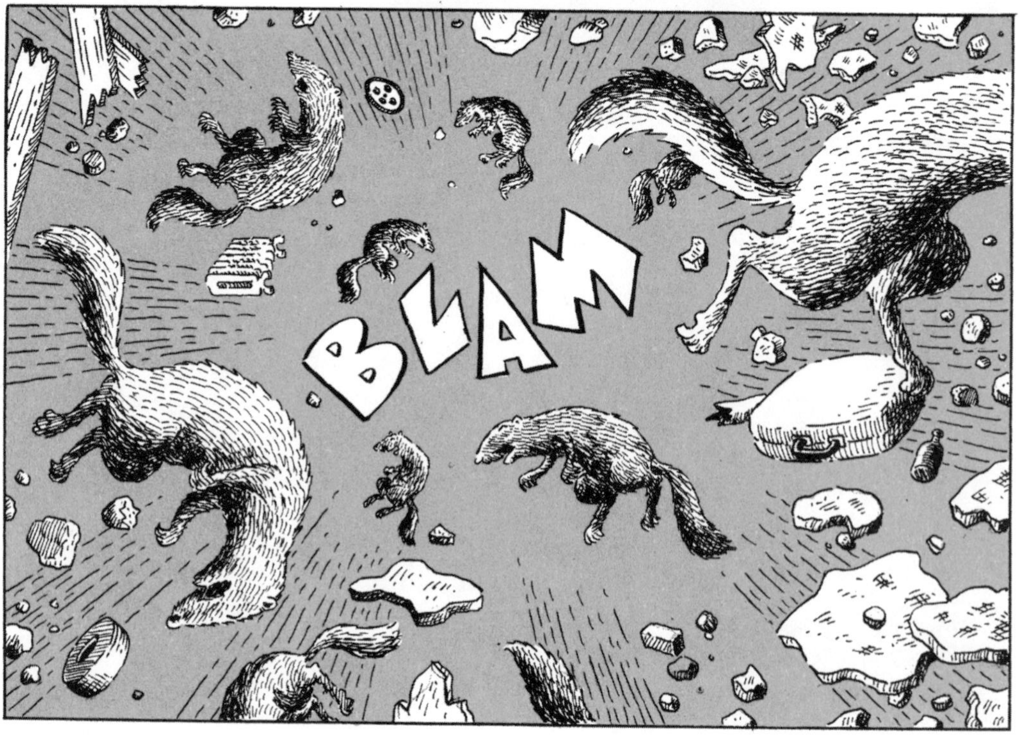
BLAM

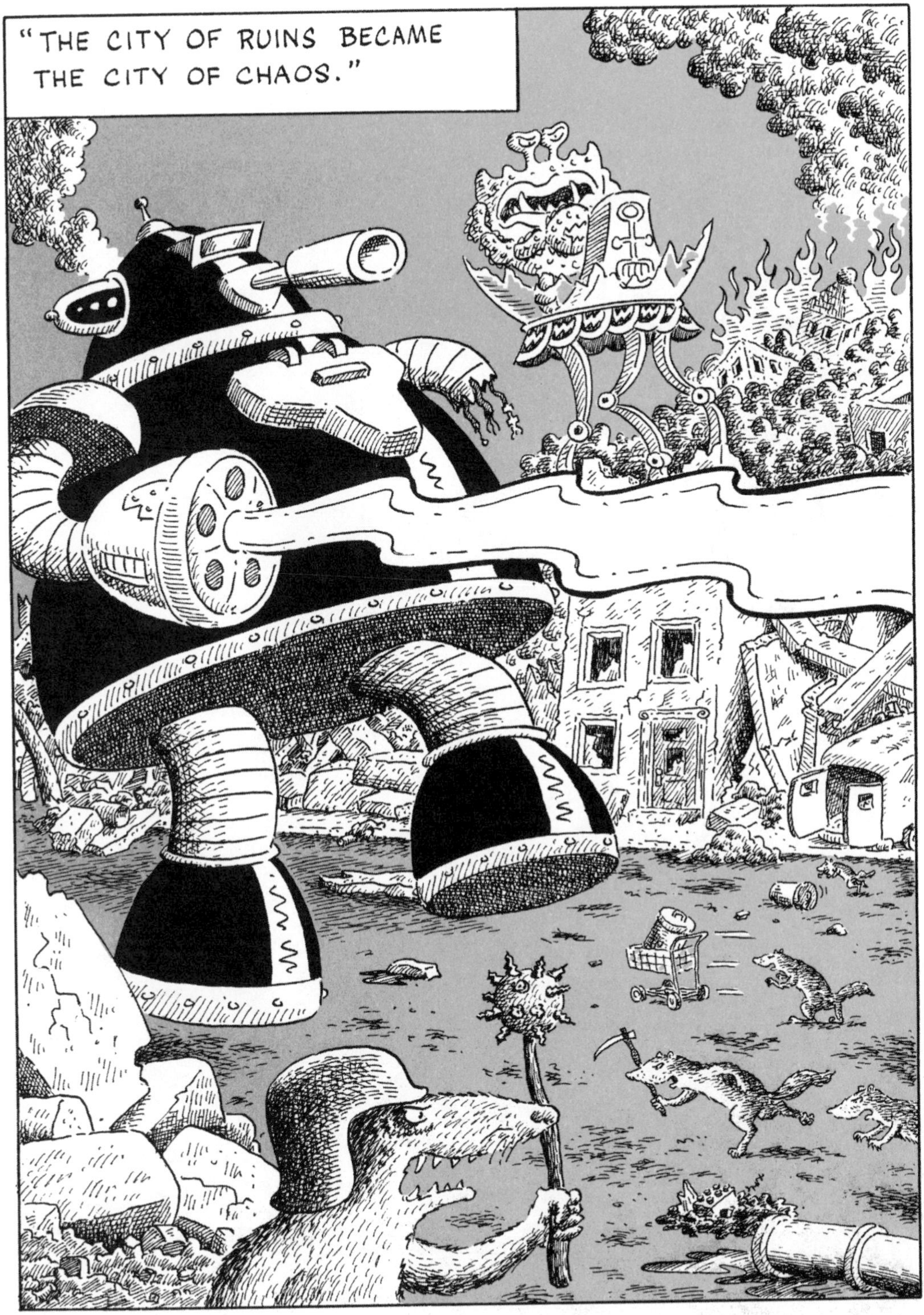
"THE CITY OF RUINS BECAME THE CITY OF CHAOS."

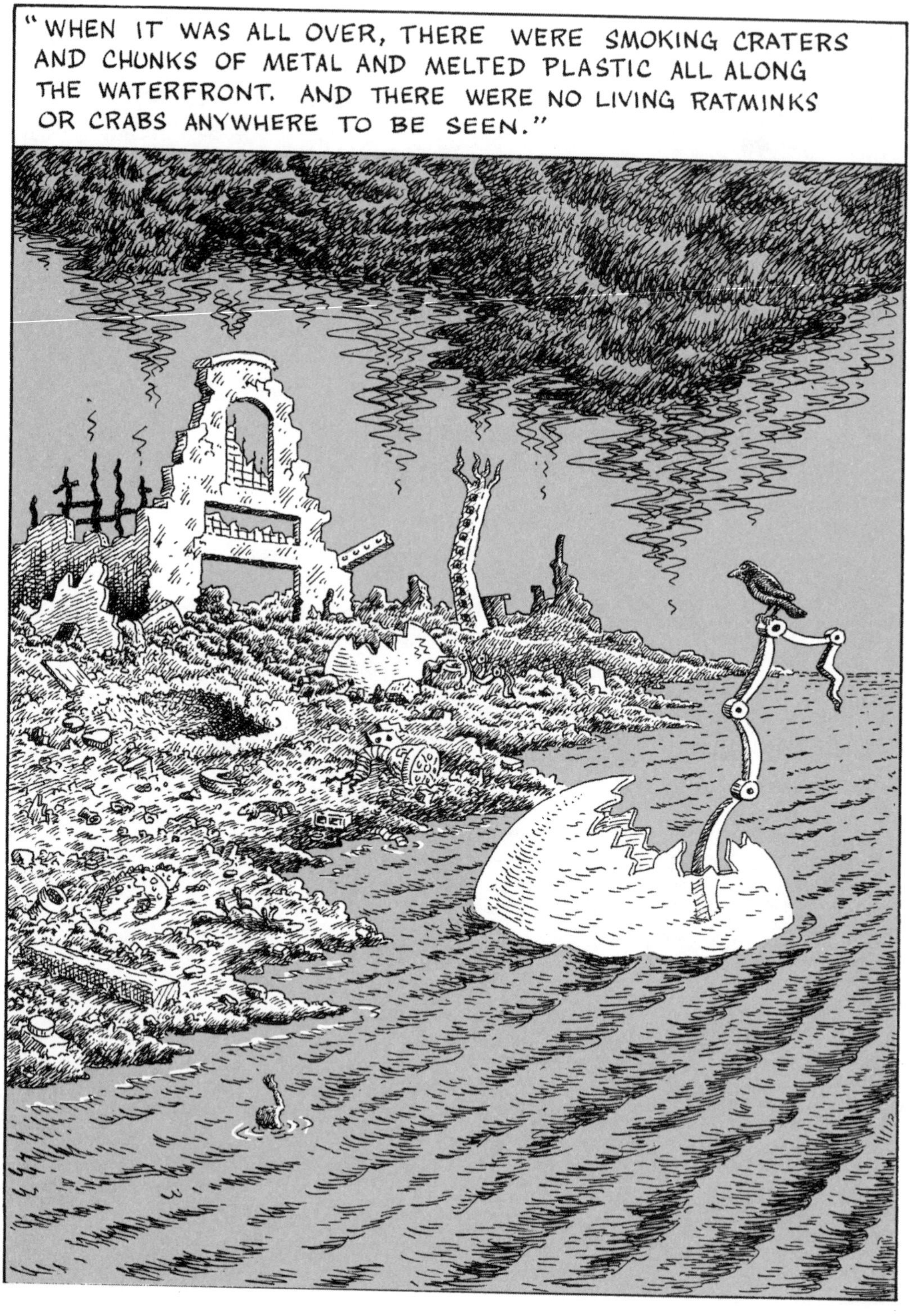
"WHEN IT WAS ALL OVER, THERE WERE SMOKING CRATERS AND CHUNKS OF METAL AND MELTED PLASTIC ALL ALONG THE WATERFRONT. AND THERE WERE NO LIVING RATMINKS OR CRABS ANYWHERE TO BE SEEN."

12

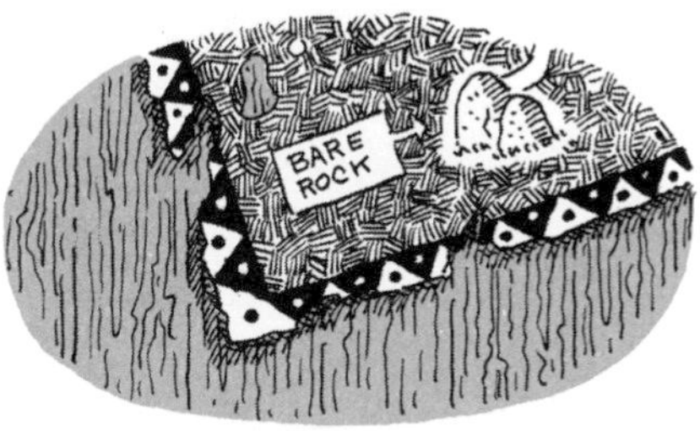
BARE
ROCK

The Old Maps

"A war of the wicked," mumbled Bill.

"So the bad guys wiped each other out?" I asked. "And it was all over before Fitz and the bears even got there?"

Morrie nodded.

"I'll bet they'll be disappointed," Brown said.

"Well, at least Fitz will be happy to see his friends again," Cluid said. "Now that the ratminks are gone, they'll be able to move back into the City!"

"You mentioned needing the bears," Upsilon reminded Morrie.

"Yeah, well, that's the bad part."

Morrie groomed under his wing for a few moments. Then he looked out the window and said, "Some of the ratminks survived."

He paused.

"And?" I prompted him.

"And the Dragon Lady." He paused again.

We waited.

"We hear they're headed for the Fog Mound."

"*The Fog Mound!*" I cried.

"Don't worry." Cluid smiled. "They'll never get in. They can't get through the deadly fog, remember?"

"The Fog Mound," Upsilon said. "That's where some of you guys live, right? What's this about deadly fog?"

"We *all* live there now," I said. "Well, except for Morrie, but he could come if he wanted to."

"The fog is all around the Mound," Cluid explained. "It keeps outsiders from getting in and protects us from predators like the Dragon Lady."

"Aren't you forgetting something?" Brown said. "The fog isn't deadly to me. It made the rest of you guys act crazy, but it didn't bother me. Remember? I had to trick you into turning around and walking out of it before you got totally zonkered!"

He turned to Upsilon. "We're assuming that for some reason reptiles aren't affected by the chemicals in the fog. And the Dragon Lady is a reptile!"

"What with the high altitude and the long winters around the Mound," Bill said, "there weren't any reptiles living in the area. I must confess I never even thought of them when I was formulating the ingredients of the fog. Let's see, should I have used more psillipyrola? Or kerriathrophlaeum, perhaps? No. Or what about tincture of the pollientia slime gland? No, no, that would be the wrong approach altogether. I must look into the components of more scents that attract—the fragrant lauroliae, perhaps. Hmmm . . ."

Meanwhile, Morrie was pacing back and forth.

"Fog, schmog!" he said. "They say the Dragon Lady has a map to some secret passage that avoids the fog."

We all looked at him.

"A map?" I said.

"To the *Secret Way?*" Cluid sounded shocked.

"Pubba handed a map to Olive when we left for Faradawn," I said. "But I don't see how the Dragon Lady could have gotten hold of it."

"What about those papers and maps that you guys left behind in Olive's warehouse?" Brown asked.

I looked at him. "What pa . . . ?" Then I remembered. "Holy cow!" I yelped. "Ragna's maps! We thought they got burned up in the fire!"

"What fire, and who's Ragna?" asked Morrie.

"Ragna was Olive's other sister," I explained. "The one who died. We found her diary and a couple of maps at Fitz's place in the City of Ruins. We meant to take them with us, but we had to leave in a hurry. And by the time Olive remembered

them, her warehouse was on fire! We thought the papers must have been destroyed. But now that I think about it, the Dragon Lady was there. I suppose she could have gotten to them before the fire did."

"Oh," Cluid cried. "She mustn't get into the Fog Mound! Think of all the Smalls! And the cows and chickens! None of them know how to protect themselves. They aren't used to predators. Oh, it would be *awful*!"

"Maybe the cold will keep her away," I said hopefully.

"I wouldn't count on it," said Morrie. "She'll think of some way around that. And she's got some ratminks with her, don't forget. They won't mind

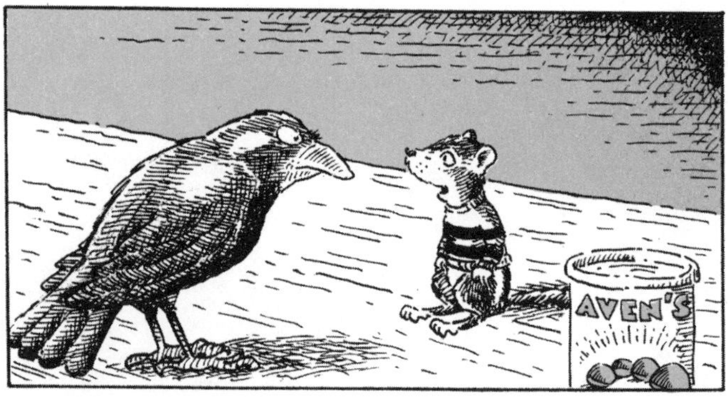
AVEN'S

the cold. No, my plan was to see if the bears would go after her and the ratminks. Bears can travel pretty fast when they want to, so I thought they would have a chance of catching up with them. And then I was going to fly to the Mound and warn the other bears there, just in case. I was hoping Olive could tell me how to get there. Now I don't know *what* to do!"

He hunkered down, dejected, letting his head sink into the space between his shoulders.

"Well," I said slowly, "for one thing, I can tell you how to get there. You just follow the same waterways that we sailed down on in our boat. I can draw you a map, no problem. But I wish I could go too!"

I racked my brain. "If only we had Olive's flying machine!" I said suddenly. "Then we could all go!"

"One of the bears has a flying machine?" Upsilon asked.

"Yeah," Brown said. "We flew in it! Me and Thelonious. We got shot at by eagles."

"And where is the flying machine now?"

"It got wrecked," I said.

"Well, so much for that," said Morrie. "Have you got something to draw with, Thelonious?"

"Warn him about the eagles," Brown said.

"There's a flying machine here at the Institute." Upsilon stretched his feet out and crossed them at the ankles.

"There is?" I climbed onto the edge of the table so I could see his face. "Where is it?"

"I wouldn't know how to fly it," he warned. "And it's not an airplane exactly."

"What is it? A helicopter?"

"No."

"A velocicopter!" I guessed.

"No, actually, it's a flying *sofa*!"

13

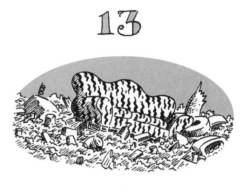

Sofa So Good

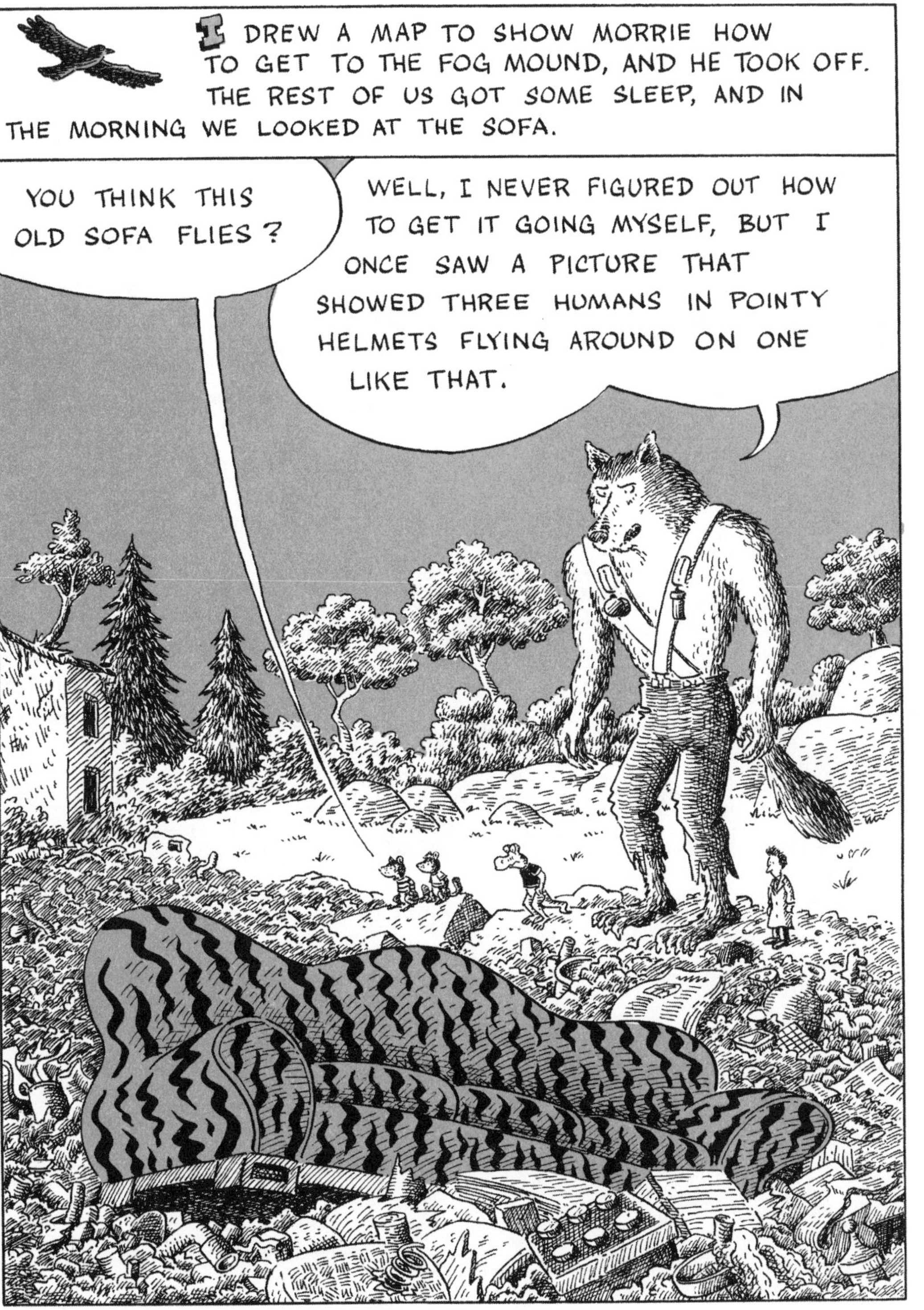
I DREW A MAP TO SHOW MORRIE HOW TO GET TO THE FOG MOUND, AND HE TOOK OFF. THE REST OF US GOT SOME SLEEP, AND IN THE MORNING WE LOOKED AT THE SOFA.
YOU THINK THIS OLD SOFA FLIES?
WELL, I NEVER FIGURED OUT HOW TO GET IT GOING MYSELF, BUT I ONCE SAW A PICTURE THAT SHOWED THREE HUMANS IN POINTY HELMETS FLYING AROUND ON ONE LIKE THAT.

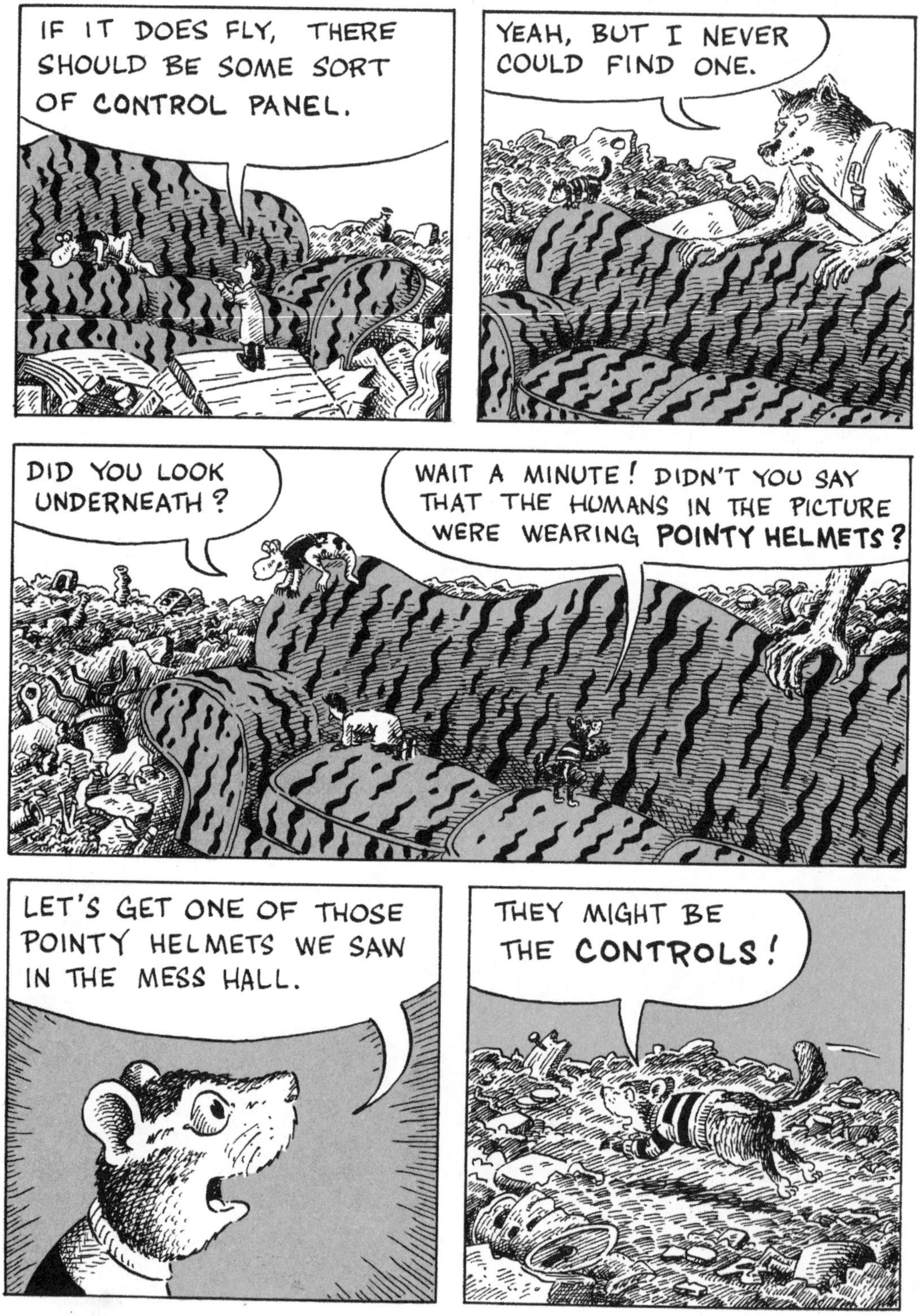
IF IT DOES FLY, THERE SHOULD BE SOME SORT OF CONTROL PANEL.
YEAH, BUT I NEVER COULD FIND ONE.
DID YOU LOOK UNDERNEATH?
WAIT A MINUTE! DIDN'T YOU SAY THAT THE HUMANS IN THE PICTURE WERE WEARING POINTY HELMETS?
LET'S GET ONE OF THOSE POINTY HELMETS WE SAW IN THE MESS HALL.
THEY MIGHT BE THE CONTROLS!

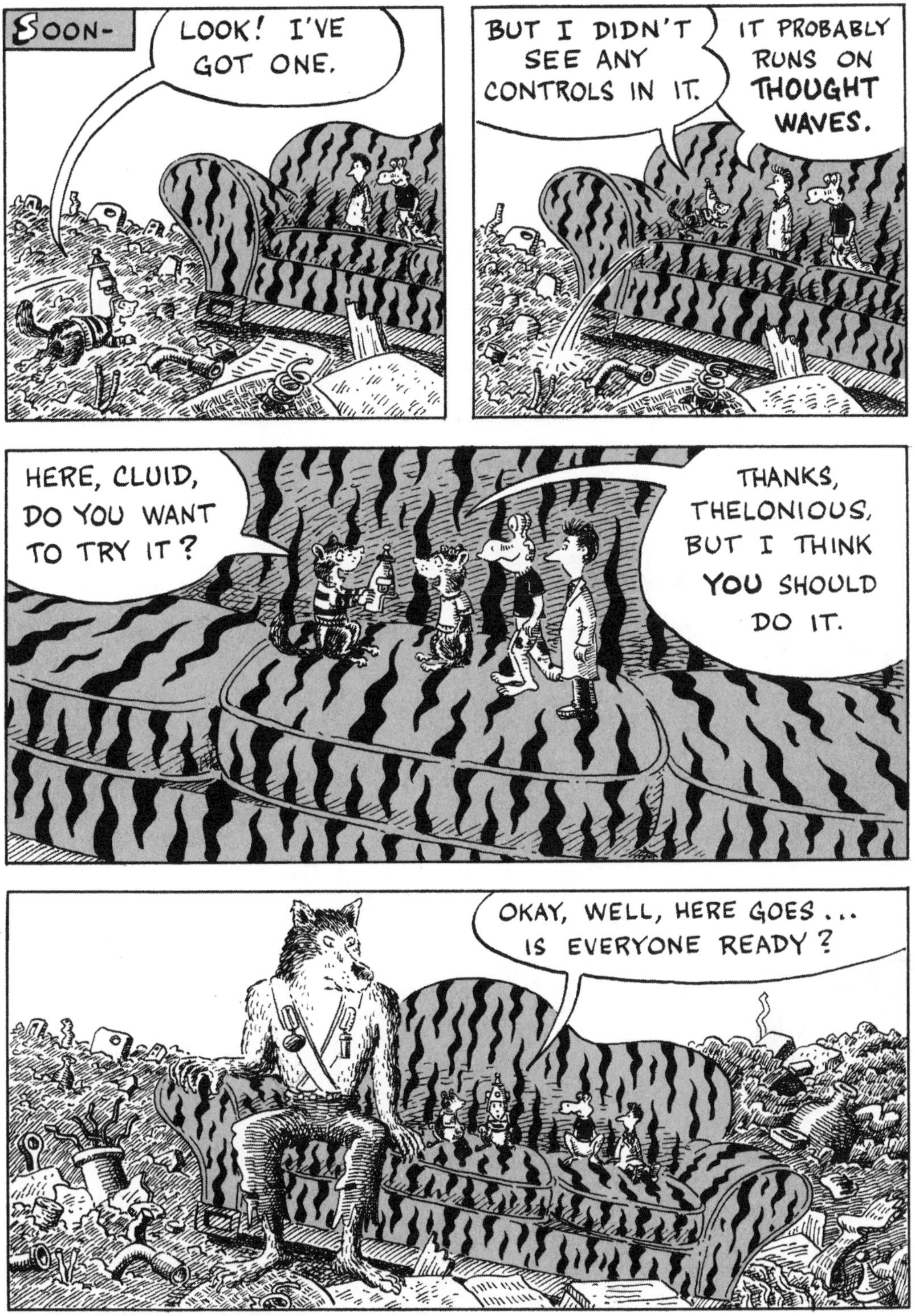
SOON-
LOOK! I'VE GOT ONE.
BUT I DIDN'T SEE ANY CONTROLS IN IT.
IT PROBABLY RUNS ON THOUGHT WAVES.
HERE, CLUID, DO YOU WANT TO TRY IT?
THANKS, THELONIOUS, BUT I THINK YOU SHOULD DO IT.
OKAY, WELL, HERE GOES ... IS EVERYONE READY?

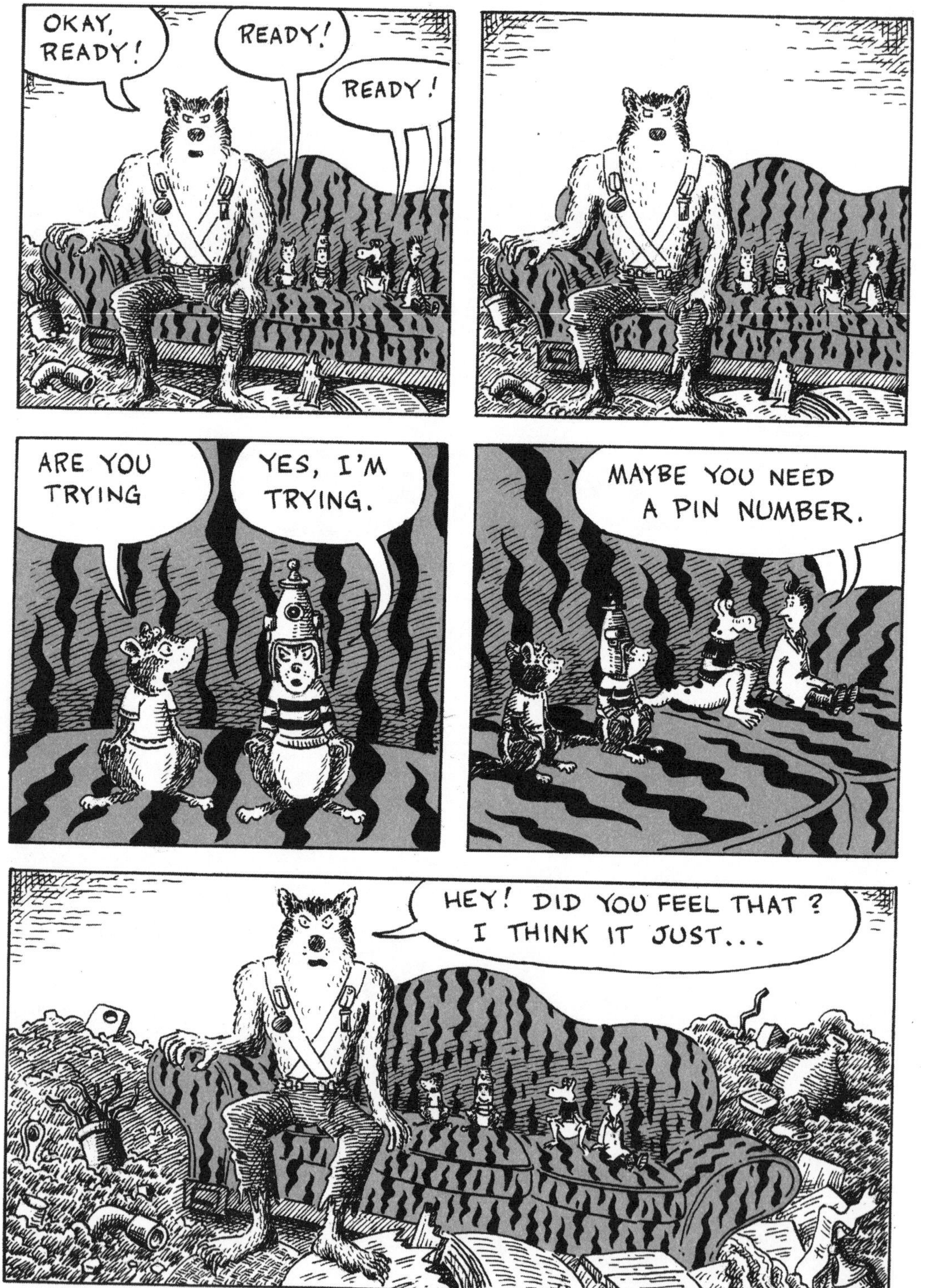
OKAY, READY!
READY!
READY!
ARE YOU TRYING
YES, I'M TRYING.
MAYBE YOU NEED A PIN NUMBER.
HEY! DID YOU FEEL THAT? I THINK IT JUST...

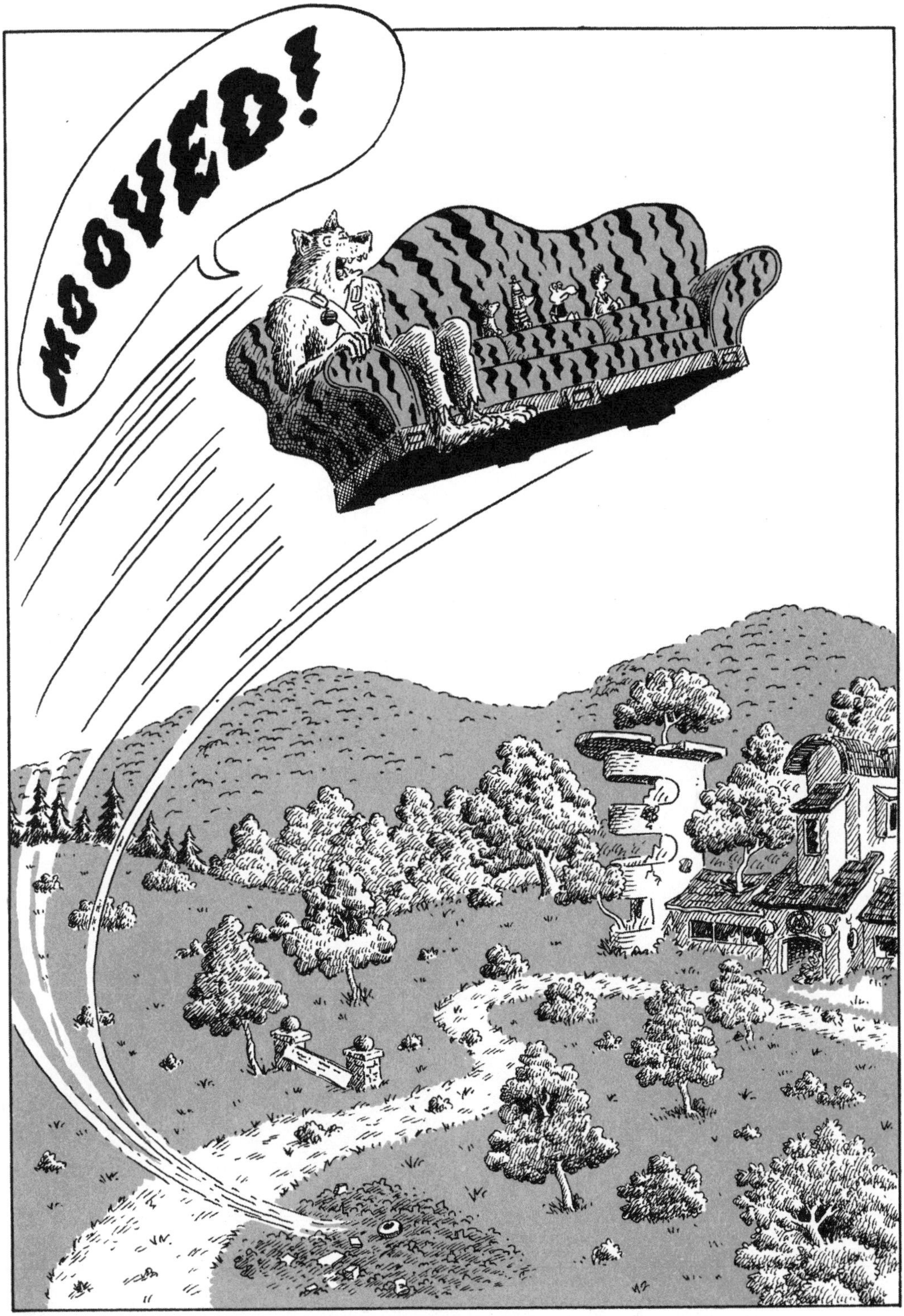
WOOVED!

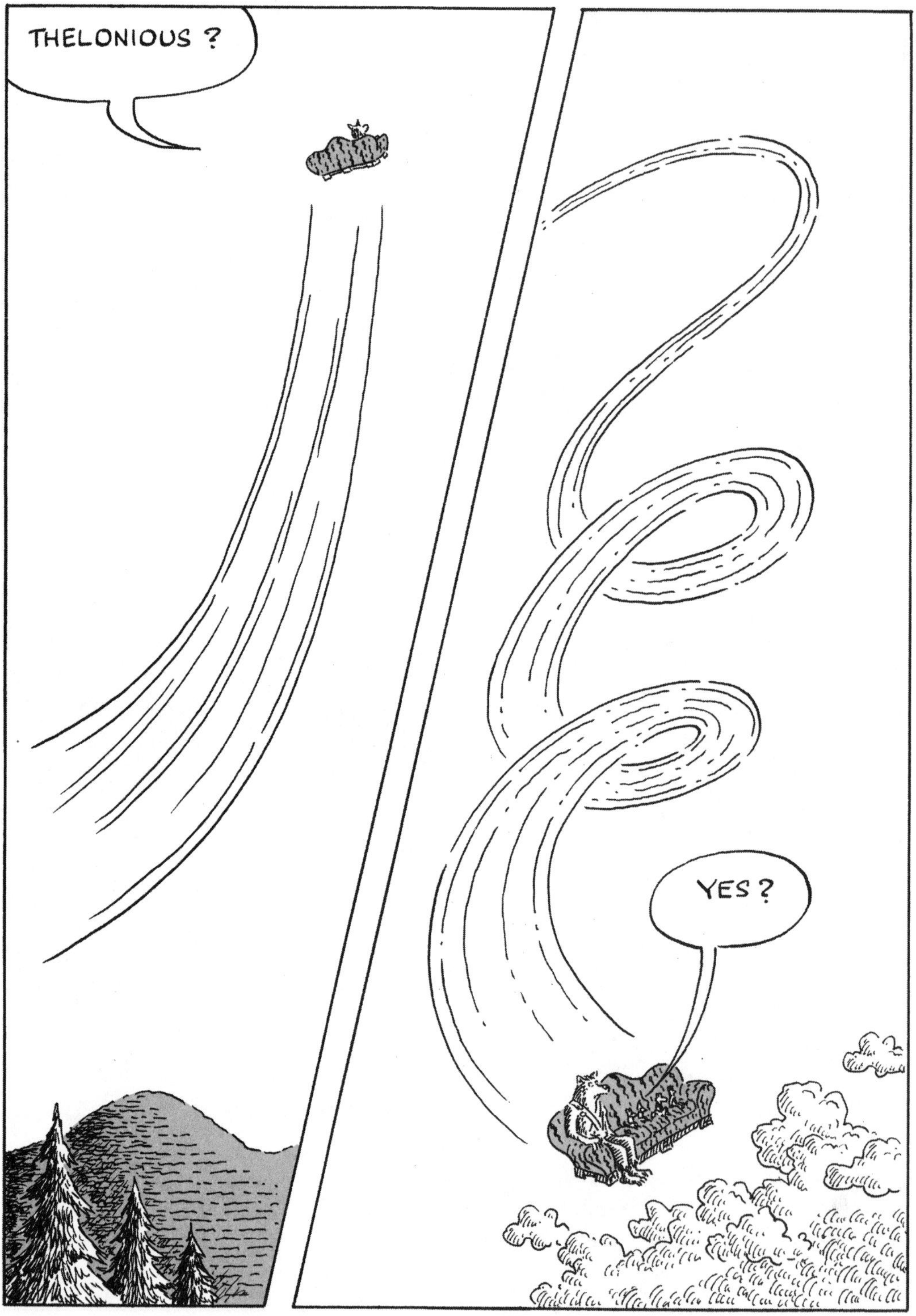
THELONIOUS ?
YES ?

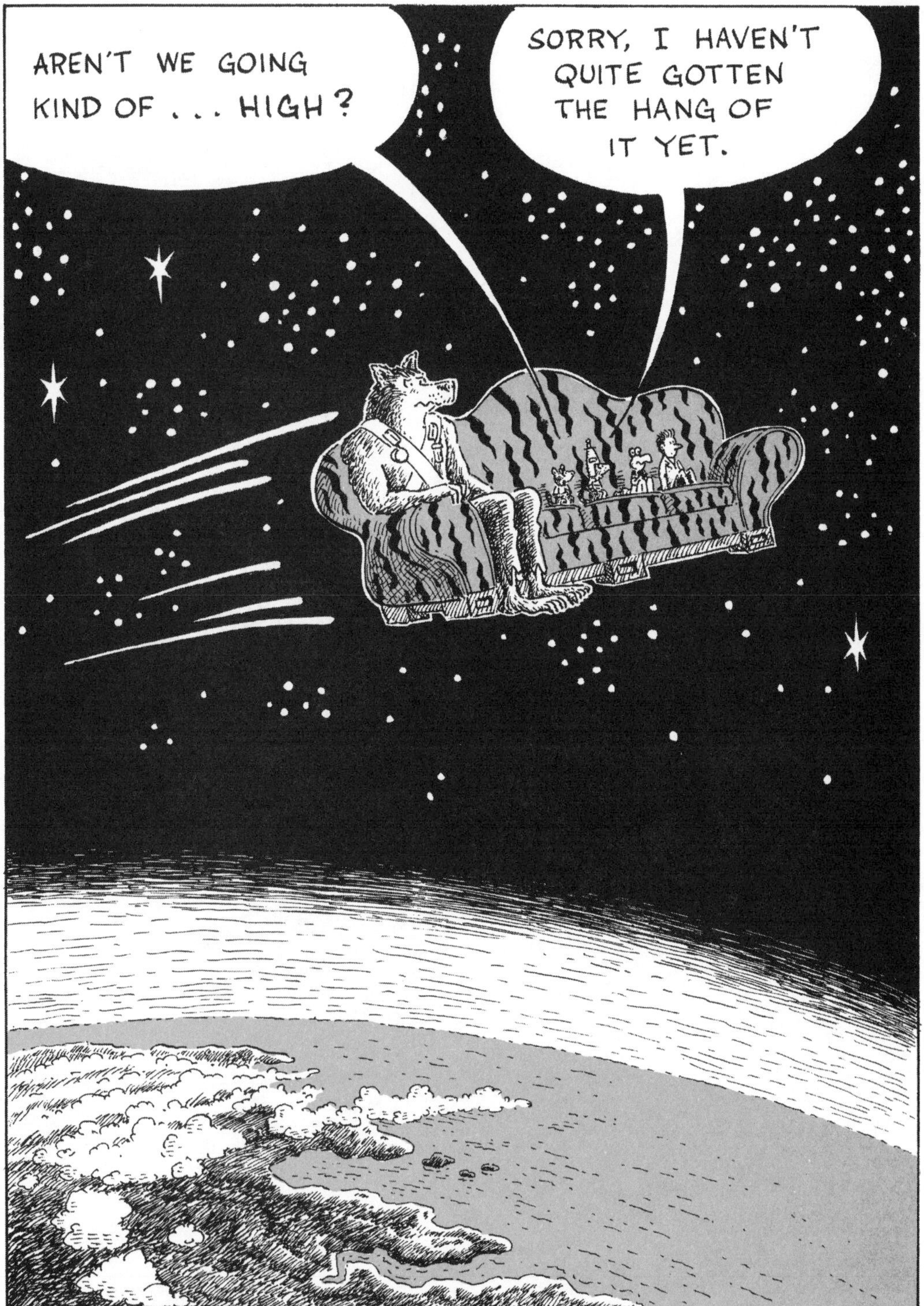
AREN'T WE GOING KIND OF . . . HIGH?
SORRY, I HAVEN'T QUITE GOTTEN THE HANG OF IT YET.

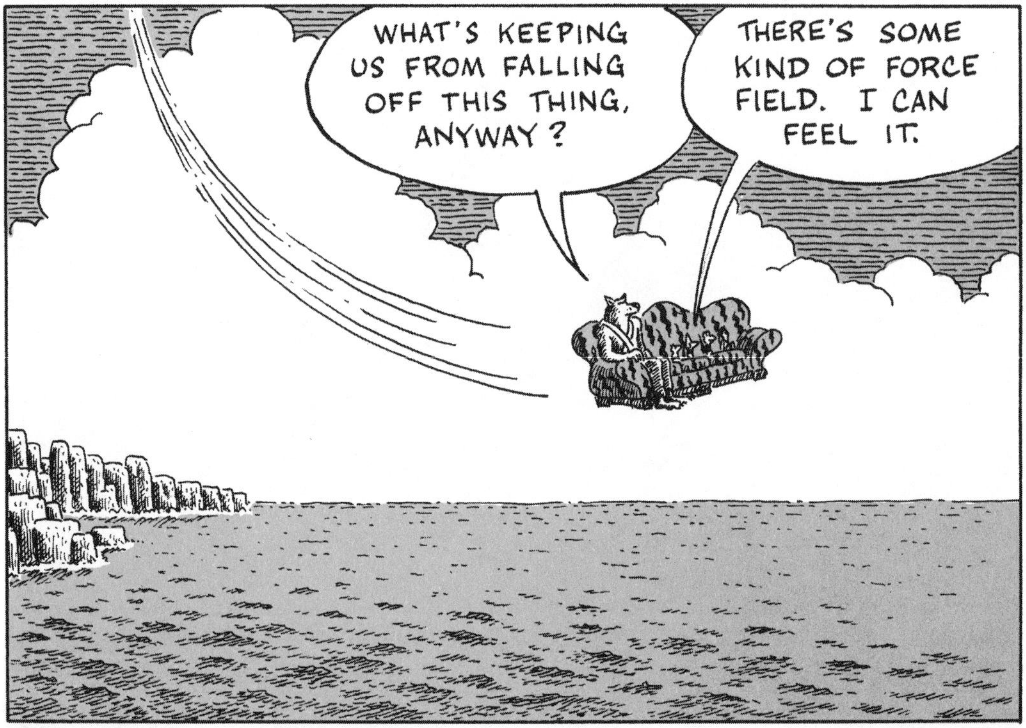
WHAT'S KEEPING US FROM FALLING OFF THIS THING, ANYWAY?
THERE'S SOME KIND OF FORCE FIELD. I CAN FEEL IT.

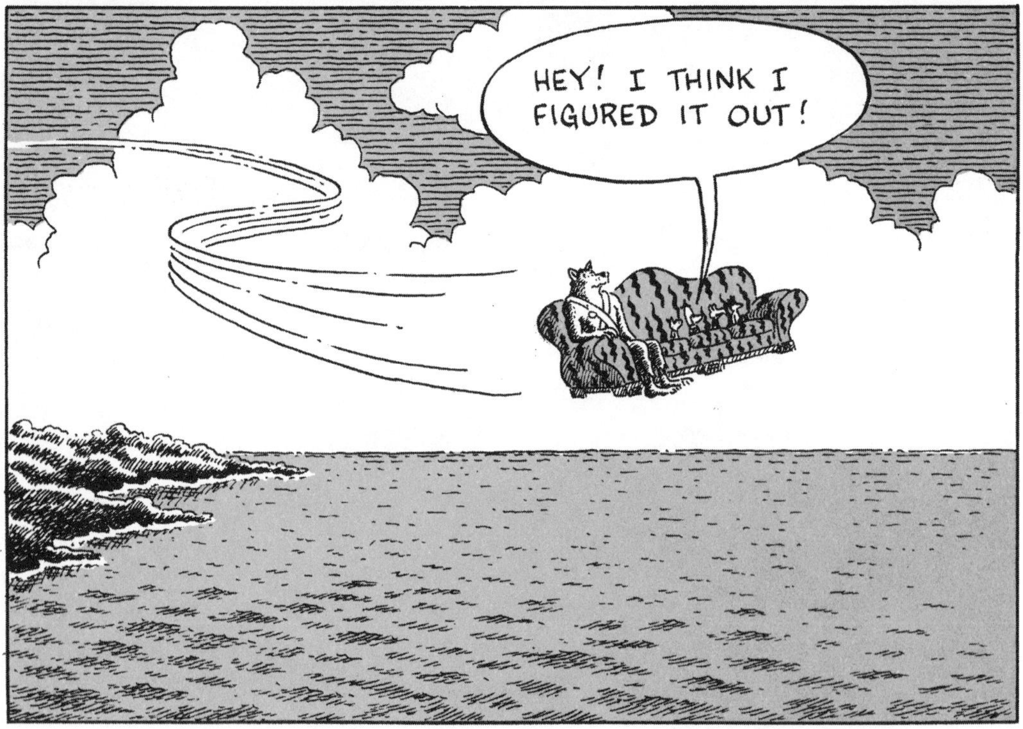
HEY! I THINK I FIGURED IT OUT!

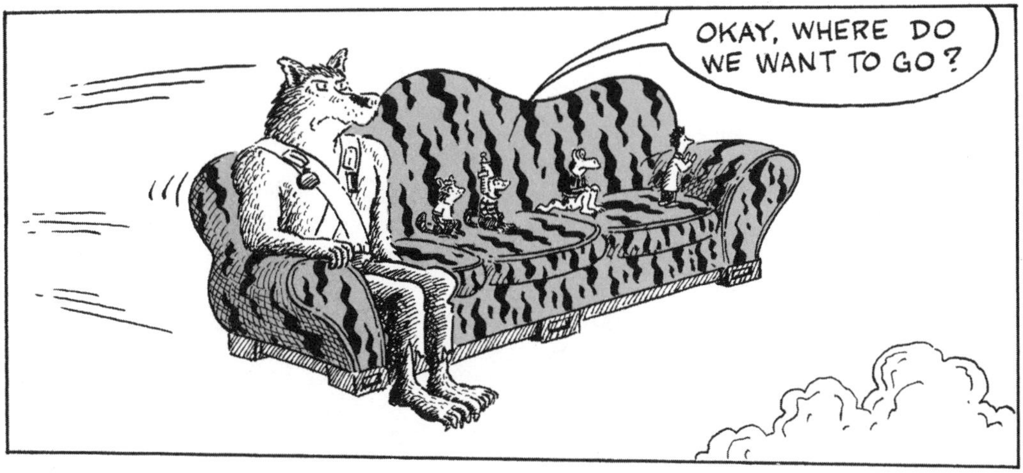
OKAY, WHERE DO WE WANT TO GO?

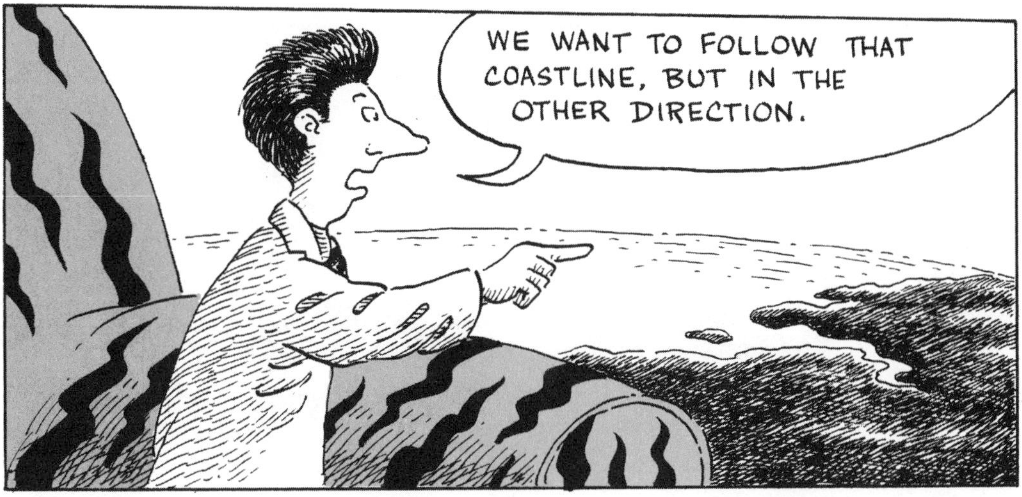
WE WANT TO FOLLOW THAT COASTLINE, BUT IN THE OTHER DIRECTION.

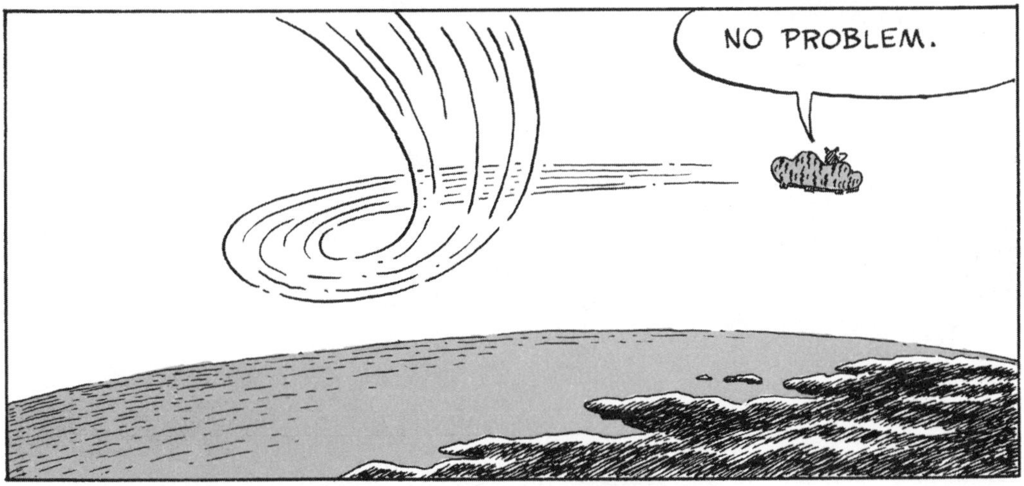
NO PROBLEM.

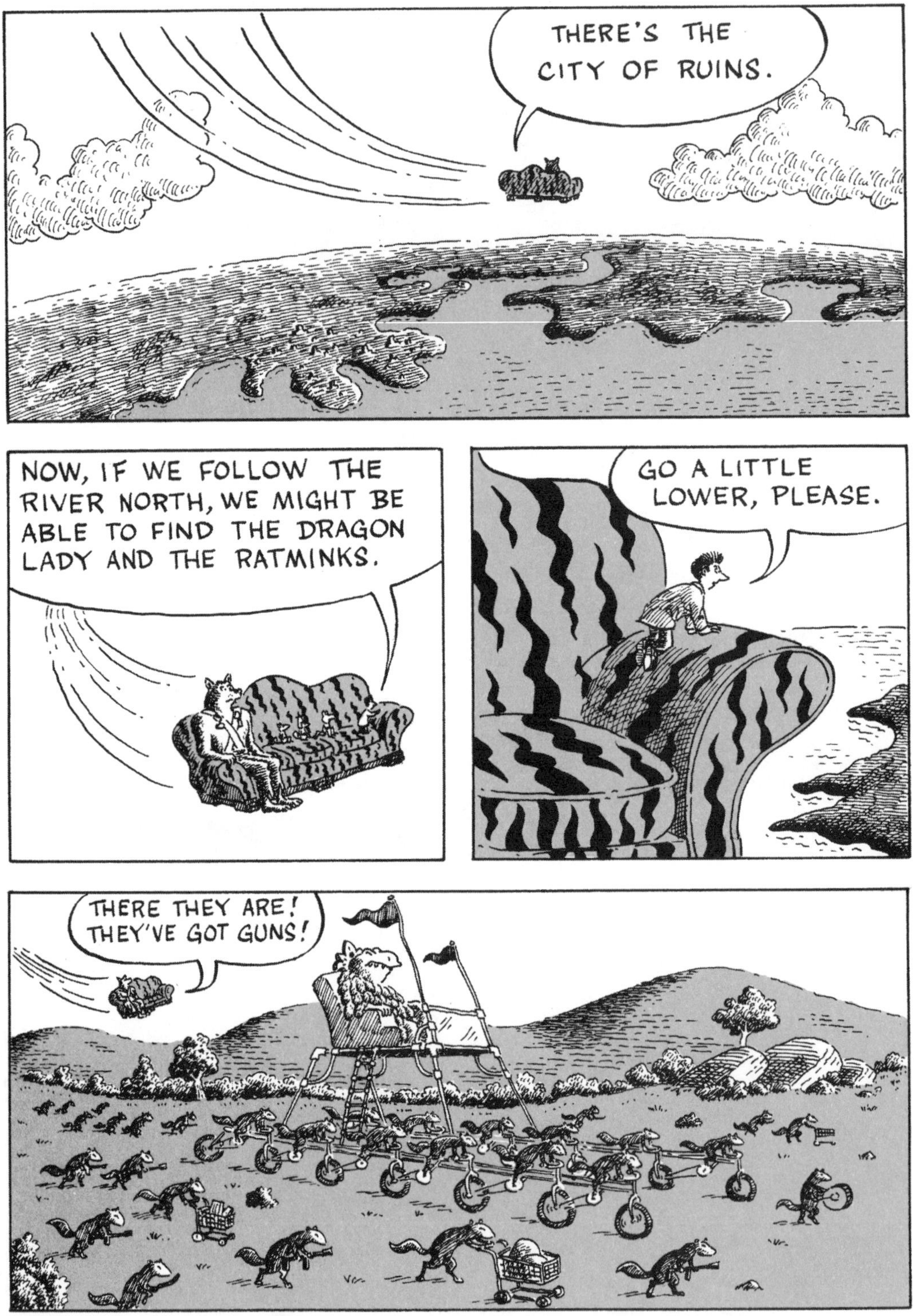
THERE'S THE CITY OF RUINS.
NOW, IF WE FOLLOW THE RIVER NORTH, WE MIGHT BE ABLE TO FIND THE DRAGON LADY AND THE RATMINKS.
GO A LITTLE LOWER, PLEASE.
THERE THEY ARE! THEY'VE GOT GUNS!

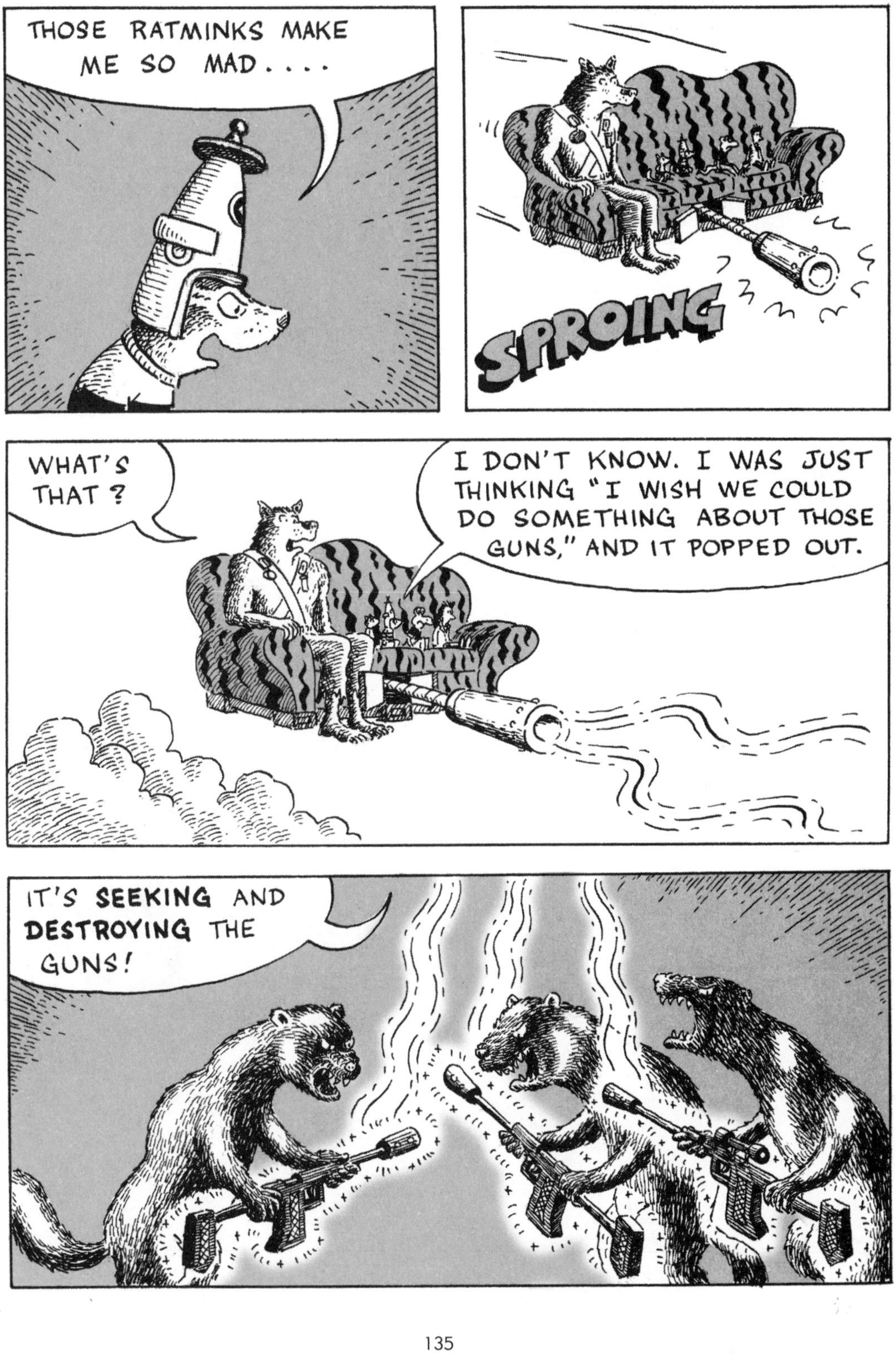

THOSE RATMINKS MAKE ME SO MAD....
SPROING
WHAT'S THAT ?
I DON'T KNOW. I WAS JUST THINKING "I WISH WE COULD DO SOMETHING ABOUT THOSE GUNS," AND IT POPPED OUT.
IT'S **SEEKING** AND **DESTROYING** THE GUNS!

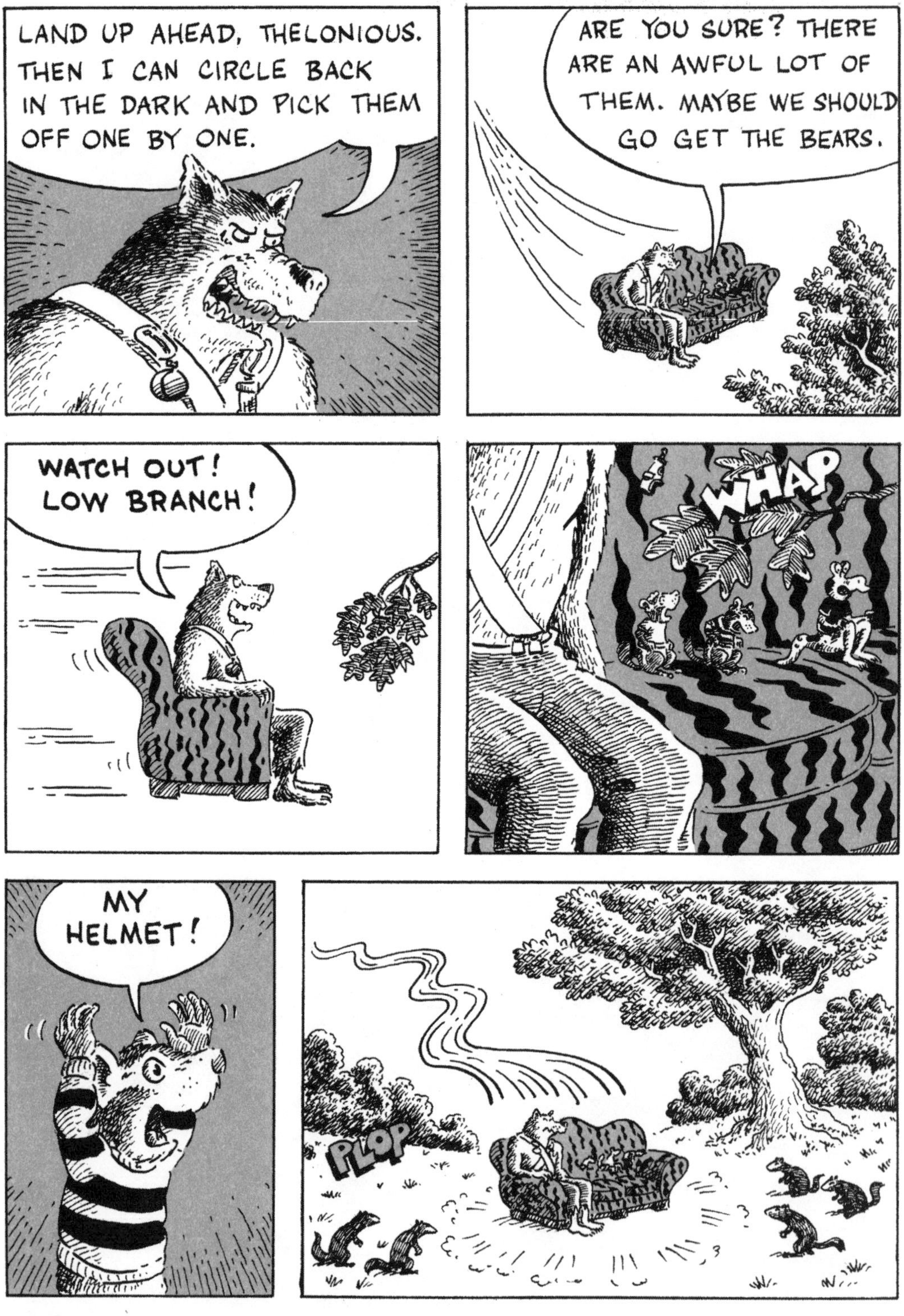
LAND UP AHEAD, THELONIOUS. THEN I CAN CIRCLE BACK IN THE DARK AND PICK THEM OFF ONE BY ONE.
ARE YOU SURE? THERE ARE AN AWFUL LOT OF THEM. MAYBE WE SHOULD GO GET THE BEARS.
WATCH OUT! LOW BRANCH!
WHAP
MY HELMET!
PLOP

14

One Against Many

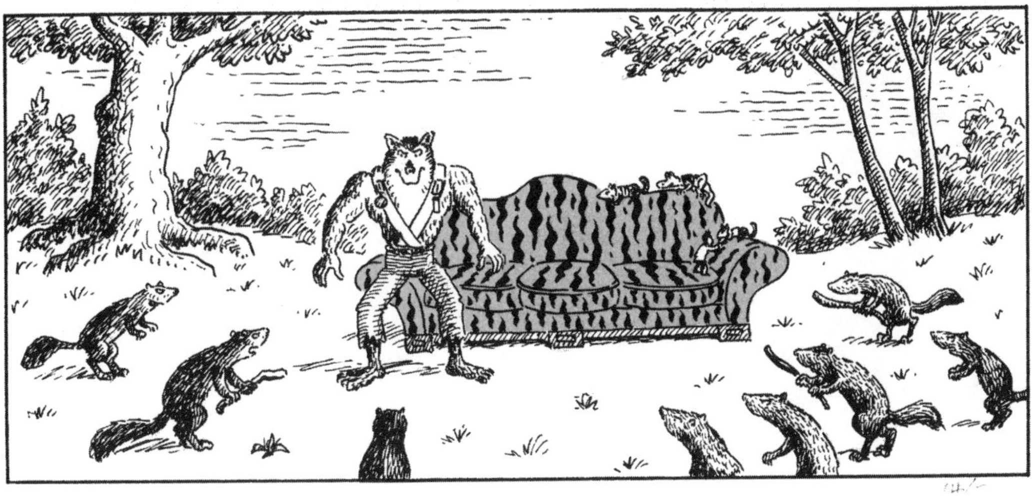

Uh-oh. This wasn't what Upsilon had wanted—to face the whole group of ratminks in broad daylight!

But there we were.

The ratminks' eyes narrowed. They picked up sticks and rocks to replace their guns and advanced toward us, growling.

Upsilon rose to his feet.

"Can you guys get Bill up the tree?" he murmured to us. "This isn't going to be pretty."

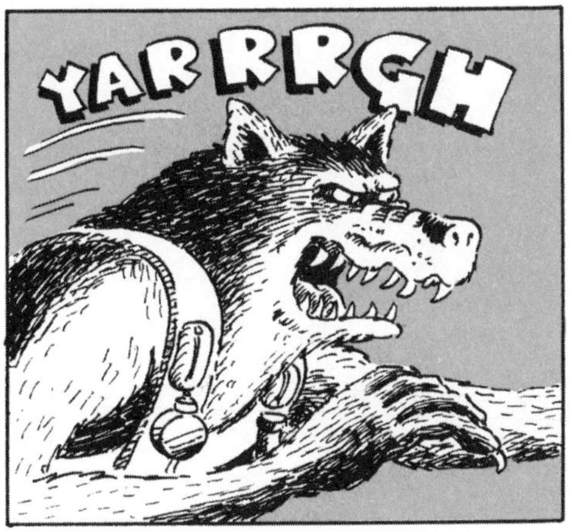
YARRRGH

Then, with a loud snarl, he hurled himself at the first of the ratminks, launching it, with one swipe of his paw, claws extended, clear across the field and *smack!* into a tree trunk. It lay there moaning.

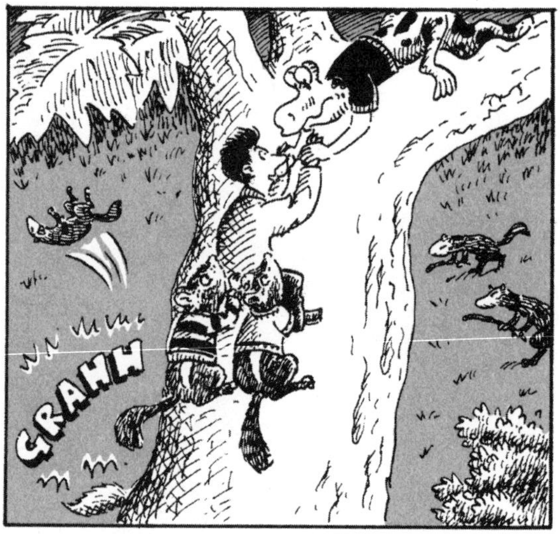
GRAHH

As quickly as we could, Cluid and Brown and I carried and pulled and pushed until we got Bill up the nearest tree to a safe spot high in the branches.

Then we crawled to the end of a branch so we could peek out through the leaves.

"What's happening?" Cluid asked.

"Your guess is as good as mine," I replied. "It just looks like a big pile of flying fur."

We could hear shrieks and roars, and we could see bleeding ratminks flying through the air.

The Dragon Lady shouted, "After him, you fools! All of you! Bite him behind the knees! Cowards! You aren't hurt! Bring him down! He's only one, and you are many! Bite! Bite!"

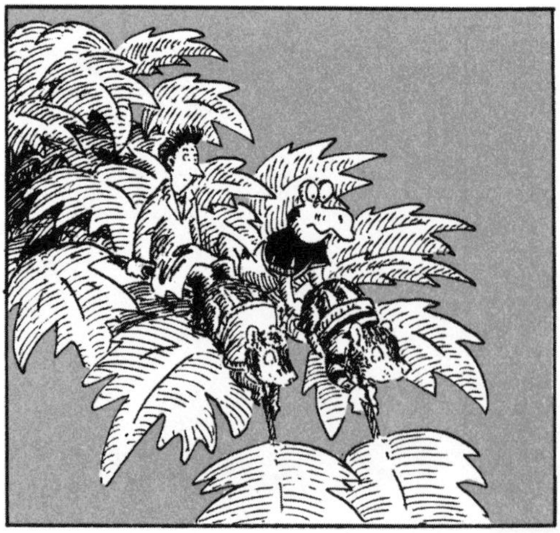

The ratminks screamed.

The Dragon Lady yelled until she was hoarse.

Upsilon's roars grew weaker.

"Uh-oh," I said, looking down, "this doesn't look good."

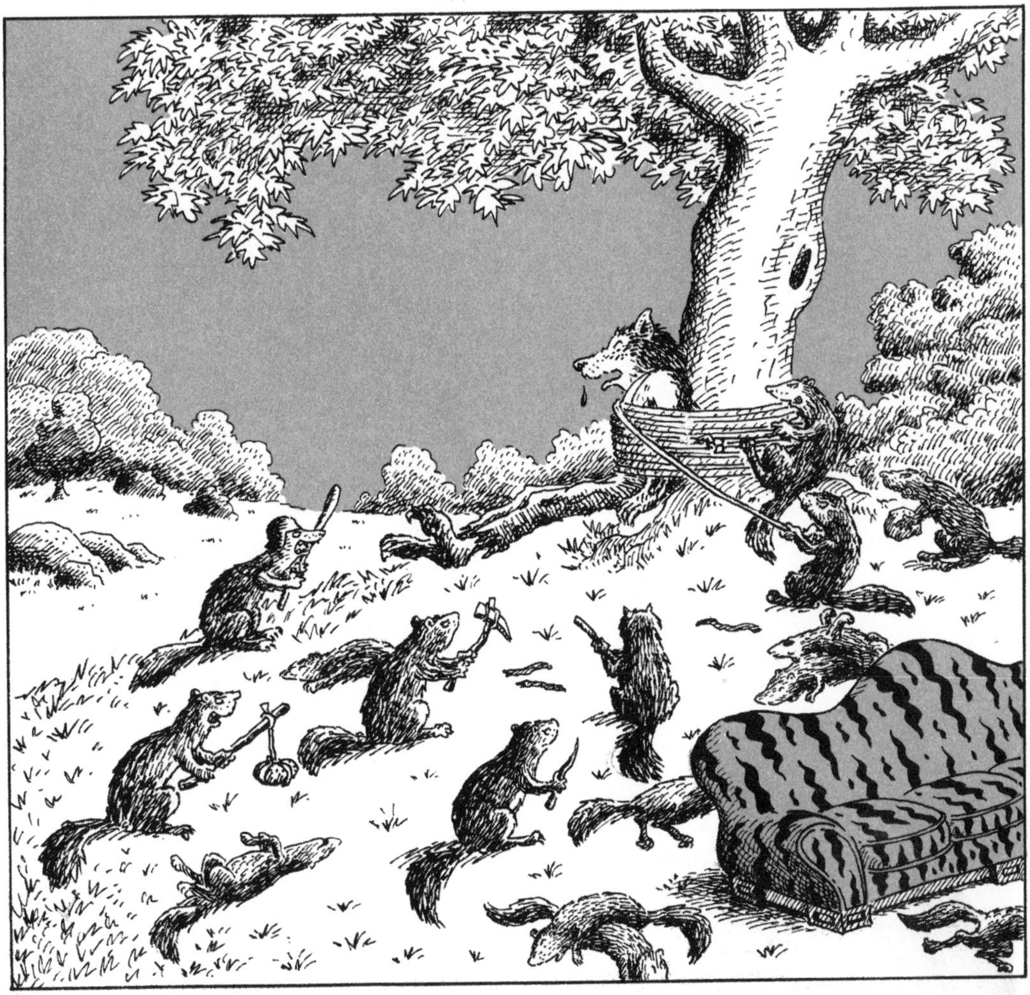

They were tying Upsilon to the very tree where we were hiding.

I swallowed hard. "They're tying him up," I said. "He looks all limp."

"He did his best," Cluid said.

"Hey, it's not over yet," said Brown. "He isn't dead, is he? If he was dead, they wouldn't have to tie him up!"

The ratminks backed up to lick their wounds, and the Dragon Lady approached Upsilon.

"I see you've taken him alive," she said, rubbing her hands together. "That's excellent! Now I can tickle his feet before I eat him!"

"Uh-oh," I said again.

"Soooo," said the Dragon Lady, with a horrible leer. "As I live and breathe, heh, heh, heh, it's the brave wolfman's son, isn't it?"

She cackled again and approached Upsilon's bare feet.

Then she stopped and whipped her head around. "What's that noise?" she said sharply.

MMMMMMMNNNNNMM-MMNNNNN, came a low humming noise from beyond the hill.

"Go see what that is!" she barked at one of the injured ratminks. "Quickly! Never mind your stupid wounds!"

The ratmink limped up the far hill as fast as it could.

MMMMMMMMNNNNNMMMMMMNNN.

The ratmink stopped at the rise, then yelped and ran for cover.

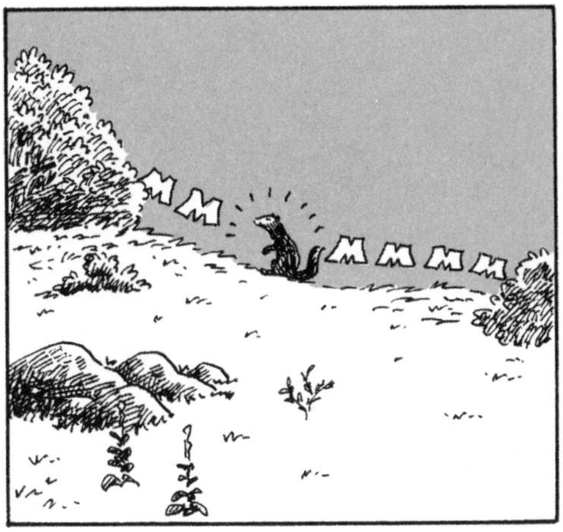
MM MMMM

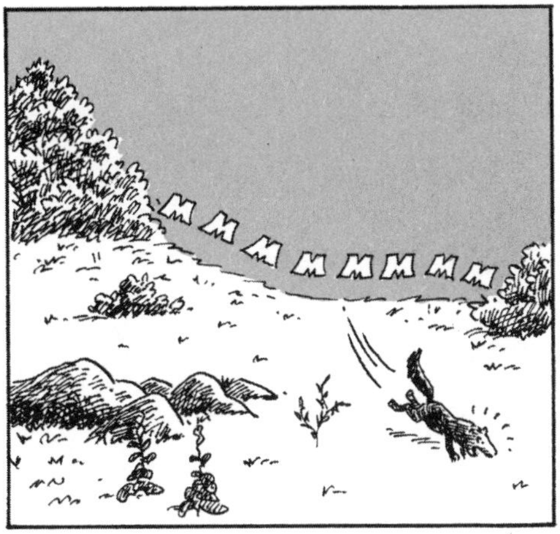
MMMMMMMMM

"WHAT IS IT?" yelled the Dragon Lady.

And then, from our spot high in the tree, we could see what it was.

15

Ragna

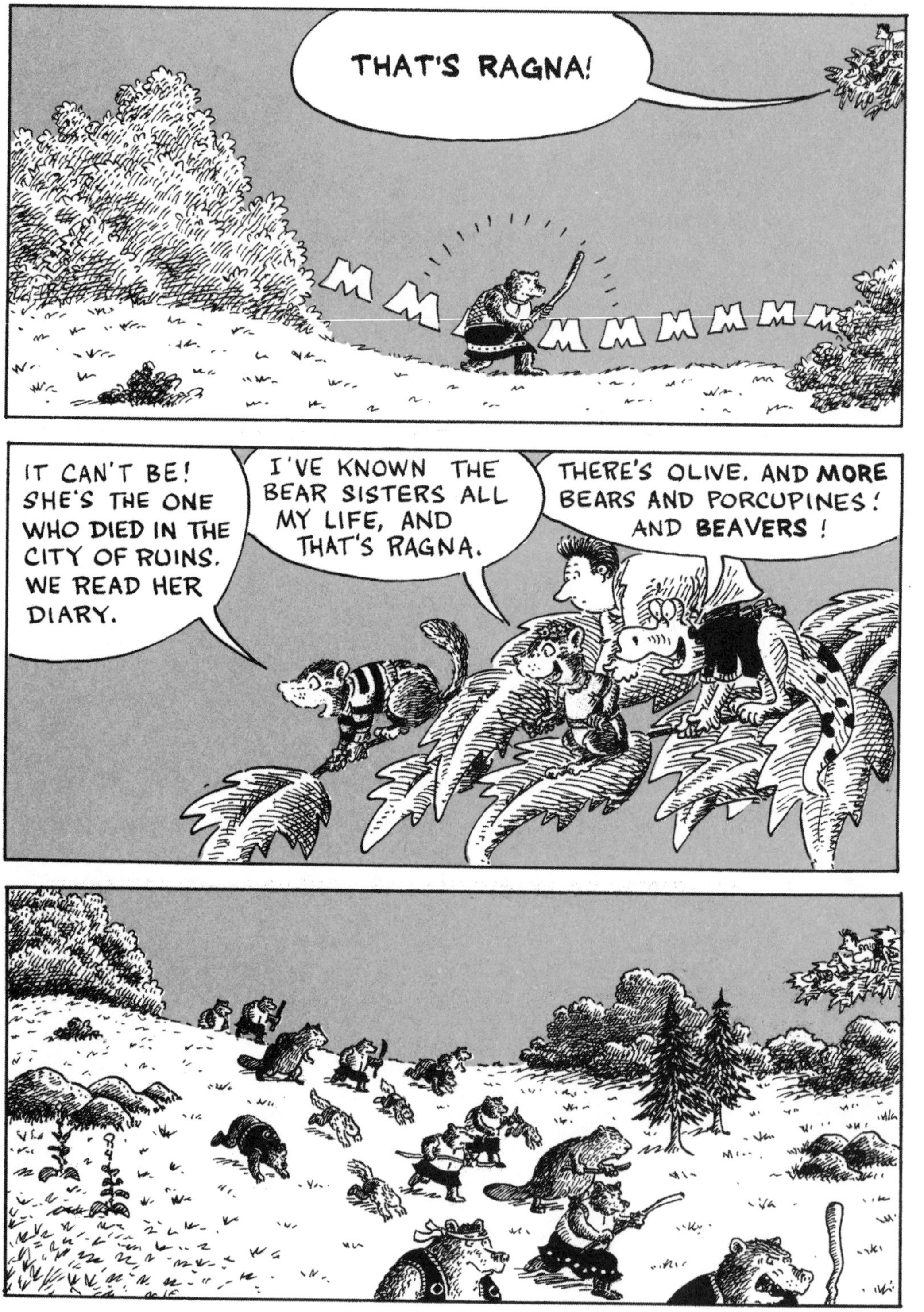
THAT'S RAGNA!
MMMMMMMMMM
IT CAN'T BE! SHE'S THE ONE WHO DIED IN THE CITY OF RUINS. WE READ HER DIARY.
I'VE KNOWN THE BEAR SISTERS ALL MY LIFE, AND THAT'S RAGNA.
THERE'S OLIVE. AND MORE BEARS AND PORCUPINES! AND BEAVERS!

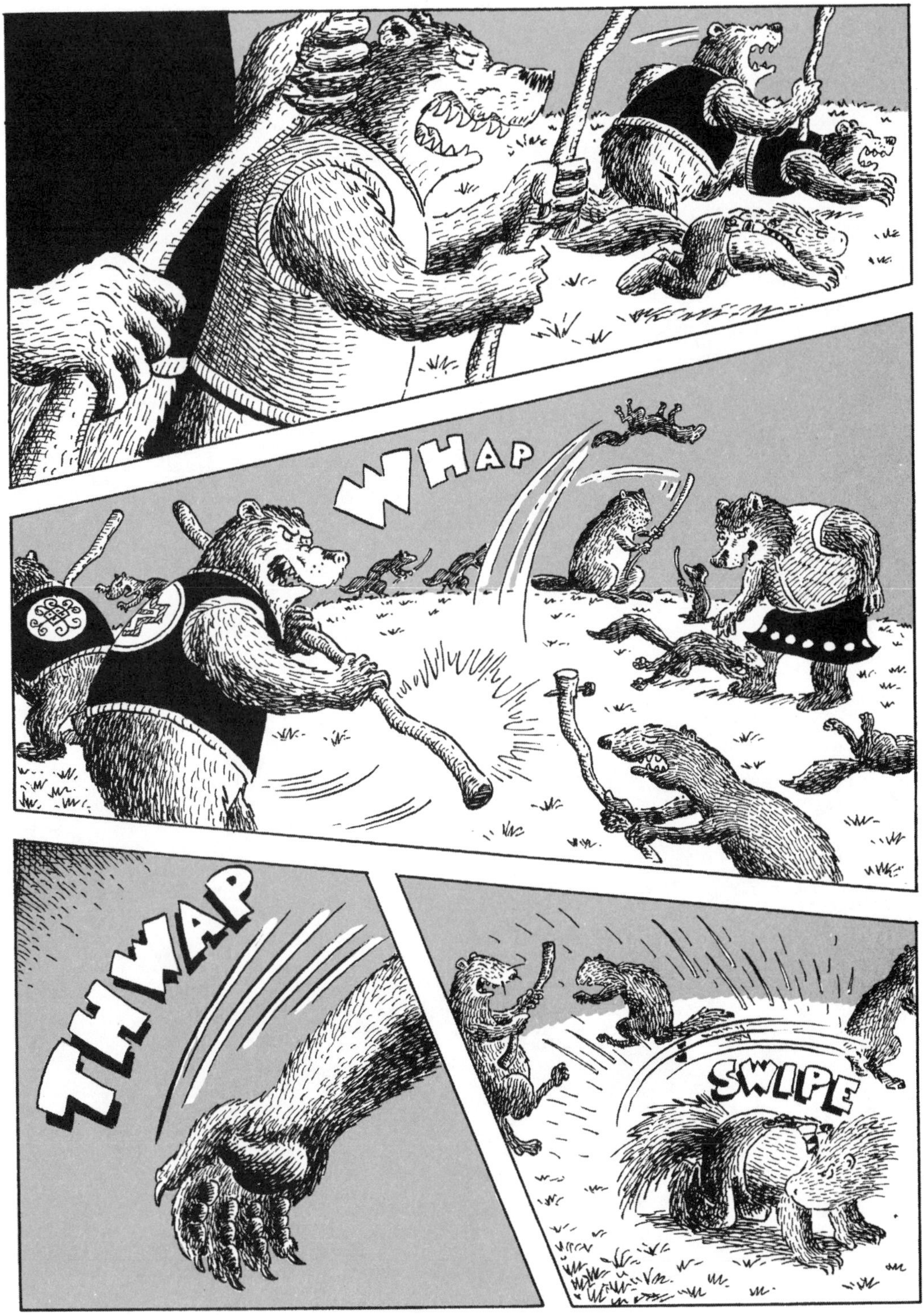
WHAP
THWAP
SWIPE

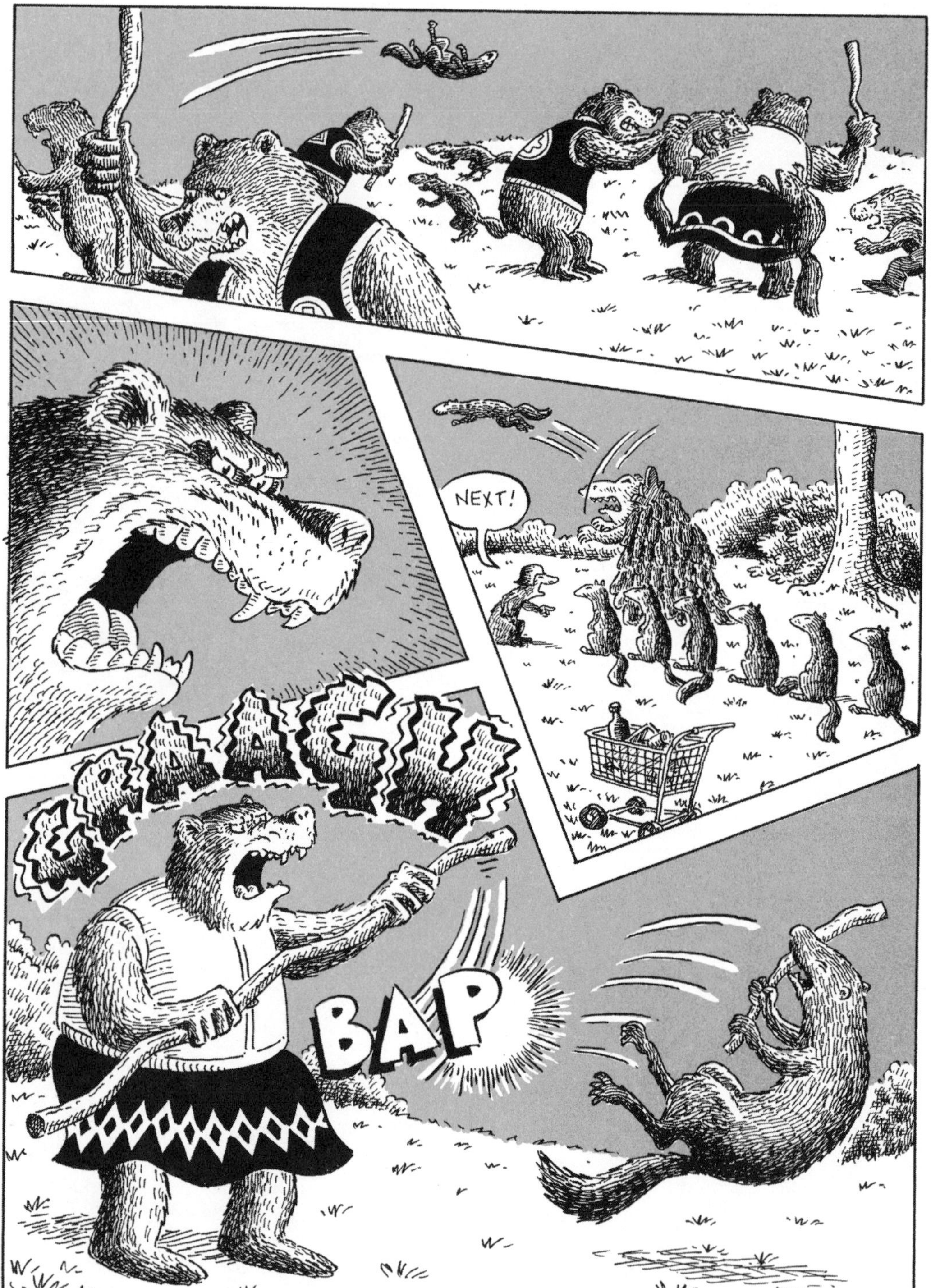
NEXT!
BAP

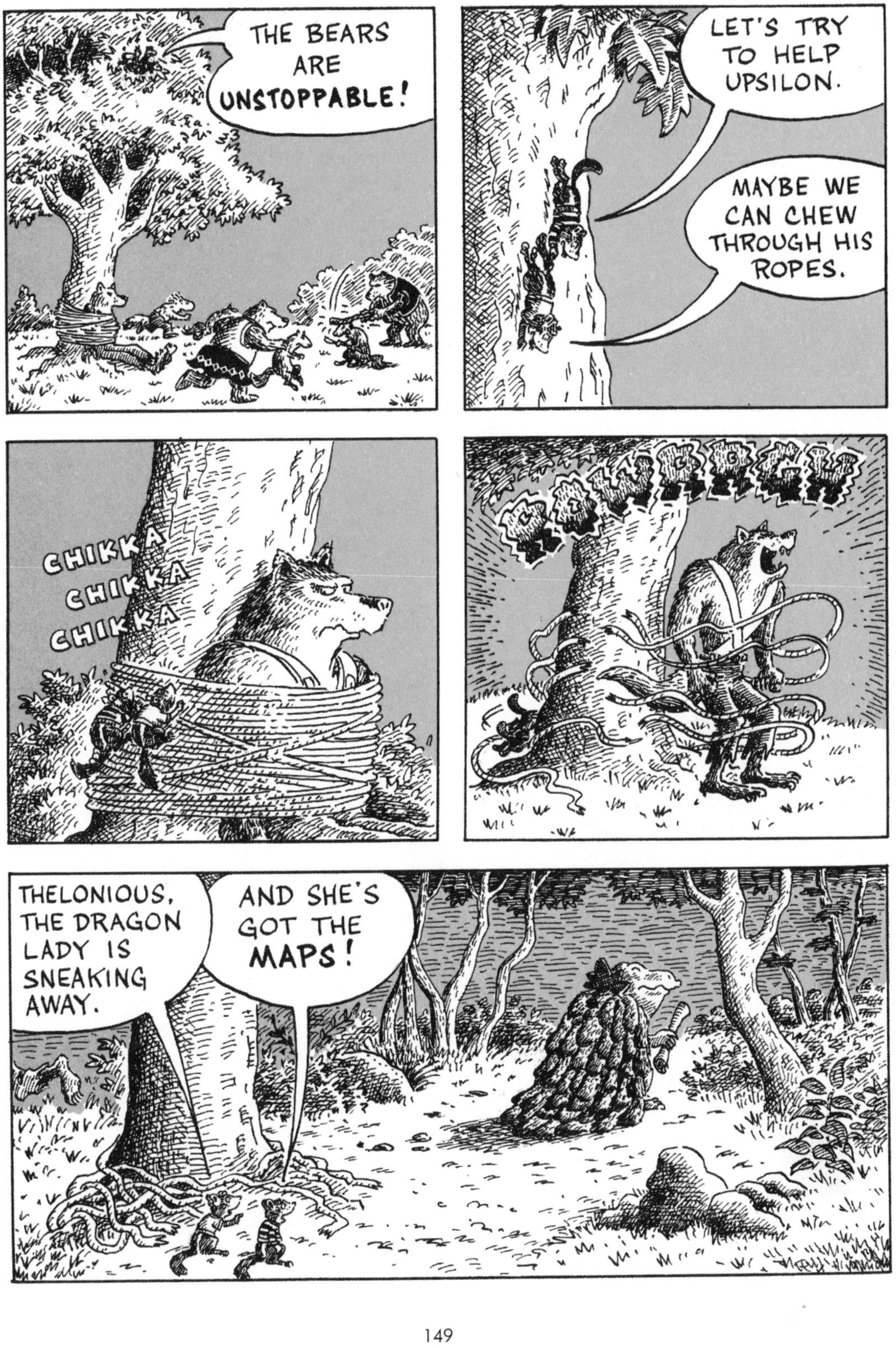
THE BEARS ARE UNSTOPPABLE!
LET'S TRY TO HELP UPSILON.
MAYBE WE CAN CHEW THROUGH HIS ROPES.
CHIKKA CHIKKA CHIKKA
THELONIOUS, THE DRAGON LADY IS SNEAKING AWAY.
AND SHE'S GOT THE MAPS!

16

The Queen
of Greed

"We've got to stop her!" Cluid was already running through the trees after the Dragon Lady.

"But what can we do?" I protested as I ran after her. "We should have a plan. Shouldn't I go get Olive or something?"

"I don't know about you, but I'm not going into that battle to look for Olive. Besides, if we did that, the Dragon Lady would get away! I'm going to follow her and see what she does next. You can come with me or not!"

"Of course I'm coming with you," I said indignantly.

"Well, hurry up, then. We've got to keep her in sight, and it's getting dark."

Luckily, the Dragon Lady didn't move too fast. I don't think she suspected she was being followed. (That's one good thing about being small—it's easy to go unnoticed.)

Cluid and I didn't speak. We trotted along behind the Dragon Lady, darting from tree to tree. We even picked up a few nuts and ate them on the run. All

the time I was thinking, *What are we going to do? We can't stop her by force. Will we be able to slip past her in the labyrinth and warn Pubba Bear? I wonder how much farther it is. I wonder how much longer I can keep this up!*

The sun went down. Still the Dragon Lady plodded on.

My little legs were starting to feel all weak and wobbly.

Then I saw Cluid stumble beside me.

I helped her up.

"Stop a minute, Cluid," I said. "We can't keep up this pace much longer. We need to think." I picked up a nut. "Here, eat this."

Cluid sat down and began to cry. "What if she gets to the Fog Mound?" she wailed. She swiped a dirty paw angrily across her cheek and struggled to her feet. "We *must* stop her!"

"No, wait," I said, pulling her down again. "It won't do any good if we exhaust ourselves. Look here—see how you can make out the trail of her tail scraping through the pine needles? We need to slow down so we don't collapse, but we can follow her trail! Sooner or later she will have to stop and rest, and then we can catch up."

"Do you think so?" Cluid asked in a small voice.

"I'm *sure* of it!" I replied, even though I wasn't. *If only I knew how far we had to go!* I thought.

We could see quite well by the light of the moon. And luck was with us: We had only been following the trail for a few hours when we came upon her quite suddenly.

Cluid drew in her breath and stopped short, holding up an arm to warn me. Silently I tiptoed up and stopped beside her.

The Dragon Lady was sleeping near a dying fire.

"Careful," Cluid whispered in my ear.

We peeked out from behind a rock. What I saw surprised me very much. It was the remains of Olive's velocicopter! Right where it had fallen when she had shaken it out of the tree!

I started to run up to it, but Cluid pulled me back.

"*Careful!*" she hissed with great emphasis.

"But that's the flying machine!" I whispered back. "I know where we are! The entrance to the Secret Way is not far at all!"

"All the more reason to take care," whispered Cluid. "Circle. Smell. Listen."

She was right, of course. And *I* was the one who'd been brought up to watch out for predators! I felt the tips of my ears get hot with shame. What if my carelessness had caused us to be captured and to fail in our mission?

Carefully we tiptoed in a wide circle around the enemy, sniffing the air and watching and listening.

The Dragon Lady snored in her sleep.

"She won't wake up," I said. "Not in this cold. We must get the maps!"

The Dragon Lady's horrible claws were closed around the rolled maps, holding them against her side.

I took a deep breath. "I'll do it," I said. "You wait here. If anything happens to me . . ."

"Shut up," said Cluid. "We'll both go."

Holding paws, we approached the sleeping dragon.

She slept on. We could see the jewels embedded in her skin. They caught the moonlight and glowed and twinkled.

She snorted.

We stopped short and stood immobile, inches from the maps.

After several moments I reached out and pulled gently on the roll of paper, holding my breath.

The paper crackled. I stopped.

The Dragon Lady slept. I pulled some more.

The maps came free!

I breathed again and, trembling, resisted the impulse to run.

Cluid picked up the other end of the roll and we tiptoed back to the cover of a small bush.

Breathing hard, we clutched our prize.

"Shouldn't we look at them?" Cluid asked.

I unrolled a corner and recognized the map I had seen in Olive's warehouse so long ago. The edge of it was charred and brittle.

Cluid and I looked at each other. "What should we do with them?" she said. "Take them to Pubba?"

I looked off in the direction of Bare Rock, which marked the entrance to the Secret Way. I looked at the sleeping dragon. I looked at the embers of the fire. And I had a revelation!

"Burn them!" I said. "I don't think we can open the Secret Way by ourselves, and the maps should be destroyed before anyone else sees them!"

"Yes!" said Cluid. "Let's burn them now!"

With one more glance at the Dragon Lady we dragged the maps to the

embers and touched one corner of the paper to the coals. It flamed up immediately.

We jumped back to the other end and fed the roll, bit by bit into the flames, watching it curl and blacken and disintegrate into ashes. But we hadn't realized that the old logs would flare up and that the heat of the fire would warm our enemy—not until her scaly hands closed suddenly and tightly around us and we were her prisoners!

She clenched her fists and shook us with rage. "MY MAPS! YOU HAVE

BURNED MY MAPS!"

She stopped shaking us and held us so close we could smell the poisonous saliva dripping off her teeth.

"Chipmunks!" she hissed, looking back and forth from Cluid to me. "Which one of you shall I eat first?"

"Let Cluid go!" I squeaked. "And I will show you the Secret Way."

"NO!" cried Cluid.

"Aha! A snitch and a hero! I will eat you both! But first you will lead me to the Fog Mound! Richest place on Earth! I will own all the jewels! I will rule the Fog Mound! No one shall dare defy me! ALL WILL SUBMIT TO MY WILL AND BE MY SLAVES!"

"But there aren't any jewels on the Fog Mound," I said.

"YOU LIE! I will eat you now!"

"No, no!" I said. "If you let Cluid go, I will show you the way." I tried to wink at Cluid, to show her I wouldn't really. Unfortunately, the Dragon Lady saw me.

"You try to trick me!" she said through her teeth. "I will eat the little lady now, unless you show me immediately the way to the FOG MOUND, to the PALACE OF JEWELS! I will eat her piece by piece. First one tiny hand, then the other. Next one tiny foot, then the other."

She lifted Cluid up to her foul mouth. Her tongue tickled Cluid's paw.

"STOP! I'll show you."

"Don't do it, Thelonious!"

"I will save the head for last!" The Dragon Lady's voice was thick with digestive secretions.

"It's over there!" I jerked my head in the direction of Bare Rock. "You have to look for a rock without any moss or lichen on it. It's called Bare Rock."

I thought to myself, *She will have to move away from the fire; then she will get colder and colder and soon she will fall asleep, like Brown.*

Unfortunately, the sun rose. The Dragon Lady stepped into the light, and her coat steamed gently, giving off a foul odor.

I would have to think of something else. And fast, too—or I would have to lead her to the Fog Mound, and Cluid would never forgive me!

17

Bite and Run

I HAD NO CHOICE. I HAD TO TELL THE DRAGON LADY HOW TO GET THROUGH THE SECRET WAY, OR SHE WOULD EAT CLUID PIECE BY PIECE. I ONLY HOPED THAT PUBBA BEAR WOULD BE ABLE TO DEAL WITH HER WHEN WE REACHED THE MOUND.

I SHOWED HER HOW TO OPEN THE ENTRANCE.

IN THE MUSHROOM CAVE, THE DRAGON LADY REALIZED SHE COULD LET ME DOWN. SHE KNEW I WOULDN'T LEAVE CLUID.

I SHOWED HER THE GROTTO AND THE ENTRANCE TO THE LABYRINTH BEHIND THE WATERFALL.

I SHOWED HER HOW TO FOLLOW THE LINE IN THE DIRT TO GET THROUGH THE LABYRINTH AND THEN I HAD AN IDEA. **IF ONLY CLUID WOULDN'T SAY SOMETHING AND GIVE ME AWAY!**

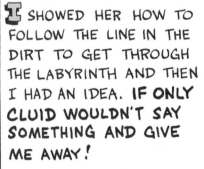

TRUST ME, CLUID.

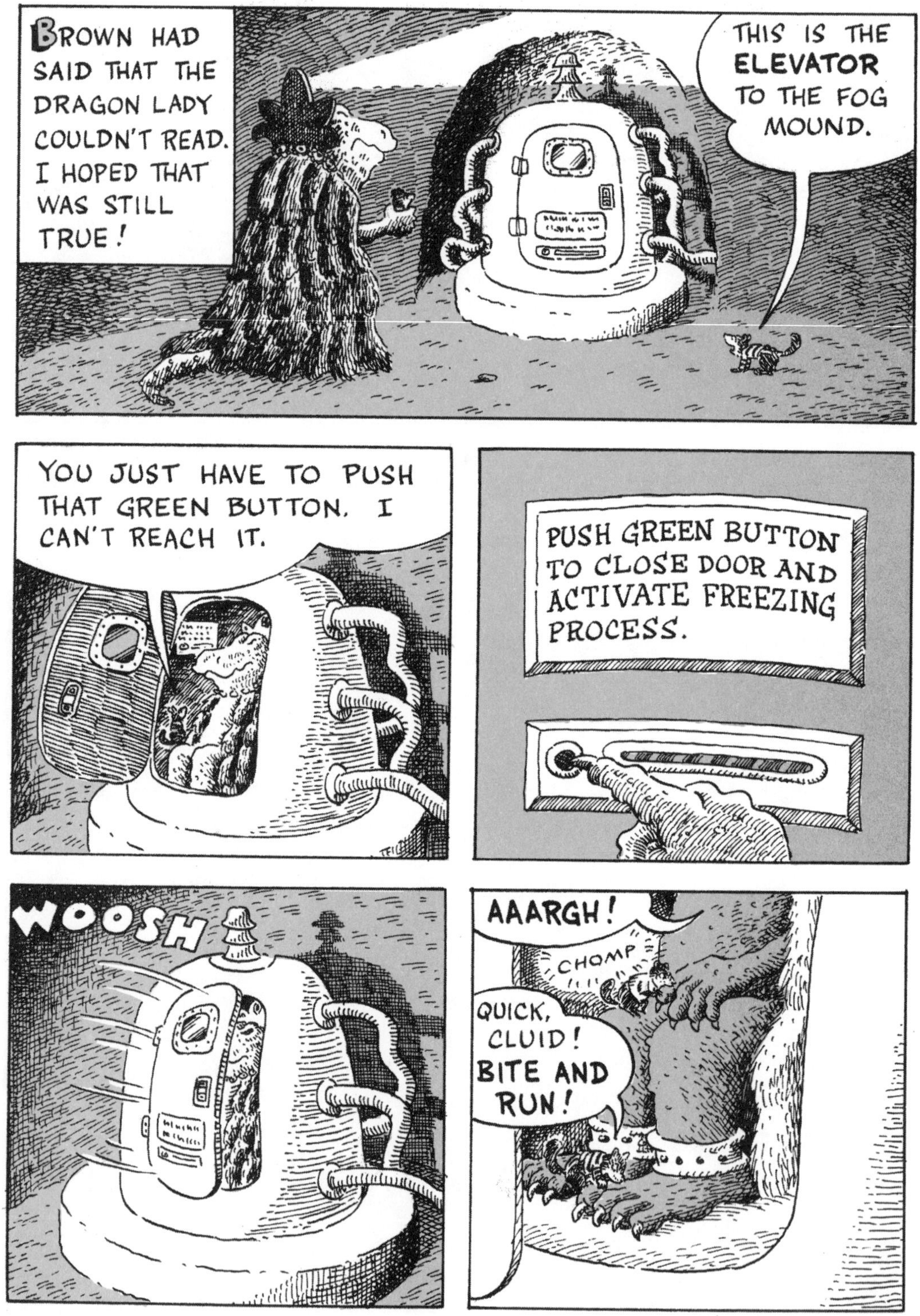
BROWN HAD SAID THAT THE DRAGON LADY COULDN'T READ. I HOPED THAT WAS STILL TRUE!
THIS IS THE ELEVATOR TO THE FOG MOUND.
YOU JUST HAVE TO PUSH THAT GREEN BUTTON. I CAN'T REACH IT.
PUSH GREEN BUTTON TO CLOSE DOOR AND ACTIVATE FREEZING PROCESS.
WOOSH
AAARGH!
CHOMP
QUICK, CLUID! BITE AND RUN!

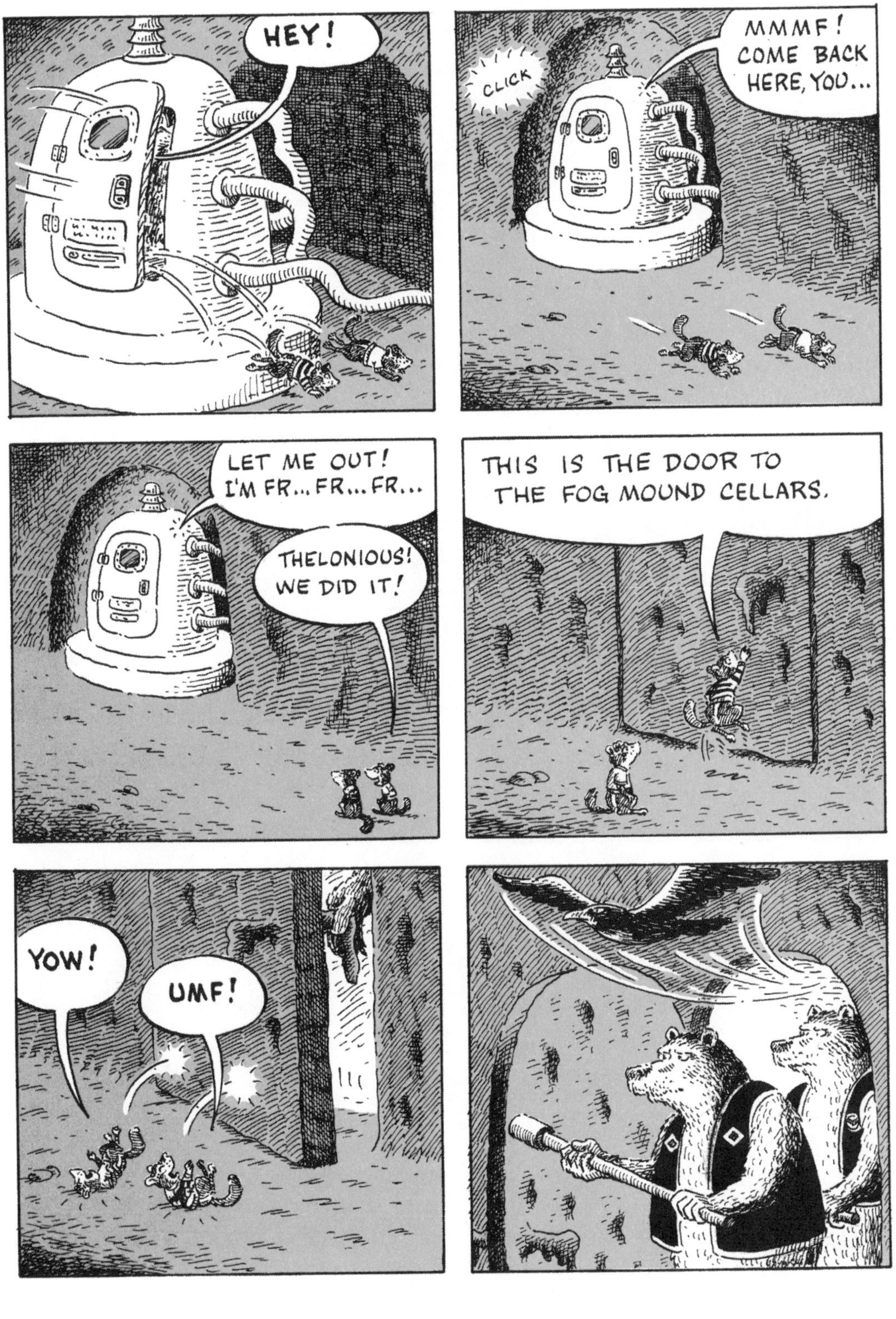
HEY!
CLICK
MMMF! COME BACK HERE, YOU...
LET ME OUT! I'M FR...FR...FR...
THELONIOUS! WE DID IT!
THIS IS THE DOOR TO THE FOG MOUND CELLARS.
YOW!
UMF!

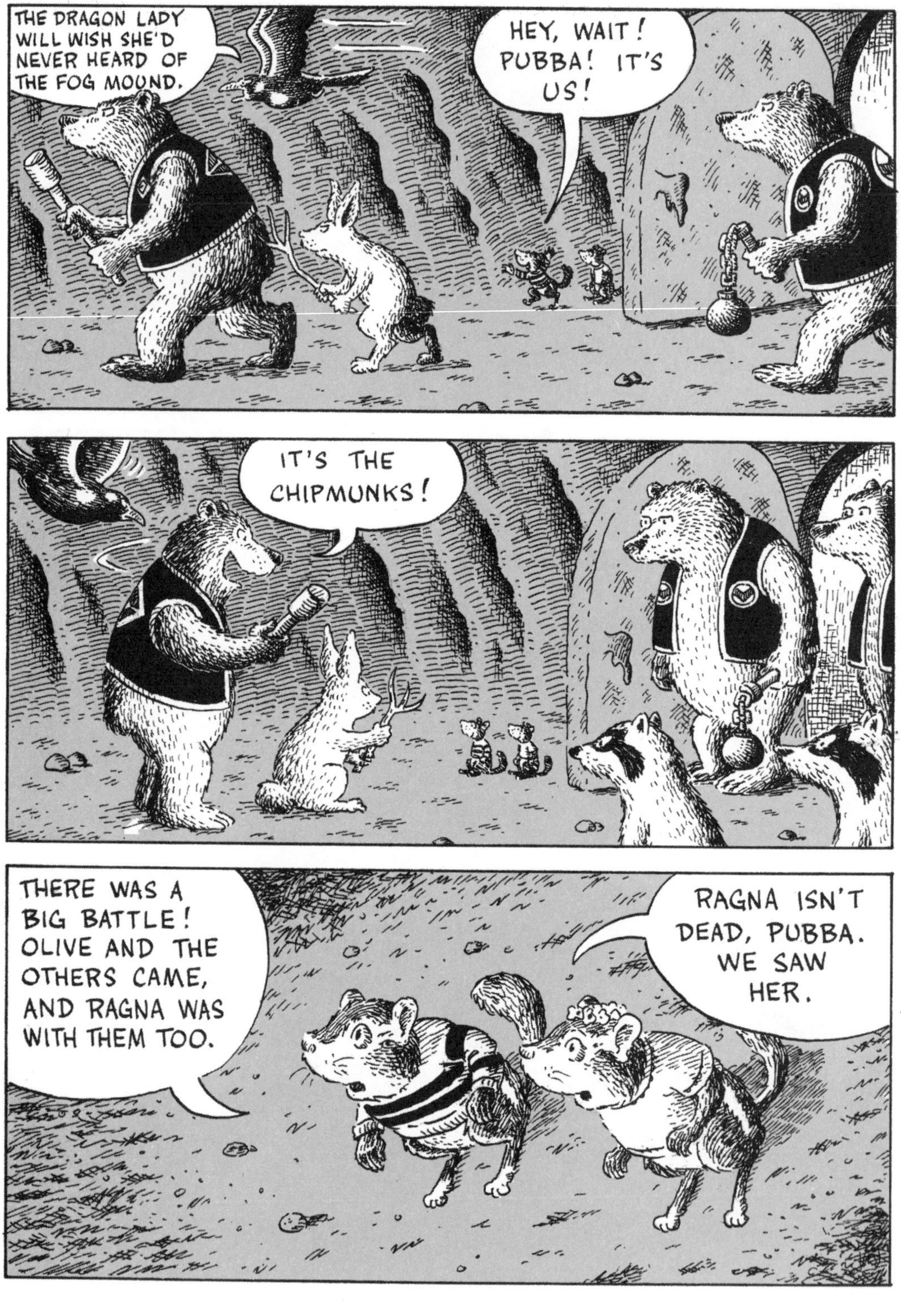
THE DRAGON LADY WILL WISH SHE'D NEVER HEARD OF THE FOG MOUND.
HEY, WAIT! PUBBA! IT'S US!
IT'S THE CHIPMUNKS!
THERE WAS A BIG BATTLE! OLIVE AND THE OTHERS CAME, AND RAGNA WAS WITH THEM TOO.
RAGNA ISN'T DEAD, PUBBA. WE SAW HER.

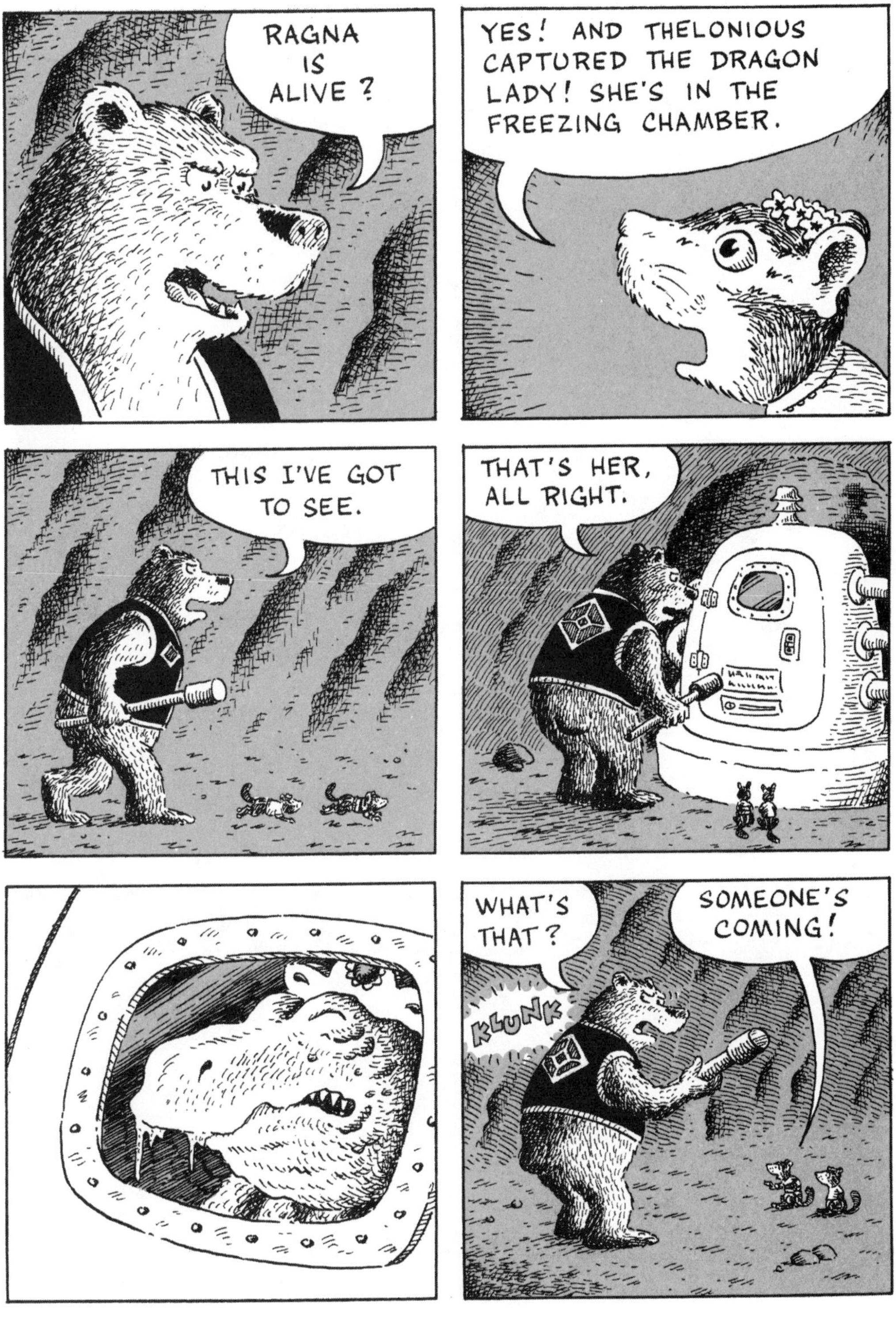
RAGNA IS ALIVE?
YES! AND THELONIOUS CAPTURED THE DRAGON LADY! SHE'S IN THE FREEZING CHAMBER.
THIS I'VE GOT TO SEE.
THAT'S HER, ALL RIGHT.
WHAT'S THAT?
KLUNK
SOMEONE'S COMING!

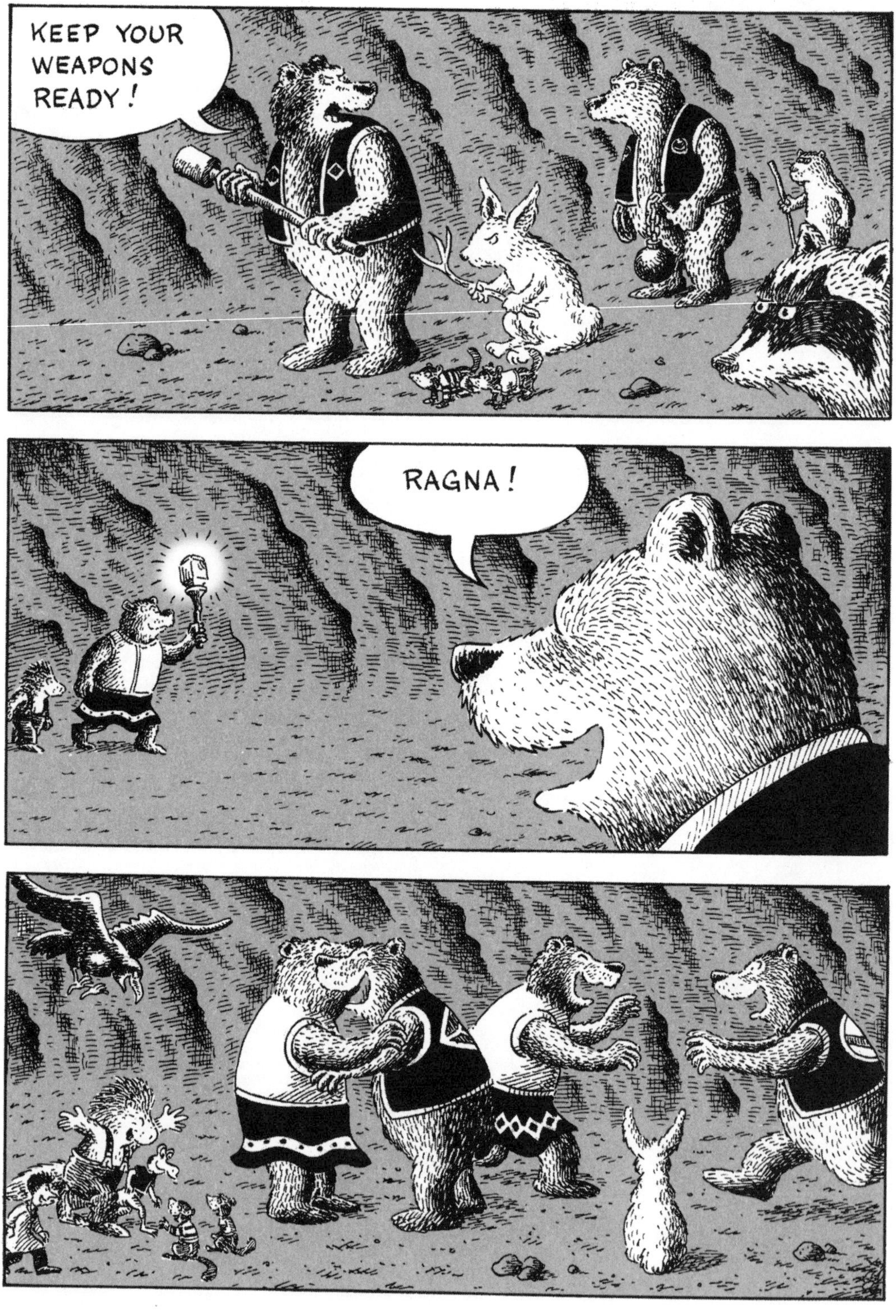
KEEP YOUR WEAPONS READY!
RAGNA!

18

The Dream Helmet

It was all over. The ratminks had been vanquished; the Dragon Lady was frozen; the Fog Mound was safe!

For a few minutes excited voices echoed throughout the Secret Way, but then Pubba boomed, "What are we hanging around here for? Follow me!"

And he led us through the door, into the Fog Mound cellars, and up into the kitchen.

Brown came over to me. I almost hugged him.

"Brown!" I said. "I was worried about you!"

"Yeah, I was worried about me too. But after you and Cluid chewed through his ropes, Upsilon defended our tree from the ratminks. *WHAM! SLASH!*" Brown jumped around, making slashing motions in the air.

"Olive thanked him herself," he said. "Here he is now."

"Upsilon is on the Fog Mound?" I whispered to Brown. "What if he gets hungry?"

"Don't worry, Chipmunk," Upsilon said, bending over us. "I guess I can survive on eggs and pancakes for a few days."

He lowered himself to the floor gracefully, like a cat, so he could talk to us. "Olive invited me to stay," he said, "and I must admit I'm curious to see the setup you have here. I think I'll be heading out after that, though. There are

171

still a few ratminks hanging around that will make good eating, and I have to do my part to preserve the balance of nature."

He pulled back his lips in a grin, showing his canine teeth. But this time I wasn't afraid of him.

"I hear you took care of the Dragon Lady, Thelonious," he said to me. "I was hoping to have that pleasure myself, but it sounds like you made a good job of it. Well done!"

Brown clapped me on the back. "Way to go, Thelonious! You're a hero!"

"We're *all* heroes!" I said.

Everybody in the room cheered and whooped, and Mother Bear poured out some raspberry cider.

"Oh, by the way, Thelonious . . ." Upsilon reached into his belt pouch. "We thought you might like this." He pulled out my helmet. "As a souvenir of the time you piloted a flying sofa!"

"My helmet!" I cried. "Cool!"

I put it on and bowed. "How do I look now?" I asked Brown.

"Like a hero," Brown said.

"All right," I said, "that's enough with the hero stuff, Brown. It's getting embarrassing!"

Suddenly I felt all worn out. I made my way to a safe spot under a chair. I lay down and closed my tired eyes . . . and I floated away—to a place where the ground was all smooth rolling hills, like ripples on the ocean. A friendly chipmunk floated beside me.

"Where are we?" I asked him. "Did I travel back in time after all?"

The chipmunk laughed. "You've just entered my dream. It's because you're wearing the helmet I left behind at Mattakeunk. By the way, my name is Simon."

"Ah," I said, understanding right away. "You're Simon, the first talking chipmunk!"

"That's me," he said. "Who are you?"

"I'm Thelonious, and I've heard of you. You're in *The Story of Bob*."

"*The Story of Bob?*"

"That's a legend I like to tell," I explained. "It's one of my favorites. It's about ancient times."

Simon and I flew close to some small humps in the ground. "So for you this is *ancient times?*" he asked. "You must be from the future, then. Cool! I guess it *is* a form of time travel."

"Yeah," I said. "And I found out that *The Story of Bob* was true, because Bill knew Bob. Hey, Bill must have known you, too! You were one of his experiments! So what do you think? Is Bill a mad scientist or is he a genius?"

Simon laughed. "A little bit of both, I guess. So Bill is all right? We were worried about him."

"Well, we found him in a freezing chamber, you know, and we thawed him out. At first he didn't talk much. And he's very small for a human. We thought it must be from being frozen for such a long time."

"Oh, no," Simon said. "All the surviving humans are small now. Bill developed a shrinking formula so humans would make less impact on the earth. He tried it on himself first and thought it didn't work, but we found out it just takes a while—sort of like growing, only in reverse.

"Some of the humans have started to grow fur on their bodies too. That was Bob's idea. And of course the next generation will be born with the changes already in place."

As he spoke, I saw several small, furry humans coming out of one of the humps in the ground.

I laughed. "The humans are starting to look like chipmunks!" I exclaimed. "Are they living in burrows, too?"

"Of course," Simon replied. "There are no trees, as you can see."

I looked at the horizon. There were no trees for forever. I realized then that what I was seeing was the legendary Barren Time that had come after the end of the Human Occupation.

"There are no trees anywhere on Earth now," Simon explained. "In fact there are

no green plants anywhere but here, and this is only a coating of algae. We've brought seeds with us, though, and we have high hopes for the future."

I was happy that all the humans hadn't died. I said so to Simon.

He said, "Died! Whatever gave you that idea?"

I told him about the GreenBerry virus and the Road Rage War and the Too Many Cleaning Products.

"Well, those things did make a dent in the human population, it's true. But not all the people died. Many of them joined the space program. Mary and Bob didn't want to leave Earth, so they got some friends together and we settled here."

"Where *is* here?" I asked him.

"It's at the end of the Earth. Come into my memory—I'll show you what

happened."

Ah. Finally! Someone was going to show me what happened!

"Hey, wait up!" I called as he hurried down a long tunnel. "Where are we, anyway?"

"We're inside my brain," Simon said.

It was a little bit like the labyrinth in the Secret Way to the Fog Mound. I hoped there wouldn't be any fog pits!

19

Inside Simon's Brain

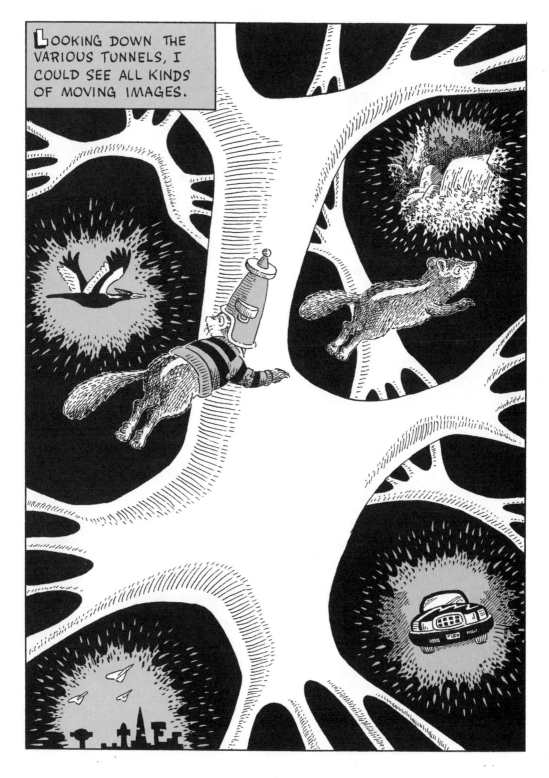

LOOKING DOWN THE VARIOUS TUNNELS, I COULD SEE ALL KINDS OF MOVING IMAGES.

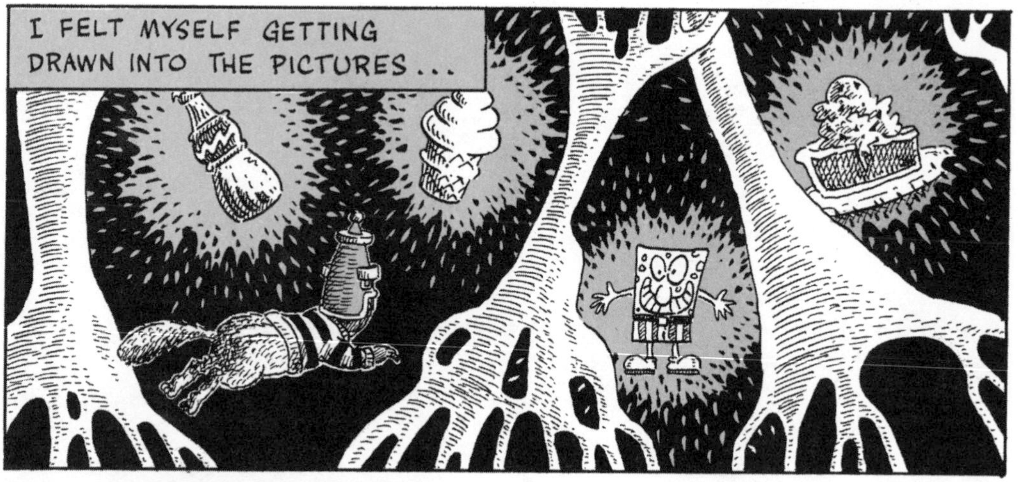
I FELT MYSELF GETTING DRAWN INTO THE PICTURES...

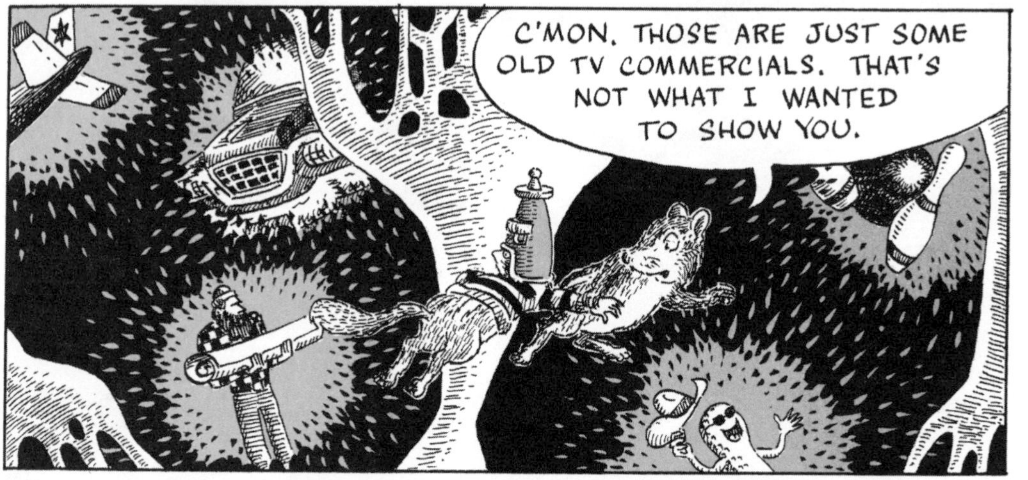
C'MON. THOSE ARE JUST SOME OLD TV COMMERCIALS. THAT'S NOT WHAT I WANTED TO SHOW YOU.

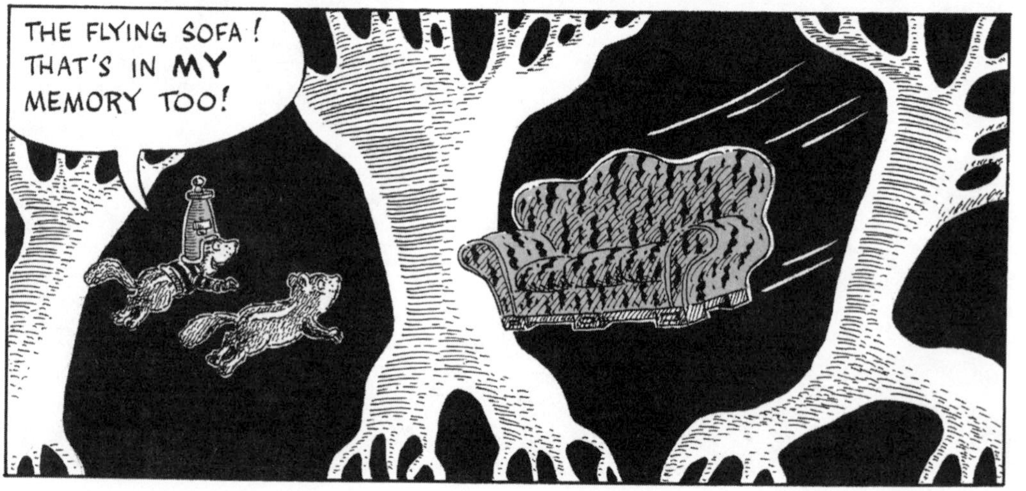
THE FLYING SOFA! THAT'S IN MY MEMORY TOO!

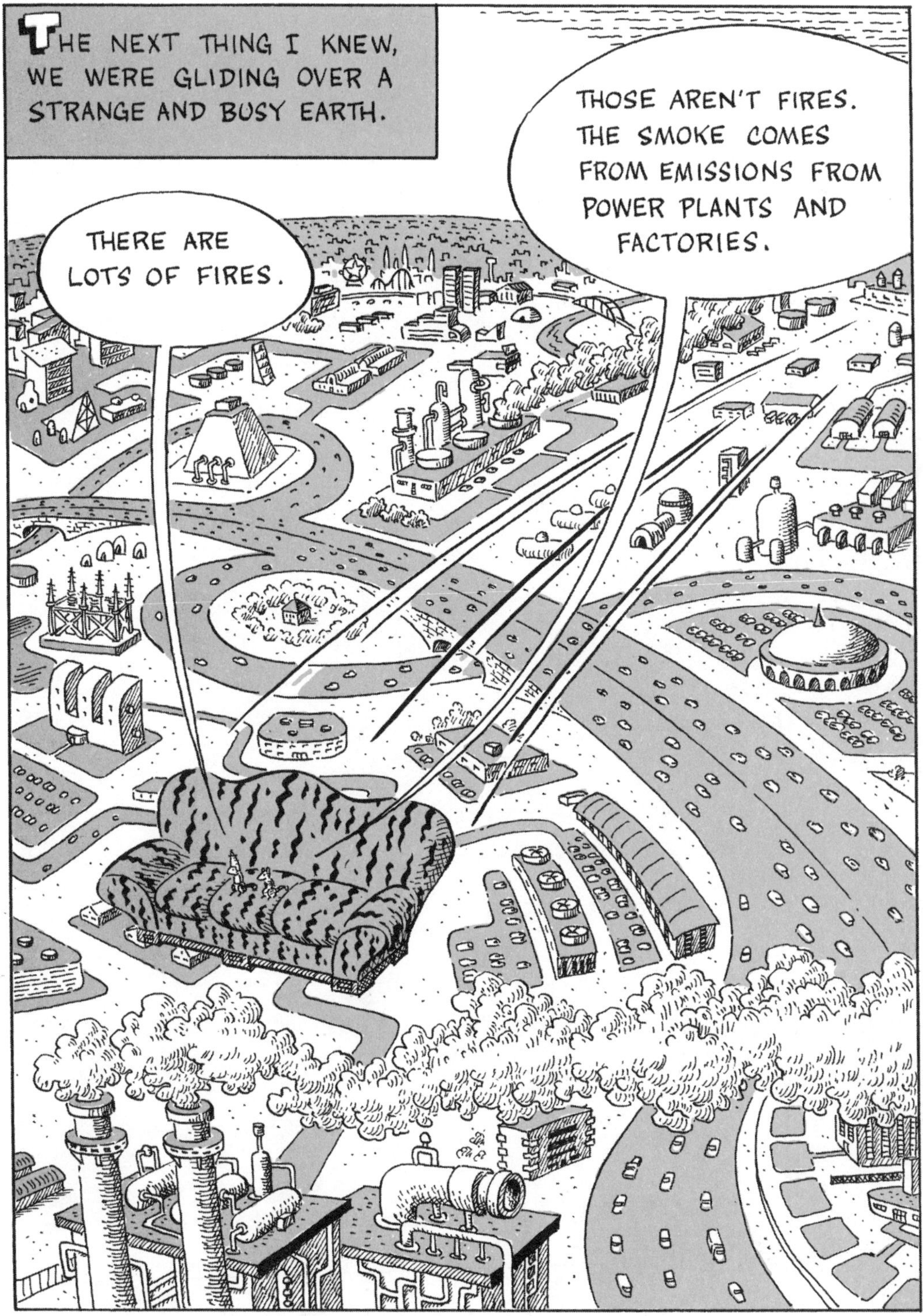
THE NEXT THING I KNEW, WE WERE GLIDING OVER A STRANGE AND BUSY EARTH.
THERE ARE LOTS OF FIRES.
THOSE AREN'T FIRES. THE SMOKE COMES FROM EMISSIONS FROM POWER PLANTS AND FACTORIES.

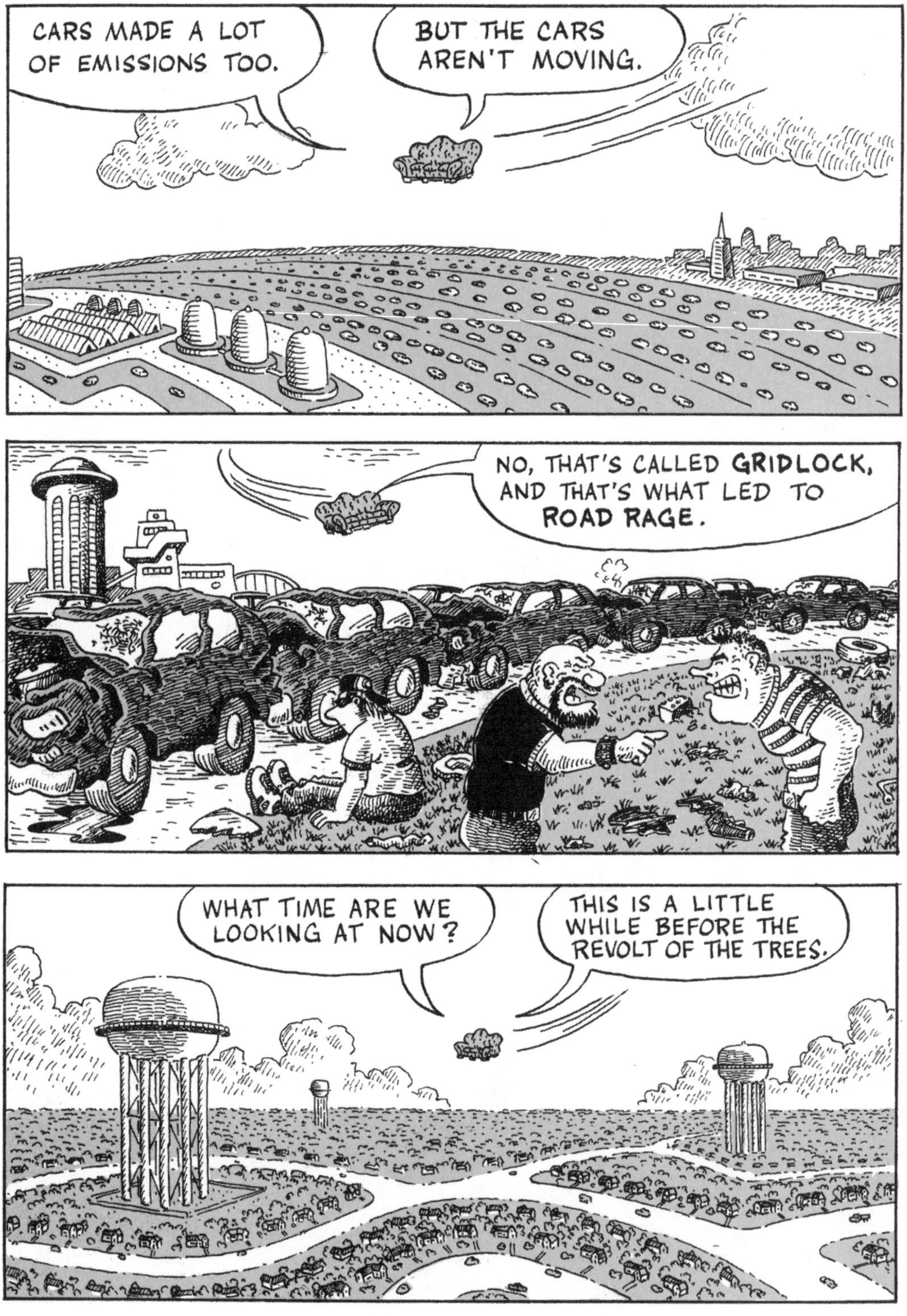
CARS MADE A LOT OF EMISSIONS TOO.
BUT THE CARS AREN'T MOVING.
NO, THAT'S CALLED GRIDLOCK, AND THAT'S WHAT LED TO ROAD RAGE.
WHAT TIME ARE WE LOOKING AT NOW?
THIS IS A LITTLE WHILE BEFORE THE REVOLT OF THE TREES.

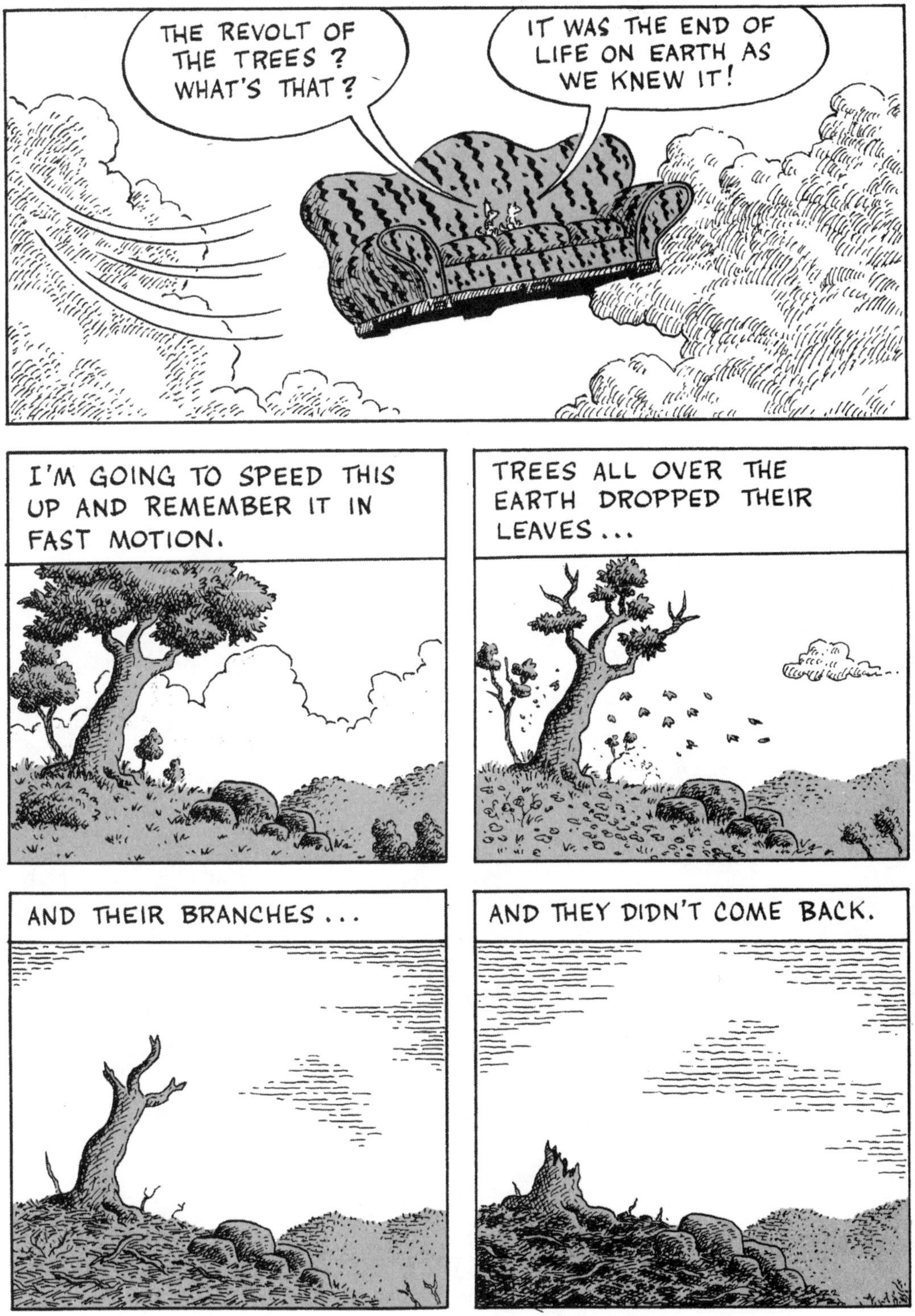
THE REVOLT OF THE TREES ? WHAT'S THAT ?
IT WAS THE END OF LIFE ON EARTH AS WE KNEW IT!
I'M GOING TO SPEED THIS UP AND REMEMBER IT IN FAST MOTION.
TREES ALL OVER THE EARTH DROPPED THEIR LEAVES ...
AND THEIR BRANCHES ...
AND THEY DIDN'T COME BACK.

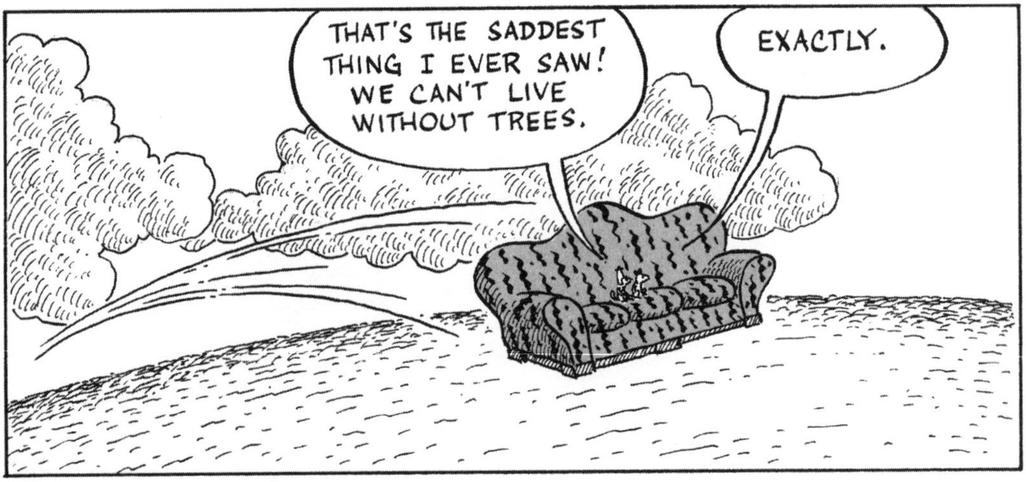
THAT'S THE SADDEST THING I EVER SAW! WE CAN'T LIVE WITHOUT TREES.
EXACTLY.

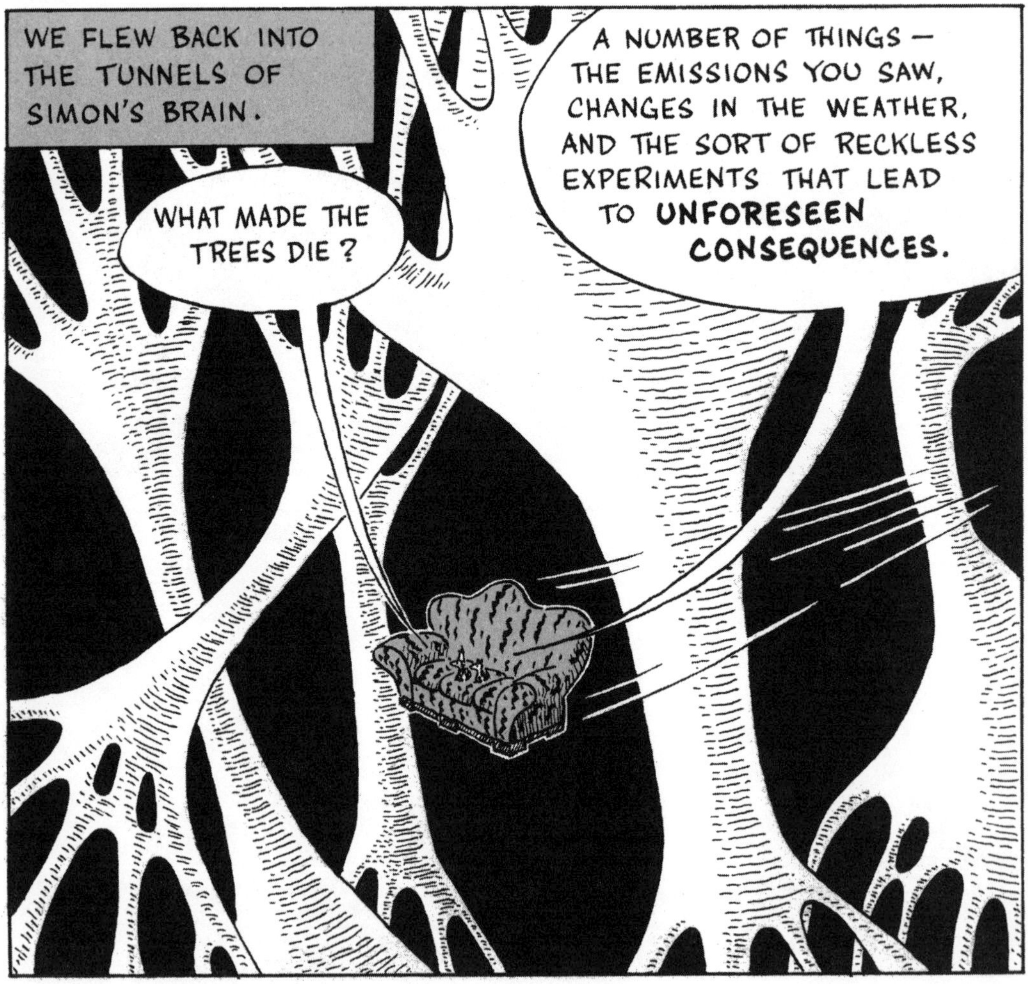
WE FLEW BACK INTO THE TUNNELS OF SIMON'S BRAIN.
WHAT MADE THE TREES DIE?
A NUMBER OF THINGS — THE EMISSIONS YOU SAW, CHANGES IN THE WEATHER, AND THE SORT OF RECKLESS EXPERIMENTS THAT LEAD TO **UNFORESEEN CONSEQUENCES.**

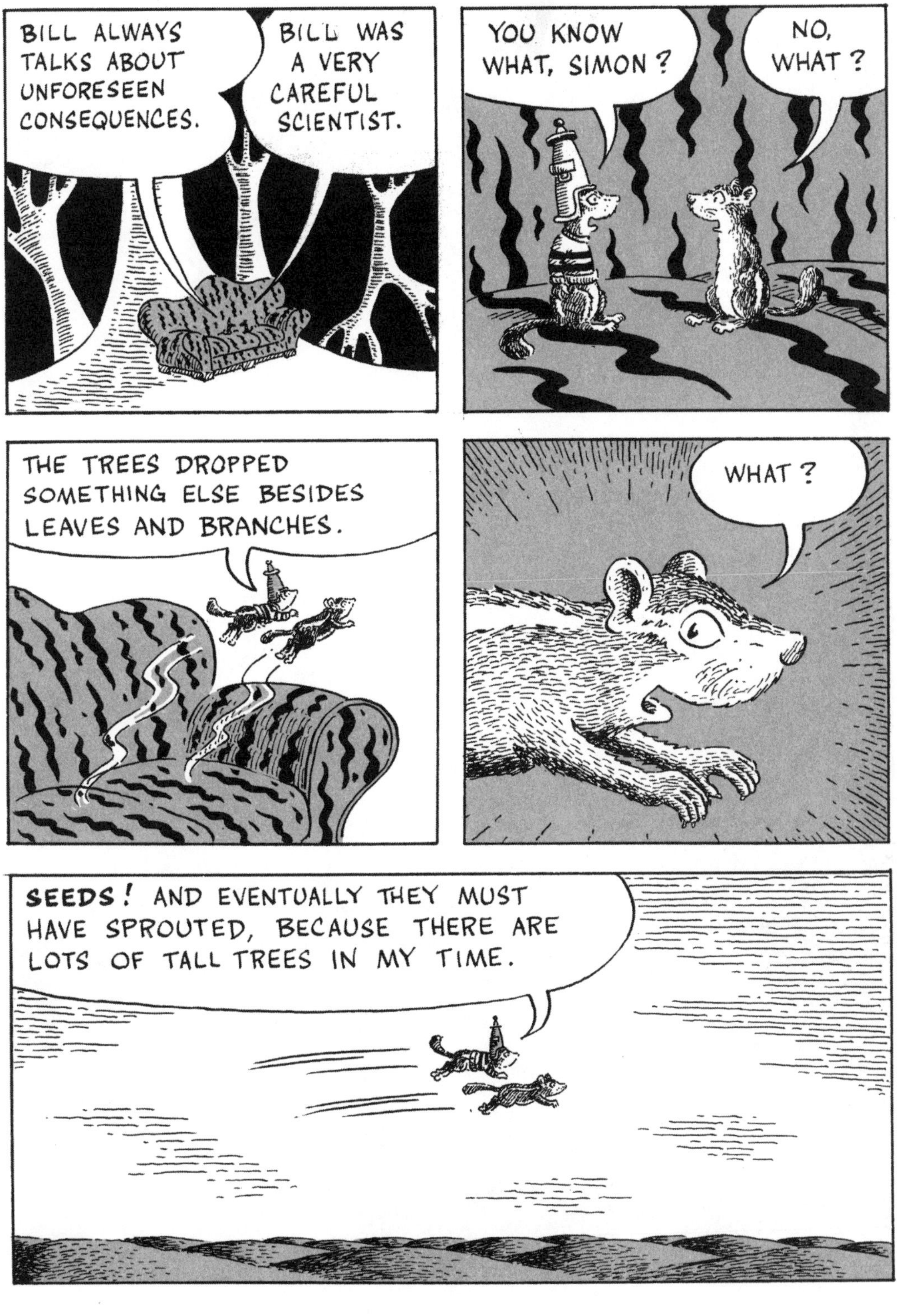
BILL ALWAYS TALKS ABOUT UNFORESEEN CONSEQUENCES.
BILL WAS A VERY CAREFUL SCIENTIST.
YOU KNOW WHAT, SIMON?
NO, WHAT?
THE TREES DROPPED SOMETHING ELSE BESIDES LEAVES AND BRANCHES.
WHAT?
SEEDS! AND EVENTUALLY THEY MUST HAVE SPROUTED, BECAUSE THERE ARE LOTS OF TALL TREES IN MY TIME.

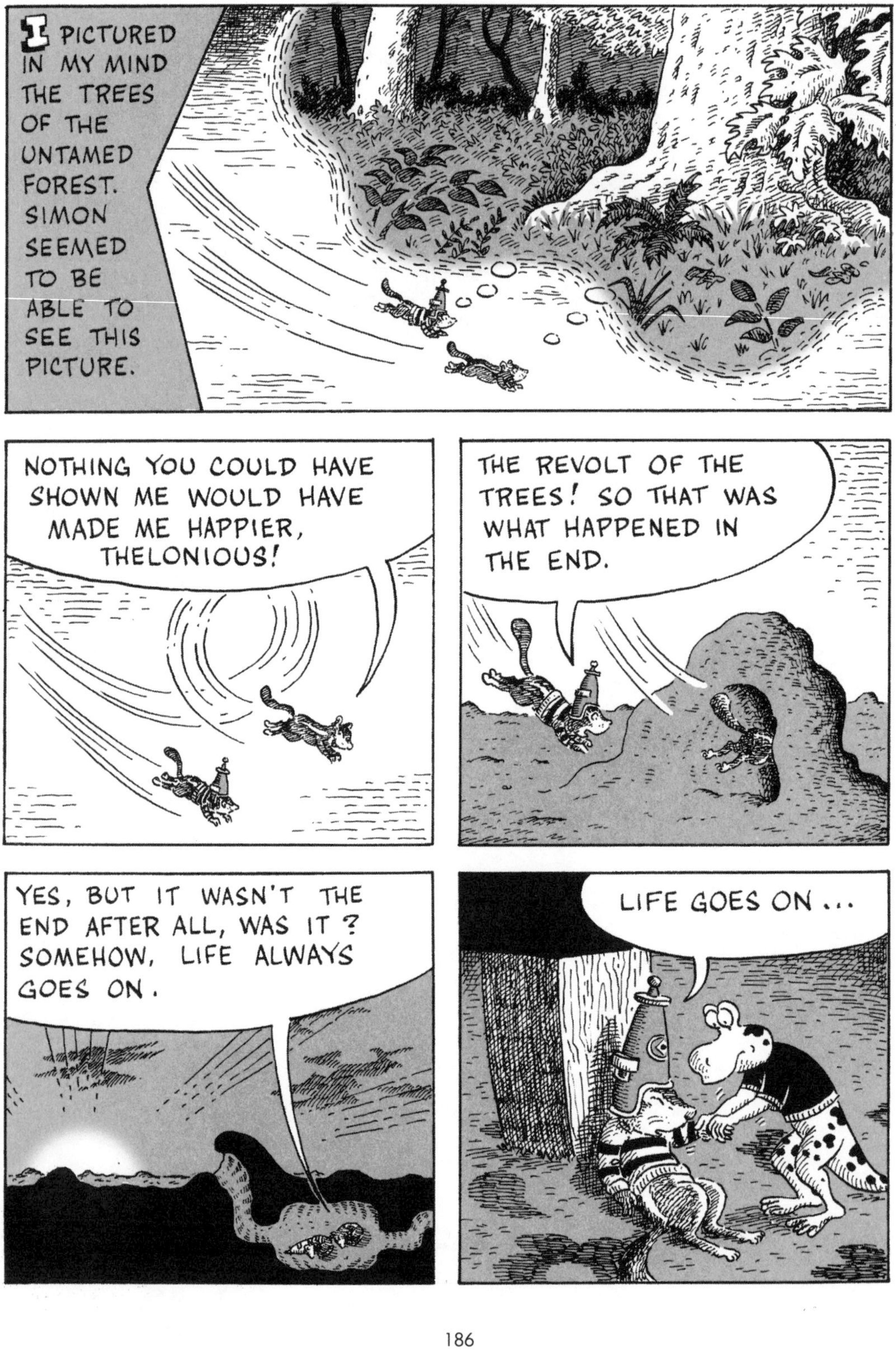
I PICTURED IN MY MIND THE TREES OF THE UNTAMED FOREST. SIMON SEEMED TO BE ABLE TO SEE THIS PICTURE.
NOTHING YOU COULD HAVE SHOWN ME WOULD HAVE MADE ME HAPPIER, THELONIOUS!
THE REVOLT OF THE TREES! SO THAT WAS WHAT HAPPENED IN THE END.
YES, BUT IT WASN'T THE END AFTER ALL, WAS IT? SOMEHOW, LIFE ALWAYS GOES ON.
LIFE GOES ON ...

20

Life Goes On

"Wake up, Thelonious. You're missing the feast!" *Brown was shaking my arm.*

"Life goes on," I said to him.

"You already said that," Brown said.

I took off the helmet and looked inside. It looked like an ordinary helmet.

Turning to Brown I said, "I know everything."

"Yeah, right," said Brown. "You're getting light-headed. Come out from under here and have something to eat."

"No, I don't mean *everything*! I mean, I know what happened at the end of the Human Occupation, and what happened to Mary and Bob and Simon!"

Bill stuck his head under my chair. "You know what happened to Mary?" he said.

I held up my helmet. "It's all in here," I explained. "If you sleep wearing the helmet,

you can enter Simon's dream. Simon and Mary and Bob went to live at the end of the Earth after the Revolt of the Trees!"

Bill and Brown just looked at me.

"Here! You try it!" I shoved the helmet at Brown.

"I'm not tired," he said. He handed it to Bill.

Bill looked it over; then he smiled and scurried away, taking the helmet with him.

"I want that helmet back when you're done with it, Bill," I called after him. "And don't do any experiments on it! They might have unforeseen consequences!"

Brown and I went to get something to eat.

I hoped Bill wouldn't wreck my helmet. It would be fun to dream in it again. Simon could show me more about what it was like when the humans ruled the Earth. And I could tell Simon more about what it was like in *our* time . . . about the Untamed Forest and the City of Ruins, about Faradawn, and the mutant crabs, and the boat that Bill gave me, and all my friends, and what it was like living on the Fog Mound now!

21

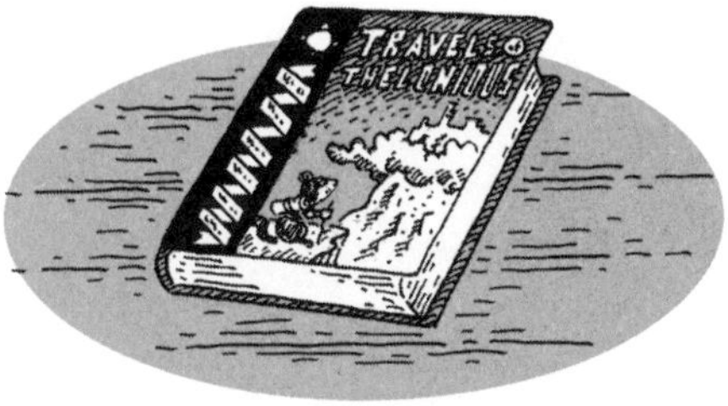
TRAVELS OF
THELONIOUS

Travels of Thelonious

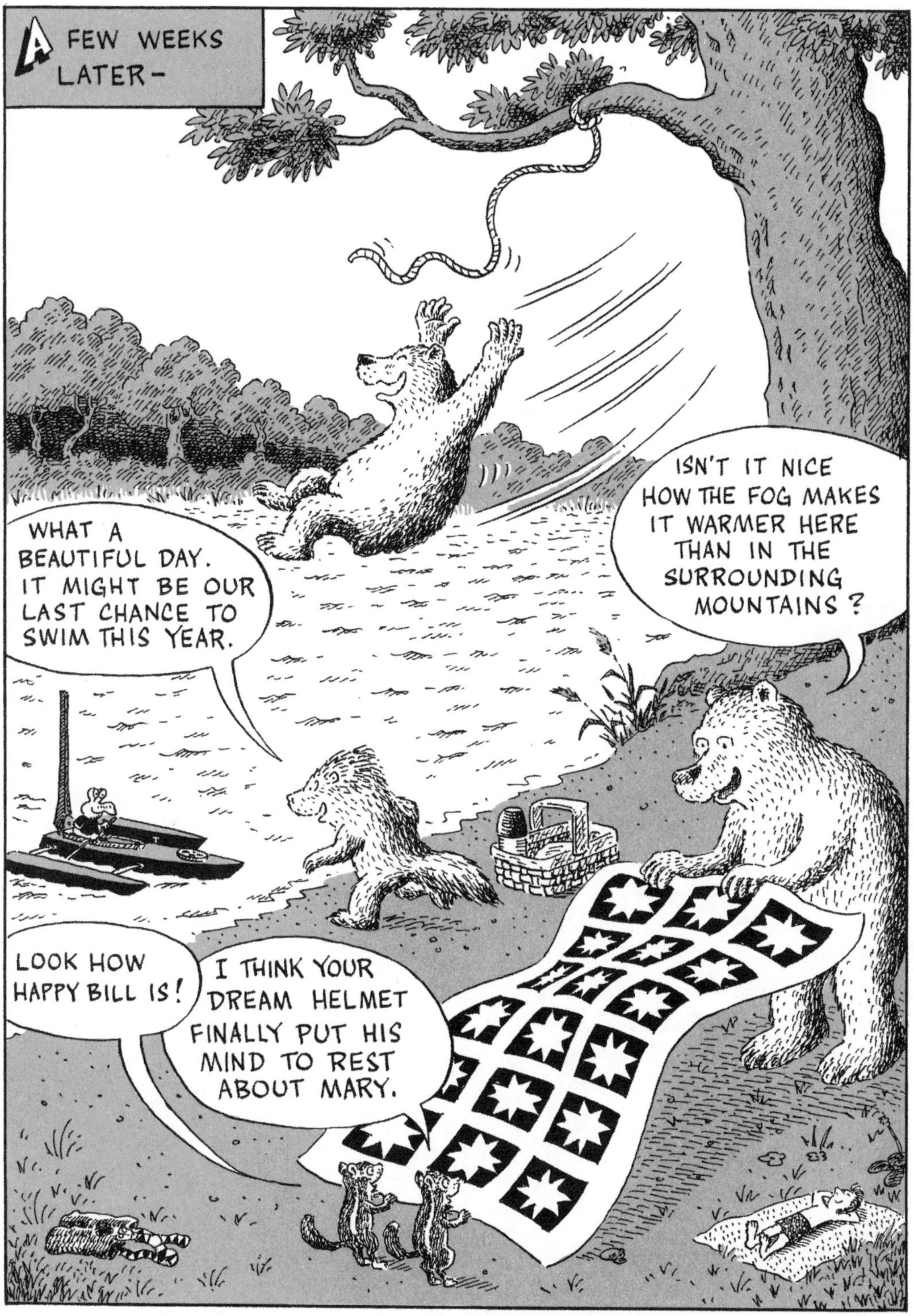
A FEW WEEKS LATER-
WHAT A BEAUTIFUL DAY. IT MIGHT BE OUR LAST CHANCE TO SWIM THIS YEAR.
ISN'T IT NICE HOW THE FOG MAKES IT WARMER HERE THAN IN THE SURROUNDING MOUNTAINS?
LOOK HOW HAPPY BILL IS!
I THINK YOUR DREAM HELMET FINALLY PUT HIS MIND TO REST ABOUT MARY.

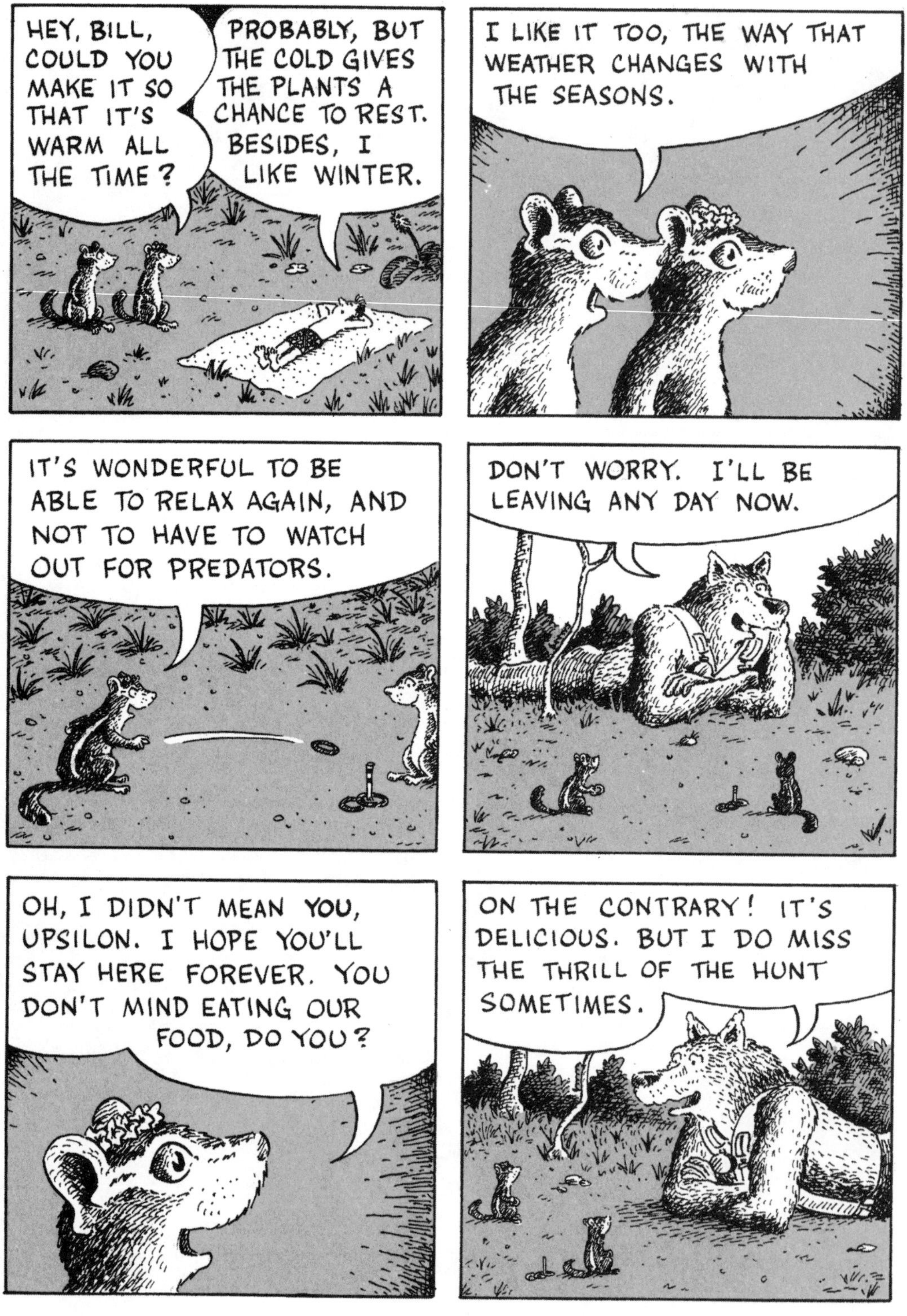
HEY, BILL, COULD YOU MAKE IT SO THAT IT'S WARM ALL THE TIME?
PROBABLY, BUT THE COLD GIVES THE PLANTS A CHANCE TO REST. BESIDES, I LIKE WINTER.
I LIKE IT TOO, THE WAY THAT WEATHER CHANGES WITH THE SEASONS.
IT'S WONDERFUL TO BE ABLE TO RELAX AGAIN, AND NOT TO HAVE TO WATCH OUT FOR PREDATORS.
DON'T WORRY. I'LL BE LEAVING ANY DAY NOW.
OH, I DIDN'T MEAN YOU, UPSILON. I HOPE YOU'LL STAY HERE FOREVER. YOU DON'T MIND EATING OUR FOOD, DO YOU?
ON THE CONTRARY! IT'S DELICIOUS. BUT I DO MISS THE THRILL OF THE HUNT SOMETIMES.

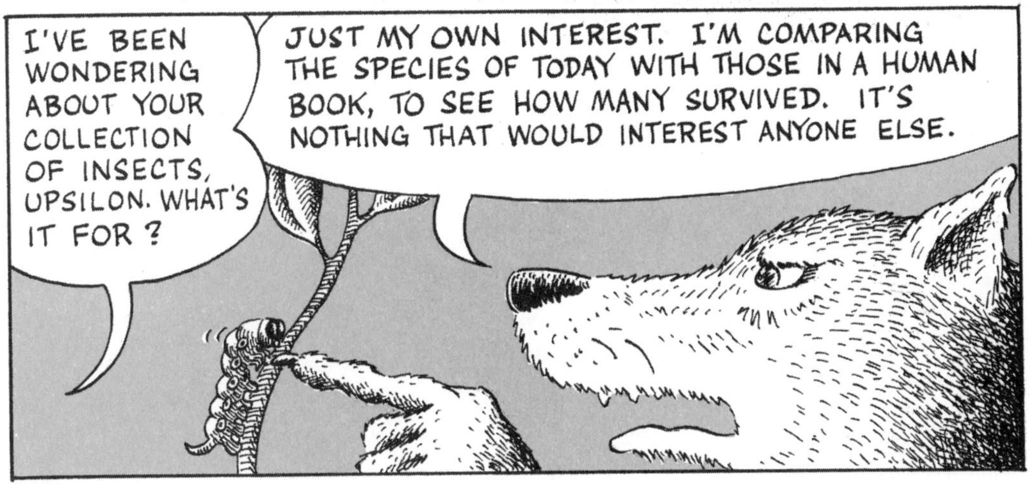
I'VE BEEN WONDERING ABOUT YOUR COLLECTION OF INSECTS, UPSILON. WHAT'S IT FOR?
JUST MY OWN INTEREST. I'M COMPARING THE SPECIES OF TODAY WITH THOSE IN A HUMAN BOOK, TO SEE HOW MANY SURVIVED. IT'S NOTHING THAT WOULD INTEREST ANYONE ELSE.

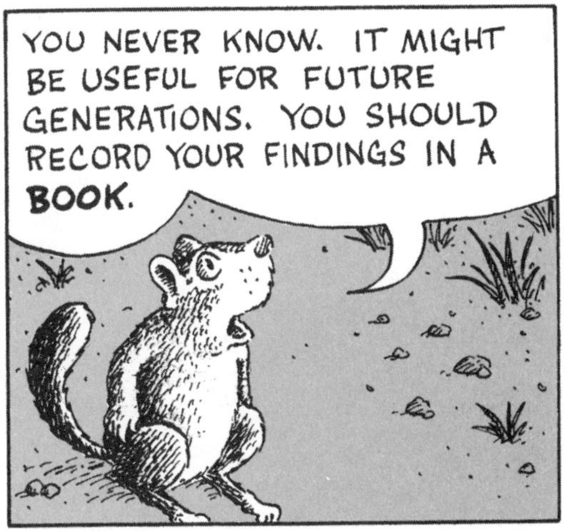
YOU NEVER KNOW. IT MIGHT BE USEFUL FOR FUTURE GENERATIONS. YOU SHOULD RECORD YOUR FINDINGS IN A **BOOK**.

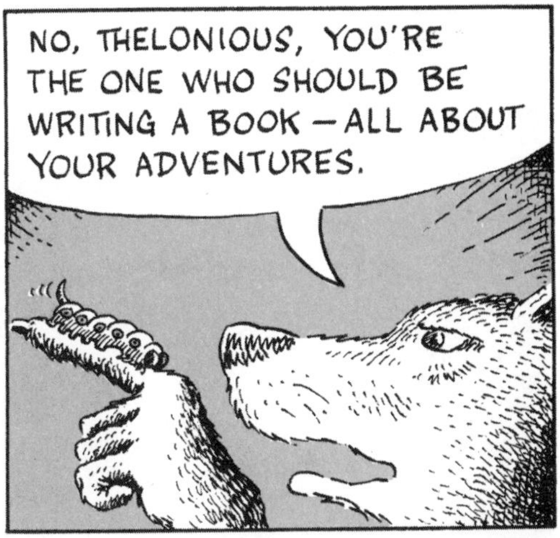
NO, THELONIOUS, YOU'RE THE ONE WHO SHOULD BE WRITING A BOOK—ALL ABOUT YOUR ADVENTURES.

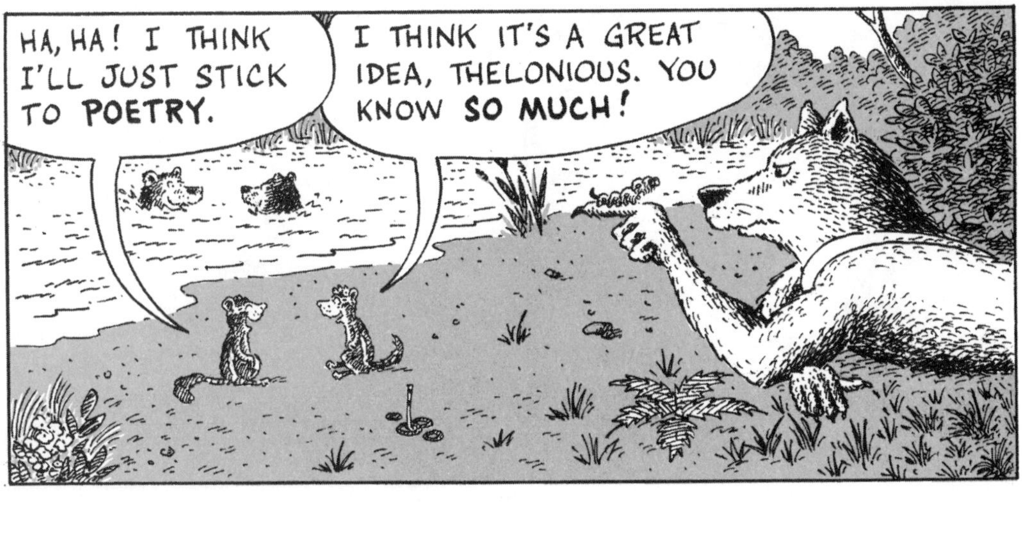
HA, HA! I THINK I'LL JUST STICK TO **POETRY**.
I THINK IT'S A GREAT IDEA, THELONIOUS. YOU KNOW **SO MUCH**!

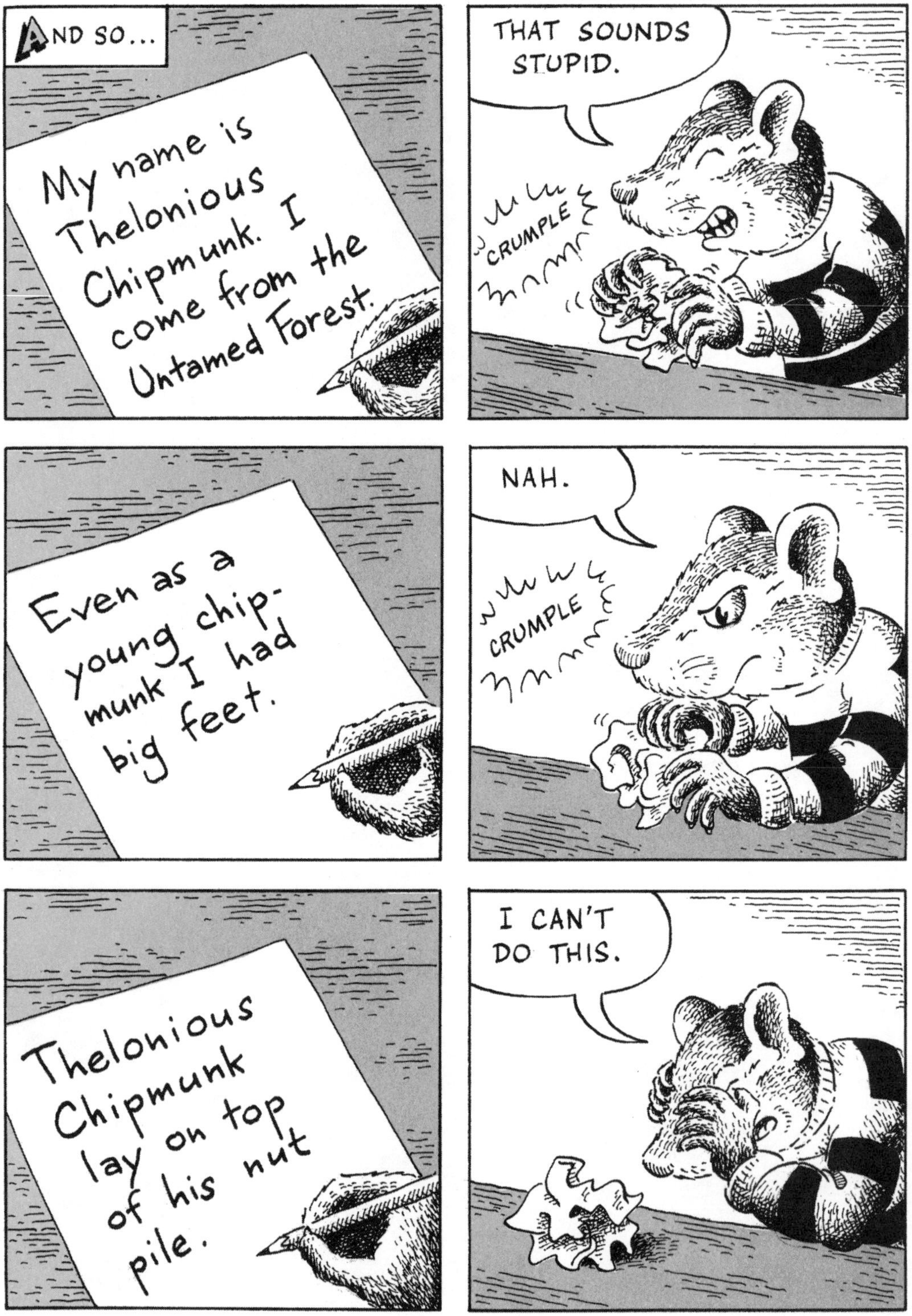
AND SO...
My name is Thelonious Chipmunk. I come from the Untamed Forest.
THAT SOUNDS STUPID.
CRUMPLE
Even as a young chip-munk I had big feet.
NAH.
CRUMPLE
Thelonious Chipmunk lay on top of his nut pile.
I CAN'T DO THIS.

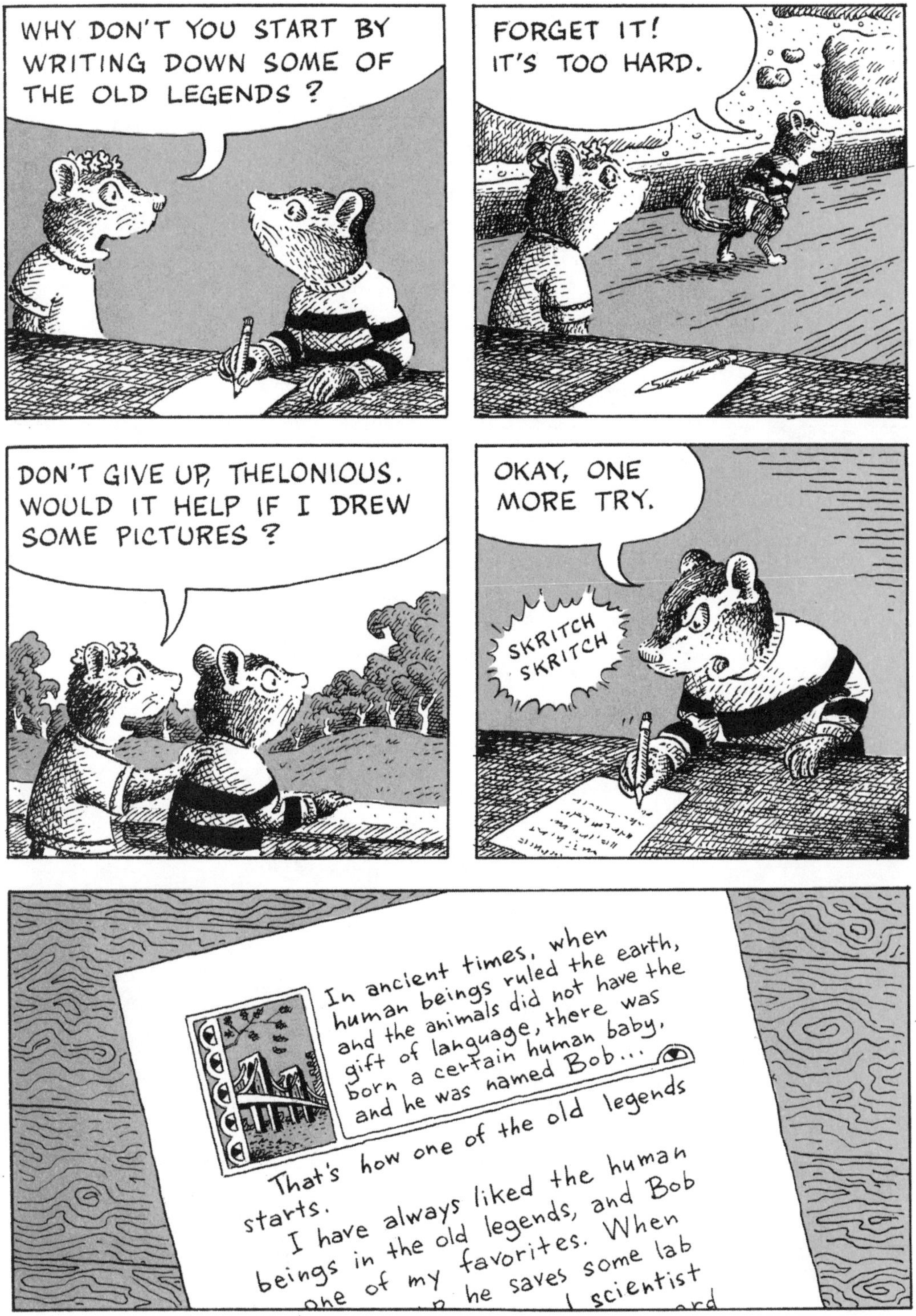
WHY DON'T YOU START BY WRITING DOWN SOME OF THE OLD LEGENDS ?
FORGET IT! IT'S TOO HARD.
DON'T GIVE UP, THELONIOUS. WOULD IT HELP IF I DREW SOME PICTURES ?
OKAY, ONE MORE TRY.
SKRITCH SKRITCH
In ancient times, when
human beings ruled the earth,
and the animals did not have the
gift of language, there was
born a certain human baby,
and he was named Bob...
That's how one of the old legends
starts.
I have always liked the human
beings in the old legends, and Bob
one of my favorites. When
he saves some lab
scientist

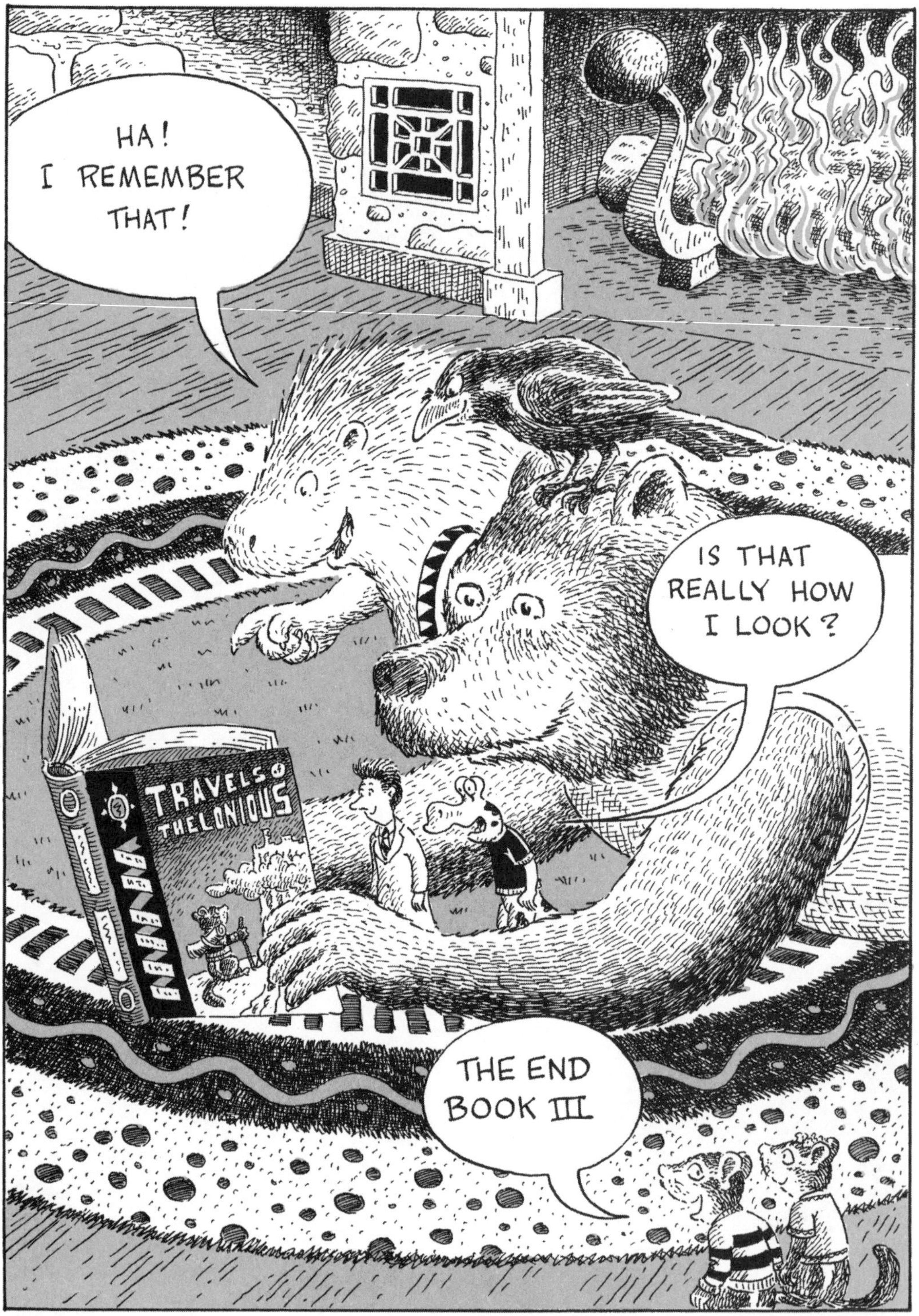
HA!
I REMEMBER
THAT!
IS THAT
REALLY HOW
I LOOK?
TRAVELS of THELONIOUS
THE END
BOOK III